KT-133-012

Graham Swift was born in 1949. His first novel, *The Sweet-Shop Owner*, was published in 1980. *Shuttlecock*, his second novel, was published in 1981 and was awarded the bi-annual Geoffrey Faber Memorial Prize in 1983. A collection of his short stories, *Learning to Swim*, was published in 1982, and will appear in Picador next year. His work has been translated into both German and Swedish. Graham Swift lives and works in London.

GRAHAM SWIFT

Waterland

PICADOR

in association with Heinemann

First published 1983 by William Heinemann Ltd
This Picador edition published 1984 by Pan Books Ltd,
Cavaye Place, London SW10 9PG
in association with William Heinemann Ltd
9 8 7 6 5 4 3 2 1
© Graham Swift 1983
ISBN 0 330 28395 2
Printed and bound in Great Britain by
Cox & Wyman Ltd, Reading

This book is sold subject to the condition that it
shall not, by way of trade or otherwise, be lent, re-sold,
hired out or otherwise circulated without the publisher's prior
consent in any form of binding or cover other than that in which
it is published and without a similar condition including this
condition being imposed on the subsequent purchaser

The author acknowledges the assistance of
the Arts Council of Great Britain.

For Candice

THE EEL.
BY MIXON

Contents

Historia, ae, f. **1.** inquiry, investigation, learning. **2.** a) a narrative of past events, history. b) any kind of narrative: account, tale, story.

'Ours was the marsh country . . .'
Great Expectations

About the Stars and the Sluice

"And don't forget," my father would say, as if he expected me at any moment to up and leave to seek my fortune in the wide world, "whatever you learn about people, however bad they turn out, each one of them has a heart, and each one of them was once a tiny baby sucking his mother's milk . . ."

Fairy-tale words; fairy-tale advice. But we lived in a fairy-tale place. In a lock-keeper's cottage, by a river, in the middle of the Fens. Far away from the wide world. And my father, who was a superstitious man, liked to do things in such a way as would make them seem magical and occult. So he would always set his eel traps at night. Not because eel traps cannot be set by day, but because the mystery of darkness appealed to him. And one night, in midsummer, in 1937, we went with him, Dick and I, to set traps near Stott's Bridge. It was hot and windless. When the traps had been set we lay back on the river-bank. Dick was fourteen and I was ten. The pumps were tump-tumping, as they do, incessantly, so that you scarcely notice them, all over the Fens, and frogs were croaking in the ditches. Up above, the sky swarmed with stars which seemed to multiply as we looked at them. And as we lay, Dad said: "Do you know what the stars are? They are the silver dust of God's blessing. They are little broken-off bits of heaven. God cast them down to fall on us. But when he saw how wicked we were, he changed his mind and ordered the stars to stop. Which is why they hang in the sky but seem as though at any time they might drop . . ."

For my father, as well as being a superstitious man, had a knack for telling stories. Made-up stories, true stories; soothing stories, warning stories; stories with a moral or with no point at all; believable stories and unbelievable stories; stories which were neither one thing nor the other. It was a knack which ran in his family. But it was a knack which my mother had too – and perhaps he really acquired it from her. Because when I was very small it was my mother who first told me stories, which, unlike my father, she got from books as well as out of her head, to make me sleep at night.

And since my mother's death, which was six months before we lay by the eel traps under the stars, my father's yen for the dark, his nocturnal restlessness, had grown more besetting. As if he were constantly brooding on some story yet to be told. So I would see him sometimes, inspecting his vegetable patch by the moonlight, or talking to his roosting chickens, or pacing up and down by the lock-gates or the sluice, his movements marked by the wandering ember of his cigarette.

We lived in a lock-keeper's cottage by the River Leem, which flows out of Norfolk into the Great Ouse. And no one needs telling that the land in that part of the world is flat. Flat, with an unrelieved and monotonous flatness, enough of itself, some might say, to drive a man to unquiet and sleep-defeating thoughts. From the raised banks of the Leem, it stretched away to the horizon, its uniform colour, peat-black, varied only by the crops that grew upon it – grey-green potato leaves, blue-green beet leaves, yellow-green wheat; its uniform levelness broken only by the furrowed and dead-straight lines of ditches and drains, which, depending on the state of the sky and the angle of the sun, ran like silver, copper or golden wires across the fields and which, when you stood and looked at them, made you shut one eye and fall prey to fruitless meditations on the laws of perspective.

And yet this land, so regular, so prostrate, so tamed and cultivated, would transform itself, in my five- or six-year-old mind, into an empty wilderness. On those nights when my mother would be forced to tell me stories, it would seem that in our lock-keeper's cottage we were in the middle of nowhere; and the noise of the trains passing on the lines to King's Lynn, Gildsey and Ely was like the baying of a monster closing in on us in our isolation.

A fairy-tale land, after all.

My father kept the lock on the River Leem, two miles from

2

where it empties into the Ouse. But because a lock-keeper's duties are irregular and his pay, set against the rent-free cottage in which he lives, is scant, and because, in any case, by the nineteen-thirties, the river-traffic on the Leem had dwindled, my father also grew vegetables, kept chickens and trapped eels. It was only in times of heavy rain or thaw that these secondary occupations were abandoned. Then he would have to watch and anticipate the water-level. Then he would have to raise the sluice which cut across the far side of the stream like a giant guillotine.

For the river in front of our cottage divided into two channels, the nearer containing the navigation lock, the farther the sluice, with, in between, a solidly built brick-faced pier, a tiny island, on which stood the cabin housing the sluice engine. And even before the river had visibly risen, even before its colour had changed and it began to show the milky brown of the Norfolk chalk hills from which it flowed, Dad would know when to cross the lock-gates to the cabin and begin – with a groaning of metal and throbbing of released water – to crank up the sluice.

But under normal conditions the sluice remained lowered, almost to the river bottom, its firm blade holding back the slow-flowing Leem, making it fit for the passage of boats. Then the water in the enclosure above it, like the water in the lock-pen, would be smooth and placid and it would give off that smell which is characteristic of places where fresh water and human ingenuity meet, and which is smelt over and over again in the Fens. A cool, slimy but strangely poignant and nostalgic smell. A smell which is half man and half fish. And at such times Dad would have plenty of leisure for his eel traps and vegetables, and little to do with the sluice, save to combat rust, grease the cog-wheels and clear away from the water the accumulations of flotsam.

For, flood or no flood, the Leem brought down its unceasing booty of debris. Willow branches; alder branches; sedge; fencing; crates; old clothes; dead sheep; bottles; potato sacks; straw bales; fruit boxes; fertiliser bags. All floated down on the westerly current, lodged against the sluice-gate and had to be cleared away with boat-hooks and weed-rakes.

And thus it was that one night, in midsummer, when God's withheld benedictions were shining in the sky, though this was several years after Dad told us about the stars, but only two or three since he began to speak of hearts and mother's milk, and the tump-tump of the pumps was drowned now, in the evening, by the roar of ascending bombers – it was, to be precise, July, 1943 – that something floated down the Leem, struck the iron-work of the sluice and, tugged by the eddies, continued to knock and scrape against it till morning. Something extraordinary and unprecedented, and not to be disposed of like a branch or potato sack or even a dead sheep. For this something was a body. And the body belonged to Freddie Parr, who lived less than a mile away and was my age, give or take a month.

2

About the End of History

Children. Children, who will inherit the world. Children (for always, even though you were fifteen, sixteen, seventeen, candidates for that appeasing term "young adults", I addressed you, silently, as "children") – children, before whom I have stood for thirty-two years in order to unravel the mysteries of the past, but before whom I am to stand no longer, listen, one last time, to your history teacher.

You, above all, should know that it is not out of choice that I am leaving you. You should know how inadequate was that phrase, so cruel in its cursoriness, "for personal reasons", that our worthy headmaster, Lewis Scott, used in his morning assembly announcement. And you should know how beside the point, by the time they were applied, were those pressures brought to bear by this same Lewis in the name of a so-called educational rationale. ("Don't imagine I like it, Tom, but we're being forced to economise. We're cutting back on history. You could take early retirement . . .") You should know, because it was you who were witness to the fact that old Cricky, your history teacher, had already in one sense, and of his own

4

accord, ceased to teach history. In the middle of explaining how, with a Parisian blood-letting, our Modern World began, he breaks off and starts telling – these stories. Something about living by a river, something about a father who trapped eels, and a drowned body found in the river, years ago. And then it dawned on you: old Cricky was trying to put himself into history; old Cricky was trying to show you that he himself was only a piece of the stuff he taught. In other words, he'd flipped, he'd gone bananas . . .

Or, as Lewis put it, "Maybe you should take a rest. A sabbatical term. How about it? A chance to get on with that book of yours – what was it now? – *A History of the Fens*?"

But I didn't take up this offer. Because, as it happened, you listened, you listened, all ears, to those new-fangled lessons. You listened to old Cricky's crazy yarns (true? made up?) – in a way you never listened to the stranger-than-fiction prodigies of the French Revolution.

And so it was not until a certain event occurred, an event more bizarre still than your history teacher's new classroom style, an event involving his wife, Mrs Crick, and – given the inescapable irony of the husband's profession – made much of, as you know, by the local press, that my departure became, at last, an absolute necessity.

Schoolmaster's wife admits theft of child. Tells court: "God told me to do it."

Children, it was one of your number, a curly-haired boy called Price, in the habit (contrary to regulations but passed over by me) of daubing his cheeks with an off-white make-up which gave to his face the pallor of a corpse, who once, interrupting the French Revolution and voicing the familiar protest that every history teacher learns to expect (what is the point, use, need, etc., of History), asserted roundly that history was "a fairy-tale".

(A teacher-baiter. A lesson-spoiler. Every class has to have one. But this one's different . . .)

"What matters," he went on, not knowing what sort of fairy-tale was about to envelop both his history teacher and his history teacher's wife, "is the here and now. Not the past. The

5

here and now – and the future." (The very sentiments, Price – but you didn't see that – of 1789.) And then – alluding rapidly to certain topics of the day (the Afghan crisis, the Tehran hostages, the perilous and apparently unhaltable build-up of nuclear arms) and drawing from you, his class-mates, a sudden and appalling venting of your collective nightmares – he announced, with a trembling lip that was not just the result of uttering words that must have been (true, Price?) carefully rehearsed: "The only important thing . . ."

"Yes, Price – the only important thing – ?"

"The only important thing about history, I think, sir, is that it's got to the point where it's probably about to end."

So we closed our textbooks. Put aside the French Revolution. So we said goodbye to that old and hackneyed fairy-tale with its Rights of Man, liberty caps, cockades, tricolors, not to mention its hissing guillotines, and its quaint notion that it had bestowed on the world a New Beginning.

I began, having recognised in my young but by no means carefree class the contagious symptoms of fear: "Once upon a time . . ."

Children, who will inherit the world. Children to whom, throughout history, stories have been told, chiefly but not always at bedtime, in order to quell restless thoughts; whose need of stories is matched only by the need adults have of children to tell stories to, of receptacles for their stock of fairy-tales, of listening ears on which to unload, bequeath those most unbelievable yet haunting of fairy-tales, their own lives; children – they are going to separate you and me. Lewis has seen to it. Forgive this emotion. I do not deserve your protestations. (We need our Cricky and all that stuff of his.) I do not expect you to understand that after thirty-two years I have rolled you all into one and now I know the agonies of a mother robbed of her child . . . But listen, listen. Your history teacher wishes to give you the complete and final version . . .

And since a fairy-tale must have a setting, a setting which, like the settings of all good fairy-tales, must be both palpable and unreal, let me tell you

6

About the Fens

Which are a low-lying region of eastern England, over 1,200 square miles in area, bounded to the west by the limestone hills of the Midlands, to the south and east by the chalk hills of Cambridgeshire, Suffolk and Norfolk. To the north, the Fens advance, on a twelve-mile front, to meet the North Sea at the Wash. Or perhaps it is more apt to say that the Wash summons the forces of the North Sea to its aid in a constant bid to recapture its former territory. For the chief fact about the Fens is that they are reclaimed land, land that was once water, and which, even today, is not quite solid.

Once the shallow, shifting waters of the Wash did not stop at Boston and King's Lynn but licked southwards as far as Cambridge, Huntingdon, Peterborough and Bedford. What caused them to retreat? The answer can be given in a single syllable: Silt. The Fens were formed by silt. Silt: a word which when you utter it, letting the air slip thinly between your teeth, invokes a slow, sly, insinuating agency. Silt: which shapes and undermines continents; which demolishes as it builds; which is simultaneous accretion and erosion; neither progress nor decay.

It came first from the coast of Yorkshire and Lincolnshire, borne on the inshore currents which flowed southwards into the ancient Wash. In the blue-black clay which lies under the soil of Cambridgeshire are deposits of silt containing traces of shells of a type occurring on the beaches and cliff-beds of north-east England. Thus the first silts came from the sea. But to these marine silts were added the land silts carried by the rivers, the Ouse, the Cam, the Welland, which drained, and still drain, into the ever-diminishing Wash.

The silt accumulated, salt-marsh plants took hold, then other plants. And with the plants began the formation of peat. And peat is the second vital constituent of the Fens and the source of their remarkable fertility. Once it supported great forests which collapsed and sank when climatic changes caused water to re-immerse the region. Today, it forms the rich, black beet- and potato-bearing soil which is second to none in the country. But without silt, there could have been no peat.

All this was still happening not so long ago. In 870 the Viking fleets sailed with ease as far as Ely, through a region which was still predominantly water. Two hundred years later Hereward, defending the same high ground of Ely, watched his Norman besiegers flounder and drown in the treacherous peat-bogs. The landscape was still largely liquid.

For consider the equivocal operation of silt. Just as it raises the land, drives back the sea and allows peat to mature, so it impedes the flow of rivers, restricts their outfall, renders the newly-formed land constantly liable to flooding and blocks the escape of floodwater. For centuries the Fens were a network of swamps and brackish lagoons. The problem of the Fens has always been the problem of drainage.

What silt began, man continued. Land reclamation. Drainage. But you do not reclaim a land overnight. You do not reclaim a land without difficulty and without ceaseless effort and vigilance. The Fens are still being reclaimed even to this day. Strictly speaking, they are never reclaimed, only being reclaimed. Without the pumps, the dykes and embankments, without the dredging programmes . . . And you do not need to remind a Fenman of the effects of heavy inland rainfall, or of the combination of a spring tide and a strong nor'easter.

So forget, indeed, your revolutions, your turning-points, your grand metamorphoses of history. Consider, instead, the slow and arduous process, the interminable and ambiguous process – the process of human siltation – of land reclamation.

Is it desirable, in the first place, that land should be reclaimed? Not to those who exist by water; not to those who have no need of firm ground beneath their feet. Not to the fishermen, fowlers and reed-cutters who made their sodden homes in those stubborn swamps, took to stilts in time of flood and lived like water-rats. Not to the men who broke down the medieval embankments and if caught were buried alive in the very breach they had made. Not to the men who cut the throats of King

Charles's Dutch drainers and threw their bodies into the water they were hired to expel.

I am speaking of my ancestors; of my father's forefathers. Because my name of Crick, which in Charles the First's day was spelt sometimes "Coricke" or "Cricke", can be found (a day's delving into local archives) amongst the lists of those summarily dealt with for sabotaging drainage works. My ancestors were water people. They speared fish and netted ducks. When I was small I possessed a living image of my ancestors in the form of Bill Clay, a shrunken, leathery carcase of a man, whose age was unknown but was never put at less than eighty, a one-time punt-gunner and turf-cutter, who had witnessed in his lifetime the passing of all but the dregs of the old wild fens in our area; who stank, even with his livelihood half gone, of goose fat and fish slime, mud and peat smoke; who wore an otter-skin cap, eel-skin gaiters and whose brain was permanently crazed by the poppy-head tea he drank to ward off winter agues. Old Bill lived with his wife Martha in a damp, crack-walled cottage not far from the Ouse and on the edge of the shrinking, reed-filled marsh known, after the watery expanse it had once been, as Wash Fen Mere. But some said that Martha Clay, who was some twenty years younger than Bill, was never Bill's wife at all. Some said that Martha Clay was a witch . . .

But let's keep clear of fairy-tales.

The Dutch came, under their engineer Cornelius Vermuyden, hired first by King Charles, then by His Lordship, Francis, Earl of Bedford. Honouring their employer's name, they cut the Bedford River, and then the New Bedford River alongside it, to divert the main strength of the Ouse from its recalcitrant and sluggish course by Ely, into a straight channel to the sea. They built the Denver Sluice at the junction of the northern end of the new river with the old Ouse, and the Hermitage Sluice at the southern junction. They dug subsidiary cuts, drains, lodes, dykes, eaus and ditches and converted 95,000 acres into summer, if not winter, grazing. Practical and forward-looking people, the Dutch. And my father's forebears opposed them; and two of them were hanged for it.

Vermuyden left (he should have been rich but the Dutch Wars robbed him of his English fortune) in 1655. And nature, more effectively than my ancestors, began to sabotage his work. Because silt obstructs as it builds; unmakes as it makes. Vermuyden did not foresee that in cutting new courses for the rivers he reduced, not quickened, their flow; since a divided river conducts at any one point a decreased volume of water, and the less water a river conducts the less not only its velocity but also its capacity to scour its channel. The Earl of Bedford's noble waterways gathered mud. Silt collected in the estuaries, where the current of the rivers was no match for the tide, and built up against the sluices.

And Vermuyden did not foresee one other thing. That reclaimed land shrinks – as anything must shrink that has the water squeezed out of it. And peat, above all, which absorbs water like a sponge, shrinks when it dries. The Fens are shrinking. They are still shrinking – and sinking. Land which was above sea-level in Vermuyden's day is now below it. Tens of feet below it. There is no exaggerating the dangers. The invitation to flooding; the diminution of the gradient of the rivers; the pressure on the raised banks; the faster flow of upland water into the deepening lowland basin. All this, and silt.

In the 1690s the Bedford River burst a sixty-foot gap in its banks. In 1713 the Denver Sluice gave way and so great was the silting below it that the water from the Bedford River was forced landwards, upstream, up the old Ouse to Ely, instead of discharging into the sea. Thousands of acres of farmland were submerged. Cottagers waded to their beds.

And at some time in all this, strangely enough, my paternal ancestors threw in their lot with the drainers and land-reclaimers.

Perhaps they had no choice. Perhaps they took their hire where they were forced to. Perhaps they responded, out of the good of their hearts, to the misery of inundated crops and water-logged homes. In 1748, among the records of wages paid to those employed in rebuilding the Denver Sluice, are the names of the brothers James and Samuel Cricke. And in the parish annals of the Crick homeland, which in those days was north of the small town of Gildsey and east of the New Bedford River, are to be found for the next century and a half, and in the same tenacious connection, the names of Cricks. "John Crick: for repairing the west bank . . ."; "Peter Crick: for scouring the Jackwater Drain and cutting the new Middle Drain . . ."; "Jacob Crick, to work and maintain the windmills at Stump Corner . . ."

They ceased to be water people and became land people; they ceased to fish and fowl and became plumbers of the land. They joined in the destiny of the Fens, which was to strive not for but against water. For a century and a half they dug, drained and pumped the land between the Bedford River and the Great Ouse, boots perpetually mud-caked, ignorant of how their efforts were, little by little, changing the map of England.

Or perhaps they did not cease to be water people. Perhaps they became amphibians. Because if you drain land you are intimately concerned with water; you have to know its ways. Perhaps at heart they always knew, in spite of their land-preserving efforts, that they belonged to the old, prehistoric flood. And so my father, who kept the lock on the Leem, still caught eels and leant against the lock-gates at night, staring into the water – for water and meditation, they say, go together. And so my father, who was a superstitious man, always believed that old Bill Clay, the marsh-man, whose brains were quite cracked, was really, nonetheless, and if the truth be known, a sort of Wise Man.

When you work with water, you have to know and respect it. When you labour to subdue it, you have to understand that one day it may rise up and turn all your labours to nothing. For what is water, children, which seeks to make all things level, which has no taste or colour of its own, but a liquid form of Nothing? And what are the Fens, which so imitate in their levelness the natural disposition of water, but a landscape which, of all landscapes, most approximates to Nothing? Every Fenman secretly concedes this; every Fenman suffers now and then the illusion that the land he walks over is *not there*, is floating . . . And every Fen-child, who is given picture-books to read in which the sun bounces over mountain tops and the road of life winds through heaps of green cushions, and is taught nursery rhymes in which persons go up and down hills, is apt to demand of its elders: Why are the Fens flat?

11

To which my father replied, first letting his face take on a wondering and vexed expression and letting his lips form for a moment the shape of an "O": "Why are the Fens flat? So God has a clear view . . ."

When the land sinks below the water-level you have to pump. There is nothing else for it: water will not flow upwards. The pumps came to the Fens in the eighteenth century, in the form of black-sailed windmills, over seven hundred of which once creaked, whirred and thrummed in the wind between Lincoln and Cambridge. And my ancestor, Jacob Crick, operated two of them at Stump Corner. When the redcoats were storming Quebec, and the citizens of New England were rising up against their British masters (and offering a model for the discontented citizens of Paris), Jacob Crick was putting his cheek and ear to the air to feel the direction and force of the breezes. He was leaning and pushing against the tail-poles of his twin mills to set the sails in the right position. He was inspecting his paddle-wheels and scoops. But in times when there was no wind or the wind blew steadily in the same quarter, requiring no resetting of the sails, he would catch eels (because he was still a water-man at heart), not only with wicker traps but with a long, many-bladed spear called a glaive; and he would cut sedge and snare fowl.

Jacob Crick manned the mills at Stump Corner from 1748 to 1789. He never married. In all those years he probably moved no further than a mile or two from his mills, which at all times he had to guard and tend. With Jacob Crick another characteristic of my paternal family emerges. They are fixed people. They have tied around their legs an invisible tether, and have enjoined upon them the stationary vigilance of sentinels. The biggest migration the Cricks ever made – before I, a twentieth-century Crick, made my home in London – was to move from the land west to the land east of the Ouse – a distance of six miles.

So Jacob Crick, mill-man and apprentice hermit, never sees the wide world. Though some would say the Fenland skies are wide enough. He never learns what is happening in Quebec or Boston. He eyes the horizon, sniffs the wind, looks at flatness. He has time to sit and ponder, to become suicidal or sagely calm. He acquires the virtue, if virtue it is, of which the Cricks have always had good supply: Phlegm. A muddy, silty humour.

And in the momentous and far from phlegmatical year 1789, whose significance you know, children, though Jacob Crick never did, Jacob Crick died.

Wifeless, childless. But the Cricks are not extinct. In 1820 it is a grand-nephew of Jacob – William – who is foreman of a gang employed in digging the southern end of the Eau Brink Cut, a new, deep channel to carry the waters of the lower Ouse by the shortest route to King's Lynn. For they are still trying to straighten out the slithery, wriggly, eel-like Ouse. In 1822, Francis Crick, perhaps another grand-nephew of Jacob, is entrusted with the operation of the new steam-pump on Stott's Drain, near the village of Hockwell. For the wind-pump is already obsolete. A windmill's use is limited. It cannot be used when there is no wind or when a gale is blowing; but a steam-pump will chug through all weathers.

So steam-power replaces wind-power in the Fens, and the Cricks adapt themselves, as we might say, to technology. To technology, and to ambition. For in this once wallowing back-water, in this sink of England, there are suddenly reputations to be made. Not only are Smeaton, Telford, Rennie and numerous other renowned engineers discovering that in the problems of drainage lies a test for their talents, but a host of speculators, contemplating the rich, dark soil that drainage produces, have already seen the wisdom of investing in land reclamation.

One of them is called Atkinson. He is not a Fenman. He is a prosperous Norfolk farmer and maltster from the hills where the Leem rises and flows westwards to the Ouse. But, in the 1780s, for reasons both self-interested and public-spirited, he forms the plan of opening up for navigation the River Leem, as a means of transport for his produce between Norfolk and the expanding market of the Fens. While Jacob Crick spears his last eels by Stump Corner and listens not just to the creaking of his mill sails but to the creaking of his ageing bones, Thomas Atkinson buys, little by little and at rock-bottom prices, acres of marsh and peat-bog along the margins of the Leem. He hires surveyors, drainage and dredging experts. A confident and far-seeing man, a man of hearty and sanguine, rather than phlegmatic, temperament, he offers work and a future to a whole region.

And the Cricks come to work for Atkinson. They make their great journey across the Ouse, leaving old Jacob at his solitary outpost; and while one branch of the family goes north to dig the Eau Brink Cut, another goes south, to the village of Apton, where Thomas Atkinson's agents are recruiting labour.

And that is how, children, my ancestors came to live by the River Leem. That is how when the cauldron of revolution was simmering in Paris, so that you, one day, should have a subject for your lessons, they were busy, as usual, with their scouring, pumping and embanking. That is how, when foundations were being rocked in France, a land was being formed which would one day yield fifteen tons of potatoes or nineteen sacks of wheat an acre and on which your history teacher-to-be would one day have his home.

It was Atkinson who put Francis Crick in charge of the new steam-pump on Stott's Drain. When I was a boy a pump still worked on Stott's Drain – though it was no longer steam- but diesel-driven and manned not by a Crick but by Harry Bulman, in the pay of the Great Ouse Catchment Board – adding its pulse-beat to that of many others on the night I learnt what the stars really were. It was Atkinson who in 1815 built the lock and sluice two miles from the junction of the Leem and Ouse, christening it the Atkinson Lock. And it was another Atkinson, Thomas's grandson, who, in 1874, after violent flooding had destroyed lock, sluice and lock-keeper's cottage, rebuilt the lock and named it the New Atkinson. A Crick did not then become lock-keeper – but a Crick would.

Yet why, you may ask, did the Cricks rise no further? Why were they content to be, at best, pump-operators, lock-keepers, humble servants of their masters? Why did they never produce a renowned engineer, or turn to farming that rich soil they themselves had helped to form?

Perhaps because of that old, watery phlegm which cooled and made sluggish their spirits, despite the quantities of it they spat out, over their shovels and buckets, in workmanlike gobbets. Because they did not forget, in their muddy labours, their swampy origins; that, however much you resist them, the waters

14

will return; that the land sinks; silt collects; that something in nature wants to go back.

Realism; fatalism; phlegm. To live in the Fens is to receive strong doses of reality. The great, flat monotony of reality; the wide, empty space of reality. Melancholia and self-murder are not unknown in the Fens. Heavy drinking, madness and sudden acts of violence are not uncommon. How do you surmount reality, children? How do you acquire, in a flat country, the tonic of elevated feelings? If you are an Atkinson it is not difficult. If you have become prosperous by selling fine quality barley, if you can look down from your Norfolk uplands and see in these level Fens – this nothing-landscape – an Idea, a drawing-board for your plans, you can outwit reality. But if you are born in the middle of that flatness, fixed in it, glued to it even by the mud in which it abounds . . . ?

How did the Cricks outwit reality? By telling stories. Down to the last generation, they were not only phlegmatic but superstitious and credulous creatures. Suckers for stories. While the Atkinsons made history, the Cricks spun yarns.

And it is strange – or perhaps not strange, not strange at all, only logical – how the bare and empty Fens yield so readily to the imaginary – and the supernatural. How the villages along the Leem were peopled with ghosts and earnestly recounted legends. The Singing Swans of Wash Fen Mere; the Monk of Sudchurch; the Headless Ferryman of Staithe – not to mention the Brewer's Daughter of Gildsey. How in the past the Fens attracted visionaries and fanatics – Saint Gunnhilda, our local patroness, who in 695, or thereabouts, built a wattle hut for herself on a mud-hump in the middle of a marsh, and resisting the assaults and blandishments of demons and surviving on nothing but her prayers, heard the voice of God, founded a church and gave her name (Gunnhildsea – Gildsey: Gunnhilda's Isle) to a town. How even in the no-nonsense and pragmatic twentieth century, this future schoolmaster quaked in his bed at night for fear of something – something vast and void – and had to be told stories and counter-stories to soothe his provoked imagination. How he piously observed, because others observed them too, a catechism of obscure rites. When you see the new moon, turn your money in your pocket; help someone to salt and help them to sorrow; never put new shoes on a table or cut your nails on a Sunday. An eel-skin cures rheumatism; a roast mouse cures whooping cough; and a live fish in a woman's lap will make her barren.

A fairy-tale land.

And the Cricks, for all their dull phlegm, believed in fairy-tales. They saw marsh-sprites; they saw will o' the wisps. My father saw one in 1922. And when echoes from the wide world began to penetrate to the Cricks, when news reached them at last, though they never went looking for it, that the Colonies had rebelled, that there had been a Waterloo, a Crimea, they listened and repeated what they heard with wide-eyed awe, as if such things were not the stuff of fact but the fabric of a wondrous tale.

For centuries the Cricks remain untouched by the wide world. No ambition lures them to the cities. No recruiting party or press-gang, foraging up the Ouse from Lynn, whisks them off to fight for King or Queen. Until history reaches that pitch – our age, children, our common inheritance – where the wide world impinges whether you wish it or not. Till history performs one of its backward somersaults and courts destruction. The waters return. In 1916, '17 and '18 there is much flooding of fields, much damage done to embankments and excessive silting in the estuaries, because of the unavailability of those normally employed in the peaceable tasks of drainage and reclamation. In 1917 paper summonses call George and Henry Crick, of Hockwell, Cambs, employees of the River Leem Drainage and Navigation Board, to be fitted out with uniforms and equipped with rifles.

And where do they find themselves, that autumn, separately but as part of the same beleaguered army? In a flat, rain-swept, water-logged land. A land not unlike their own native Fenland. A land of the kind where the great Vermuyden earned his reputation and developed those ingenious methods which nonetheless proved inappropriate to the terrain of eastern England. A land where, in 1917, there is still much digging, ditching and entrenching and a pressing problem of drainage, not to say problems of other kinds. The Crick brothers see the wide world – which is not a wondrous fable. The Cricks see – but is this only some nightmare, some evil memory they

16

have always had? – the wide world is sinking – the waters are returning – the wide world is drowning in mud. Who will not know of the mud of Flanders? Who will not feel in this twentieth century of ours, when even a teenage schoolboy will propose as a topic for a history lesson the End of History, the mud of Flanders sucking at his feet?

In January 1918 Henry Crick is shipped home, an obliging shrapnel wound in his knee. By that time plans are already afoot in Hockwell to raise the war memorial that will bear, amongst others, the name of his brother. Henry Crick becomes a hospital case. Henry Crick limps and blinks and falls flat on his face at sudden noises. For a long time he finds it hard to separate in his mind the familiar-but-foreign fields of the Fens and the foreign-but-familiar mudscapes he has come from. He expects the ground to quake and heave under his feet and become a morass. He is sent to a home for chronic neurasthenics. He thinks: there is only reality, there are no stories left. About his war experiences he says: "I remember nothing." He does not believe he will one day tell Salty Tales of the Trenches: "In some of the big old shell-holes – there were eels . . ." He does not believe he will ever talk to his son about mother's milk and hearts.

But much will happen to Henry Crick. He recovers. He meets his future wife – there indeed is another story. In 1922 he marries. And in the same year Ernest Atkinson brings indirect influence to bear on his future employment. Indirect because the Atkinson word is no longer law; the Atkinson empire, like many another empire, is in decline, and since before the war, when he sold most of his share in the Leem Navigation, Ernest Atkinson has been living like a recluse, and some would say a mad one at that. But in 1922 my father is appointed keeper of the New Atkinson Lock.

4

Before the Headmaster

And Lewis says, "We're cutting back History . . ."

Just like that. As if there's no need to go into the actual and embarrassing reasons for my inevitable departure, these being fully acknowledged (if never discussed) between us. As if we can play the game that it is not under a cloud of personal disgrace that I am to make my exit, but over a simple matter of curricular rethinking.

But hold on, Lewis. Cutting back History? Cutting *History*? If you're going to sack me, then sack *me*, don't dismiss what I stand for. Don't banish my history . . .

Children, our commendable and trusty headmaster – if I may waive professional discretion for a moment – regards me and my department (whatever he says) as a thorn in his flesh. He believes that education is for and about the future – a fine theory, an admirable contention. Thus a subject, however honoured by academic tradition, which seeks as its prime function to dwell on the past is, *ipso facto*, first to go . . .

Children, there's this fellow called Lewis – better known to you, indeed to me, as Lulu – who's trying to make out that I'm a bad lot, that I'm even just a bit off my rocker. And that this is the inevitable result of my long dabbling in the hocus-pocus of this self-same History.

"Early retirement, Tom. On full pension. Half the staff would jump at it."

"And the closure of my department?"

"Not closure. Don't be ridiculous. I'm not *dropping* History. It's an unavoidable reduction. There'll be no new Head of History. History will merge with General Studies."

"Amounts to pretty well the same thing."

"Tom, let's be clear about this. This isn't my personal decision. I don't, it's true, have a taste for your subject. I've never disguised my views. You don't care for physics. Nor, so you've made clear, for headmastership. We've been sparring partners for years – " (a weak smile) " – it's been the basis of our friendship. A little healthy academic animosity. But there's no question here of a vendetta. You know how the cuts are biting. And you know the kind of pressure I'm under – 'practical relevance to today's real world' – that's what they're demanding. And, dammit, you can't deny there's been a steady decline in the number of pupils opting for History."

"But what about now, Lew? What about in the last few weeks? You know as well as I do there've been no less than six requests by students doing other subjects to transfer to my 'A' level group. I must have some attraction."

"If you call a complete departure from the syllabus 'attraction', if you call turning your classes into these – circus-acts – 'attraction'."

He snorts and starts to lose patience.

"I gave you my advice, Tom – my sympathetic advice. I said take a rest, a period of leave . . ."

(And come back to no bloody History Department.)

"If you chose to persist – "

He gets up, taking deep breaths. He stands by the window, hands in pockets, leaning, sideways-on, in the angle formed by the window-frame and a filing cabinet. Four-thirty. Lessons over. Dusk enveloping the playground.

"It just so happens, Tom, that I agree with the powers-that-be. Equipping for the real world. It just so happens that I think that's what we're here for." A demonstrative hand waved towards the playground. "Send just one of these kids out into the world with a sense of his or her usefulness, with an ability to apply, with practical knowledge and not a rag-bag of pointless information – "

(So there we have it.)

A good, a diligent, a persevering man. Truly. Sometimes when I leave school I see Lewis's light still on, on the first floor, suspended like a lantern amid the darkened classrooms. He cares; he strives; he endeavours. And where he can't prevail he worries, as if in penitential reparation. Worries for his pupils's sake. Worries that in the 1980s he can't provide them with golden prospects. Worry's donated him an ulcer, which he douses with whisky from a filing cabinet (I know about that too).

Children, a brief sketch of our Headmaster:

Once upon a time, in the bright mid-sixties . . . But you won't remember the bright mid-sixties. Okay to be revolutionary then, quite possible to be revolutionary then. The product (let's put it into historical perspective) of temporary affluence, educational expansion and a short-term good outlook. A sort of revolution of the young . . . The period also of the cold war, the Cuba crisis and the intercontinental ballistic missile . . .

Once upon a time, in the bright mid-sixties, when you were being born and Lewis, apart from being appointed Head (his only rival a history teacher, a senior man who nonetheless wanted to remain in the classroom), was busy begetting his own little ones, there was plenty of future on offer. Good times for headmasters. Our school a new ship bound for the Promised Land. Lewis, our doughty captain, a teacher of physics and chemistry (technology then in its white-hot days), confidently striding the deck.

It's still his ship. But he's no longer captain. He's become – a figurehead. Steadfast and staunch, but still a figurehead. Tap him. Beneath the varnish, solid wood (and worms of worry). Our ship's figurehead is a replica of a headmaster of fifteen years ago.

Watch him at morning assembly. (You do? And listen too? Yes, yes, he casts a certain spell.) You won't catch old Lulu looking glum. You won't see him up on the dais without his chin held high and determinedly jutting, a smile and a joke to hand. He sees that as his role now: hold firm, keep smiling. But it's hard work, masking the marks of worry. Gives you ulcers.

And he's good with kids. Has three of his own. Corners you with them in the staff room (my David, my Cathy –) At a private dinner party (guests Tom and Mary Crick) he announces, not a little worse for drink, that he's considering installing a domestic fall-out shelter: "For the kids, you know, for the kids' sake . . ." If he can no longer be a bountiful Santa Claùs, if there are no longer enough of those gift-wrapped promises to go round, he's still free with pats on the head and genial exhortation. Just work hard at your lessons, be good in class. Your education will save you. A school is a microcosm, so if the school works well . . . He's good with kids.

It's just the cares of grown-ups, it's just the addled adult world he's not so keen on. He wants to be close to his pupils: keeps his distance from his staff. When *they* have problems they get short shrift . . .

He must have worked it out with the Authority. Seized the excuse of their pressure to impose cut-backs. The man's got to go. No question of that. But how to avoid all that adult mess? Departmental reshuffling. Budgetary directives . . . And the relevance of the subject to the real world . . .

(But since when have you been living, Lew, in the real world?)

So he says, "We're cutting back History . . ."

He doesn't say: "If it were anything else . . . But child theft. *Child* theft. A schoolmaster's wife. You can't deny the repercussions. And those damned press reports . . ."

He doesn't say: "I'd stand by you, Tom, I'd defend you. But, in the circumstances – these lessons – these circus-acts . . ."

He doesn't say: "How is she, Tom?"

(She's what in days gone by they might have called mad. She's in what, in days gone by but not any more, they called an asylum.)

He doesn't ask: "Why?"

He says – But he can't even say what he'd planned to say: he's opening his filing cabinet, he's going to offer me whisky. No reasons, no explanations, no digging up what's past. He'd rather pretend it isn't real. Reality's so strange, so strange and unexpected. He doesn't want to discuss it.

Mr Lewis Scott, Headmaster, had "no comment" today when faced with angry reaction from parents.

He'd like it over and done with and out the way:
Early retirement. Full pension. We're cutting History.

A Bruise upon a Bruise

It bobbed gently. It swivelled and rocked in the eddies, face down, arms held out, bent at the elbow, in the position of someone quietly, pronely asleep. But it was dead, not asleep. Since bodies do not sleep which lie face down in the water, least of all if they have been lying thus, undetected in the darkness, for several hours.

For that night (July the twenty-fifth, 1943), as chance would have it, Dad had not been plagued by his usual restlessness. That night he had slept soundly till woken by the dawn, at which he had risen, along with Dick who, never suffering himself from disturbed nights, woke every morning at five-thirty, to depart at six-thirty on his motor-cycle for the outskirts of Lynn, where he worked on a dredger in the Ouse. Only a commotion coming from the front of the cottage, a hoarse shout from Dad, the clanking of someone running over the cat-walk of the sluice, denied me the extra hour's sleep I was allowed as a studious schoolboy (schoolboy then on holiday, and not so exclusively studious) and prevented me from being woken, as I usually was, by the coughings and garglings of Dick's motor-bike.

And when I went into Dick's room to look out over the river, Dad and Dick were standing on the cat-walk, bent forward, eyes lowered, and Dad was prodding something in the water, tentatively, nervously, with a boat-hook, as if he were the keeper of some dangerous but sluggish aquatic animal and were trying to goad it into life.

I flung on my clothes; went downstairs, heart jumping.

At that time of year the river was low. The barrier of the sluice itself, the vertical brick-facing of the adjacent river bank and the pier between sluice and lock formed a deep, three-sided enclosure from which no body, alive or dead, could be lifted with ease. Dad must have been considering this fact and was scrambling back to the cottage to look for better tools than the boat-hook, when he met me, scrambling in the opposite direction, by the sluice engine. His face had the look of a criminal caught in mid-crime.

"Freddie Parr," he said.

But I had already recognised the checked summer shirt, the grey cotton trousers, the prominent shoulder-blades, the dark hair which, even when soaked with river water, formed unsmoothable tufts at the back of Freddie's head.

"Freddie Parr."

He brushed past me. I joined Dick on the cat-walk. He held the boat-hook and was giving gentle, deliberate pokes to the body.

"Freddie Parr," I said.

We could not get beyond this repetition of a name.

"Freddie Parr," Dick said. "Freddie Parr-Parr."

For that was how Dick spoke, in a sort of baby-language.

He turned his face to me; a long, potato-coloured face, with a heavy jaw and a slack mouth which hung invariably open, emitting a thin, unconscious wheeze. His eyelids flickered. When Dick was moved, only his eyelids showed it. The muddy complexion neither flushed nor paled; the mouth remained limp; the eyes themselves stared. The eyelids alone registered emotion. But although they registered emotion it was impossible to tell merely from their movement what emotion was being signalled.

"F-Freddie Parr. Dead. D-dead Freddie. Deddie Freddie."

He stirred the body with the boat-hook. He was trying to get it to float face upwards.

Dad had disappeared into the lean-to shed abutting the cottage. Here were kept more boat-hooks, ropes, life-belts and the rakes and grappling hooks he used for clearing debris from the river. Our punt, which would have been the most serviceable piece of equipment at this moment, was lying upturned on a pair of trestles by the tow-path, a section of its bottom removed for repair.

He emerged again, empty-handed. It was clear that he had given thought to the ropes and hooks, but though they were effective for tree branches and the carcasses of sheep, he baulked at using them on the raw flesh of a dead boy.

He stood, facing us, on the tow-path. Then quite deliberately, for a matter of several seconds, he turned to look the other way. I know what he was doing. He was hoping that all this was not happening. He was hoping that no drowned body had floated one bright summer's morning against his sluice-gate. He was hoping that if he turned his back, counted ten, whispered a covert entreaty, it would go away. But it didn't.

The sun was still low, glinting on the river. Above the fields, larks were twittering in a milky-blue sky. All over the globe, at this very hour, a war was being fought. Our troops were pushing hard, so we were told, in Sicily; the Russians, also, were pushing. Meanwhile, in the Atlantic . . . But except for the Lancasters and B24s which favoured for their roosts the flat and strategic country of East Anglia, no hint of this universal strife reached us in our Fenland backwater.

Dad hobbled back over lock and cat-walk and took the boat-hook from Dick's hands. There was nothing for it but, by means of this boat-hook, to steer the body through the water to a point where it could be manhandled onto dry land. This meant manoeuvring it around the central pier, across the head-gate of the lock, then upstream a few yards along the tow-path to where landing-steps led down to the water and where, had it not been upturned with a hole in its bottom, our punt would have been moored.

I watched Dad decide between the collar of Freddie's shirt and the belt of his trousers. He settled for the collar. It would have been better, in the long run, if he had chosen the belt. Slipping the end of the boat-hook between the shirt-collar and the white nape of Freddie's neck, he gave a twist and succeeded in getting a hold. He began to walk, slowly, holding the boat-hook with great, indeed, trembling concentration, along the cat-walk and up the central pier. We followed him.

The position of Freddie's outward-bent arms did not facilitate this journey through the water. It also gave the illusion that he was propelling himself in some crude, floundering way over the surface – a semblance counteracted by the evident stiffness of both arms and legs, and by the well known fact, only confirmed by this morning's discovery, that Freddie Parr could not swim.

As Dad tried to guide the body round the upstream end of the central pier he ran into difficulties. When he pulled the body across-stream the legs swung out into the current. The right hand and forearm, at the same time, caught against the brick-work, increasing the feet-first swing. By applying sideways pressure with the boat-hook, Dad attempted to correct this tendency and to disengage Freddie's hand – which nonetheless remained caught – from the wall of the pier.

The combined effect of all these movements and counter-movements was that the twist in Freddie's collar by which he was attached to the boat-hook, twisted still further, to the point where it could twist no more without Freddie twisting with it. All at once, the body, left leg and shoulder first, turned face upwards, and this, unlike the unconvincing imitation of swim-ming, gave every appearance that Freddie Parr had suddenly woken from his nose-down slumber and, annoyed by the boat-hook that was both probing his neck and threatening to throttle him, was angrily alive.

Whether it was in frantic response to this illusion or whether he had decided anyway to abandon his plan and haul the body out of the water there and then, Dad began to pull mightily on the boat-hook. Freddie reared out of the water, as far as his waist, and hung, elbows out, wrists raised in a gesture of sur-render, still several feet below Dad. The head fell back and hit the brickwork of the pier. Water flowed out of the mouth. The twisted shirt-collar which could not support the weight of the hanging body, tore apart. The boat-hook caught first under Freddie's jaw, then, as the body fell back into the water, gouged upwards through cheek, eye-socket and temple.

And it was then, children – as Freddie Parr plunged but bobbed up again, and as it became clear that the inadvertent wound to his head had drawn blood, but not blood of the usual kind, vivid red and readily mingling with water, but a dark, sticky, reluctant substance, the colour of blackcurrants – that I came out of a dream. That I realised. I realised I was looking at a dead body. Something I had never seen before. (For I had seen Mother dying but not dead.) And not just any dead body, but the dead body of my friend (true, a devious friend, a friend to be suspected on more than one count – but a friend). Freddie Parr. Whom I had talked to the day before yesterday. With whom, not so long ago, I used to sit and jibe and banter on the high banks of the Hockwell Lode where it joins the Leem, not far from where the Leem meets the Ouse. Along with Dick, and Mary Metcalf and Shirley Alford and Peter Baine and David Coe, most of us half-naked and muddy-limbed, because this was our favourite spot for swimming.

Save that Freddie Parr couldn't.

Dick's eyelashes whirred. Dad swore – the soft oath of a godfearing man who swears never in anger but only in distress – and fished once more with his boat-hook amongst Freddie's clothes.

We got Freddie Parr out of the water. Between us, we lifted him up the landing-steps – a water-logged body is not light – and carried him onto the concrete stretch of tow-path in front of the cottage. There, because it is the recommended position for the resuscitation of the not-quite-drowned, Dad had him placed chest-down on the ground. And there, because Dad had at one time under the auspices of the Great Ouse Catchment Board (which subsumed the Leem Drainage and Navigation Board) been given token instruction in the Holger-Nielsen Method of Artificial Respiration, he began to press between Freddie's prominent shoulder-blades, to raise and lower his stiffened arms and to continue to do so for a full quarter of an hour. Not because he did not know, any less than Dick and I knew, that Freddie was dead, but because Dad, being superstitious, would never exclude the possibility of a miracle, and because this ritual pretence at resuscitation staved off the moment when he must face the indictment of truth. That the corpse of a boy had been found in his lock, a boy who – had his lock-keeper's vigilance not failed him that night – might have been saved; that because it was his lock, it was his responsibility; that it was the corpse of the son of a known neighbour of his; that in retrieving this corpse he had cack-handedly wounded it about the head with a boat-hook, and to wound the dead was perhaps a sin more heinous than to wound the living; that the appropriate authorities must be informed and summoned; that, once again, Trouble was invading his quiet, riverside life.

For when a body floats into a lock kept by a lock-keeper of my father's disposition, it is not an accident but a curse.

More water flowed from Freddie Parr's mouth, but no blood flowed from the mulberry gash in his temple. Water flowed from Freddie Parr's mouth in rhythmic spurts according to the pressure of the persevering hands between his shoulders. For there is such a thing as human drainage too, such a thing as human pumping. And what else was my father doing on that July morning than what his forebears had been doing for generations: expelling water? But whereas they reclaimed land, my father could not reclaim a life . . .

Thus I see us, grouped silently on the concrete tow-path, while Dad labours to refute reality, labours against the law of nature, that a dead thing does not live again; and larks twitter in the buttery haze of the morning sky, and the sun, shining along the Leem, catches the yellow-brick frontage of our cottage, on which can be observed, above the porch, a stone inset bearing the date 1875, and, above the date, in relief, the motif of two crossed ears of corn which, on close inspection, can be seen to be not any old ears of corn but the whiskered ears of barley.

The water slops out, in astonishing quantities. And no amount of rhythmic pressing and pulling on Dad's part, no amount of dogged application of the Holger-Nielsen Method can hide the fact that he is desperate. That though his lips do not move he is praying, that he is thinking of Jack and Flora Parr who do not know, at this moment, that their son is dead. And I too am praying and hoping – I do not know if it is for Freddie Parr's sake or for my father's – that Freddie Parr will miraculously revive. Because it seems to me that in his futile pumping at Freddie's body, Dad is trying to pump away not just this added curse, but all the ill luck of his life: the ill luck that took away, six years ago, his wife; the ill luck that had his first son born a freak, a potato-head (for that's what Dick is). And more curses, more curses perhaps, as yet unknown.

Only Dick, of the three of us, shows no dismay (but what can you tell of the feelings of a potato-head?). For him, this removal of a body – even a familiar body – from the river is perhaps not

27

essentially different from his daily task (for which he will be late today) of removing silt, by means of bucket-dredging apparatus from the bottom of the Ouse. For Dick is a good worker, potato-head though he is, there is no doubt about that. There is no doubting his manual strength, his stamina, his sullen willingness to get on with the chores he is set. Dick smells of silt. He goes now to the edge of the tow-path. He is holding the boat-hook. He leans on it and spits – a great gob of the old Crick phlegm which, though thick and in good supply, has momentarily failed to quell my father's inner agitation – into the lock-pen. He watches it float, bubble, sink. His cow-lashes flutter over his fish-eyes.

And only Dick sees, through blinking eyes, as we try to raise the dead, that two lighters are approaching in the distance, upriver, from the Ouse, and will require passage through the lock. Drowned body or not, the lock-gates must be opened and closed. And soon this riverside calamity which is known only to us will be known to others too, the news carried up the Leem by the lightermen of the Gildsey Fertiliser Company. Soon the desperate silence on the tow-path will be broken by the voices of those for whom this drowned boy is only something on the periphery, not at the hub of their concern. "Ent much sense squeezin' the water outa dead body" (first lighterman). "Boat-'ook? What d'you use a boat-'ook for? Coulden you dive in an' pull the bugger out?" (Why not indeed? Because it's bad luck to swim in the same water as a drowned body.) By the voices of policemen and ambulancemen, with questions and note-books, for whom this sort of thing is not exactly everyday, but not unusual.

And why make a fuss about one drowned boy when over the far horizon and in the sky a war is being fought; when mothers are losing their sons every day and every night the bombers are taking off and don't all return? The wide world takes priority. And even Dad, who once watched the wide world drowning in Flanders yet lived to tell the tale, will one day tell perhaps, with a flick of cigarette ash and a shake of his head, how he fished that poor drowned lad out of the New Atkinson.

For the reality of things, children – be thankful – only visits us for a brief while.

But – for a brief while – the scene which seems endless: the tow-path; the glinting Leem; lighters approaching downstream; Dick by the lock-pen; Dad labouring in vain, but not knowing how to stop, at the water-filled body of Freddie Parr.

And Dad does not see, in his agitation, something to make this scene even more endless and indelible. For under and around the gash on Freddie Parr's right temple is a dark, oval bruise. Or perhaps Dad does see it, which is why he goes on levering Freddie's arms, not wanting more Trouble. And perhaps Dick sees it, which is why he turns away and spits in the lock-pen. Perhaps we all see it; but I am the only one to consider (notwithstanding my ignorance of how speedily a corpse bruises) that the bruise on Freddie's right temple, which is a dull yellow at the edges, was not made by the boat-hook.

But the lighters are approaching. Dick is opening the tail-gates and the lightermen at the same time are seeing something on the tow-path which will justify a break in their upstream journey. They clamber ashore to inform us of what we know already but do not want to know, that Jack Parr's son is dead, sure as they're alive; and to be the means at last of making Dad cease his relentless squeezing and pulling. The lightermen gabble. Dad is quiet; then suddenly remembers he is a lock-keeper, with official duties in cases of emergency.

Twenty-five minutes have passed since Freddie was hoisted from the river (the perimeter of the puddle in which he lies is already beginning to dry). And it will be another thirty-five minutes before the policeman from Apton and the ambulance from Gildsey will arrive. By which time (because dead bodies, like picked fruit, do indeed bruise) a new bruise, caused by the boat-hook, will have begun to form over the old bruise which could not have been caused by the boat-hook, rendering the two bruises, in due course, to appear, to the casual eye, as one. And because of this; because in giving his account to the policeman Dad stressed more than once, with contrite insistence, that the wounds to Freddie's head were made by his own inexcusable clumsiness with a boat-hook (to which I and a grunting Dick bore witness); because the policeman was satisfied; because time elapsed while the unfortunate parents were informed and summoned (another endless, indelible scene) and the body was transported to the mortuary in Gildsey, and time blurs details; and because the examining pathologist, having been informed of the business of the boat-hook, did, indeed, have a casual eye and was concerned only to ascertain that Freddie's lungs were water-logged, and to note the further conclusive fact that the subject's congealing blood contained a substantial infusion of alcohol – the preliminary verdict on Freddie Parr was that he died (being a non-swimmer and also drunk at the time) by drowning, between the hours of 11 p.m. and 1 a.m. on the night of the twenty-fifth to the twenty-sixth of July, 1943.

Children, why did fear transfix me at that moment when the boat-hook clawed at Freddie Parr's half-slipping, half-suspended body? Because I saw death? Or the image of something worse? Because this wasn't just plain, ordinary, terrible, unlooked-for death, but something more?

Children, evil isn't something that happens far off – it suddenly touches your arm. I was scared when I saw the dark blood appear but not flow in the gash on Freddie's head. But not half so scared as when Mary Metcalf said to me later that day: "I told him it was Freddie. Dick killed Freddie Parr because he thought it was him. Which means we're to blame too."

And that same evening, after I'd cycled back from my tryst with Mary (because she and I had one of those youthful things going, which, though youthful, are not always innocent and which, though they happen in your youth, can affect the rest of your life), something else floated down the Leem, was seen and fished out only by me.

The swallows are skimming the water above the sluice. The late July evening is only just beginning to darken. Gnats are jitter-bugging above the rushes. And I am lying in a little cavity in the river-bank, under a willow, upstream from the cottage on the far side; a place where I have often sat or lain and fed my hunger for books. Where I have polished off *Hereward the Wake*, *The Black Arrow* and *With Clive in India*. And, more recently, chewed thoughtfully, if distantly, over school textbooks (does it surprise you, children, that your tiresome teacher was once a tiresome swot?) or concocted my high-flown essays (wince again) on the Jacobite Rebellions or The Effects of the Seven Years' War. But I have not brought history with me this evening (history is a thin garment, easily punctured by a knife blade called Now). I have brought my fear.

Through willow branches, I watch Dad. He is walking to and fro, sentry-like, along the far tow-path. Sometimes he looks at the gently gliding river and sometimes he looks at the sky. He is talking, soundlessly, to himself. And now and then he rubs his right knee, the right knee wounded all those years ago in 1917. He rubs it because he has made the mistake earlier in the day of kneeling (the worst possible thing for that still susceptible knee) on a hard surface (concrete) for several minutes. Yet he was scarcely to have considered . . . And now he walks, up and down, the twilight darkening his profile, nursing and flexing the suffering joint, but still not really thinking of it. He won't go to set eel-traps tonight; but he won't go to bed either. When it's dark and nearer dawn than dusk he'll still be rubbing his knee at the lock-side. Because, last night, for want of vigilance . . .

And Dick is by the lean-to against the left-hand wall of the cottage, doing what he will always be found doing when there is nothing else to do – "mending" his motor-cycle. That is to say, removing parts of it (for, though it's old, there's nothing wrong with that motor-cycle), oiling them, holding them up to the light, blowing on them, rubbing them, and putting them back again. Dick has a way with machines. Every day he coaxes into continued action the antiquated gear of a bucket-dredger which, were it not for the war, would have been declared obsolete long ago. And it is conceivable that, but for the lack of something up top, this way with things mechanical, which in Dick's case is less a skill than a sort of kinship, might have taken Dick far in some relevant field – hydro-engineering, say, for which there is constant demand in the Fens.

Dick lacks, indeed, certain accomplishments which even the mechanically-minded find useful. Dick cannot read or write. He is not even good at putting a spoken sentence together. He has received a rudimentary schooling at the village school. But the strange thing is that whereas it would seem that

Dick's shortcomings required extra and extensive attention, his education was in fact curtailed, even, one might say, deliberately abandoned by the parents. To the younger son was given the privileged role of the bright schoolboy of whom much was expected and who was therefore to be protected from all things menial; while to the elder (who did not seem to mind) was assigned a lifetime of daily toil. And while this determined policy on the part of the parents might have expressed the simple recognition that their first-born was, after all, irreclaimable, this did not account for the rigour with which it was pursued: for that moment, for example, when the younger son, thinking it only right to impart to his less fortunate brother some of his, albeit frugal, learning, embarked (the future teacher in the making) on a programme of secret tuition; and, being found out, was not only stopped short in his scheme of enlightenment but was roundly told by the provoked father (who was not a man, it was true, easily roused to great temper or severity, especially since the sad death of his wife): "Don't educate him! Don't learn 'im to read!"

And it was that same night that the father (composure regained) told the younger son about mother's milk and everyone having a heart . . .

Dick works at his motor-bike. It could be said that Dick's love of machines, if love it is, springs from the fact that Dick himself is a sort of machine – in so far as a machine is something which has no mind of its own and in so far as Dick's large, lean and surprisingly agile body will not only work indefatigably but will perform on occasion quite remarkable feats of dexterity and strength. This despite the clumsy mental faculties that go with it and its deceptive air of ineptitude. Dick wants to know why other people are not like machines. Perhaps Dick too wants not to be like a machine. Dick stumbles helplessly or blenches in a kind of puritanical horror at any event which proves that human behaviour is not to be regulated like that of a machine. Except when he descends to foolish attempts to imitate, by mechanical means, the idiosyncracies he sees around him, Dick can give the impression that he looks down from his lofty and lucid mindlessness, half in contempt and half in pity at a world blinded by its own glut of imagination. That he knows something we don't.

And this impression – this pose – can lend Dick, in the eyes of others, a certain rugged pathos; can even invest him (for there's no getting away from it, Dick has an ugly mug) with a perverse appeal. But it makes Dick lonely. It makes him suffer. Which is why he talks, for solace, to his motor-bike, more than he talks to any living thing. And why it has even been said (and Freddie Parr was one of the chief rumour-mongers) that Dick is so fond of his motor-bike that he sometimes rides it to secluded spots, gets down with it on the grass and . . .

Dick crouches by the lean-to. As well as silt, Dick smells of oil. He holds up some bit of engine to inspect. Dick has big, powerful hands. But I cannot see his eyes.

And Dad walks. And in walking, as he passes the cottage, he steps perceptibly to one side, round the spot on the concrete where . . .

To and fro; up and down. His figure, on the river-bank, looms darker against the fading sky and takes on for me some of that pitiful charisma Dick too can exert. He must imagine I'm up in my room, nose buried in my books. For if he knew I wasn't, his head would be turning and his neck craning in even greater fretfulness. He'd be searching along the river. For he's one of those who believe that sorrows seldom come singly, and he's already witnessed, this morning, one father and his drowned boy.

To and fro. Perhaps he's thinking, on this day when there's so much else to think on, of the old conundrum of his two sons. How one pores over books, one over motor-bikes; how one is a moron, and one has brains, will be a clever man. He doesn't guess how the brainy one is hiding from the brainless one.

Because the brainy one's scared.

About-turn. Pause. Flex leg. Rub knee.

And then something catches my eye amongst the rushes. Perhaps it has just, that very moment, drifted there, or perhaps it has been there all the while. A bottle. And since it is a habit if you live by a river to fish out the debris it brings down, I reach out, hook one finger into its neck and retrieve it. A bottle. A beer bottle. A bottle of thick dark brown glass, but not a sort of bottle that is seen any more around the Fens – or has been seen for over thirty years. Label-less, undirtied, with a slender neck and an upright, slim rather than squat appearance.

All this I observe before, as darkness gathers, I take the bottle and carry it along the river-bank, to below the sluice, from where it will float down to the Ouse, and even, perhaps, in time, to the sea. An old-fashioned, but quite unmuddied beer bottle, with round the base, embossed in the glass, the words: ATKINSON GILDSEY.

6

An Empty Vessel

But there's another theory of reality, children, quite different from that which found its way into my fraught after-school meeting with Lewis. Reality's not strange, not unexpected. Reality doesn't reside in the sudden hallucination of events. Reality is uneventfulness, vacancy, flatness. Reality is that nothing happens. How many of the events of history have occurred, ask yourselves, for this and for that reason, but for no other reason, fundamentally, than the desire to make things happen? I present to you History, the fabrication, the diversion, the reality-obscuring drama. History, and its near relative, Histrionics . . .

And did I not bid you remember, children, that for each protagonist who once stepped onto the stage of so-called historical events, there were thousands, millions, who never entered the theatre – who never knew that the show was running – who got on with the donkey-work of coping with reality?

True, true. But it doesn't stop there. Because each one of those numberless non-participants was doubtless concerned with raising in the flatness of his own unsung existence his own personal stage, his own props and scenery – for there are very few of us who can be, for any length of time, merely realistic. So there's no escaping it: even if we miss the grand repertoire of

34

history, we yet imitate it in miniature and endorse, in miniature, its longing for presence, for feature, for purpose, for content.

And there's no saying what consequences we won't risk, what reactions to our actions, what repercussions, what brick towers built to be knocked down, what chasings of our own tails, what chaos we won't assent to in order to assure ourselves that, nonetheless, things are happening. And there's no saying what heady potions we won't concoct, what meanings, myths, manias we won't imbibe in order to convince ourselves that reality is not an empty vessel.

Once upon a time the future Mrs Crick – who was then called Metcalf – as a result of certain events which took place while she was still, like some of you, a schoolgirl, decided to withdraw from the world and devote herself to a life of solitude, atonement and (which was only making a virtue of necessity) celibacy. Not even she has ever said how far God came into this lonely vigil. But three and a half years later she emerged from these self-imposed cloisters to marry a prospective history teacher (an old and once intimate acquaintance), Tom Crick. She put aside her sackcloth and sanctity and revealed in their stead what this now ex-history teacher (who is no longer sure what's real and what isn't) would have called then a capacity for realism. For she never spoke again, at least not for many years, of that temporary communing with On High.

But it must have been always there, lurking, latent, ripening like some dormant, forgotten seed. (Seed indeed!) Because in the year 1979, a woman of fifty-two, she suddenly began looking again for Salvation. She began this love-affair, this liaison – much to the perplexity of her husband (from whom she could not keep it a secret) – with God. And it was when this liaison reached a critical – in the usual run of liaisons not unfamiliar, but in this case quite incredible – pitch, that your astounded and forsaken history teacher, prompted as he was by the challenging remarks of a student called Price, ceased to teach history and started to offer you, instead, these fantastic-but-true, these believe-it-or-not-but-it-happened Tales of the Fens.

Children, women are equipped with a miniature model of reality: an empty but fillable vessel. A vessel in which much can be made to happen, and to issue in consequence. In which dramas can be brewed, things can be hatched out of nothing. And it was Tom Crick, history-teacher-to-be, who, during the middle years of the Second World War, not knowing what reactions, what repercussions, and not without rivals (though none of them was God) was responsible for filling the then avid and receptive vessel of Mary Metcalf, later Mrs Crick.

But on the afternoon of July the twenty-sixth, 1943, he was about to know what repercussions.

7

About Holes and Things

For at four o'clock on that same afternoon, after I had assisted in retrieving the body of Freddie Parr from the River Leem but before I had plucked from the same river a certain brown bottle, I was riding on an ancient bicycle along the narrow, pot-holed but otherwise dead-flat road which runs between the Fenland villages of Hockwell and Wansham, to meet, at an appointed time and place, the fore-mentioned Mary Metcalf. I had taken the main Gildsey to Apton road which runs eastwards, close by the lock-keeper's cottage at the Atkinson Lock, following the south bank of the Leem. But I had not turned left – which would have been my quickest, and my usual route – onto the road which crosses the Leem by Hockwell bridge and heads north-wards to Wansham and Downham Market, but continued along the Apton road a further quarter of a mile, wheeled my bike across the footbridge which spanned both the river and a line of the Great Eastern Railway, and thence, by a circuitous route, involving travelling along three unnecessary sides of a rectangle, regained the road to Wansham. I had not crossed the Leem by the Hockwell bridge because on the other side of the bridge, only a little distance from it, yet hidden by the raised banks of the river, a line of trees and a bend the road makes on the northern side, was a level-crossing. And the keeper of this level-crossing was Jack Parr, Freddie Parr's father.

All of which meant that, what with the troubled events of the day, I was late for my rendezvous.

But Mary was not late. She sat in the hollow of sheltered ground formed by an angle in the banks of the man-made waterway known as the Hockwell Lode. To her left was a line of sunken, vivid grass, dotted with clumps of rushes and marsh weed, marking a silted-up drain, and to her front and right (masking her from me as I strode with my bike along the top of the embankment) a group of those trees so characteristic of temperate flatlands – poplars. Perched on an outwork on the landward side of the Lode bank, which formed the termination of the defunct drain, were the remains of a windmill. That is to say, the tarred, cracked wooden shell of the mill's lower portion, no more than six feet in height, devoid of its internal workings, open to the sky, but preserving still, minus its door, the tiny access-way through which the millman had once ducked to enter. And leaning against the derelict mill, on top of the mill emplacement, beside the weed-choked brick culvert and rusted cog-wheels which once conveyed water from the old drain up to the Lode, sat Mary, in a red-check skirt, knees drawn up to her chin and clasped in her arms, waiting for me to appear.

The silting up of the old drain – when abandoned in favour of a new pumping station to the north – had left the adjacent land wet and spongey, fit only for summer pasture. So Mary shared her vigil with a score or more of munching cows, which cropped the lush grass and released their splatterings of dung between her and the poplar spinney. The cows belonged to Farmer Metcalf, whose chief business was beets and potatoes; but who, not wasting an acre of land, kept also a small herd of Friesians which roamed every summer up and down the margins of the Lode and sent their milk to a dairy in Apton. Thus it was not only mother's milk but Farmer Metcalf's milk which Dick and I drank when we were boys. And it was her father's milk – but, alas, never her mother's – that Mary Metcalf grew up on.

For Mary was a farmer's daughter. Her father owned the fields, thick at that moment with creamy-flowered potatoes, which she could see if she looked to her left, across the narrow ditch dividing pasture from ploughland. And away in front of her, hidden by poplar spinney and twisting banks, lay Harold Metcalf's brick farmhouse and clustered farm buildings, looming abruptly and starkly amidst the flat fields, as is the manner of Fenland farms, and in no way nestling or huddling like the farms of picture-books. A Polt Fen Farm had existed since the days when Thomas Atkinson drained Polt Fen, and the Metcalfs, who built the new farmhouse in 1880, were the second family to own it.

Polt Fen Farm, like many farms of the region, was not large but made up for size with intensity of yield. Harold Metcalf employed three permanent hands and an additional contingent of cursing, raw-fingered temporary labourers during the long and malodorous winter beet harvest. But now, in the summer of 1943, neither permanent nor temporary hands, excluding the lame or one-eyed variety, were available. Instead, into Farmer Metcalf's farm, as into other neighbourhood farms, fluttered coveys of Land Girls, in boiler-suits and dungarees and tightly fastened head-scarves, their forearms growing muscular and sunburnt, their urban decorum evaporating in the summer heat. Broken-down trucks ferried these creatures from their hostels in Apton and Wansham to the scenes of their labours, to the leers and jeers of the local inhabitants. It was said that the land girls brought to our Fenland byways an atmosphere of subversion and simmering sexuality. But simmering sexuality – as you may well know, children – is always there.

Freddie Parr claimed that he had enjoyed the utmost favours of one of these female migrants – an auburn-haired beauty called Joyce, whose well-formed rump, upturned as she worked in the fields, Freddie spent many hours watching from the banks of the Hockwell Lode. And it was true that after they shed their initial ladylike airs, the land girls would often wave to us local kids, tell us their names and share their field-side lunches with us (though they persistently declined our invitations to bathing parties in the Hockwell Lode). And it was even true that this same auburn-haired Joyce used to wave with smiling condescension at Freddie in particular (for perhaps she was touched by his moony attentions); and only stopped one day when she saw that Freddie (who was barely fourteen at the time) was not only vigorously waving back with one hand but with the other doing something of unmistakable import in the region of his trouser buttons. After which Joyce was seen no more in the fields around Hockwell.

So, doubtless, Freddie Parr was lying.

And now, in any case, Freddie Parr was dead.

And the land girls, anyway, were not for us. At night, healthily exhausted, they were swooped up by roaming airmen from the bases, whom bad weather kept from their missions. And if the girls gave themselves readily to these heroes of the skies, then it was not for anyone to protest and was even regarded as proper, since these same brave fliers might be dead tomorrow.

But Freddie Parr was dead too.

Farmer Metcalf had no idle fancies about acquiring for the length of the war a temporary harem. A grave, reserved, hard-headed man, he regarded the land girls as replacement labour and made no concessions either to their sex or to the patriotic motives which brought them to his acres. Nor did he look upon them as fit companions for his only daughter. For years, with the earnestness of a good beet- and potato-grower secretly emulating the role of gentleman-farmer, he had discouraged all tendencies on her part to help out either in the fields or in the farmyard, to become the archetypal farmer's daughter – dung on her boots and straw in her hair. With a view to her becoming a cultivated and elegant lady, an embodiment of everything above beets and potatoes, he sent her, at his own expense, to the St Gunnhilda Convent School in Gildsey.

For Harold Metcalf was not only a farmer with ambitious notions but also a Roman Catholic. That is to say, he had married a Catholic wife, a fact which might have had no effect on the dour disposition of Harold Metcalf, were it not that Mrs Metcalf had died, in the second year of their marriage, and in remaining faithful to her memory – Harold never remarried and those land girls could not snare him – he conferred the articles of her faith on his daughter. Thus "Mary" became this daughter's inevitable name, and thus Harold Metcalf would have turned her, if he only could, into a little madonna, who would be transformed, in due course, into a princess. And Mary might have met her father half-way over this arrangement,

39

which, in effect, was that she should be a distilled and purified version of her mother, had she known at all what her mother had been like. For Mary's mother had died in giving birth to Mary. And perhaps it was this common factor – the absence of a mother – that (amongst other things) drew her and Tom Crick together.

So Farmer Metcalf, intending his daughter for Higher Things, but scarcely consulting her own inclinations, sent her to the St Gunnhilda School for Girls (more exclusive by far than the Gildsey High School for Girls), firmly believing his outlay and his efforts must have results. Just as his neighbour, Henry Crick, a humble lock-keeper, seeing his younger child, without any paternal effort or outlay, win a scholarship to Gildsey Grammar School (for Boys) and begin to immerse himself in history books, drew the converse conclusion that his son must have a vision which he lacked, and began consciously and apologetically to see to it that this son should not soil his hands on sluice engines.

Yet Henry Crick once had a wife whom Harold Metcalf might have doted on for a daughter . . .

And so it was on the little four-carriage train that called at Hockwell Station (not a stone's throw from Jack Parr's signal-box and level-crossing) and went on via Newhithe to Gildsey, that Mary and I got to know each other. That, to the accompaniment of clacking bogie-wheels and passing steam-puffs, irrepressible symptoms began to appear and steps were taken, tacit or overt, to relieve them.

Yet for a long time, children, even before these hesitant but tell-tale traits broke surface, your history-teacher-to-be was in love with Mary Metcalf. For a long time the very feelings that drew him towards her placed her also, in his eyes, at an impossible distance, and made him melancholy and mute.

He is timid, he is shy – this fledgling adolescent. He has a sorrowful streak. He believes he is fated to yearn from afar. And why is he these things? Why sad? Why this gap between him and the world (which, for better or worse, he attempts to fill with books)? And why, even when he cannot deny certain distinct signs – that Mary Metcalf, it seems, might have feelings about him too (because his reticence and plaintiveness have not failed to lend him an air of mystery, and Mary cannot resist a mystery) – can he scarcely believe that it can really be happening? That this unattainable girl – ? That he – ?

Because his mother is not long dead. Because she died when he was nine years old. Mary's mother is dead too, but Mary cannot be said to miss her, never having known her. Whereas this son of a lock-keeper has not yet got over missing his mother.

So even more, perhaps, than Farmer Metcalf, Tom Crick has turned Mary – in spite of the facts – into an untouchable madonna (that red sacred heart, emblem of the blessed St Gunnhilda, that burns so tantalisingly, so ambiguously, on the breast pocket of her school blazer). Yet he knows – he has evidence – that Mary Metcalf is no demure convent girl. And Mary Metcalf knows that although Tom Crick has a Platonic disposition and a brainy head . . .

Thus the Great Eastern Railway which brought these two young people into twice-daily contact – she in a rust-red uniform, he in inky black – is to be held responsible for loosening inhibitions which, without its nudging and jostling, might have stuck fast, and for a merging of destinies which might otherwise never have occurred. For while the shadow of the engine – westward-slanting in the morning, eastward-slanting in the evening – rippled over the beet fields, the unattainable was attained. Certain notions were gradually (and not unpainfully) dissolved, certain advances made and, less falteringly, encouraged, and, at last (but this was the work of two years' railway travel), an undeniable intimacy mutually – but always circumspectly – achieved.

And why were we so circumspect – beyond the normal discretion in such cases – on these schoolward and homeward journeys? Why did we choose our carriage and compartment with care and last-minute changes (which no doubt earned us more attention)? Why did we sometimes, on the return journey, deliberately miss the ten-past-four from Gildsey and pick up the next train from Newhithe, thereby not only avoiding the usual carriage-loads of passengers but allowing various fondnesses to occur on the walk from Gildsey, across the mud-grey Ouse,

41

past the decaying lighter wharves of Newhithe, along the tree-screened fringes of celery and onion fields?

Because on that four-ten train could be Freddie Parr and Peter Baine and Shirley Alford, not to mention other contemporaries from Hockwell and Apton, pupils, for the most part, at the Gildsey Secondary School (blue uniform) and the Gildsey High School (dark brown and green uniform).

But Freddie Parr above all. There was no suppressing Freddie Parr. Freddie lacked subtlety, had a crude tongue. Freddie was often drunk at four-thirty in the afternoon on secret supplies of whisky stolen from his father, who in turn procured it, by nefarious means, from an American air base. Freddie, at sixteen, had the mind of an advanced roué and a complex about the size of his penis – which was average. I might have been intimidated by Freddie Parr were it not that I knew, at least, that I could swim and he could not – a distinct failing in a watery region. But there remained Freddie's leering eye, and his talent for gossip. For, no doubting it, Freddie would have hastened to tell my brother how Mary and I always sat together (and not just that) on the Gildsey train. Because, by the summer of 1943, it was a well known fact (how well I knew it) that Dick Crick often took solitary evening walks along the banks of the Hockwell Lode in the direction of Polt Fen Farm.

Freddie would gladly have implanted in Dick's mind the seeds of revenge for the thwarted designs that he, Freddie, had on Mary; were it not that he feared that Dick might suspect him; that he spurned the ignominious role of pander; and were it not that he stood in awe, in any case, of my brother. Because Dick Crick, it was generally rumoured – even his own brother was unable to refute it – possessed a penis of fabulous dimensions. And had it not been my opinion that even if Dick had had a penis like a marrow he would not have known how to use it; had I not innocently believed that brothers, after all, are brothers; had Freddie Parr not curbed his tongue; and had I not wanted to keep Mary so much that instead of taking jealous exception, I myself had already pandered to her fascination with Dick (for she couldn't resist a mystery), not least with his much wondered-at parts – I might have been afraid of my brother.

As afraid before as I was after that day we pulled Freddie from the river with a new bruise and an old bruise on his head . . .

But in the school holidays, when the Great Eastern Railway no longer provided us with a travelling rendezvous, we would meet in the late afternoon by the stump of the old windmill, near the poplar spinney, by the bend in the Lode, out of sight of the farmhouse of Polt Fen Farm.

Why here? And why at this particular hour?

Because it was here that one day in August 1942 (defeat in the desert; the U-boat stranglehold) we first explored, tentatively but collaboratively, what we called then simply "holes" and "things".

Hesitantly, but at Mary's free invitation, I put the tip of my index finger into the mouth of Mary's hole, and was surprised to discover what an inadequate word was "hole" for what I encountered. For Mary's hole had folds and protuberances, and, so it seemed to me, its false and its genuine entrances, and – as I found the true entrance – it revealed the power of changing its configuration and texture at my touch, of suggesting a moist labyrinth of inwardly twisting, secret passages. The dark curled hairs – only recently sprouted – between Mary's thighs, on which at that moment broad Fen sunlight was genially smiling, had, on close inspection, a coppery sheen. I dipped one finger, up to the first, the second knuckle into Mary's hole; then a second finger alongside it. This was possible, indeed necessary, because Mary's hole began to reveal a further power to suck, to ingest; a voracity which made me momentarily hold back. And yet the chief and most wondrous power of Mary's hole was its capacity to send waves of sensation not only all over Mary's body, but all over mine; and this not by some process of mental association but by a direct electric current which flowed up my arm, flushed my face and gathered in the part of me to which Mary was simultaneously applying her hand.

For just as inexorably as I explored Mary's hole, Mary explored my thing. Indeed, she was the bolder of the two of us. It was she whose fingers first got the itch and were at work before I dared, and only then at her prompting – her grabbing

43

and guiding of my hand, her pulling up and pulling down of clothing – to use mine.

Mary itched. And this itch of Mary's was the itch of curiosity. In her fifteen-year-old body curiosity tickled and chafed, making her fidgety and roving-eyed. Curiosity drove her, beyond all restraint, to want to touch, witness, experience whatever was unknown and hidden from her. Do not smirk, children. Curiosity, which, with other things, distinguishes us from the animals, is an ingredient of love. Is a vital force. Curiosity, which bogs us down in arduous meditations and can lead to the writing of history books, will also, on occasion, as on that afternoon by the Hockwell Lode, reveal to us that which we seldom glimpse unscathed (for it appears more often – dead bodies, boat-hooks – dressed in terror): the Here and Now.

When I had finished exploring Mary's hole, Mary continued our homage to curiosity by verbal means. She spoke of hymens and of her monthly bleedings. She was proud of her bleedings. She wanted to show me when she bled. She wanted me to see. And it was as she spoke of these mysteries, and of others, while the sun still shone on coppery hairs, that I thought (so too perhaps did Mary): everything is open, everything is plain; there are no secrets, here, now, in this nothing-landscape. Us Fenlanders do not try to hide – since we know God is watching.

Within the windmill by the Hockwell Lode curiosity and innocence held hands. And explored holes. Within its stunted, wooden walls we first used those magic, those spell-binding words which make the empty world seem full, just as surely as a thing fits inside a hole: I love – I love – Love, love . . . And perhaps the windmill itself, empty and abandoned since steam and diesel power encroached, and the Leem Drainage Board in its wisdom reviewed its pumping system, found in our presence a new-found windmill-purpose.

But this was when Mary was fifteen, and so was I. This was in prehistorical, pubescent times, when we drifted instinctively, without the need for prior arrangement, to our meeting-place. How had it arisen that in the space of a year our encounters were now a matter of appointment and calculation; that during the summer months we would meet to love each other (and sometimes merely to talk) only between the hours of three and five-thirty in the afternoon?

For two reasons. Because between the hours of three and five-thirty, at least, Dick would still be at work on the dredger, watching the dripping silt of the Ouse disgorge itself from the river-bed. Thus, needing time to ride home and eat his supper, he could not – for want of a better phrase – go awooing along the Hockwell Lode till seven at the earliest. At six-thirty every evening Mary ate her own supper at Polt Fen Farm, under the austere eye of her father, who daily shook his head (having given up remonstrating) over his reprobate daughter; and thus would not be free to present herself to be wooed till nearer seven-thirty. By which time I would be hard at my history books.

Secondly: to avoid Freddie Parr. For though Freddie Parr, a pupil at the Gildsey Secondary School, had, like ourselves, the freedom of the summer days, he would be engaged most weekday afternoons on certain business for his father, signalman and guardian of the Hockwell level-crossing, for which Freddie earned good pocket-money; thus gaining an advantage over us neighbouring children whose own pocket-money (with the exception of Mary's – till her father stopped it) was negligible, and thus acquiring a small-time monopoly in various black-market goods, ranging from Lucky Strikes to condoms.

At two-thirty or so Freddie would set out from Hockwell with one, sometimes two sacks under his arm. Forsaking his bicycle – because he would never know that on his return his sacks might not be heavily and bulkily laden – he would walk by road and field in the direction of Wash Fen Mere, and, in particular, in the direction of the marsh-hut occupied in the summer months by Bill Clay, whose age no one knew.

No one knew either what it was that Bill Clay and Jack Parr had in common; unless it was something that had stemmed from some favour in the past. Unless Jack Parr, who was a superstitious man, more superstitious even than my father, had once as a boy – long before he became a trainee signalman – made visits to the old fowler (he was old even then) and had been prepared, as few were, to sip his lethal poppy tea and listen to his half comprehensible yarns. Yet everyone knew that Jack Parr's present dealings with Bill Clay were of a more material kind. That Jack Parr, renowned for his ability to pass clandestine messages up and down the lines of the Great Eastern Railway and thus obtain from near and far all sorts of unauthorised consignments, to which the company guards turned a blind eye, merely kept Bill supplied with certain articles hard to come by in these belligerent times. And that the sacks which Freddie Parr carried to Wash Fen Mere were not always empty but sometimes contained canisters of gunpowder and bottles of rum and whisky.

Bill Clay still shot duck during the winter floods on Wash Fen Mere. In the summer, when there were no big flights, he grew torpid like the Mere itself which became in places little more than a stagnant bog, and contented himself with eeling and setting springes in the reed beds. Bill Clay sent his winter bags of fowl legitimately to market but his summer bags were sold locally and without licence to all comers – much to the irritation of the inspectors of the Ministry of Food. An official was duly sent from the food office in Gildsey to appeal to Bill's patriotic instinct and sense of fair play in these days of rationing; to be met by the 6-bore barrel of Bill's punt-gun, a muzzle-loader for which supplies of gunpowder were essential.

It was for these same illicit summer fowl that Freddie Parr brought his sacks. Indeed Jack Parr was Bill Clay's chief customer. Within hours of Freddie's return with his haul, the sack or sacks of birds would be on their way by the evening train to a station on the Mildenhall line. Here (guard and station-master taking their share) they would be collected by a jeep of the United States Air Force, whose driver would convey them to certain officers at the nearby base, who took solace in having their orderlies serve up for them what they regarded as the traditional fare of the region before they took off on their insane daylight missions, to be killed – or live for another feast. In return for these regular banquets, the officers were prepared to pay at a good American rate; and back up the line every week, despatched by the self-same corporal in his jeep, would come sometimes foodstuffs, sometimes tobacco, but always, and most importantly for Jack Parr, several bottles of Old Grand-dad Kentucky Bourbon.

Jack Parr could not desert his signal-box and level-crossing. So every alternate afternoon, between half-past two and half-past five, Freddie Parr would make his way to Bill Clay's marsh-hut. He would hand over the smuggled contents of his sack. Then the two of them would set off round the margins of Wash Fen Mere. While Mary and I nestled in the old windmill, Bill Clay would inspect his springes. If a bird were caught, he would grasp it with a fowler's firm yet pacifying grip, unsnare it, and with a casual action, as if he were shaking out a tea-towel, wring its neck. Freddie – so he told us – learnt to do likewise. While Mary and I engaged in caresses that were no longer exploratory yet far from unadventurous, three, four, six or more birds, snagged by the neck or leg, would struggle, flap, thrash at approaching footsteps, be stilled by Bill Clay's horny hand and dispatched. Doubtless, throughout all this Bill Clay talked, and, doubtless, Freddie listened. For Freddie, who was a great blabber-mouth and divulged everything about his father's dealings with the U.S. Air Force, told us – me, Mary and the others – much about Bill Clay, which may or may not have been embellished. How, though Bill wasn't the wisest man in the world, he was certainly the most extraordinary. How he ate water-rats; hypnotised animals; how he was over a hundred; how he knew about the singing swans. How, though he left his cottage and lived alone for weeks on end in his tiny marsh-hut, he was still 'married' to Martha Clay and they still 'did it' (a remarkable sight it was too) in the open air amongst the reeds.

But I never told Freddie what Mary and I did on summer afternoons.

Freddie Parr. My own brother. You see the shape of my dilemma – and the extent of Mary's curiosity. And why I was obliged to meet Mary only at selected and predetermined times.

But on July the twenty-sixth, 1943, I was late for my rendezvous. Because – because, in a word, Freddie Parr was dead. And Mary was squatting on top of the windmill emplacement, chin on knees, arms round shins, rocking to and fro in agitation.

Scarcely, it's true, the agitation of the impatient mistress kept waiting by her lover. Because she must have heard by now – Because by now the whole of Hockwell had heard– But Mary's agitation had another source too. For three weeks now there'd been no misreading the signs. For Mary – if you haven't guessed already – was pregnant.

Beyond the poplar spinney, I wheeled my bike down the landward side of the Lode bank, let it drop in the long grass, ran the last few paces, because of the steepness, onto level ground, then continued to run, helter-skelter, though I didn't have to, across the wedge of meadow between bank and windmill.

A simple but edifying scene in which Mary and I embrace to confirm the power of our love in the face of the unforeseen perils of the world and the frailty of flesh, as witness the death of a mutual friend. Not to be. Mary doesn't unclasp her shins. Because a new bruise on an old bruise . . .

"Dead, Mary. Dead. Right there on the tow-path. Dead. I saw him."

But she cuts me short, lifting her chin from her knees. Dark brown hair. Smoke-blue eyes. She must be braver than me. No wasted emotions. Facts. Facts.

"Listen – did anyone say anything? Your Dad? The police?"

"Say?"

"About how Freddie died."

"He drowned."

Mary bites her lip.

"About *how* he drowned."

"He fell in the river. Couldn't swim, could he?"

The schoolboy game. Act innocent: you'll be innocent. Act ignorant: people will think you don't know.

But Mary has buried her face in her knees again. She shakes her head. Poplar trees rustle. When she looks up she seems three times older than me, as if she's become a hard-featured woman with a past. Then I see it's because something's gone from her face. Curiosity's gone.

"Freddie didn't fall in. Someone made him fall in. Dick made him fall in."

"Mary."

"I saw them together last night, down near the footbridge. Freddie was drunk."

"But – "

"Because I told him. Because I thought sooner or later he'll have to know. I told him. He looked so pleased. Because he thinks – And I said, No, Dick. Not yours. And now I think maybe I should have said Yes. If I'd said Yes, yours –. Then he just stared at me, so I had to say something. I said it was Freddie. I told him it was Freddie's."

I look at Mary. I'm trying to interpret her words. At the same time I'm thinking: Dick came in last night, at about half-past eight, then left again with something in the pocket of his windcheater.

But all this must look to Mary like disbelief.

"I said it to protect *you*. Maybe I shouldn't."

She lowers her chin, then looks up again with the air of a martyr.

"It's true. I told him it was Freddie. Dick killed Freddie Parr because he thought it was him. Which means we're to blame too."

The cattle in the meadow have moved round a bend in the banks. The landscape is emptying.

"How do you know?"

"Because I know Dick."

I look at her.

"*I* know Dick."

"Perhaps you don't."

"Perhaps I don't know anything."

Soft cotton-wool clouds drift across the July sky. We let them drift for a full minute.

"Mary – *is* it Freddie's?"

"No, it's not Freddie's."

Which still keeps me guessing.

"Is it Dick's?"

"It couldn't have been Dick's."

"How do you know?"

"Because – " she looks at the ground, " – because it was too big."

"Too big?"

"Too big."

"To go in?"

"Yes."

"But if it was too – why should he think – ?"

"You know, you know. Because he didn't know how, in any case. He thought you could have one just by thinking about it. He thought you could have one – just by loving."

Which still keeps me guessing. Because I don't believe that if Dick didn't know how, Mary wouldn't have taught him. Wasn't that why Dick made his evening trips to the Lode? To be taught? Why Mary and I took pity? Poor Dick, who wasn't allowed to be educated . . . Poor Dick who wanted to know about love.

That – and Mary's itching curiosity. Which has suddenly gone.

"It was too big. It wouldn't – But that's not the main thing any more now, is it?"

And I'm still guessing after we part on the Lode bank and Mary walks off, without a backward glance, in the direction of the farmhouse. Brown hair; erect carriage; flat land. I don't know what to guess, what to believe. Superstition's easy, children; to know what's real – that's hard.

I'm still guessing that same evening, on the river-bank under the willow tree, as I watch Dick tinkering with his motor-bike. (No, he's not going wooing tonight.) But that same evening too I pick out from the river a beer bottle of curious appearance. I know what was in that bottle. I know where that bottle came from. Guesswork forms conclusions (which don't quell fear). So Dick comes home from seeing Mary and goes out again with something in the pocket of his wind-cheater. He waylays Freddie near the footbridge. He knows that Freddie, like his father, never refuses a drink, and though Dick is never known to drink himself, he offers him something special – a beer like no other. With the result that Freddie, who can't swim anyway, will be in no state to save himself. "Freddie want drink?" They sit on the footbridge. For good measure, before pushing him in, Dick hits him with the empty bottle. On the right temple. Then Dick

50

throws the bottle into the river too. And, like Freddie, the bottle floats downstream . . .

I take the beer bottle and carry it, unseen, beyond the obstacle of the sluice, meaning to throw it in once more, to float away for good this time, perhaps to float all the way to the sea. But at the last moment something stops me. I thrust it inside my shirt and smuggle it up to my bedroom. And that night, as I go to bed and Dick goes to bed, I do something I've never done before. I take the old, rusty, never-used key to my room from a hook on the wall and lock the door.

8

About the Story-telling Animal

I know what you feel. I know what you think when you sit in your rows, in attitudes of boredom, listlessness, resentment, forbearance, desultory concentration. I know what all children think when submitted to the regimen of history lessons, to spooned-down doses of the past: "But what about Now? Now, we are Now. What about Now?"

Before you a balding quinquagenarian who gabbles about the Ancien Régime, Rousseau, Diderot and the insolvency of the French Crown; behind you, beyond the window, grey winter light, an empty playground, forlorn and misty tower blocks . . . And around you this stale-smelling classroom in which you are suspended, encaged like animals removed from a natural habitat.

Now. What about Now?

Price pipes up – one of his numerous attempts to subvert the French Revolution – to disrupt disruption – and says: "What matters is the here and now." But what is this much-adduced Here and Now? What is this indefinable zone between what is past and what is to come; this free and airy present tense in which we are always longing to take flight into the boundless future?

How many times, children, do we enter the Here and Now? How many times does the Here and Now pay us visits? It comes so rarely that it is never what we imagine, and it is the Here and Now that turns out to be the fairy-tale, not History, whose substance is at least for ever determined and unchangeable. For the Here and Now has more than one face. It was the Here and Now which by the banks of the Hockwell Lode with Mary Metcalf unlocked for me realms of candour and rapture. But it was the Here and Now also which pinioned me with fear when livid-tinted blood, drawn by a boat-hook, appeared on Freddie Parr's right temple, and again when, after a certain meeting with Mary Metcalf, I hid a beer bottle in my shirt and, retiring to my bedroom, locked the door.

And so often, children, it is precisely these surprise attacks of the Here and Now which, far from launching us into the present tense, which they do, it is true, for a brief and giddy interval, announce that time has taken us prisoner. So that you can be sure that on that July day in 1943 your juvenile history teacher ceased to be a babe. As you may be sure that when during the French Revolution the hair of Marie Antoinette who once played at Little Bo-Peep and other childish pranks in the gardens of Versailles, turned, in a single coach journey from Varennes to Paris, white as a fleece, she was aware not only of the Here and Now but that History had engulfed her.

And yet the Here and Now, which brings both joy and terror, comes but rarely – does not come even when we call it. That's the way it is: life includes a lot of empty space. We are one-tenth living tissue, nine-tenths water; life is one-tenth Here and Now, nine-tenths a history lesson. For most of the time the Here and Now is neither now nor here.

What do you do when reality is an empty space? You can make things happen – and conjure up, with all the risks, a little token Here and Now; you can drink and be merry and forget what your sober mind tells you. Or, like the Cricks who out of their watery toils could always dredge up a tale or two, you can tell stories.

Children, my becoming a history teacher can be directly ascribed to the stories which my mother told me as a child, when, like most children, I was afraid of the dark. For though my mother was not a Crick, she had the story-telling knack in no small measure, and, in any case, as I did not then know – as only later historical researches would reveal – she had cause of her own to be no stranger to fairy-tales.

My earliest acquaintance with history was thus, in a form issuing from my mother's lips, inseparable from her other bed-time make-believe – how Alfred burnt the cakes, how Canute commanded the waves, how King Charles hid in an oak tree – as if history were a pleasing invention. And even as a schoolboy, when introduced to history as an object of Study, when nursing indeed an unfledged lifetime's passion, it was still the fabulous aura of history that lured me, and I believed, perhaps like you, that history was a myth. Until a series of encounters with the Here and Now gave a sudden urgency to my studies. Until the Here and Now, gripping me by the arm, slapping my face and telling me to take a good look at the mess I was in, informed me that history was no invention but indeed existed – and I had become part of it.

So I shouldered my Subject. So I began to look into history – not only the well thumbed history of the wide world but also, indeed with particular zeal, the history of my Fenland forebears. So I began to demand of history an Explanation. Only to uncover in this dedicated search more mysteries, more fantasticalities, more wonders and grounds for astonishment than I started with, only to conclude forty years later – notwithstanding a devotion to the usefulness, to the educative power of my chosen discipline – that history is a yarn. And can I deny that what I wanted all along was not some golden nugget that history would at last yield up, but History itself, the Grand Narrative, the filler of vacuums, the dispeller of fears of the dark?

Children, only animals live entirely in the Here and Now. Only nature knows neither memory nor history. But man – let me offer you a definition – is the story-telling animal. Wherever he goes he wants to leave behind not a chaotic wake, not an empty space, but the comforting marker-buoys and trail-signs of stories. He has to go on telling stories. He has to keep on making them up. As long as there's a story, it's all right. Even in his last moments, it's said, in the split second of a fatal fall – or when he's about to drown – he sees, passing rapidly before him, the story of his whole life.

And when he sits, with more leisure but no less terror, in the midst of catastrophe, when he sits – as Lewis can see himself sitting, for the sake of his children – in his fall-out bunker; or when he only sits alone because his wife of over thirty years who no longer knows him, nor he her, has been taken away, and because his schoolchildren, his children, who once, ever reminding him of the future, came to his history lessons, are no longer there, he tells – if only to himself, if only to an audience he is forced to imagine – a story.

So let me tell you another. Let me tell you

9

About the Rise of the Atkinsons

Some say they were originally Fenmen. But if they were, they moved long ago, tired of wet boots and flat horizons, to the hills of Norfolk, to become simple shepherds. And it was on the hills of Norfolk (low and humble hills as hills go, but mountain ranges by Fen standards) that they got Ideas – something the stick-in-the-mud Cricks rarely entertained.

Before Vermuyden came to the Fens and encountered the obstinacy of the Fen-dwellers, an Atkinson forefather, on his bleating hillside, conceived the idea of becoming a bailiff; and his son, a bailiff born, conceived the idea of becoming a farmer of substance; and one of the fourth, fifth or sixth generation of idea-conceiving Atkinsons, while land was being enclosed and the wool trade fluctuating, sold most of his sheep, hired plough-men and sowed barley, which grew tall and fruitful in the chalky upland soil and which he sent to the maltster to be transformed into beer.

And that is another difference between the Cricks and the Atkinsons. That whereas the Cricks emerged from water, the Atkinsons emerged from beer.

Those acres of land he ploughed must have been special, and Josiah Atkinson must have known a thing or two, because word got around that the malt made from his barley was not only exceptional but there was magic in it.

The good – and exceedingly good-humoured – villagers of west Norfolk drank their ale with relish and, having nothing to compare it with, took for granted its excellence as only what true ale should be. But the brewers of the nearby towns, eager men with a flair, even then, for market research, sampled the village produce on foraging excursions and inquired whence came the malt. The maltster in his turn, a simple fellow, could not refrain while praise was being heaped on his malt from declaring the source of his barley. Thus it came about that in the year 1751 Josiah Atkinson, farmer of Wexingham, Norfolk and George Jarvis, maltster of Sheverton, entered a contract, initiated by the former but to the advantage – so it appeared – of the latter, whereby they agreed to share the cost of purchase or hire of wagons, wagoners and teams of horses to convey their mutual product, for their mutual profit, to the brewers of Swaffham and Thetford.

This partnership of Jarvis and Atkinson thrived. But Josiah, who had already conceived another idea, did not deny himself in this agreement the right to send his barley, if he so wished, to be malted elsewhere. Atkinson foresight told him that in his son's or his grandson's lifetime, if not in his own, the brewers in their market towns would find it expedient to operate their own malting houses, close at hand, and that Jarvis, who for the present believed Atkinson to be tied by their joint commitment to the brewers, would suffer.

So he did – or, rather, so did his successors. While across the Atlantic the first warning shots were being fired in what is known to you, children, as The War of American Independence, William Atkinson, Josiah's son, began sending his barley direct to the brewers. Old George's son, John, perplexed, enraged but powerless, could only fall back on local trade. His malting business declined. In 1779, with the boldness of a man only pursuing an inevitable logic, William Atkinson offered to buy him out. Jarvis, humbled, broken, agreed. From that day the Jarvises became overseers of the Atkinson malting house.

William, nothing compunctious, had only to complete the well laid stratagem of his father. On his sorrel horse, in his high boots, with his tricorn hat on his head and his brown-cloth riding cloak over his shoulders, he went visiting the brewers of Swaffham and Thetford. He announced that as for his barley, there was none finer, as they well knew, in the region; nor was there any shortage of it (for was he not even now bringing more land under the plough?) but henceforth no brewer was to have it unless it was malted at the Atkinson maltings.

The brewers protested, arched their eyebrows, pushed back their carved oak chairs, snapped the stems of their clay pipes. What of their own malting houses, built at considerable expense and for the express convenience of proximity? William replied that, by all means, they should continue to use them – to produce an ale that their customers would surely judge inferior. That as for the question of proximity, had not his own wagons given reliable service in the past?

The brewers huffed, scowled, loosened their itching periwigs; and at length yielded to compromise. The early 1780s in Swaffham and Thetford witnessed a phenomenon as yet unheard of. Ale was, henceforth, no longer ale but a twin-headed creature, one face bearing the accustomed character of ale but costing a halfpenny more, the other, at the old price, unfamiliar and insipid.

William Atkinson rode away, well pleased, from further consultations with the brewers, at which he is to be imagined, perhaps, sitting in their tap-rooms, jovially clinking tankards. For William owed his success not merely to the prescience of his father, or his own acumen, but to infectious good cheer. It was that magical liquor, cupped in their hands, winking and beaming even as they spoke, which prevailed, as much as Will's wily brain. Good cheer: was not this the ultimate aim of his – and their – business? And was good cheer to be propagated by rancour and hard feelings? Could he not tell these begrudging brewers how once his father, old Josiah, had taken him out into the barley fields where the wind rustled like a thousand silk petticoats through the ripening ears, and, stooping low and cocking his head to one side, had said: "D'ye hear that? D'ye hear that now? That's the sound of loosening tongues, that's the sound of ale-house laughter – that's the sound of merriment."

William's wagons lumbered from Sheverton to Swaffham and from Sheverton to Thetford with their sacks of malt. In time, brewers from Fakenham and Norwich, who had tied up no capital in maltings of their own, found it worth their while to send to Sheverton for their malt.

But William, who was growing old and already conferring much of his affairs on his son, Thomas, knew that success could not continue unthreatened. Other Norfolk barley-growers, showing the farming enterprise he and his father had shown, must compete for the brewers' favours. Besides, Will Atkinson was still having ideas. He dreamed that the Atkinsons would one day follow the wondrous barley-seed from its beginning to its end without its passing through the hand of a third party. That the former shepherds who now farmed and malted would one day brew, and in a style far surpassing the tin-pot brewers of Thetford and Swaffham.

Picture a scene not dissimilar from that in which Josiah and William once stood listening to what the barley had to say, but in which it is now William who, leaning on a stick, commands his son's attention and directs his gaze towards the west, to where the Fens lurk in the misty distance. To where the peaty soil, such as has been won back from water, albeit admirable for oats and wheat, will never yield malting barley like that nourished by the furrows on which they stand. Drawing his outstretched hand across the view, he explains to young Tom how the people of the Fens import their malt from the uplands of southern Cambridgeshire, Hertfordshire and Bedfordshire. Very good barley country too, and very good malt, except that the numerous tolls levied on it as it is brought in barges down the Cam and Ouse make it expensive; and the natural hazards of those same waterways, which have a troublesome habit of bursting their banks, changing their course and every so often becoming choked with silt, ensure that supplies are unreliable, sometimes unforthcoming and, when forthcoming, often in poor condition. In short, the Fenmen pay hard for irregular and indifferent ale. And, as if this were not enough, the Fens are such a backward and trackless wilderness, that few Fenmen can lay their hands on what ale is available.

Looking down from his hilltop in an expansive and prophetic manner (which perhaps explains how, when I tried to visualise that God whom Dad said had such a clear view, I would sometimes see a ruddy, apple-cheeked face, beneath a three-cornered hat, with snowy hair tied back in the eighteenth-century fashion), looking down from his Norfolk hills, William clasped his son's shoulder and said perhaps some such words as these: "We must help these poor besodden Fenlanders. They need a little cheer in their wretched swamps. They cannot survive on water."

Picture another scene, in the parlour of the red-brick farmhouse that Josiah built in 1760 (still standing in all its Georgian solidity on the outskirts of Wexingham) in which Will unfurls a map specially purchased from a Cambridge map-seller and points with a nut-brown index finger to the region of the Leem. He takes as a centre the little town of Gildsey near the confluence of the Leem and Ouse. He compares the distance, by way of the Leem, from their own farmland to Gildsey, with that by way of the Cam and Ouse from the barleyland of the south. He draws his son's attention, for which no map is necessary, to the hamlet of Kessling, but a few miles west of Wexingham – a run-down cluster of dwellings amidst rough heathland and pasture where the young Leem, after its journey from the hills, begins to slow and gather itself – from which most of the inhabitants have already departed to become Atkinson labourers. He taps the map with his pipe-stem. "The man who builds a malting house at Kessling and has the keys of the river will bring wealth to a wasteland. And himself."

Thomas looks at the map and at his father. The keys of the river? He sees no river; only a series of meres, marshes and floodlands through which perhaps a watery artery is vaguely traceable. Whereupon William, pipe-stem back in the corner of his mouth, utters a word which falls strangely and perplexingly on the ears of a man who lives on top of a chalk hill: "Drainage."

So Thomas Atkinson, spurred by his father, who goes to his rest in Wexingham churchyard, year of our Lord 1785, begins to buy water-logged land in the Leem catchment and discovers that Drainage is indeed a strange, even magical, word – as magical as the grains of his own barley. Because in five or six years' time he can sell the same land, with the water squeezed out of it, at a ten-fold profit.

While on the continent the millennium arrives, while the Bastille tumbles, Jacobins oust Girondins and there is widespread draining away of blood, Thomas Atkinson studies the principles of land drainage; of river velocity and siltation. How the efficacy of artificial drainage is measured by the increased water dischargeable through the natural drain of a river. How the velocity of a river increases as a fraction of the increase of water but siltation decreases as a multiple of the increase of velocity. He applies these principles with palpable results. He consults and hires surveyors, engineers and labourers, none of whom complain of his ignorance or his impatience or his parsimony as an employer. And amongst those who come to work for him are the Cricks from across the Ouse.

Thomas learns it isn't easy. And it's never finished. Little by little. The obstinacy of water. The tenacity of ideas. Land reclamation.

But, lest it be thought that amidst these arduous toils Thomas has lost sight of his father's Good Cheer, his account books record the provision of regular supplies of ale, made with Atkinson malt, to be brought from Norfolk, at some cost and hardship considering the problems of transport, for the refreshment of his Fenland workers. And when in 1799, grown rich from land-speculation, and appointing an agent to run his Norfolk farm, he moves from Wexingham to Kessling – where, to the astonishment of the handful of villagers, he has not only had a house built but drawn up plans for the digging of a basin in the River Leem and the construction beside it, in due course, of a malting house of large and most up-to-date pattern – it is to bring with him a young and spirited bride of eighteen. And the man-servant, maid-servant, cook and stableman who have followed him from Wexingham cannot refrain from exchanging nudges, winks and leers at the unmistakable sounds that emanate thereafter from their master's chamber. Thomas, with good eighteenth-century uninhibitedness, is begetting heirs.

Who was this frolicsome and – so it proved – fecund young bride? She was Sarah Turnbull, only surviving child of Matthew Turnbull, brewer, of no great fortune, of Gildsey, Cambridgeshire – to whom Thomas Atkinson had one day come with the astonishing proposition that if he, Matthew, were to sell him, Thomas, one full half of his business, he, Matthew, would one day be a rich man. Whereupon Matthew had reflected deeply, paced several times around the sparsely furnished brewery office, and Thomas had spied, through the window, in the brewery yard below, the brewer's comely, lightly-stepping daughter, and, after discreet inquiries as to the health of the brewer's family, evolved a means of securing his aims in Gildsey more effective than any buying up of shares.

By the year of Trafalgar, Thomas had drained 12,000 acres along the margins of the Leem; dykes had been dug by the score; some sixty or so wind-pumps were in operation; and tenant farmers were paying the lucrative rents and drainage levies that went with equally lucrative soil. From Kessling, where by now almost every villager received Atkinson wages, to Apton – a distance, by water, of nine miles – the river had been embanked and sluices and staunches built to control the flow.

But the remaining section between Apton and the Ouse proved difficult. Thomas suffered the fate of all men of initiative whose single-handed ventures pay off: he came up against a wall of rivalry, vested interests and parliamentary machination. For fifteen years he had waged war on water, mud and winter weather, but he encountered no enemy more stubborn than the elders of Gildsey and their elected representatives when they perceived that the navigation of the Leem was indeed feasible and land prices were rocketing. While Napoleon made his lightning marches against Austrians, Prussians and Russians, Thomas Atkinson got bogged down in protracted litigation and labyrinthine wrangles over navigation rights, land tenure and the constitution of drainage boards.

A lesser man would have been dissuaded. A lesser man would have cut his losses and returned to the dry and stable vantage point of his Norfolk hills. But in 1809, at long last, the Leem

Navigation is officially, if grudgingly, ceded to him. Simultaneously, he gains the chairmanship – albeit over a divided and unruly board – of the Leem Drainage Commission.

He sets to work once more. The new banks of the river progress westward. Where he cannot buy land he buys co-operation. The Hockwell Lode is dug to assist the drainage of the particularly intractable region north of the lower Leem. A location is fixed, two miles from the junction with the Ouse, for the construction of a combined sluice and navigation lock, to control the entrance to the river. The barge pool at Kessling is completed and a site on the west bank of the Ouse on the northern outskirts of Gildsey purchased for development as wharves. Though no boat has yet made the auspicious journey between Kessling and Gildsey, numerous craft are already plying their way with materials and waste between Kessling and Apton, Apton and Gildsey, and overtures have been made to the boat-builders in Ely and Lynn regarding the construction of a permanent fleet of lighters.

In 1813, while Napoleon, whose army once advanced so proudly in the opposite direction, retreats from Leipzig to the Rhine, Thomas Atkinson begins building the maltings at Kessling. He is now in his fifty-ninth year.

In his fifty-ninth year he is still a hale and hearty – and a merry – man; a man who would claim no affinity with the vainglorious Emperor of the French. With his young wife (who now affects the loose gowns and coal-scuttle bonnets made familiar to us through pictures of Lady Hamilton and the mistresses of Byron), he strolls round the barge-pool at Kessling and inspects progress on the works. Is it merely coincidence that it is in the year 1815 that the large and lofty building is completed and christened, by inevitable choice, the Waterloo Maltings? Is it merely coincidence that at the outset of that year his father-in-law, the brewer of Gildsey, falls ill and is declared by his doctor to be not long for the world? Is it coincidence alone that the dignitaries of Gildsey, amidst the flush of national rejoicing, decide to forget their differences with this Norfolk upstart and to welcome him instead as one of their own, the bringer of prosperity to their town and a living emblem of the spirit of Albion? And is it no more than a sop to the times – or a sign of personal exultation, or a mark of willingness to be turned into a symbol – that when on a September day in 1815, amidst cheering and the fluttering of red, white and blue bunting, a little gang of four newly built lighters manoeuvres, by means of sail and quant-pole, across the Ouse, then, linked to a beribboned draught-horse, enters the Leem from Gildsey and passes through the newly completed Atkinson Lock, the foremost of this gang – the flagship, as it were – should bear on its bows, beside the bright red stem-post and the device, soon to be familiar, of two crossed yellow barley-ears above a double wavy blue line, the name *Annus Mirabilis*?

Children, there is a theory of history which may be called – to borrow a word from the ancient Greeks – the theory of hubris. This doctrine provides that there can be no success with impunity, no great achievement without accompanying loss; that no Napoleon can go carving up the map of Europe without getting his comeuppance.

You sneer. Who administers this grand and rough justice? The gods? Some supernatural power? This is getting all too much like fairy-tales again. Very well. But even nature teaches us that nothing is given without something being taken away. Consider water, which, however much you coax it, this way and that, will return, at the slightest opportunity, to its former equilibrium. Or consider the handsome wife of Thomas Atkinson, formerly Sarah Turnbull, of Gildsey. Between the years 1800 and 1815 she bears Thomas three sons, two of whom live and one of whom dies; and a daughter, who lives, but only till her sixth year. For the techniques of land-drainage may have improved considerably but medical science is still in its infancy.

Sarah watches, on the arm of her lauded husband, the lighters passing into the River Leem, but tempers the pleasure in her lovely face with due signs of decorum and restraint. For it is only three weeks since her father – who never saw, save in his daughter's good fortune, the riches Thomas Atkinson promised him – went to his grave. And watching also, perhaps, somewhere along the banks of the Leem, are the Cricks – the father William and the brothers Francis and Joseph. But they do not cheer as heartily as other spectators. Too much enthusiasm never went with their phlegmatic natures. And though they draw pride from their part in the making of this newly navigable, brightly gleaming river, they know that what water makes, it also un-makes. Nothing moves far in this world. And whatever moves forwards will also move back. It is a law of the natural world; and a law, too, of the human heart.

The townsfolk cheer. They drink ale (but not Atkinson Ale, for the town brewery remains as yet in the name of Turnbull and it would not do to dishonour the dead). There is jubilation and merriment. But just for a moment, perhaps, Thomas Atkinson wonders if this is the sort of merriment he wants – the merriment that goes with grand openings and speeches and toasts to the hook-nosed vanquisher of Bonaparte.

In the winter of 1815 to 1816 rain swells the River Leem which bursts its banks between Apton and Hockwell and floods six thousand acres of newly ploughed farmland. A grievous but sufferable disaster: Atkinson resourcefulness takes care of it and within three months the damage is repaired. In 1816 the price of wheat doubles and those same tenant farmers whom Thomas had provided with rich farmland can no longer pay either their rents or their labourers. Napoleon is beaten: the poor starve. In Ely a mob runs riot and sabre-waving dragoons who but a year before held the field at Waterloo are summoned to crush their own countrymen. Jubilation? Merriment?

Thomas surveys the stricken Fenlands and the inconstancy of history. But this too he can bear. Because he is a rich man – and a barley-man, not a wheat-man to boot – he can be accommodating to his tenant farmers. He hands out shillings and finds food for the hungry (his dear wife herself does not shirk from ladling gruel beside the maltings at Kessling). And it is only because of these charitable acts and because in these hard times he continues to provide employment, as he has in the past, that no mob runs loose in Gildsey and storms, as it surely would have done, the local Bastille of the town brewery.

In 1818 – when violence has ceased but there is no less hardship – Thomas fits out the ground floor of his house in

Kessling as offices for his maltings and makes the second move of his life, from Kessling to Gildsey, to a grand residence, Cable House (which still stands, children), north of the market square, but a minute's walk from the brewery, with a view down the narrow lane, which was known then and is still known, though it is a wide thoroughfare now with a Boots and a Woolworths, as Water Street. The brewery is enlarged and ceases to bear the name it has borne for three respectful years, of Turnbull. The townsfolk taste, for the first time under its proper title, the inimitable flavour of Atkinson Ale made with Atkinson malt from Atkinson barley. The landlords of the Gildsey inns, whose names reflect the watery world which surrounds them – The Swan, The Dog and Duck, The Jolly Bargeman, The Pike and Eel – regale their indigent yet thirsty customers.

Does it soften their grievances – a dose or two of tawny Merriment? Does it soften old Tom's?

For something is happening to Thomas, now a still robust sixty-three. He is becoming a monument. Man of Enterprise, Man of Good Works, Man of Civic Honour. The portrait painted of him in this same year shows a countenance of undoubted character, but it does not have the twinkle of his father's eye or the soft creases of his father's mouth – nor will his two sons, George and Alfred, revive these features of their grandfather. Thomas is becoming aloof. He can no longer stand by one of his new drains and clap the shoulder of the man who has helped to dig it. The labourers who once worked beside him – the Cricks perhaps amongst them – now touch forelocks, venerate him, regard him as a sort of god. And when, with the express purpose of showing he is not aloof, he enters the tap-room of The Swan or The Bargeman and orders a pint for every man, a silence descends on these haunts of mirth, like the hush inside a church.

He does not wish it – he cannot help it – but he feels himself measured up and fitted out for the stiff and cumbersome garments of legend. How he made the River Leem from a swamp. How he brought Norfolk beer to the Fens. How he fed the hungry by the barge-pool, became a pillar of . . . And, deep inside, he thinks, perhaps, how better and brighter things were that day in the old house at Wexingham, when the summer breezes blew through the window the sound of whispering barley and his father uttered the curious password: Drainage.

But even this he could bear, even this would be all right – for, God knows, Thomas Atkinson never believed in heaven on earth – if it were not for the matter of his wife. In 1819 she is thirty-seven. The playful, girlish looks which once won his fancy (and suited his business ends) have been transformed by the years into something richer and mellower. Mrs Atkinson is beautiful; with a beauty which is apt to remind Mr Atkinson of the beauty of an actress – as if his wife occupies some strongly lit stage and he, for all his public eminence, watches from a lowly distance. It seems to him that he has worked hard and achieved much and yet failed to give due attention to this wonderful creature with whom, once, he bounced so casually through the rituals of procreation.

In short, Sarah Atkinson is in her prime; and her husband is growing old and doting – and jealous.

In his sixty-fifth year attacks of gout confine Thomas within doors and disturb his usually even temper. He cannot accompany his wife on their accustomed walks, drives and visits. From the window of the house in Market Street, he watches her step into waiting carriages and be whisked away, and the constant paperwork before him, which concerns plans for the modernisation and further enlargement of the brewery, the extension of the Ouse wharves and the conveyance of Atkinson Ale by river or road to ever more numerous points of consumption, cannot stop his thoughts, while she is gone, returning repeatedly to her.

Several men fall under his suspicion. His own brewery manager; a King's Lynn corn merchant; the younger members of the Drainage Commission; the very doctor who calls to treat his gout. And none of them can explain, for fear of imputing to the Great Man of Gildsey a slander which he has not openly voiced, that Mrs Atkinson is innocent, innocent, and has nothing but loyalty and devotion for her husband, whom everyone knows she adores.

One night in January, 1820, an incident occurs for which no first-hand account exists yet which is indelibly recorded in

65

innumerable versions in the annals of Gildsey. That January night Sarah returned from an evening spent, so it happened, in the irreproachable company of the rector of St Gunnhilda's, his good wife and assembled guests, to a Thomas more than usually plagued by the pains of gout. It is not known exactly what passed between them, only that – according to what was unavoidably overheard by the servants and what Atkinson himself later gave out as confession – Thomas was gruff, grew surly, angry, and, whilst giving vent to the most unwarranted accusations and abuse, rose up from his chair and struck his wife hard on the face.

Doubtless, even if this action had not had the terrible consequences it did, it would have been regretted infinitely. Yet Thomas had indeed cause for infinite regret. For, having been struck, Sarah not only fell but in falling knocked her head against the corner of a walnut writing-table with such violence that though, after several hours, she recovered consciousness, she never again recovered her wits.

Whether it was the knock against the writing-table or the original blow which caused the dreadful damage, whether it was neither of these things but the moral shock of this sudden fury of her husband's, whether, as some have claimed, the knock against the writing-table was only an invention to hide the true extent of Thomas's violence – is immaterial. In a distraction of remorse over the motionless body, Thomas calls his sons and in a voice heard by the whole house announces: "I have killed my wife! I have killed my darling Sarah!" Horror. Confusion. Plenty of Here and Now. The sons, inclined at first, at what they see, to believe their father's bald summary of the case, send for the doctor – the self-same doctor whose innocent attentions have contributed to this terrible scene – who is obliged not only to tend the stricken wife but to administer copious draughts of laudanum to the husband.

On that night in 1820 Thomas Atkinson is supposed to have lost completely all the symptoms of gout. At least, he no longer took heed of them. Far worse torments awaited him. All through the next day and on into the next night he must watch by the bedside, praying for those sublime eyes to open and those exquisite lips to move. He must experience the rushing relief and joy of seeing, indeed, the lips part, the mouth flutter, only to suffer the redoubled agony of knowing that though the eyes open they do not see him, or if they do, do not recognise him. And though those lips move they will never again utter to Thomas Atkinson a single word.

Sarah Atkinson is thirty-seven. Fate has decreed that, knocks on the head or no, she will live a long life. She will not go to her rest till her ninety-third year. For fifty-four years she will sit on a blue velvet chair before the window in an upper room (not the room once shared by her husband but a room to be known simply as Mistress Sarah's room), staring now straight before her down the cluttered thoroughfare of Water Street to the Ouse, now to her left over the rooftops to where, in 1849, the tall chimney of the New Brewery, on its site by the Ouse wharves, will rise.

But it is doubtful whether she will see these things. She will retain the paradoxical pose of one who keeps watch – but over nothing. She will not lose her beauty. Her upright, forward-looking posture will convey an undeniable grace. Even in old age when her flesh has shrunk but the firm mould of her bones remains (for in such a state her portrait will be painted, in a black dress with a diamond necklace, at the instigation of her sons – and what a perfect sitter she will make!), she will preserve the sadly imperious demeanour of an exiled princess.

At regular times servants will come, with meals on a tray, to comb her hair, light the fire, prepare their mistress for bed, or merely to sit beside her at the window, through bright mornings or sombre twilights, offering unanswered comment on the activity in the street below. And so too will come Thomas, to sit by his wife, often for hours on end, to clasp and wring his hands, to utter God knows what entreaties – but Sarah will never make the barest sign that she knows who he is.

All this he must endure. But first he must watch the doctor come daily, for prolonged visits. He must watch him look grave, thoughtful, shake his head and finally declare that he can do no more and the advice of specialists must be sought. Thomas will arrange, at great expense, for eminent physicians to come from Cambridge to examine his wife. He will conduct Sarah like

67

some rare exhibit round the consulting-rooms of that learned city. He will take her to London to be examined, tapped, probed and considered by still more eminent men of medicine, and will donate to St Bartholomew's Hospital the sum of £500 for "the Further Investigation and Better Relief of Maladies of the Brain".

He will offer a fortune to the man who will give him back his wife; but no man will claim it. He will return to Gildsey, to the silent, unrelenting enmity of his sons and the judgement of a whole town. For will they not, considering all he has done for them, his works and undertakings, the prosperity he has brought them, forgive him this one act of human weakness? No, it seems not. There are even those few, yet die-hard disciples of Temperance who add to the existing rumours the embellishment that when Thomas struck Sarah he was blind-drunk from his own fine ale – and does this not prove the truth of the old saying that (far from spreading good cheer) brewers are the breeders of brawlers?

And if others have it in them to forgive Thomas, Thomas will not wish to be forgiven, not wishing to forgive himself. In The Jolly Bargeman and The Pike and Eel, where Temperance does not enter, they still smack their lips over Atkinson Ale, for its flavour remains ever true, ever conducive to the forgetting of troubles; and, besides, the Atkinson business is now in the hands of young George and Alfred – long may they thrive. But as for old Tom, they preserve a dour brevity of comment or shake their heads, as once the doctor did over his poor wife.

The times cannot be numbered when Thomas Atkinson will ask, Why? Why? And again Why? (For heartache, too, inspires its own sad curiosity.) Not content with the verdict of physicians, he will embark, himself, on the study of the brain and the nervous system. To his library in Cable House he will add volumes in which are contained what human knowledge, in the 1820s, has to offer on the mystery of the human mind. Where once he pored over the topography of the Fens and the innumerable complexities of drainage, flood control and pumping systems, he will pore over the even more intricate topography of the medulla and the cerebellum, which have, so he discovers, their own networks of channels and ducts and their own dependence on the constant distribution of fluids.

But this is an internal land which cannot be redeemed, cannot be reclaimed, once it is lost.

Abandoning science, he will turn to religion. The good church-goers of Gildsey who have hitherto observed Thomas, alongside his wife and two sons, uttering his Amens with the calm air of a man who regards the Sunday service as a wholesome if unabsorbing social duty, now witness the bent and furrowed brow, the forever restless lips of the sinner wrapped in penitential prayer.

He no longer attends to the expanding affairs of Atkinson and Sons. He no longer reads his newspaper (Castlereagh has cut his throat; Canning takes his place). History has stopped for him. He has entered the realms of superstition. It is even said that when God did not answer him, when God, even with his clear view, could not explain Why, Thomas sent out into the undrained Fen, for the services of one of those ancestors of Bill Clay, whose potions and charms were still regarded with respect. And that the reply of the wizened occultist (who had no cause to help Atkinson whose drainage schemes spelt the doom of his kind) drove the last rivet of grief into old Tom's soul: that Thomas Atkinson, as Thomas himself well knew, was only receiving the punishment he merited, and that, as for his wife, no magic in the world could bring her out of the state which she herself – had not Thomas looked closely enough into her eyes? – wished to remain in.

For two, three, four years, Thomas will look closely into his wife's eyes. For four years he will continue to sit with her in the upper room, wringing her hand and his own heart. And then in December, 1825 – story has it that it was in this self-same upper room, in his wife's presence, that death occurred, and that the two were discovered, the one stone dead, the other not batting an eyelid – this once vigorous and hearty man, who a decade ago, though sixty then, would have been credited with another twenty or thirty years, worn out with remorse, is released from his misery.

He is buried with due dignity, ceremony and appreciation of his Works, but with what seems also a certain haste, in St

Gunnhilda's churchyard, a little distance from the south transept, in a grave capped by a massive marble monument, its corners carved in high relief in the form of Ionic columns. An inscription on the south face gives Thomas's dates and a record in Latin of his deeds (*qui flumen Leemem navigabile fecit . . .*) but not his misdeed; and the whole is surmounted by an enormous, fluted, krateriform marble urn, half covered by a shroud of marble drapery on which, where it extends onto the flat surface of the monument, lie (an incongruous touch on such a classical edifice, but no visitor fails to be caught by it or to note the extraordinarily life-like rendering) two sorrily strewn ears of barley. In his last will and testament Thomas leaves it to God, Time and the people of Gildsey, but, before all these, to Sarah herself – "whom Providence restore swiftly to that wholeness of mind so to pass judgement but long to await its execution" – to determine whether his dear wife shall one day, again, lie beside him.

And shall we leave it too, children – possessing though we do the gift of hindsight – to see what God, Time and the people will decide – and make no comment, as yet, on what, if anything, lies beside old Tom's grave in St Gunnhilda's churchyard; nor make any moralising and wise-after-the-event comparisons between the simple headstone, which stands gathering moss and lichens in Wexingham, of William Atkinson who died content and the grand tomb of Thomas Atkinson who died wretched?

To Thomas's sons, George and Alfred, mere striplings of twenty-five and twenty-three, yet already fashioned by regrettable circumstances into brisk and earnest young men of business, it seems that the air is cleared, purified. Their debt of shame has been paid and now with renewed righteousness, with renewed purpose, they can start once more. History does not record whether the day of Thomas's funeral was one of those dazzling mid-winter Fenland days in which the sky seems to cleanse every outline and make light of distances and the two towers of Ely cathedral can not only be seen but their contrasting architecture plainly descried. Nor does it record whether the people of Gildsey, who so confidently scorned the genuine grief of Thomas for his wife, failed to notice the lack of grief of Thomas's sons for their father.

But such things would have been appropriate. For the town, no less than its two young champions, feels, as it enters, indeed, its heyday, this ever-recurring need to begin again, to wipe the slate, erase the past and look to the sparkling landmarks of the future.

Has not the shrewdness of old William been borne out? No Fenland brewer, dependent on barley from the south, can compete with Atkinson barley malted at the Atkinson maltings and brought down the Leem in Atkinson lighters without a single toll charge. Soon not only the people of Gildsey but the people of March, Wisbech, Ely and Lynn will appreciate the fine quality and fine price of Atkinson Ale. And if Atkinson lighters can carry Atkinson Ale to all these places, and beyond, why should they not carry other things? Why should the Atkinsons not avail themselves of their favourable position at the junction of Ouse and Leem, and of the general improvement of the waterways, to turn Gildsey into an *entrepôt* of the eastern Fens? The Atkinson Water Transport Company along with the New Brewery is perhaps already a living creature in the minds of young George and Alfred as they drive away from their father's burial.

And what creature stirs in the mind of Sarah Atkinson? If anything stirs in the mind of Sarah Atkinson. Popular opinion will not entertain the possibility that Sarah Atkinson is stark mad. (Was it not her husband who was the mad one when he struck his wife for no cause at all?) Popular opinion learns scarcely anything of Sarah Atkinson, though it knows that she sits constantly in that upper room, surveying the town like a goddess. And it begins to tell stories. It tells, for example, how although Sarah Atkinson never uttered a word to her husband after that fatal day, nor ever gave him a single glance of recognition, such was not the case with her two sons. That to them indeed she imparted, perhaps in plain words, perhaps by some other, mystical process of communication, wisdom and exhortation. That it was from her, and not from their father, that they got their zeal and their peculiar sense of mission. Not only this, but the successes that came to the Atkinson brothers came to them not from their own stirling efforts but from this wronged Martyr.

In short, children, that that blow on the head had bestowed on Sarah that gift which is so desired and feared – the gift to see and shape the future.

Thus it was she who so uncannily predicted the exact timing of the repeal of the Corn Laws; it was she who devised a cunning strategy to outface the Challenge of the Railways; it was she who divined, and even caused to be, the boom years of the mid-century and who envisaged, even as they stood by their father's grave, her George and Alfred, masters respectively of the Brewery and the Transport Company and jointly of the Leem Navigation and the Atkinson Agricultural Estates, as kings in their own country.

Yet some imaginative Gildsey souls went much further than this. For when that portrait of Sarah in her old age, in her black satin dress and diamonds, was painted, and donated by the brothers, in a gesture both poignant and magnanimous, to the town, to be hung in the lobby of the Town Hall, it became the object of no small local pilgrimage. And it was not long before someone asked: did not the gaunt yet angelic features of Sarah bear a striking resemblance to those of St Gunnhilda, in the precious Gunnhilda triptych (then still in the church of her name) – to St Gunnhilda who looked out over the devil-ridden Fens and saw visions?

Whether any of this contains a grain of truth; whether the brothers themselves regarded their mother as oracle, priestess, protectress, or merely allowed these rumours to circulate as a means of securing the favour of the town, no one can tell.

But a further story – which supports the stark-mad theory – which has been handed down and repeated too often to be lightly dismissed, relates that, whatever the bonds between Sarah and her sons and whatever the true description – serene, dumb, inscrutable – of her long and stationary vigil in the upper room, she would be seized every so often by a singular form of animation.

It began with a trembling and twitching of her nostrils; then a wrinkling of her nose and an energetic and urgent sniffing. This would be followed by a darting of her eyes hither and thither in an alert fashion and a claw-like tightening of her hands. Then her lips would rub furiously at themselves and while her face contorted and her body wriggled and bounced so violently in her chair that its oak legs sometimes lifted from the floor, she would utter the only words specifically attributed to her in all the years following her husband's dreadful fit of rage. Namely: "Smoke!", "Fire!", "Burning!", in infinite variations of repetition and permutation.

The servants – and this bespeaks their devotion – would exert themselves to calm her. The butler would undertake a tour of the house, checking every fireplace and chimney. A maid would look from the window and affirm that neither smoke nor fire were visible – unless one included the fumes wafting from the brewery chimney, which were nothing but a good sign, or unless the wind was blowing from the direction of Peter Cutlack's smoking-house at the far end of Water Street, where Peter Cutlack turned slithery, olive-green Ouse eels into crooked, copper-brown walking-sticks. Another maid would be despatched to the kitchen to ensure that whatever assailed their mistress's nostrils was not a portent that dinner was ruined. A boy would even be sent to inquire in the streets.

But all these steps were to no avail. Sarah would go on sniffing and wriggling and popping her eyes and hollering "Smoke!" and "Burning!" till exhaustion overcame her.

These fits, it is claimed, grew more frequent, and it is a fact not without irony, if entirely coincidental, that in 1841 the Atkinsons, amongst others, were responsible for bringing to Gildsey its first, custom-built fire-engine.

Not only more frequent but more distressing. And more embarrassing too. It is even suggested – though here scepticism must step in, for the principal evidence is that of one of the Atkinson servants dismissed for being in a shameless state of pregnancy and thus having a motive to invent malicious lies – that the spasms grew so severe and convulsive that, far from continuing to adore and sanctify their mother, the brothers packed her off to an Institution; though, for the sake of the townsfolk, they continued to preserve the legend (for example, by having a certain picture painted of Sarah in black dress and diamonds when in fact she was trussed up in a strait-jacket) that their Guardian Angel still watched over them.

All this, it is true, was much later, in the 1870s – Sarah, indeed, was a long time adying – when the brothers themselves were past their peak and young Arthur, Sarah's grandson, George's son, was already the driving force of the Atkinson machine. Yet even in 1820, the year of the shocking event, it was put about by certain omen-loving and sourly witty parties that when Thomas Atkinson devised his company emblem – so neatly denoting both his Brewery and Navigation interests – of the crossed barley ears over a symbolic representation of water, and cast about for a motto to go with it, he chose unwisely. For the motto which he chose – *Ex Aqua Fermentum* – which was once engraved in huge arched capitals over the main entrance to the New Brewery and which appeared on the label of every bottle of Atkinson beer, does indeed mean, simply, "Out of Water, Ale", and can even be construed, as perhaps Thomas intended, "Out of Water, Activity"; but it can also be interpreted, as surely Thomas never meant: "Out of Water, Perturbation".

Children, you are right. There are times when we have to disentangle history from fairy-tale. There are times (they come round really quite often) when good, dry, textbook history takes a plunge into the old swamps of myth and has to be retrieved with empirical fishing lines. History, being an accredited sub-science, only wants to know the facts. History, if it is to keep on constructing its road into the future, must do so on solid ground. At all costs let us avoid mystery-making and speculation, secrets and idle gossip. And, for God's sake, nothing supernatural. And, above all, let us not tell *stories*. Otherwise, how will the future be possible and how will anything *get done*? So let us get back to that clear and purified air and old Tom tucked up in his new white grave. Let us get back to solid ground . . .

In 1830 – when in Paris the barricades go up again, the mob once more invades the Tuileries and the air is full not only of smoke and revolution but of the heady scent of *déjà vu* – George Atkinson marries Catherine Anne Goodchild, daughter of the leading banker of Gildsey. A marriage in every way predictable, laudable and satisfactory. In 1832 – for the brothers conducted their lives to a pattern and in almost all things Alfred, being two years the junior, did what his brother did, only two years later – Alfred married Eliza Harriet Bell, the daughter of a farmer who owned land on both banks of the Leem to the west of Apton, once drained and sold to him by Thomas. A marriage less predictable and laudable, for though everyone can see how Alfred is consolidating the navigation interest, this is not a prosperous time for farmers of the likes of James Bell.

Was this Sarah's work? Was it she who saw what a handsome profit James Bell's wheat would fetch in the post-Repeal era of the '50s and '60s? And was it she who saw how the Norwich, Gildsey and Peterborough Railway, which in 1832 was but a tentative pencil-mark in some planner's rough-book, must one day pass through James Bell's land, either north or south of the river? When the time came, James Bell would be readily per-suaded to hold out for two years to the railway company – not just so that, when he finally sold, it would be at double the price, but so that Eliza's husband and brother-in-law could complete in the interval the replacement of draught-horses, quant-poles and sails by steam-barges and narrow steam-tugs on the Leem.

Thus the brothers Atkinson would ensure that steam would compete with steam, and that when the railway came it would still be cheaper to freight bulk goods to and from Gildsey by river. And thus the Norwich, Gildsey and Peterborough Railway was mainly a passenger service; just as it was still when, as part of the Great Eastern Railway, its varnished teak carriages were the scenes of daily assignations between a boy in a black uniform and a girl in a rust-red one.

Sarah's work perhaps. But let us keep to the facts. In 1834 Catherine Anne gives birth to a strapping son, Arthur George. In 1836 Eliza Harriet bears a daughter, Louisa Jane. In 1836, likewise, but after the birth of Louisa Jane, Catherine Anne is delivered also of a daughter, Dora Emily. In 1838– But in 1838, for once, Alfred does not observe the two-year principle and does not complete the square by fathering a son of his own. And there, indeed, in 1838, with a round total of three – and only one male child, what's more, on whom to place the hopes of the future – the Atkinson progeny reaches its limit. No unusual thing in our own times, but unusual in 1838 when successful men of business were given to make children as they made money, and were further spurred by the knowledge – George and Alfred had but to think of their own short-lived brother and sister – that to be certain of one heir it is well to beget several.

If they had not so revered the two brothers, if the brothers' fortunes were not so inseparable from their own and if the brothers had not built such a fine tomb for their unhappy father, the people of Gildsey might have reflected on this state of affairs. They might have reflected upon the four-year period after marriage before, in the case of both couples, conception was achieved. They might have connected the brothers' habitual air of stern and implacable purpose with a certain frosty forlornness about both their otherwise charming wives; and connected this in turn with a certain fulsome affection they were wont to display, even in public, to their be-ribboned and be-crinolined daughters. They might have concluded that the nuptial squeaks and squeals that once old Tom and Sarah had raised at Kessling did not find an echo in the pious atmosphere of Cable House; and that this was how the Guardian Angel wrought her magic. In short, the brothers were inhibited by that woman up there in that upper room. In short, the townsfolk might have diagnosed, had they been acquainted with a form of magic not then invented, the classic symptoms of the Mother Fixation, not to say the Oedipal Syndrome. And was it not possible that the tireless industry of George and Alfred was nothing other than Sexual Energy (ah, you strenuous Victorians) which, like Fenland water, cannot be subdued but can be pumped into new channels?

But, facts, facts. In 1833 the new wharves, known collectively as Gildsey Dock, with their warehouses, derricks, pony-pulled railway trucks and their sister installation across the Ouse at Newhithe, are officially opened. Simultaneously, the Atkinson Water Transport Company, with its soon-to-be extended fleet of three steam-tugs, four steam-barges, six sail-barges and forty-six lighters – not to mention the craft already at work on the Leem – is inaugurated. Within a few years, malt and barrels of ale are no longer the prime, though they are still the most honoured cargo of the Atkinson vessels. Nor is the Leem the chief artery of their trade. The Atkinson barges go as far afield as Huntingdon, Bedford, Peterborough and Northampton. They ship grain to King's Lynn and Tyne coal and continental produce back again. They carry iron, timber, agricultural machinery, bricks, stone, hemp, oil, tallow, flour.

When work begins, in 1839, on the Norwich and Gildsey, and the Ipswich, Bury and Gildsey Railways, it is the Atkinson Transport Company which brings supplies and even Atkinson expertise which advises on such matters as drainage and embanking. The townsfolk are dismayed. Will we not lose our trade, they demand, to the railways? And the brothers reply: And would you lose your markets to some other town served by the steam-trains? For the brothers foresee (Sarah's work?) that what the railway may take in long-haul trade, they regain in short-haul traffic in goods brought by the railway itself. Can trains deliver coal to every pumping-station in the region? Can trains bring goods to every village in this land where people are naturally settled beside water? And, pray, compare our rates of carriage with those of the Railway Company.

Besides, the brothers hold substantial shares in the railways. In these times of change, it is best to be sure.

And not the least of those many materials ferried into the new Dock (and in this case not ferried out again) were the materials used between 1846 and 1849 in the construction of the New Atkinson Brewery. For let us not forget that the name of Atkinson is first and foremost the name of a beer. Even as the dock is completed, space has been set aside for the grand building which must one day replace the enlarged but soon to be inadequate old brewery. And, little by little, in those mid-century years, the edifice rises.

It is not vast, by modern standards; but as its foundation stones give way to its part brick and part stone-faced walls, and as its brick and stone-faced walls give way to elaborately embellished cornices and friezes (a chain of barley sheaves and beer casks) and to a roof part gabled and part widely arched in the manner of railway termini, and as this roof leads on, in turn, to a four-sided chimney, sixty-six feet high, the sides tapering upwards and faced with brickwork fluting, and the whole crowned, beneath the vent, by more ornate moulding and friezing (of indeterminate style but said by the architect to suggest an Italian campanile) and, for good measure, a clock, by which all Gildsey, and half the Fens if they possess a spy-glass, can tell the time – as all this rises up and draws with it the gaze of the gaping inhabitants, a joke originates: that the New Brewery must surely cause a new flooding of the Fens, but not a flooding of water – a flooding of beer.

Sarah hears, in her room, the sounds of work in progress. There comes a time when above the crooked house-tops on the northern side of Water Street appear scaffolding, the tops of cranes and hoists, then the iron skeleton of the roof itself, over which workmen crawl and strut, as if on some giant flying-machine. Then the chimney, phallically rising to abash the Fenland sky. Does she notice? Does she care? Is she pleased, is she proud? No record notes that she is present among the guests of honour on that day in June, 1849, outdoing for splendour even that former day of triumph in 1815, when a band played once more, when no less than two Lords were in attendance, when speeches rang out first from a flag-bedecked rostrum and again at the Grand Reception in the Town Hall; when the Atkinson bargees raised their caps and sounded the horns of their steam-barges, when the crowd hurrahed and the first, ceremonial shovelfuls of malt-grist were loaded into the mashing tuns. But was she there in spirit? Was she cheering with the rest of them? Or was she still, in her upper room, keeping her watch over Nothing?

When can we fix the zenith of the Atkinsons? When can we date the high summer of their success? Was it on that June day in 1849? Or was it later, in 1851, when amongst the products privileged to be represented at the Great Exhibition was a bottled ale from the Fens, known appropriately as Grand '51, which, in the face of strong competition, won a silver medal for excellence, outdoing even the noble brewers of Burton-on-Trent? Was it before that, in 1846, when, having served his six years as alderman of the town, George Atkinson was unanimously elected mayor? Or was it in 1848 (two years later) when his brother Alfred succeeded to the same office, and the tacit principle became established that whoever, thereafter, would be nominal and official mayor, the true mayoralty of the town would belong always to its brewers?

Was it in 1862? When George and Alfred, stout men now with greying whiskers, as old as the ageing century, decided that their labours had earned them the right to stylish seclusion, to a rural retreat to complement the bustle of the town; and so had built at Kessling, though not near the maltings and their father's former residence but a good mile or more to the south, an opulently ugly country mansion, Kessling Hall, complete with gargoyles and turrets, happily concealed by thick woods, where at weekends or for longer sojourns George and Catherine would occupy one wing and Alfred and Eliza another, but would meet together in the Long Room or the Dining Room to entertain visiting men of rank and their families; and where the cousins, Dora and Louisa, young ladies in their mid-twenties – but not so young that they did not give cause for recurrent concern – would suffer and deter, on the Terrace, or the Croquet Lawn, suitor after suitor. For they preferred, above all suitors, their darling Papas, and to the company of young men that of each other, and perhaps a volume of moody verse.

Or was the pinnacle not yet reached, even in the luxury of Kessling Hall? Was it not, indeed, to be reached during the ascendancy of George and Alfred but during that of Arthur, who, as his father and uncle puffed their proud cigars at Kessling, was already assuming command at Gildsey, and who, in 1872 – as Atkinson Ale was in demand over all the eastern counties, and as a special pale brew known as Atkinson India Ale was being regularly shipped thousands of miles to Bombay for consumption by Her Majesty's Forces – added yet another province (in well-tried manner) to the Atkinson dominions, by marrying Maud Briggs, daughter of Robert Briggs, owner of the Great Ouse Flour Mills?

Is there no end to the advance of commerce? But should we speak only of the advance of commerce, and not of the advance of Ideas – those Ideas which the Atkinsons cannot help conceiving? For these present Atkinsons, brothers and son, though they would be the first, if need be, to point with rigid fingers to facts – to figures of Profit and Sale, to sacks of malt, barrels of ale, chaldrons of coal – are apt also, when the mood takes them, which it does more and more, to make light of these material burdens, and to assert in almost self-renouncing tones that what moves them is indeed none other than that noble and impersonal Idea of Progress.

Have they not brought Improvement to a whole region, and do they not continue to bring it? Do they not travail long and indefatigably in the council chamber as well as in the board-room, for the welfare of the populace? Have they not established, out of their own munificence, an orphanage, a town newspaper, a public meeting-hall, a boys' school (black uniform), a bath-house – a fire-station? And are not all these works, and others, proof of that great Idea that sways them; proof too that all private interest is subsumed by the National Interest and all private empires do but pay tribute to the Empire of Great Britain?

What is happening to our little Fenland outpost, once but a mud hump with a wattle chapel, once so removed from the wide world?

How many times does the Union Jack flutter above the arched and motto-inscribed entrance to the New Brewery to mark some occasion of patriotic pride? How often does the *Gildsey Examiner* (founded with Atkinson money and an organ for Disraeliite Toryism) refer in its columns, in the same breath and the same tone, to the March of Industry and the Might of Albion? How many times do George and Alfred and Arthur pause in their boardroom addresses, hands on lapels, to allude to some new instance of imperial prowess? And how often do those barrels and bottles of Atkinson Ale find new wonders to celebrate? "The Grand '51"; "The Empress of India"; "The Golden Jubilee"; "The Diamond Jubilee" . . . ?

Children, why this seeking for omens? Why this superstition? Why must the zenith never be fixed? Why has the spread of merriment been transformed into the Idea of Progress? And why has land reclamation in the eastern Fens become confused with the Empire of Great Britain? Because to fix the zenith is to fix the point at which decline begins. Because merriment never made history. Because if you construct a stage then you must put on a show. Because there must always be – do not deny that there must always be – a future.

And yet when, in 1874, Arthur Atkinson is elected Member of Parliament for Gildsey and concludes his maiden speech with the much-applauded phrase, "For we are not masters of the present, but servants of the future", does he know what he means? Does he mean what he says? Is he merely masking behind that gesture towards duty and sacrifice the smug knowledge that he is, indeed, master of the present, and is that why his words receive, from his Tory-democratical compeers, such loud and self-congratulatory "hear-hears"? Does he see the future as only a perpetuation of the present? Does he see what the future will bring? Does he see that the fate of the future (my father's and my own, early twentieth-century present, when there were still plenty of copper pennies bearing the rubbed-away profile of Victoria) will be only to lament and wearily explain the loss of his confident sentiments?

Which way do we go? Forwards to go backwards? Backwards to go forwards? What is Progress?

Does Sarah know? who in 1874 has seen ninety-two years and yet, since that bang on her head, has forgotten the date of her birthday and has perhaps been oblivious of the passage of time? Does Sarah know, who now, so old yet so vigilant in her eyrie above Water Street, is required to add to her various guises – Guardian Angel, Holy Mother, Saint Gunnhilda-come-again – yet another? To take in her left hand a trident and in her right a shield, to submit her wrinkled scalp and thin white locks to a plumed helmet, to allow her blue velvet chair to be transformed into a sea-girt rock and to evoke an intrepid Britannia, staring, staring – To where?

How do the Atkinsons mark, in 1874, the ninety-second birthday of Sarah? With beer and merriment? With raised tankards and toasts? For once, being a brewer's daughter, Sarah enjoyed her beer. Once she liked nothing better than to sit cradling a pewter pot in her lap. Once, before she became a lady of the town and all the other, more remarkable apparitions that fate would turn her into, she downed many a cheery draught with – her darling husband. But now, though it has been pushed at times hopefully before her, not a drop will pass her lips. No match, perhaps, for those raging inner fires.

They mark Sarah's birthday by building an asylum. Between Gildsey and Ely, a mile from the Ouse, discreetly sealed from the world by dykes and poplar brakes, no less than is Kessling Hall by its enshrouding woods, it stands at the beginning of 1874, almost finished. Further evidence of the Atkinson belief in progress. Further proof that in their commercial zeal they do not overlook the claims of the distressed and needy; of how they extend their concern even to those poor Fenland madmen and melancholics, who in a less enlightened age would have been pilloried, burnt or whipped to the next parish.

It is completed in March (no flags, no speeches). And here, in the same year, the brothers George and Alfred, with the assistance of Arthur, because they have always been so devoted to their mother, install Sarah as guest of honour, in the best apartments, with the most diligent attendants at her disposal. Because in Gildsey tongues have begun to wag. They have begun to say that Sarah Atkinson is perhaps, after all, just stark-raving. Heads have begun to turn in Market Street and Water Street, upwards towards the window, where everyone knows . . . but from where now, even from behind the secondary panes of glass that have recently been fitted, shrieks of the most unco-operative and defiant, of the most hideous and alarming kind have begun to emanate.

And if – when the shrieks, quite suddenly, stop – tongues should begin to wag again, self-contradictorily as tongues are apt to wag; if they should start to say: the only reason why the Atkinsons built that asylum was to put their mother in it, because they wanted to take away our saintly, blameless Sarah and lock her up in a cage for cretins, then they are answered by the patient assertions of the Atkinson servants (whose private wardrobes, in the 1870s, acquire an unusual fineness): Mrs Atkinson is in her room where she has always been. She is confined to her bed. A specialist is prescribing drugs. (Hence the cessation of screams). If you really must know (a confiding yet disdainful expression enters the face of the spokesman),

Mrs Atkinson is dying. Yes, dying. Now – must you profane the passing of our dear mistress with your ignorant gossip?

Who will go to Wetherfield Asylum, to that house of horrors, to check?

And, besides, in the autumn of 1874, Sarah Atkinson does die.

It is announced, in a black-bordered column, in the *Gildsey Examiner*. All Gildsey is hushed. There are those who regard her death with loyal and poignant remembrance. There are those, a majority perhaps, who regard her death as, when all is said, a merciful release. And there are those – the ones who believed it was always Sarah and never George, Alfred or Arthur who fostered the fortunes of the town – who regard her death with anxiety and foreboding.

But everyone wants to know one simple thing. Will all be reconciled, will all be resolved in good old story-book fashion – in a fairy-tale ending to make the heart melt? Will the brothers bury Sarah beside old Tom?

What is going on in the house in Market Street where the blinds are drawn and few lights burn? Has anybody seen the undertaker, or the rector, come and go? Are there tears, quarrels? Is there dissension in the family?

Then it is given out: Mrs Atkinson will be buried in St Gunnhilda's churchyard in the plot (which no other parishioner has dared claim) adjoining the grave of her husband. God rest both their souls. In honour of one so beloved and lamented not just by her children and grandchildren but by the whole town, the brewery will be closed on the day of interment and public houses and shops are requested to suspend business. The hearse will pass down Water Street, along the Ousebank, past the brewery gates and thence to St Gunnhilda's. The funeral service will be at eleven.

The town is overjoyed – if overjoyed a town can be at a funeral. Because there is nothing like a good ending to turn mourning into smiles, and stop the asking of a thousand questions. And nothing like a little pageantry to lift the heart even in the midst of sorrow.

In his yard beside the Ouse, not far from Cutlack's smoking-house, with its own small wharf where Atkinson lighters offload his supplies of stone, granite and marble, Michael Jessop, Monumental Mason and Stone-cutter, is up all night with his apprentices, lovingly carving a most special and esteemed commission. He pauses as he labours perhaps, trying to revive the delicate touch of his grandfather who once fashioned the stone that is this one's twin, trying to render, as once old Toby Jessop did, the feathery likeness of two scattered barley ears, and sheds – most unlikely thing for a monumental mason – a tear.

And yet is it a tear, or only a drip from one of the many troublesome leaks in the rickety wood and tarred canvas canopy under which he works? For outside it has begun to rain.

It is still raining on the morning of the funeral. Not heavily, not torrentially, but with a steadiness, a determination that Fenlanders have come to know cannot be ignored. All over the country of the Ouse and the Leem that morning they are watching water-levels, fuelling auxiliary pumps, tending sluices and flood-gates. The Cricks – my father's grandfather and his brethren – are spitting into the mud and saying to themselves there is work to be done. And the rain increases. Moreover, if it was raining that day, in the Fens, it was raining also over those upland regions to the south and west whence the rivers descend for which the Fens are a basin; and it was raining with particular intensity, with particular intentness, some will assert later, over Kessling, Kessling Hall and those Norfolk hills where the Leem has its source.

The brothers, who, since the decision to bury Sarah by her husband, have been elevated from the status of stern businessmen to that of sentimental heroes, do not mind the rain. Rain is good for a funeral: it masks human tears and suggests heavenly ones. Furthermore, rain is peculiarly reassuring when old Sarah had ranted so much about fire. The cortège proceeds down Water Street, and the mourners feel that the rapid ruination of so much black crape, black horses' plumes and black funeral outfits can only add to the impression of authentic and unself-regarding sorrow. Likewise, amongst the shopkeepers and artisans who dutifully line the streets, bareheaded, while water trickles down their necks, those who hold that the rain is a good sign (compare the unbefitting sunshine of old Tom's funeral day) far outnumber those who hold it is bad.

The cortège moves at a steady pace past the brewery, and the only signs of unseemly impatience on this solemn occasion are in the porch of St Gunnhilda's church, where the waiting rector, sexton and grave-digging party mentally urge the hearse to quicken its pace, because, despite temporary coverings, the grave is filling with water, and there is nothing worse than a neat grave which disrespectfully subsides in the middle of the ceremony – or than lowering a coffin into a puddle.

The ceremony is indeed a somewhat brisk affair – for the ladies, at least, must not be exposed overlong to the risk of chills. The rector intones the service; raindrops drip off his nose and are caught in his lower lip. The rain hides the bowed and veiled faces of the mourners and seems to cast its own veil of obscurity over this sad ritual, cutting it off, as it were, from all around. But whether this briskness and concealment are purely accidental or in some way fortuitous and appropriate, no one yet asks.

It is done; it is over. Mrs Atkinson lies again at the side of her husband.

But the rain doesn't stop. It doesn't stop for two days and two nights. For two days watery palls unfurl themselves over the Fens; for two nights God's arrested stars are blotted out. But thoughts of divine weeping and so forth are soon put to one side as the flood takes hold. The folk of Gildsey know from long observation that however brown, swirling and threatful their old Ouse becomes, they have little to fear from a flood confined to that river alone. A few traders near the banks will receive a wetting and be bailed out literally and, if they are lucky, financially, by their drier neighbours. Nothing worse. But if the Leem floods simultaneously with the Ouse then the effect of the torrents discharged by the former into the latter will be like a liquid dam causing the Ouse to flow back on itself and spill out in every direction. All of which could make the position of Gildsey, so near the junction of the rivers, a disastrous one on which to build a town – were it not for the fact that Gildsey rests upon a hill, the one-time mud-isle of St Gunnhilda, a mere bump to a non-Fenlander, but enough to keep the community from drowning.

The waters rise. At first with a steady increase, and then with a sudden rush which signals that the Leem has indeed thrown in its forces. The watermen along the Ouse embankment haul in their boats and punts; the eel fishermen bring ashore their nets. Wagons carry shop-wares, livestock and household furniture to the safe vicinity of the church and the market-place. But no one can move in a hurry Michael Jessop's stock of stone and marble, nor his cumbersome stone-cutting gear, and the floodwaters immerse them, mysteriously stealing away several slabs that two men could not carry and demolishing the wood and tarpaulin canopy – though it is not the first time that canopy has been removed, hence its perpetually makeshift nature. Nor does Peter Cutlack, fish-smoker, quite have time to rescue all his stock: several crates of his coppery eels find themselves stiffly swimming once more in their old element.

The waters rise. They creep up the slopes of Water Street. The lower buildings are, as everyone expected, inundated, and here and there a forlorn if defiant figure – in many cases not unused to the situation – squats immovably on a roof. They creep further. They dump a ton or more of mud into the hastily cleared cellar of The Jolly Bargeman, but they do not reach The Pike and Eel; nor do they reach – much to the intense glee or disappointment of some of the populace for whom floods, notwithstanding their being natural catastrophes, are also sources of excitement and much laying of bets – the white-painted mark at the base of a chemist's shop which records the furthest encroachment of floodwater up the street hitherto commemorated, and which, apart from historical interest, has much to do with the fixing of rents in Water Street.

The Gildsey Dock and the Brewery remain undamaged. For the brothers, in their wisdom, have taken great pains to guard against this perennial danger, and the elaborate system of locks, sluices and channels incorporated into the dock complex do their work. Not only this but the two Relief Channels, one to the north and one to the south of the town, dug with public funds but largely at Atkinson instigation in 1868, are fully tested for the first time and prove equal to their task. From the air (though there are no helicopters in 1874 – no flickering newsreel shots of beleaguered rooftops and engulfed cars), Gildsey must look like a moated settlement drawn in on itself and hoisting up its skirts for defensive action; its lower extremities submerged, the brewery and the dock like separate outworks, the two relief channels forming a mud-brown horseshoe, diverting the floodwater to the meadows to the west and thus returning the town to its ancient island state.

But if the Gildseyites can pride themselves on their capacity for self-protection, they have little other cause for gladness. A country town, especially a Fenland town, depends upon the region which serves it; and from the outlying – outwallowing – districts, the news is bleak. In the floods of October, 1874, eleven thousand acres of land are rendered uncroppable for a year. Twenty-nine people are drowned, eight missing, presumed so. Eight hundred head of cattle and twelve hundred head of sheep perish. The damage to houses, highways, bridges, railways, drains and pumps is beyond clear reckoning.

But what is abundantly clear is that the River Leem, navigable water-course and traffic-lane of the Atkinson malt barges, is temporarily no more. The rain has indeed been heavy – malignly heavy – over the westernmost hills of Norfolk. It has caused the Leem to show such contempt for its confines that the helicopter panorama would reveal its raised embankments, over long stretches, only as dark parallel lines against a watery sheen, like scratches on a mirror. The Hockwell Lode has overflowed into Wash Fen. The bridge is threatened at Apton. At the Atkinson Lock the lock-gates have been wrenched loose and the iron sluice-gate, so accustomed to restraining water, has been torn bodily from its supports and flipped like a slate into the current, watched by the lock-keeper and his family who are forced to pass four days in their attic. While at Kessling, the barge-pool has vanished; water flows through the front doorway of Thomas Atkinson's one-time home, and despite the heroic efforts of the pool manager, refugees from the flood, already astonished enough, encounter to their amazement, for miles around Kessling, empty lighters, broken free of their moorings, their red stemposts and painted insignia plain to see, drifting at random over former fields of wheat and potatoes.

But what is the greater cause for astonishment that hangs over Kessling? What is the greater cause for alarm that presses, amidst all this destruction and confusion, on Kessling Hall, where on the second morning of the rain, while the roads are still passable – on the morning after Sarah's funeral – the Atkinson family, with the exception of Arthur and his wife, have come in what must be considered, despite the natural desire of the bereaved for privacy and seclusion, a certain fugitive haste?

Rumour is unleashed with the floodwaters. Rumour has it that on the night of the twenty-fifth of October the figure of a woman dressed in the style of fifty years ago, is seen on the rain-soaked terrace of Kessling Hall, amongst the dripping urns and stone pineapples, tapping on the French windows for admittance. Dora Atkinson – for she is the witness – is roundly scolded for this fanciful vision. It is the product of reading too much Tennyson. And, in any case, how could Dora, who had not even been born at the time a certain fateful blow was struck on a certain head, be sure that what she had seen was the younger image of her grandmother? Her grandmother who was *buried yesterday*.

Yet that Dora is shaken – by something – is plain. For the female servant who unloosed this rumour onto the world (though she did not do it till years afterwards, till old George and Alfred were both safely dead) found cause to loose another on its heels. Namely, that when Dora went to bed that night it was not to her own room but to that of her cousin, Louisa; it being a well known fact that these two confirmed spinsters would occasionally, in times of stress – thunderstorms, floods, the like – curl up in the same bed together, just like little children.

Rumour is but rumour. But several rumours, of similar vein, from different sources, cannot be ignored. On the same night of the twenty-fifth, Jane Casburn, the wife of the sexton of St Gunnhilda's, sees in the churchyard the form of a woman, in outmoded dress, bending imploringly over the grave of Sarah. She sees it – she is sure that she sees it – but she does not tell her husband till some time later, because the Ouse is in flood and the good man is helping with emergency arrangements.

Back at Kessling, by the barge-pool and the maltings, more than one mystified if not frightened witness will later claim to have seen during these confused times a female shape, moving about the hithes and moorings in the manner of someone searching; seeming to glide, some say, over the rising water; seen in the maltings and seen again, more than once, outside the evacuated manager's residence – at the door where Thomas Atkinson brought his young bride – seeming to implore entrance. Which was soon granted – if not to her, then to the swollen waters of the Leem.

And at Gildsey, in the house overlooking Water Street (which is earning its name), in the room where – ?

But nobody knows what spectral visitations, if any, have occurred in the house which at present Arthur and Maud are occupying. The only rumour to emerge from that quarter – but it is a precise and corroborated one – is that in the early morning of the twenty-seventh the Atkinson doctor arrives, with some urgency.

The waters rise: the waters return. Has she returned, too, not just from the dead but from the former life that was hers before a knock on the skull dislodged her brains and for ever jumbled up for her past, present and future? Has she come back, to Gildsey, to Kessling, to seek her lost husband, her lost bridegroom who was once merry and not jealous?

Ah, do not ghosts prove – even rumours, whispers, stories of ghosts – that the past clings, that we are always going back . . . ?

But if Sarah Atkinson lies in her new grave, beside Thomas's old grave, in St Gunnhilda's churchyard, where the rain, soaking the soil, is already beginning the process by which their dust will be commingled, is she not already spiritually reunited with her lost husband for ever?

The waters rise. They wash up rumours and strange reports of many kinds, but they also flow over them again and sweep them aside. The brothers will perhaps be grateful (though why should they be grateful?) for these floods which so dominate attention and divert thoughts to practical matters. When news is flying hither and thither of houses ruined, livestock lost, roads impassable, what heed is to be paid to hysterical gossip about ghostly women? And when the flood at last begins to abate and grim costs have to be reckoned, what will the ramblings of a few housewives, bumpkins and servants count against the praise-worthy efforts of George and Alfred to bring order again to a stricken countryside – or against the labours of Arthur, who while he shares the local burdens of his father and uncle, still has energy left to speak out from his bench in the Commons, on far weightier and wider matters, on matters of State and Empire?

Yet someone will ask – when these floods have become a memory, when the Leem once more flows contentedly within its banks, when a new lock and sluice, beside a new lock-keeper's cottage which will one day be the home of Henry Crick, regulate and guard its currents – how do we *know* that Sarah Atkinson lies in that grave beside her husband in St Gunnhilda's church-yard?

And somebody will dig up again that preposterous and much scorned and suppressed imputation that Sarah Atkinson was not only incarcerated in Wetherfield Asylum but, being a woman of uncanny powers, also escaped from it – some days before her own funeral. That, giving her custodians the slip and eluding pursuit, she scrambled (a woman of ninety-two, mark you) in nothing but her shift, across ditch and field, till she reached the banks of the Ouse. And here – so the ludicrous testimony of a bargee has it – she dived "like a very mermaid" beneath the water never to surface again.

But two things, for ever connected with those floods of '74, are less in dispute. One is that numerous patrons of The Swan and The Pike and Eel and even of The Jolly Bargeman, who do not let a mere flood or even a cellarful of mud keep them from their tankards, notice a subtle change in their pints of ale. The beer is weak. It is watery. Is this a mental illusion brought about by so much rain and inundation? Or is it really the case that the floods have somehow infiltrated the Atkinson barrels, invaded the bowels of the brewery, and what they are drinking is – God forbid – part river-water? The brewers affirm that no such shameful dilutions have occurred, that the ale in question is none other than the good old fortifying ale, made in the good old Atkinson manner. Yet the beer does not improve; and a large body of Gildsey opinion will rigidly maintain that – river-water and bad barrels apart – the beer brewed by the Atkinsons after those floods, after poor Sarah's funeral, never was the same as the beer brewed before; that after 1874 – until a certain memorable time in the next century – Atkinson Ale, which for over fifty years had been the pride of Gildsey, was an inferior stuff. And whether this is true or not, the profits of Atkinson beers in the last quarter of the nineteenth century and the first decade of the twentieth show a gradual yet distinct decline.

And the second thing concerns that doctor's visit in the early morning to Cable House. What has brought him in such haste? Has something terrible taken place within? No – or, that is, no and perhaps yes too. For Mrs Arthur Atkinson, three weeks before her expected time, is being delivered of a son.

What has induced this premature birth? Some sudden shock, at something seen, perhaps, in that upper room where Sarah, we are given to believe, breathed her last? The stress and agitation – which, who knows, might have betokened guilt as well as grief – attendant upon that rain-drenched funeral? Or was it that the swelling waters of the Fens, the bursting dykes, the rising river – already, through the window, visibly lapping at the foot of Water Street – awoke a mysterious affinity in Mrs Atkinson's system and caused her own waters to break in sympathy? No one knows. But certain it is that on the twenty-seventh of October, 1874, Maud Atkinson is delivered of a baby son. And the baby lives and is healthy . . .

And that, children, is how, amidst floods and flying rumour, my grandfather, Ernest Atkinson, future owner of the Atkinson Brewery and the Atkinson Water Transport Company, came into the world.

Meanwhile, the rain continues. It transforms the lands around the Ouse and Leem into an aqueous battlefield, it turns them back into the old swamp they once were.

Drainage. Begin again. The Cricks get to work.

And down the swirling, swelling, slowly relenting Leem come willow branches, alder branches, fencing posts, bottles . . .

10

About the Question Why

And when you asked, as all history classes ask, as all history classes should ask, What is the point of history? Why history? Why the past? I used to say (until Price reiterated the question for the umpteenth time but with a new slant to it – and that distinctly trembling lip): But your "Why?" gives the answer. Your demand for explanation provides an explanation. Isn't this seeking of reasons itself inevitably an historical process, since it must always work backwards from what came after to what came before? And so long as we have this itch for explanations, must we not always carry round with us this cumbersome but precious bag of clues called History? Another definition, children: Man, the animal which demands an explanation, the animal which asks Why.

And what does this question Why imply? It implies – as it surely implies when you throw it at me rebelliously in the midst of our history lessons – dissatisfaction, disquiet, a sense that all is not well. In a state of perfect contentment there would be no need or room for this irritant little word. History begins only at the point where things go wrong; history is born only with trouble, with perplexity, with regret. So that hard on the heels of the word Why comes the sly and wistful word If. If it had not been for . . . If only . . . Were it not . . . Those useless Ifs of history. And, constantly impeding, deflecting, distracting the backward searchings of the question why, exists this other form of retrogression: If only we could have it back. A New Beginning. If only we could return . . .

'*Historia*' or 'Inquiry' (as in Natural History: the inquiry into Nature). To uncover the mysteries of cause and effect. To show that to every action there is a reaction. That Y is a consequence because X preceded. To shut stable doors, so that next time, at least, the horse– To know that what we are is what we are because our past has determined it. To learn (the history master's hoary standby) from our mistakes so it will be better, in future . . .

And to illustrate both our pressing need to ask the question why and the proposition that history begins with our sense of wrong, I used to ask you to liken the study of history to an inquest. Suppose we have on our hands a corpse – viz., the past. A corpse not always readily identifiable but now and then taking a specific and quite personal form. For example, the headless trunk of Louis XVI. Do we say of this corpse, Well a corpse is a corpse and corpses don't revive? No, we do not. We ask: Why did this corpse come to be a corpse? Answer: by accident – or because on a certain day in Paris when a certain guillotine was descending, Louis XVI happened to have his neck in the way. At which you would laugh, and prove your inquisitive minds, your detective spirit – your historical consciousness.

But why, we ask, did Louis' neck happen to be – ? Because . . . And when we have gleaned that reason we will want to know, But why *that* reason? Because . . . And when we have that further reason, But why again – ? Because . . . Why? . . . Because . . . Why? . . . Until, in order to find out why Louis died, it is necessary not only to reanimate in our imaginations his troubled life and times but even to penetrate the generations before him; by which stage that incessant question Whywhywhy has become like a siren wailing in our heads and a further question begins to loom: when – where – how do we stop asking why? How far back? When are we satisfied that we possess an Explanation (knowing it is not a complete explanation)? How – if only for a moment's peace – do we turn off that wretched siren? Might it not be better (it can happen in extreme cases – witness my father's one-time reply to inquiries about his Great War experiences) if we could acquire the gift of amnesia? But would not this gift of amnesia only release us from the trap of the question why into the prison of idiocy?

Children, I always taught you that history has its uses, its serious purpose. I always taught you to accept the burden of our need to ask why. I taught you that there is never any end to that question, because, as I once defined it for you (yes, I confess a weakness for improvised definitions), history is that impossible thing: the attempt to give an account, with incomplete knowledge, of actions themselves undertaken with incomplete knowledge. So that it teaches us no short-cuts to Salvation, no recipe for a New World, only the dogged and patient art of making do. I taught you that by for ever attempting to explain we may come, not to an Explanation, but to a knowledge of the limits of our power to explain. Yes, yes, the past gets in the way; it trips us up, bogs us down; it complicates, makes difficult. But to ignore this is folly, because, above all, what history teaches us is to avoid illusion and make-believe, to lay aside dreams, moonshine, cure-alls, wonder-workings, pie-in-the-sky – to be realistic.

So when your history teacher's teachings are put to the test, when his wife, who is yet to be branded by the local press as "The Baby Snatcher of Lewisham" and "The Child Thief of Greenwich", delivers herself one Sunday afternoon of an inexplicable announcement, he obeys both human instinct and academic training. He drops everything (even the French Revolution) and tries to explain.

But he already knows – though he carries on, in defiance of his professional superiors, risking, indeed, his whole career – that it's not explaining he's doing. Because he's already reached the limits of his power to explain, just as his wife (a once dogged and patient woman) has ceased to be realistic – has ceased to belong to reality. Because it's the inexplicable that keeps him jabbering on nineteen-to-the-dozen like this and scurrying further and further into the past. Because when there's no way forward the only way is – Because his children, who have bad dreams, suddenly want to listen, and although he's trying to explain he's really only telling a –

94

11

About Accidental Death

So when the pathologist had presented his report and the witnesses — notably my father, Henry Crick, and Police Constable Wyebrow — had given their testimonies, the inquest into the death of Frederick Parr, sixteen, of Hockwell, Cambs, held at Gildsey Coroner's Court on July 29th, 1943, reached the verdict that the deceased had died by accident. End of story.

But sir! Sir! That can't be all. What about that double bump on the head? What about that freaky brother? And this thing with you and Mary what's-her-name? (Hey, we never knew you —) What about our detective spirit? Don't stop, keep telling. That can't be the end.

Very well. No end of story.

Because, for one reason, when the Coroner recorded a verdict of accidental death and the death certificate was signed and the order for burial drawn up, my father was still asking Whywhywhy. I could see the question tying new knots in his forehead, causing new twinges in that chronically troublesome knee and making him, when enough seemed enough, turn once more and continue pacing, on his evening sentry-walks on the tow-path. A coroner's court is a court of law; though an inquest is not a trial. But my father, a simple and impressionable man, summoned by the coroner's officer to attend as witness, was under every apprehension that he stood accused; that the purpose of this official gathering was not to ascertain how Freddie Parr had died but how he, Henry Crick, lockkeeper of the Atkinson Lock, had by his own negligence suffered a sixteen-year-old boy to drown in his sluice and had further compounded his crime by defacing the body of the same with a boat-hook. My father, in a hot courtroom, in an unaccustomed stiff collar under which the sweat prickled and trickled, awaited the judgement: Henry Crick, we find you guilty of manslaughter, of murder, of death, of the sins and wrongs of all the world . . .

Coroner: "At what time, in your opinion, did death occur?"

Pathologist: "As near as I can judge, between the hours of 11 p.m. of the twenty-fifth and 1 a.m. of the twenty-sixth."

Coroner: "Mr Crick, between those hours, did you hear any sounds to alarm you – splashings, cries for help – in the vicinity of the lock?"

My Father: "No sir. I'm afraid, sir, I was asleep . . ."

Coroner: "Doctor, the wound and contusion on the right side of the deceased's face – can you explain how and when they were caused?"

Pathologist: "By a rigid, semi-sharp object or instrument, some hours after death had occurred."

Coroner: "On the last point you are sure?"

Pathologist: "Yes, sir."

Coroner: "Mr Crick, could you give your account of how exactly this wound came to be caused?"

My Father: "He were heavy. I'm sorry, sir. The boat-hook slipped – got him."

Coroner (patiently): "Do not be sorry, Mr Crick – but be more precise. Rest assured, you have no cause to reproach yourself in this matter . . ."

But my father does not rest assured. He walks up and down the tow-path asking Whywhywhy. He asks, how do these things happen? (And I ask, watching him, does he suspect? – Mary, Freddie, Dick, me?). He casts back over his life (just as I, one day, will cast back over his life, going even so far as to unearth dusty inquest transcripts), looking for wrongs requiring expiation, omens to be fulfilled. And on his face, as he stares from flat river to flat fields, is imprinted an expression of exaggerated vigilance.

And Freddie Parr's father, with even greater cause, is asking Whywhywhy. No repetition of that neat word "accident" can stop that siren in his brain, or close the chasms of responsibility, of blame that yawn inside him . . .

Coroner: "In plain terms, how would you describe the proportion of alcohol present in the deceased's blood?"

Pathologist: "As considerable, sir."

Coroner: "Sufficient to have rendered the deceased drunk?"

Pathologist: "Certainly."

Coroner: "Incapacitated by drink?"

Pathologist: "Very likely."

Coroner: "To an extent where he might have been more liable than usual to a slip or fall from the riverside?"

Pathologist: "Quite probably."

Coroner: "And finding himself in the water, less able than usual to save himself?"

Pathologist: "Again, very probably."

Coroner (frowning): "The deceased was sixteen years of age. Was he in the habit of getting drunk?"

P.C. Wyebrow (circumspectly, the deceased's parents not being present): "I believe he was, sir. With all respect to the bereaved, I believe he took after his father."

Coroner: "Mr Parr is a heavy drinker? Mr Crick, are you able to substantiate this?"

My Father: . . .

Coroner: "Mr Crick?"

My Father: "He likes a drop, sir."

Coroner: "Mr Parr is a known drinker. And Mr Parr is a signalman – and level-crossing keeper . . ."

And why did these facts – so the coroner might have pursued had his business not been in another area – not strike constant trepidation into the hearts of the motorists, cyclists and other road-users in the habit of relying on Jack Parr's gates, not to mention the footplatemen, guards and passengers of the Great Eastern Railway? And why had the railway authorities never got to hear of the unfortunate weakness of their employee – fuelled as it was (though the coroner didn't know this) by illicit liquor conveyed on their own rolling-stock?

For the simple reason that it was Mrs Parr – and this was

common knowledge too, P.C. Wyebrow might have added – who manned the gates and the signals during the periods of her husband's debility. It was she who heaved back and forth as to the manner born the clanking signal-switches; it was she who received and passed on the telegraph messages from Apton to Newhithe, from Apton to Wansham, that the nine-ten to Gildsey was twelve minutes late, that a goods train had been rescheduled; it was she who on icy winter dawns unfroze with the aid of a blow-lamp the hinges of the level-crossing gates while her husband lay snoring off the effects of a hard night's Kentucky Bourbon.

And what was the cause of this shameless laxity on the part of the husband and this remarkable forbearance on the part of the wife?

Hearsay holds that in the early and sober days of Jack Parr's signalmanship a terrible accident very nearly occurred at the Hockwell level-crossing. That the nightmare which haunts all level-crossing keepers one day became reality, and Jack Parr forgot to close, when needed, his life-saving gates. Perched in his signal-box, he suddenly awoke not only to this dreadful omission but to two other facts. That a scarlet Post Office van was idly mounting the Leem bridge on the southern side from where the railway line, on the northern side, was hidden by that fatal combination of bend, river embankment and line of trees; whilst, further to Jack Parr's left, down the dead-straight track in the direction of Apton, the all-too-punctual King's Lynn express was thunderously approaching. Jack Parr alone saw the full horror of the complete scene which was denied to any of its human components. With the alacrity of the panic-stricken, he leapt from his signal-box, descended in two bounds the flight of iron stairs and began turning, as only terror can make a man turn, the crank-wheel of the crossing-gates.

The scene implodes. In one unthinkable, if perfectly harmless, moment gates close, Post Office van screeches to a halt and King's Lynn express, brakes likewise screaming their utmost, hurtles through. No one is scathed. Jack Parr's professional record remains unblackened. But so great was the shock, so terrible was the thought of what *might* have happened and so unendurable was the possibility that at some time another lapse might occur, that Freddie Parr's father took to earnest drinking, thus forestalling any future forgetfulness through regular alcoholic oblivion.

But this whole story is possibly only the justificatory fabrication of Jack Parr's drink-sodden fancy. Jack Parr drank, perhaps, for no other reason than a good many other of his Fenland countrymen reached for the bottle. Because he was oppressed by those flat, black Fenland fields and that wide, exposing Fenland sky. Because he grew tired of looking every day, unable to move from his post, at featureless river-banks, phlegm-hued river-water, at rows of beets and potatoes, at straight railway track and files of spindly poplars; at the wind-swept platforms of Hockwell Station, at the dykes and drains intersecting and receding, imprinting on the brain their intolerable geometry. Because all this, together with the awesome fixity of his duties – this terrible combination of emptiness and responsibility – was too much for him.

Ah, children, pity level-crossing-keepers, pity lock-keepers – pity lighthouse-keepers – pity all the keepers of this world (pity even school teachers), caught between their conscience and the bleak horizon . . . Sometimes I wonder why my father, turning and turning yet again on the Leem tow-path, did not also take to drink.

Assuredly, Jack Parr did not drink to be merry – he who never raised a laugh, a true, a mirthful laugh, so it was said, after the day of that accident that never happened. And assuredly it is not for mirth's sake that he grasps again the neck of his Old Grand-dad on the night of the twenty-ninth of July, 1943, the date that it is officially recorded that his son has died – by another accident. He tilts and tilts again the bottle in order to silence that dreadful wail. Whywhywhy . . .

Because (he gulps) my Freddie was drunk and fell, with no one to save him, into the river. And why . . . ? Because he learnt to drink from his father, who was a worthless drunkard, who even went to the despicable lengths of sending his son on black-marketeering missions with the sole object of procuring alcohol. And why . . . ? Because his father was a hopeless good-for-nothing, content to train his son in dishonesty and

vice, a sinner who is rightly punished by this death of his first-
and only-born. But why . . . ?

And as each Why opens its bleating mouth Jack Parr stops it
with a swig, and another swig, endeavouring to efface the crime
of drink with yet more drink.

But it's not enough; it won't work.

For what do these unquellable and guilt-inflicting Whys lead
Jack Parr to do on this same July night? They lead him to
clamber over the gates of his own level-crossing, bottle in hand,
and to sit down with an air of great finality on the rails. The
desperate efforts and frantic protestations of Mrs Parr will not
budge him. He says nothing. Moonlight gleams on the lines.
Freddie Parr's father sits down and waits for the 00.40 Gildsey
or the one o'clock goods (the time-table is blurred) to run him
down.

But he is not run down. He is still there, drawing breath, in
the morning. Because Mrs Parr, abandoning her futile pleas
and assuming her old resourcefulness, has mounted to the
signal-box, as so often during her husband's bouts of mental
absence, thrown switches, tapped messages, phoned P.C.
Wyebrow – who hastily institutes a traffic diversion – to announce a "failure" at the level-crossing, communicated with
other signalmen up and down the lines and thus effected a
telegraphic conspiracy: lights winking over half the eastern
Fens, trains cancelled, diverted, unaccountably delayed, much
to the chagrin of late-night passengers and freight-shippers and
a good many mystified officials of the Great Eastern Railway.

Thus Jack Parr spent a whole night under the stars – which,
according to my father, hang in perpetual suspension because
of our sins – stupid with alcohol, waiting for iron-wheeled death
which never came. Thus he sat – lay – snored – dreamed. Till he
awoke, amidst the twittering of skylarks, to discover that he was
not dead but alive and that by his calculation (for Flora Parr
said nothing) two passenger trains and three goods had roared
over him without leaving a single mark. And thus Jack Parr,
who was a superstitious man and that very morning swore to
forsake drink, came to believe that God, who sometimes brings
about by way of punishment inexplicable cruelties and drowns
a man's own son, also performs inexplicable wonders.

Because, despite everything, despite emptiness, monotony, this Fenland, this palpable earth raised out of the flood by centuries of toil, is a magical, a miraculous land.

12

About the Change of Life

Mary – wherever you are, now you're gone, still here but gone, somewhere inside yourself, now you've stopped and all that is left for anyone else is your story – do you remember (can you still remember?) how once we lay in the shell of the old windmill by the Hockwell Lode and how the flat, empty Fens all around us became, too, a miraculous land, became an expectant stage on which magical things could happen? Do you remember how we looked up at the sky, into blue emptiness, and how out of the sky (because I told you: my homespun religiosity for your Catholic sophistication) God looked down on us; how He'd lifted off the roof of our makeshift home of love, and we didn't mind? How no one else could see us in our windmill bower but He could; and we let Him?

And was it the same God, looking down on us then, who spoke to you – ?

Children, once upon a time there was a history teacher's wife called Mary, with blue, curious eyes and brown hair, who before she was a history teacher's wife was the daughter of a Cambridgeshire farmer. Who lived in a stark, sturdy, sallow-brick farmhouse, amidst beet fields, potato fields and geometrically disposed dykes. Who during the years of the Second World War attended the St Gunnhilda (Convent) School for Girls in Gildsey, thus furthering her acquaintance with the future history teacher, then also attending school in Gildsey. Who, to her widower father's delight and pride, was praised by the sisters of the St Gunnhilda School for being a bright and eager pupil with a thirst for knowledge, but who, to her father's bitter disappointment, could not keep from exercising her curiosity out of school hours, particularly in matters sexual. Whose investigations, in this area, did not stop with the future history teacher. Who was adventurous, inquisitive, unrestrainable. Who was the last person one could imagine imitating the patron saint of our local town and shutting herself up, hermit-fashion, for over three years in that stark farmhouse; though she did, to her own mortification and her father's mounting dismay, in the autumn of 1943, her curiosity – and much else – having come in that same year (her seventeenth) to a sudden halt.

Many years ago there was a future history teacher's wife who resolved upon a certain drastic course of action. Who said to the future history teacher (causing consternation to engulf him, for he had no notion what he, in the circumstances, would do): "I know what I'm going to do." Who said to him, at a later date, much having occurred in the interval: "We must part." And then buried herself in that lonely farmhouse – as he buried himself in history books.

Some would say that this withdrawal on her part was not so much a voluntary act of penance as a punishment inflicted by her shamed and angered father, a man capable of stern measures, who, having once had hopes for his daughter, but being now only too aware of her wickedness, determined to lock her away from further mischief. But your history teacher (frightened witness to his wife-to-be's resolve) knows that the father, punitive though he was, played only a secondary part. He knows that Mary locked herself away of her own free will. Though he does not know, being denied at the time even the rights of visits or written communication, what occurred during that three-year period. Whether God spoke to her (then too) as He spoke, above the howls of demons, to St Gunnhilda; whether she found Salvation; whether, perhaps, she was visited by the ghost of Sarah Atkinson, the Brewer's Daughter of Gildsey, who, so local lore has it, offers her companionship to those whose lives have stopped though they must go on living . . . Or whether the truth of those three years was that nothing, nothing at all, occurred and that the future Mrs Crick, gazing day after day from her farmhouse cell at the level fields, was only, wittingly or unwittingly, preparing herself for her later marriage – which would be a sort of fenland.

Whatever the truth of the matter – for the future history teacher's wife is destined never to disclose it, and the future history teacher, called away early in 1945 to do military service, is in no position to glean anything at first-hand – whatever the truth of the matter, true it is that Farmer Metcalf's shame and anger relent and turn, in three years, to anxiety for his daughter's health and her future welfare.

Swallowing his pride – resigned to the fact that his daughter is not to rise in a world whose natural propensity appears to be to sink – and breaking a vow never to speak to the man again, he pays a visit to his neighbour, Henry Crick.

Though Harold Metcalf is, like Henry Crick, a widower and has grown accustomed to the ambience of seclusion, he is struck by the ramshackle solitariness of the lock-keeper who now lives alone in the lockside cottage and whom he finds, perhaps, mending eel-traps or conversing with his chickens.

Henry Crick receives him with an apprehensive and round-mouthed stare. They beat about the bush. The one laments the declining river-traffic, the other the iniquities of the War Agricultural Committee. They avoid more tender spots. Farmer Metcalf, at length, asks Henry if he has heard from his son, now stationed in Cologne – and so broaches his subject.

By the banks of the Leem, rapidly coming to an accord, less rapidly overcoming mutual shyness, the two men stammer, sigh, nod heads sagely (Henry Crick rubs his knee) and agree that enough is enough of anything, it can't go on, and that Time, after all, is the great reconciler. In short, Farmer Metcalf proposes that Henry Crick write a letter to his son, hinting that a second letter, of a certain drift, be sent in turn from the son to the Metcalf farmhouse. And though Henry Crick, being no letter-writer and no master of diplomacy, inwardly blenches at this undertaking, he agrees; for (to judge, indeed, by his own experience) he believes that marriages are made by Destiny, and Destiny is a great force; and where Destiny lends its hand even the most daunting tasks may be accomplished.

Yet he need not have agonised over that momentous letter. Because his son, a member of His Majesty's Army on the Rhine but now approaching the term of his period of service, is already, as the two fathers meet, resolving to put pen to paper and break a long, prohibitive silence. He writes, indeed, the sort of letter in which Destiny impregnates each word. But he too beats about the bush. He describes, with faltering eloquence, gutted cities, refugees, soup kitchens, mass graveyards, bread queues. He attempts to explain how these things have given him a new perspective, have made events by the River Leem seem, perhaps . . . Though he leaves out how they have deepened his desire to fathom the secrets of History and aroused, moreover, a belief in Education. He hints that he has undergone his own penance, though does not dare to suggest that this is of a kind that can possibly match hers, or that two years' barrack life and fitful meditation on the ruins of Europe can offer absolution. He makes no allusion to the wider future, but only asks that, upon his forthcoming demobilisation and return to England, they should, at least, meet.

And – as if to prove the hand of Destiny – it is only two days after he posts this letter that he receives another, tortuously and painstakingly composed, from his father. So that Farmer Metcalf is amazed, taking from his mail-box an envelope marked Cologne and addressed to his daughter, at the speed and efficiency with which Henry Crick has carried out his mission. Thereafter (since neither is disabused) he is inclined to take fresh stock of the lowly lock-keeper whom – setting aside the recent business of the latter's son and his own daughter – he had always regarded as a credulous simpleton (brains bashed about in Flanders) who had made that preposterous marriage.

Thus it is that in February, 1947, the future history teacher's wife waits at Gildsey station for the arrival of her husband-to-be. Thus it is that ex-serviceman Crick (now fully determined to become a teacher) makes his journey home in the guise of the returning Prince ready to pluck aside briars and cobwebs and kiss his Princess out of whatever trance has possessed her for the last three years. He expects to find – and accept – a nun, a Magdalen, a fanatic, a hysteric, an invalid . . . But he sees, even as he steps from the train, a woman (no girl) who impresses him with her appearance of toughness, endurance, as if she has made the decision to live henceforth without any kind of prop or refuge. And he realises that though this three-year separation has fostered the illusion that, should they reunite, *he* would be a prop to *her* (the specious sense of having grown up, the hardening effects of army life, acquaintance with the wide – and devastated – world), it is quite the opposite: that she will be a prop to him; that she will always be, just as she was in those days when she lost her curiosity, stronger than him.

It is a freezing winter. Hard snow covers the Fens and though, on this February day, the sun shines brilliantly, the air bites. In the White Rose Tea Room, near Gildsey station, in a scene evoking for the outsider but not for the protagonists certain cinema-screen reunions (no moon-faced café proprietor observes with a wink that they haven't touched their tea), the future history teacher's wife and the future history teacher deliberate their life together. It is clear that bonds exist between them stronger, and sterner, than those which link many couples who rush into wedlock; it is clear that if they are not meant for each other, then what other persons could there be for whom each of them, separately, is meant? It is clear that though certain things must be, though they cannot dispose of the past . . .

He breaks off his stumbling speechifying. They look into each other's eyes. Hers are still a smouldering blue: she is – has she forgotten it? – a desirable woman. She wears (to fuse the image of ex-schoolgirl and ex-soldier?) a simple black beret. He talks to her through wreaths of smoke from his Camel cigarettes, several packs of which he has specially hoarded to prepare the ground with Harold Metcalf. It is clear that if they have not been lovers in deed for three-and-a-half years, they are still lovers in spirit.

They leave the White Rose Tea Room (tea untouched) in order to be free to kiss and twine arms. Their breaths form a mingled cloud. They cross Market Street, walk down Water Street. On the Ousebank they embrace. Heavy winter clothing muffles and mutes unfamiliar closeness. They kiss. It is not a kiss which revives drowned curiosity, which restores the girl who once lay in a ruined windmill. But nor is her kiss, so it seems to him, the kiss of a woman who still seeks Salvation.

And so, by the icy Ouse, as they walk arm in arm between piles of cleared snow (watching spies, had there been any, might have scurried back to inform a relieved Farmer Metcalf and Henry Crick that all is well), it is decided. And it is there too, on the Ousebank, that the future history teacher's wife says two things. Firstly (looking at the heaped snow): "There'll be a bad thaw. Father can't move his cattle. Those idiots at the Catchment Board will have a lot to answer for." And then (looking straight at him): "You know, don't you, that short of a miracle we can't have a child?"

Children, once upon a time there was a future history teacher's wife who wore a rust-red schoolgirl's uniform and wore her deep-brown hair in a straight fringe, in the regulation fashion, under a schoolgirl's beret or straw hat; but who – wearing little or nothing at all – invited the future history teacher to explore the intricacies of her incipient womanhood, to consider the mysteries of her menstrual cycle – and to offer reciprocal invitations. Who liked to find things out, to uncover secrets, but then ceased to be inquisitive. Whose life came to a kind of stop when she was only sixteen, though she had to go on living.

Once, long ago, there was a future history teacher's wife who, though she said to the future history teacher they should never meet again, married him three years later. And the future history teacher took her away with him, in 1947, from the Cambridgeshire Fens where they were both born, to London. Though not before in the spring of that year a great flood had drowned the larger part of those same native Fens. And not before this same flood, which caused Henry Crick to contract broncho-pneumonia while he kept, tenaciously, vigilantly, in a half submerged cottage, to his post of lock-keeper, had brought about the death of the future history teacher's father.

But that, children, is another story . . .

They moved to London. He becomes a teacher. And she, after some years as only a history teacher's wife (seeing him off to school each morning – the inevitable ironies, the mother-son charades this prompted), finds work, for reasons never fully explained, in a local government office concerned with the care of the elderly.

They settle in Greenwich, in a suburb of London noted for its historical features: a Royal Observatory; a park where Henry VIII once wooed and hunted; a former palace; a Queen's House turned Maritime Museum; not to mention the dry-docked Cutty Sark, bowsprit permanently pointing to the Isle of Dogs. He teaches at a Grammar School (resited and rein-corporated as a comprehensive in 1966) in Charlton. She works at the municipal buildings in Lewisham.

They acquire regular habits, spiced with unspectacular variations. Sunday walks in the Park (the Observatory and back). Exchanges of hospitality with his teaching colleagues and her age-care associates. Joking comment is passed (do the couple accept it as joking?) at these sociable occasions about their respective professional spheres – he amongst schoolkids, she amongst the senile. (What has become of the middle bit of life?) A visit, approximately every six weeks, to her father (who won't leave his farm, who won't have any of this nursing-home nonsense) in Cambridgeshire. A slap-up meal in a restaurant every birthday and wedding anniversary. Trips to the theatre. Weekend excursions. Holidays: he, true to form, prefers historical associations; she is incurious.

Not having a family – and inheriting, in 1969, part of the proceeds of the sale of a Fenland farm – they do not lack for money, indeed are almost embarrassingly comfortable: the "enviable Greenwich home" (Regency, porticoed front door) of which much will be made in certain newspaper reports.

They acquire regular habits and regular diversions. So much so that three decades pass as if little has happened, as if without event, and it does not seem long before they are both in their fifties: he a Head of Department who refuses a headmaster's desk; she having decided, for reasons no more explicit than those which made her begin, to give up her work with her Old Folk. And as they take their Sunday walks in the park (walks during which it might be observed that should they lean on one another, it is he who leans on her rather than she on him), they are joined by a third party – a golden retriever, called Paddy. It lopes and fawns about them and causes them now and then to smile and utter words of encouragement or command. A golden retriever bought by her for him on his fifty-second birthday, for which the official justification (a prod at his stomach) is the inducement to more exercise in sedentary middle age. But brief examination of the fact that when the wife made her sudden decision to leave work it was during the onset of a late and troubled menopause, suggests a different explanation . . .

They walk now, in chill January sunshine, Paddy padding behind them, along the path to the Observatory. Eyes blinking in the dazzling light; Sunday morning thick heads receiving frosty purgation. For this is the morning after a certain dinner party at the house of Lewis and Rebecca Scott.

Over-freeness with the pre-dinner gins and the mid-dinner wine; Mrs Scott a bustling, cerise-clad hostess; the Scott children (unable to sleep: all this adult chatter from below) suddenly paraded, exhibited in the dining-room in pyjamas and dressing-gowns, offering bashful smiles or performing impudent tricks, being whisked off again briskly to bed; the subject of nuclear shelters emerging through the coffee and brandy . . .

And all of it, according to him – though she said, as they drove to the Scott home, he should curb his paranoia – a piece of sinister manipulation. A way of buttering him up. (When did Lewis last ask the Cricks to dinner?)

He'd been getting the rumours ("Drink up, Tom"): phasing out the History Department . . .

Gloves and scarves. Silvered asphalt underfoot. Breaths forming vapour-trails. They walk in silence, each lost in misty thoughts. Paddy keeps a tactful distance.

She speaks, stealing from him the words he was about to say to her.

"You're quiet. What's up?"

"O – I was just thinking of one of my kids. Bit of a trouble-maker. Price."

He smiles, shrugging aside the subject.

"Tell me about him."

So he tells her about Price. His classroom declaration: history is coming to an end. A schoolmaster's explanatory theory: Price as would-be revolutionary. Like every active-minded young man, Price wants to change the world. Yet Price knows that all the old authentic revolutions are over. Old hat. Hence his disruption, despite the seeming affinity, of a lesson on the French Revolution. How can you have a revolution if history's coming to an – ? The frustrated revolutionary turns radical reactionary. Price doesn't want to change the world, he wants to –

"Save it?" Her words anticipating his again.

She takes his arm, squeezes it. (It'll be the last time they'll walk so closely, familiarly in the old park.)

"But I don't mean that. I meant tell me about *him*."

"Price? He's sixteen. Curly-haired. Skinny. Sort of underfed and homeless-looking. But surly with it. Not that he hasn't got a home. His father's a garage manager. I asked him, 'How are things at home?' He said, '*They*'re happy.' He wears this stuff – don't ask me why – a sort of dirty-white greasepaint . . ."

He rambles on, evidently needing to speak, about this teenage thorn in the flesh.

"He's actually quite clever. I think he blames me. For history. He's – likeable . . . I think he's frightened."

She listens, questions. Breath-smoke. Keen eyes. Frost-sharp air.

"It's not like you to let a student under your skin."

And it's not like Mary to be curious.

Once upon a time there was a future history teacher and a future history teacher's wife for whom things went wrong, so – since you cannot dispose of the past, since things must be – they had to make do.

And he made do precisely by making a profession out of the past, out of this thing which cannot be eradicated, which accumulates and impinges – whose action, indeed, was imitated by the growing numbers of books (works of history, but – more recently – also of natural history) which filled the first-floor room of the Greenwich house which the history teacher made his study, and spilled out onto landing and staircase. He made a profession – a life's work – out of the past, for which his justification was the children to whom he offered daily the lessons that the past affords. To them he presented the equivocal gift of history – burdensome yet instructive – to carry into their futures. And thus the history teacher – though his relation with his young charges echoes first the paternal, then the grand-paternal, though he sees in their faces (but does not admit it) less and less the image of the future, more and more that of something he is trying to retrieve, something he has lost – could always say (he acquires a penchant for paradox) that he looked back in order to look forward.

But she made do (so he thought) with nothing. Not believing either in looking back or looking forward, she learnt how to mark time. To withstand, behind all the stage-props of their marriage, the empty space of reality. So that whereas he could not do without his history classes and his schoolkids, she could readily dispense with her Old Folk – witness that voluntary, indeed adamant decision. And whereas he had to keep going back every day to school, there was always this grown-up woman to return to, who was stronger than him (he believed) at facing the way things must be – whom he needed indeed, when it came to it, more than he needed all the wisdom and solace of history.

So that your history teacher's wife, children, may be said to have been the inspiration of all that he taught you . . .

Once upon a time there was a history teacher's wife who, for quite specific and historical reasons, couldn't have a child. Though her husband had lots: a river of children – new lives, fresh starts – flowed through his classroom. Who could have adopted a child (many times, in the early years, the husband warily – hopefully – raised the subject); though she never adopted a child, for the simple and intractable reason, so the husband supposed, that to adopt a child is not the real thing, and his wife was not a woman to resort to make-believe.

Once there was a history teacher's wife who, as if to prove that she could live without children, chose to work with old people, with those people who, since their lives have come to a virtual halt, have themselves become burdens, embarrassments, anxieties to their own children and consequently have to be taken off their hands and put in Homes. Who engages in this work for twenty-odd years. But in her fifty-third year – in the same year in which she purchases for her husband's birthday a dog called Paddy – she suddenly but deliberately stops work with her old people, leaving herself with no other occupation but to survey the flat and uniform terrain of thirty years of marriage while he surveys his rows of teenagers.

A history teacher's wife who (so the history teacher thought) was realistic. Who did not need (since she had learnt her lessons) to go back to school. Who did not believe any more in miracles and fairy-tales, nor (having experimented in her younger days) in New Life and Salvation.

But in her fifty-third year, in the year 1980, it begins to seem to the history teacher that this one-time schoolgirl who could not leave a secret unexplored, is herself harbouring a secret. Why is she taciturn? (Yet keen-eyed.) What does she do with the time on her hands while he holds forth before his classes? Why is she so often out when he returns from school in the late afternoons? Is this a case (like old Thomas Atkinson, should Mr Crick strike Mrs Crick and let all hell loose?) of doting solicitude leading to jealous imaginings? For Mrs Crick, you'll have observed, children, even from those atrocious newspaper photographs, is a well-preserved woman.

At length she confesses she has been talking to a priest. She confesses she has been to confession – something she has not done for nearly forty years. But she will not say more. She brings home books whose very titles ("If Jesus Returned"; "God or The Bomb") appal him. He watches her read (while he marks exercise books). She reads with the earnest and receptive gaze that now and then, in luckier moments, will steal over his listening students. The history teacher says to himself – with a sense that she is drifting away from him, with a sense that some picture he has had of things has been turned upside down – my wife is becoming a child again. He wants to draw her back, to keep her safe. But on Sunday mornings and afternoons, customary times for their strolls in the Park, she begins – the first occasion is a week after their talk about Price – to insist on taking walks alone (he is left to the company of a dog): walks whose object, he strongly suspects, is to attend church.

Mary, do you remember our Sunday walks, with which we trod and measured out the tenuous, reclaimed land of our marriage?

*

111

On the top of Greenwich Hill, in Greenwich Park, stands an Observatory, founded by Charles II to search the mysteries of the stars. By the Observatory, set in the asphalt, much bestridden and photographed by visiting sightseers, a metal plate marks the line of longitude 0°. Near longitude 0°, perched on a plinth, becloaked and tricorned, stands General Wolfe, in bronze, staring to the Thames. And beneath General Wolfe, imitating his vigilant pose, stands the history teacher, in coat and scarf, taking in for the umpteenth time the famous view. The Maritime Museum (relics of Cook and Nelson); the Naval College (painted ceiling depicting four English monarchs). History's toy-cupboard. The pastime of past time. The history teacher himself, here in Greenwich at the head of end-of-term outings, his worthy Subject reduced to ice-cream guzzling and clambering over cannons. The river: a steel serpent coiling through clutter – derelict wharves and warehouses, decaying docks . . .

From the top of Greenwich Hill it is possible not only to scan the inscrutable heavens but to peel back past panoramas (windjammers in the India Dock; royal barges, under Dutch-Master skies, bound for the Palace), to imagine these river approaches to London as the wild water-country they once were. Deptford, Millwall, Blackwall, Woolwich . . . And, away, out of sight to the east, the former marshes where, in 1980, they are building a flood barrier.

He stands alone and contemplates the view. Every Sunday, weather permitting, by varying routes, to the Observatory and back. To longitude 0° and back. Pause on the belvedere; admiration of the view; silent, simultaneous but separate musings; then he to her or she to him (a smile; a shiver at the cold): "Home?" But now he stands alone, beneath the Hero of Quebec.

He stands alone – save for a golden retriever which rubs and nuzzles at his legs and begs to be indulged in more stick-throwing games. Because his wife no longer comes on walks with him. She goes her own way. As if, he thinks, she is already (but her husband lives) a widow. But widow's not the right word. Widow suggests an old woman. And she is getting younger. She is leaving him. She reminds him of a woman in love . . .

Low winter sun over Flamsteed's Observatory. Fiery highlights on the roof of the Maritime Museum. The history teacher stands, surveys the outstretched view. Thinks of a student called Price. The only important thing . . . If the truth be known, he is frightened. If the truth be known, he doesn't know what to think. He is telling himself stories. (How a girl and a boy once . . . How . . .) He dreads going home. Dreads, now, weekends, Sundays. Dark evenings.

He turns. Stoops suddenly to ruffle vigorously the neck of the impatient Paddy, who, tail-wagging and panting, anticipates the return of his favourite game. He leaves the belvedere and the asphalt, strikes out onto the grass, overtaken by an ecstatic dog. In his gloved right hand he carries an already tooth-marked and saliva-dampened stick. "Here, Paddy! Here!"

The history teacher throws the stick, watches the dog run – a blond flurry attached to a long winter shadow – pick up, return, demand more. He throws again. And again. Mary, what became of our love? . . . And again, watching instinct at work. Pursue; pick up; return; pursue again.

Retriever. Golden retriever.

For two, three weekends he goes alone to the Park; throws sticks for a dog. Then one Sunday she wants to come walking with him again. He is, restrainedly, overjoyed. They put on coats. Paddy comes too. There's a feeling of newness. Her face, winter-rouged, is aglow with something. They turn at the Observatory. She wants to sit for a moment on a bench. February twilight gathering (the Park closes at dusk). And then suddenly she announces: "I'm going to have a baby. Because God's said I will."

Children, don't stop asking why. Don't cease your Why Sir? Why Sir? Though it gets more difficult the more you ask it, though it gets more inexplicable, more painful, and the answer never seems to come any nearer, don't try to escape this question Why.

13

Histrionics

Because when I was your age and Jack Parr was asking Whywhywhy and my father was asking Whywhywhy, how sweet and redeeming sounded that neat and neutral phrase "Accidental Death". How sweet and blessedly – fraudulently – normal seemed the view from the Wansham Road (blessed flat fields, blessed monotonous dykes) as I cycled, on that same day of Jack Parr's miraculous survival, to meet Mary by the Lode. Because that neat phrase – it was official – meant that no one was guilty. If death was accidental then it couldn't have been murder, could it, and if it couldn't have been murder then my brother couldn't have been – And if my brother wasn't, then Mary and I weren't– And that only left the little problem (but it was only a little problem, a not even visible problem, and when the time came, we'd sworn, we were going to go first to Mary's father, then to mine . . .) of that little thing in Mary's tummy.

And so I said (I wasn't late this time; I got there first, and Mary appeared, minutes later, through the poplar spinney): "It's all right. Haven't you heard? Accidental death. So it's all right. All right. Nothing's changed."

And Mary looked at me – how can I convey that look which seemed to pile years upon her and strip them from me (and she still does it – or rather did it – my mother-wife who packed her husband off to school)? Mary looked at me and said: "It's not all right. Because it wasn't an accident. Everything's changed."

And what did your history-teacher-in-the-making do after taking in these words and receiving that gaze? He looked around at the innocent fields and dykes and saw in them treacherous conspirators. He couldn't bring himself to face the face which faced him and which seemed to be accusing him of childish stupidity. He threw a (childish) tantrum. He kicked the brick base of the former windmill by the Hockwell Lode. He marched up the bank of the same Lode, savagely tearing up as he went a clump of grass, and stood at the top of the bank, throwing bits of that same torn-up clump, equally savagely, this way and that. So he was still in the same mess, after all – just as he was thinking that a neat phrase had hauled him out. Just as he was succumbing to the illusion that everything was all right, like it was before, and they might even, inside the ruined windmill . . . And she had to spoil it all.

As if it were all against *him*, this conspiracy. As if being guilty, as if having to accept that what has happened really happened and can't unhappen, were a kind of unjust trick played upon him.

Another seized-up clump of grass. The future history teacher indulges in histrionics. He struts and fumes like a true male member of the species. Are you watching me, Mary? Can you see how *outraged* I am? Throws more tufts of futile grass into the air. Stares at the Lode (the sheeny eye of the Lode stares back at him). While Mary stands at the bottom of the bank, arms drawn round herself, not really noticing, not impressed. He's alone. She's alone. He's blustery-raging alone; and she's rooted, patient alone.

He turns. On this warm July afternoon he suddenly feels cold. Suddenly he knows for certain that the fear he felt by the river-bank and in his own locked room four days ago can't be allayed by two official words – nor by seizing up and throwing to the wind each and every tussock along the Hockwell Lode. He descends the Lode bank. He stands before the motionless girl. He would have liked (hated too) this sixteen-year-old, warm-bodied, stern-eyed, ten-weeks-pregnant, no-longer-curious creature, in whom he sees suddenly qualities of iron, to hold him. But her arms stay wrapped round her own shoulders. He sits down, weakly, at the foot of the bank. She remains standing. He looks up and asks (he wants someone suddenly to come up with the answers): "*You* told him. *You* told him. So what are we going to do?"

And Mary says firmly: "I know what I'm going to do."

And turns and leaves him sitting beneath the bank and

doesn't move her head or speak when he gets up and shouts: "What's that then, Mary? *What* are you going to do? Mary – ?"

He cycles back to his lock-cottage home, not knowing when he will see Mary again, whether she will ever meet him again by the stump of the old windmill. His father, who has been lifting potatoes (lifting potatoes so as to stop asking why) from the vegetable plot behind the cottage, wipes earthy hands, says, though not in the voice with which he was once apt to tell fireside yarns: "Jack Parr – have you heard? Sat down on the railway line . . ." Sits down himself, on an upturned barrel beside the chicken coop. Takes out and lights a Lucky Strike (forgetting: courtesy of the U.S. Air Force, via Jack Parr, via Freddie . . .) Wonders, perhaps, looking at his son's face – his son's troubled face which mirrors his own – whether this is the time, this time of universal strife and reckoning, and now that a drowned body . . . to tell him everything, the whole story, all he will one day learn for himself. But says, blowing smoke, paternally, confidingly, solicitously: "Is it serious – you and Mary?"

Is it serious?!

Broody chicken sounds. Innocent cluck-clucks. Quiet river. Mocking late-afternoon mellowness. Because life continues. "Sat down on the railway lines . . ." Because life goes on and July afternoons turn to old gold, despite drowned bodies and inquests, and even despite wars which assert themselves in wireless announcements and evening blackouts. Dad gets up: the six o'clock bulletin. A daily ritual. A daily homage to history. Stands at the back door, shakes his head (another singeing for the inhabitants of the Ruhr), rubs his mouth, conflating things local and things cosmic. Returns to his vegetable plot. Gets on vigorously with his potato lifting.

And even now, on sunlit airfields, bomber crews are being briefed. And even now, down the Gildsey road comes a sound not unreminiscent of a distant bomber. Dick on his motor-cycle. That familiar sound, every evening, a little after six. Dick's motor-bike; Dick coming home from the dredger. This joke-truth: life goes on. And is it possible that for Dick this is just another day? Home after six. That he has forgotten – ? That for

116

him present eclipses past? That he possesses those amnesiac, those time-erasing qualities so craved by all guilty parties – ? No Before, no After. Just another day. Another day on the dredger. Silt-shifting.

Father and son watch the motor-bike approach. Watch the machine-and-man entity buzz towards them down the straight and level Gildsey road, then slow down and reveal its bipartite nature as Dick brakes, sits up in the saddle, and the two observers hear, faintly, through the noise of the engine and a flurry of dust as Dick turns into the track to the cottage, the tuneless wail, the wordless, endless song of love to his motor-cycle that Dick always sings as he rides.

Father leans on his fork. And son picks up a potato (an Ulster Chieftain), starts to tear at it with his bare nails, to flay it, to gouge it, and asks himself (again, yet again): "And what am *I* going to do?"

14

De la Révolution

It goes in two directions at once. It goes backwards as it goes forwards. It loops. It takes detours. Do not fall into the illusion that history is a well disciplined and unflagging column marching unswervingly into the future. Do you remember, I asked you – a riddle – how does a man move? One step forward, one step back (and sometimes one step to the side). Is this absurd? No. Because if he never took that step forward –

Or – another of my classroom maxims: There are no compasses for journeying in time. As far as our sense of direction in this unchartable dimension is concerned, we are like lost travellers in a desert. We believe we are going forward, towards the oasis of Utopia. But how do we know – only some imaginary figure looking down from the sky (let's call him God) can know – that we are not moving in a great circle?

It cannot be denied, children, that the great, so-called forward movements of civilisation, whether moral or technological, have invariably brought with them an accompanying regression. That the dissemination of Christian tenets over a supposedly barbarous world has been throughout the history of Europe – to say nothing of missionary zeal elsewhere – one of the prime causes of wars, butcheries, inquisitions and other forms of barbarity. That the discovery of the printing press led, likewise, as well as to the spreading of knowledge, to propaganda, mendacity, contention and strife. That the invention of the steam-engine led to the miseries of industrial exploitation and to little children working sixteen hours a day in coalmines. That the invention of the aeroplane led to the widespread destruction of European cities along with their civilian populations during the period 1939 to '45 (here I can offer you my two-fold eye-witness account: the nightly flights of bombers from East Anglian bases from 1941 onwards; the ruins of Cologne, Dusseldorf and Essen).

And as for the splitting of the atom –

And where history does not undermine and set traps for itself in such an openly perverse way, it creates this insidious longing to go backwards. It begets this bastard but pampered child, Nostalgia. How we yearn – how you may one day, if that day comes, yearn – to return to that time before history claimed us, before things went wrong. How we yearn even for the gold of a July evening on which, though things had already gone wrong, things had not gone as wrong as they were going to. How we pine for Paradise. For mother's milk. To draw back the curtain of events that has fallen between us and the Golden Age.

So how do we know – lost in the desert – that it is to the oasis of the yet-to-come we should be travelling anyway, and not to some other green Elysium that, a long while ago, we left behind? And how do we know that this mountain of baggage called History, which we are obliged to lug with us – which slows our pace to a crawl and makes us stagger off course – is really hindering us from advancing or retreating? Which way does salvation lie?

No wonder we move in circles.

So then. Let us throw down our baggage, let us cast aside all this cumbersome paraphernalia, and see. Every so often, there are these attempts to jettison the impedimenta of history, to do without that ever-frustrating weight. And because history accumulates, because it gets always heavier and the frustration greater, so the attempts to throw it off (in order to go – which way was it?) become more violent and drastic. Which is why history undergoes periodic convulsions, and why, as history becomes inevitably more massive, more pressing and hard to support, man – who even without his loads doesn't know where he's heading – finds himself involved in bigger and bigger catastrophes.

What is this thing that takes us back, either via catastrophe and confusion or in our heart's desire, to where we were?

Let's call it Natural History.

Children, do you remember when we did the French Revolution? That great landmark, that great watershed of history. How I explained to you the implications of that word "revolution"? A turning round, a completing of a cycle. How I told you that though the popular notion of revolution is that of categorical change, transformation – a progressive leap into the future – yet almost every revolution contains within it an opposite if less obvious tendency: the idea of a return. A redemption; a restoration. A reaffirmation of what is pure and fundamental against what is decadent and false. A return to a new beginning . . .

The turmoil of great revolutions is the last setting in which one would expect Nostalgia to thrive. But so it does. Reflect for a moment on the wilful and cultivated *naivety* of those French revolutionaries. How they demanded not the rights of citizens but the rights of *Man*. How they took up good old Rousseau's cry of back to nature and "*l'homme né libre*". How when in 1790 they thought the revolution was over (naive in that too) they celebrated by dressing up, in Arcadian simplicity, as swains and shepherdesses and by planting tender young trees of liberty. Consider the growing religiosity – pious feasts to the Supreme Being – of a movement whose initial animus had in part been anti-clerical if not atheistical. And consider the dangers of this naivety. How this yearning after purity and innocence is only a step from Robespierre's famous, and infamous, incorruptibility; how liberation turns to Grand Purge; how this revolution, which they thought was over so quickly, is forced, in order to satisfy its insistence on first principles, to renew itself again and again, with ever more ruthless zeal, till exhaustion allows compromise – if not reaction.

And those revolutionary messiahs – Robespierre, Marat, the rest – of whom we think we can say, though they terrify us, that at least they were prepared to go to extremes in order to create a new world – did they really have in mind a Society of the Future? Not a bit of it. Their model was an idealised ancient Rome. Laurel wreaths and all. Their prototype the murder of Caesar. Our heroes of the new age – good classicists all – yearned, too, to go back –

"But Sir!"

It's corpse-pale Price who interrupts. Provocative hand raised. Another of his lesson-sabotaging sallies.

And the teacher feels, through Price's rebellious eyes, the unrest, and anticipation of the whole class.

Sir! Hang on a moment! We're not living in the eighteenth century. What about –?

"This nostalgia stuff, sir" – shifting in his desk with an air of ironic puzzlement – "how would nostalgia make these hungry workers go on the rampage then?"

Titters and murmurs from the class. (A mob gathering.) Nervous shifting of weight on feet by teacher.

(They've all noticed it: Something just a bit edgy of late, something just a bit vulnerable about old Cricky.)

"I'm glad you asked that, Price." (How a teacher announces a side-step.) "Because it raises the question of how you define a revolution – sociologically speaking. Just as a revolution moves in paradoxical directions, so its social location is elusive. You mention the hungry workers. Do these make a revolution? Or do the overtaxed bourgeoisie? Is a revolution merely a spontaneous external event or is it the expression of a particular party or parties? Surely a revolution cannot be called a revolution unless before it is even an act it is the expression of a *will*? But whose? Where do we place the revolutionary will? The petit bourgeois? The hungry masses? The political clubs? As you try to define the revolution you imitate precisely the action of the revolution itself – eliminating with a mental guillotine those who do not fit some impossibly absolute notion of revolution. Where is the revolution truly embodied? In Danton? He wanted to call it a day and retire to the country. Robespierre? He, on the other hand, was a ruthless fanatic. Thus one comes to the obligingly vague notion of 'the people' – *Vox populi, vox Dei*. Translate, someone."

Judy Dobson, front row left (a perky answerer): "The voice of the people is the voice of God."

"Very good. But true? And who, in this case, were the people? The professional men who flocked to the National Assembly? They for the most part were fired by personal ambition and the prospect of power. The masses? The mob?" (The mob, the mob.) "Are they our true revolutionaries? Study the history of the Paris mob from 1789 to 1795 and the one constant feature you'll find is inconsistency . . ."

(Stop this waffle. Price doesn't want a lecture – and he can see through your smoke-screen.)

"The mob supports this party, then that, but once its particular grievances are met, once it is no longer hungry, it will follow a Napoleon as readily as a Danton. There can be no revolution, perhaps, without a mob, but the mob are not the revolutionaries . . ."

Teacher fingers tie-knot, paces, like a blustering general before mutinous troops.

"Where then does the revolution lie? This starting-point of our modern age. Is it merely a term of convenience? Does it lie in some impenetrable amalgam of countless individual circumstances too complex to be analysed? It's a curious thing, Price, but the more you try to dissect events, the more you lose hold of what you took for granted in the first place – the more it seems it never actually occurred, but occurs, somehow, only in the imagination . . ."

Teacher pauses. Price's response to all this suddenly seems important.

He hesitates a moment. Then, boldly, almost insolently: "Should we be writing this down, sir? The French Revolution never really happened. It only happened in the imagination."

"Don't be literal, Price."

"No, but I think it's true. We don't know the half, so a good half must be make-believe."

Suppressed chortlings around the class.

"And are we really supposed to believe that in 1789 everyone wanted to put the clock back?"

More giggles and outbursts. Price turns, surveys the class.

(So is that your game? All it is? Just the old bash-the-teacher stuff? The old schoolroom power-contest: Class-mates beware! Don't be fooled by our teacher's attempts to turn a thing into its opposite. To call revolution retrogression. What all this clever-talk amounts to is that our Cricky's over the hill. Like all the oldies, he can only look backwards. He can't bear the notion of anything new . . .)

"I'm speculating, it's true, Price. But we're all free to inter-pret."

"You mean, so we can find whatever meaning we like in history?"

(Actually I do believe that. I believe it more and more. History: a lucky dip of meanings. Events elude meaning, but we look for meanings. Another definition of Man: the animal who craves meaning – but knows –)

"Price," (side-step again), "I draw attention to the backward-tending element of the Revolution to illustrate that even re-volutions with their claims to construct a new order are subject to one of the most ingrained historical beliefs. That history is the record of decline. What we wish upon the future is very often the image of some lost, imagined past."

He frowns. For the first time in this classroom set-to he looks unsure.

(Will you have a lost past, Price? When you are my age – ?)

"I don't understand that, sir. I mean that's really *weird*, isn't it?"

Open laughter in class. Teacher's eyes fasten on the view beyond the window.

"It's no more weird – no more superstitious than saying that at some magical time in the future paradise will arrive."

Price bites his pen. He's not laughing with the others. He'll wait for another lesson for his Big Statement.

122

The only important thing . . .

"I never said that, sir. Never said anything about paradise. But – I want a future." (The class has gone quiet.) "We all do. And you – you can stuff your past!"

And so, children, having examined all the evidence, we must ask ourselves some big questions. Why was it that this revolution in the name of liberty and equality ended with an emperor? Why was it that this movement to abolish for good the *ancien régime* ended with a reincarnation of the old Sun King?

Why was it that this revolution which did indeed achieve lasting reforms could not do so without fear and terror, without the piling up, in the streets of Paris alone, of (at a modest estimate) six thousand corpses, not to mention the thousands of corpses in greater France or the unnumbered corpses of Italians, Austrians, Prussians, Russians, Spaniards, Portuguese, Englishmen – which were to be strewn over the battlegrounds of Europe? Why is it that every so often history demands a bloodbath, a holocaust, an Armageddon? And why is it that every time the time before has taught us nothing?

Follow me, said the Corsican, and I will give you your Golden Age. And they followed him – these regicides, these tyranthaters.

How it repeats itself, how it goes back on itself, no matter how we try to straighten it out. How it twists, turns. How it goes in circles and brings us back to the same place.

So if you're thinking of going somewhere. If you want your Here and Now. If you're tired of school and lessons, if you want to be out there, in the real world of today, let me tell you

15

About the Ouse

The Great Ouse. Ouse. Say it. *Ouse*. Slowly. How else can you say it? A sound which exudes slowness. A sound which suggests the slow, sluggish, forever oozing thing it is. A sound which invokes quiet flux, minimum tempo; cool, impassive, unmoved motion. A sound which will calm even the hot blood racing in your veins. Ouse, Ouse, Oooooouse . . .

Once upon a time there was a river which flowed into another river which one day men would call the Rhine. But in those days there were no men, no names and no North Sea and no island called Great Britain and the only beings who knew this river which flowed into the nameless Rhine were the fishes which swam up and down it and the giant creatures which browsed in its shallows and whose fantastic forms we might never have guessed at were it not for the fact that now and then they lay down to die in circumstances that would preserve their fossilised bones and so, millions of years later, became a subject for human inquiry.

Then there was an ice age, or, to be precise, a series of glacial advances and withdrawals, during which time the sea interposed itself between the conjunctive Ouse and Rhine, and the land mass later known as Great Britain began to detach itself from the continent. And during this same lengthy period the first men, or their ape-like ancestors, coming from no one knows exactly where, perhaps from Africa, perhaps from China, or even, by way of an evolutionary detour, out of the sea, migrated across the continental shelf and began to inhabit this not yet severed peninsula, thus setting a precedent many times to be followed, but for the last time successfully in 1066.

What these first men and their waves of successors called the Ouse we have no idea, having no inkling of their language. But

124

how the Ouse regarded (for let us adopt the notion of these primitive peoples who very probably thought of the Ouse as a God, a sentient Being) these two-legged intruders who by daring to transmute things into sound were unconsciously forging the phenomenon known as History, we can say readily: with indifference. For what did such a new-fangled invention matter to a river which flowed on, oozed on, just as before. What did the three Stone Ages, the Beaker Folk, the Bronze Age, Iron Age, the Belgic Tribes and all their flints, pots, axes, bangles, brooches and burial customs signify to a river which possessed as no man did, or does, the secret capacity to move yet remain?

Then the Romans came. What they called the Ouse we do not know either, but we know that they called the Wash "Metaris". And they were the first to impose their will on the sullen, disdainful Ouse. For they employed several miles of it in the construction of their great catchwater channel, the Car Dyke, which ran, and can still be traced, from the Cam to the Witham – from near Cambridge to near Lincoln – round the whole western flank of the Fens, thus providing yet another example of that Roman skill in engineering and dauntlessness before nature at which modern man still gasps in admiration.

But in those days the Ouse took a different course from that which it takes today. It is a feature of this footloose and obstinate river that it has several times during its brush with human history changed direction, taken short-cuts, long loops, usurped the course of other rivers, been coaxed into new channels and rearranged its meeting-place with the sea. All of which might be construed as a victory for history (for it is human ingenuity which in so many cases has effected these changes), yet which is more aptly to be interpreted as the continued contempt of the river for the efforts of men. Since without the old Ouse's perpetual if unhurried unruliness, without its ungovernable desire to flow at its own pace and in its own way, none of those cuts and channels and re-alignments, which are still being dug, and which enmesh the tortuous, reptilian Ouse in a net of minor waterways, would ever have been necessary.

In Roman times and in that period known as the Dark Ages but which, as many, notably Charles Kingsley, the Fenland fabulist, have opined, was for the Fens their most lustrous and legendary era – the Ouse flowed northwards, nearly to March, before meeting with the old River Cam. In that period in which Canute, who could no more stop rivers flowing than he could bid waves retreat, was mesmerised by the singing of the monks as he was rowed past Ely in his royal barge, the Ouse, giving a free ride to its brother Cam, met the sea at Wisbech (which is now ten miles from the coast).

But in the Middle Ages, under licence of great floods, the Ouse took it upon itself to flow eastwards up one of its own westward-flowing tributaries and by way of this channel to meet the Cam where it still meets it, some dozen miles downstream of Cambridge. At much the same time it abandoned its outfall at Wisbech to the encroachment of silt, and found a new exit at Lynn. Thus the old river became extinct and a new river, a great ragged bow thrown out to the east, was formed, much to the rejoicing of the people of Ely and the tiny community of Gildsey who now found themselves not only on the water-route between Lynn and Cambridge but also on that between Lynn and Huntingdon. And much to the disgruntlement of the corn merchants of Huntingdon, whose way to the sea was now extended by many miles.

Then, as we know, Vermuyden came, to put matters right, and dug the Bedford and New Bedford Rivers – straight strings to the bow of the rebellious river – to the glee of the men of Huntingdon who now had better access than ever to the coast, and the dismay of the men of Cambridgeshire whose three-centuries-old waterway was reduced to little more than a land drain. And thus the fate of that true and natural, if wayward, Ouse (and still called "Great" despite the sapping of its waters along the Bedford Rivers) was to lie thenceforth (for we have now moved into a period which even historically speaking is recent and which in the limitless life of a river is but yesterday) in the hands of those local men of ambition so characteristic of this island which as a nation was approaching the peak of its world-wide ambitions – not least amongst whom were the Atkinsons of Norfolk and later of Gildsey.

The Ouse flows on, unconcerned with ambition, whether local or national. It flows now in more than one channel, its waters diverging, its strength divided, silt-prone, flood-prone. Yet it flows – oozes – on, as every river must, to the sea. And, as we all know, the sun and the wind suck up the water from the sea and disperse it on the land, perpetually refeeding the rivers. So that while the Ouse flows to the sea, it flows, in reality, like all rivers, only back to itself, to its own source; and that impression that a river moves only one way is an illusion. And it is also an illusion that what you throw (or push) into a river will be carried away, swallowed for ever, and never return. Because it will return. And that remark first put about, two and a half thousand years ago, by Heraclitus of Ephesus, that we cannot step twice into the same river, is not to be trusted. Because we are always stepping into the same river.

It flows out of the heart of England to the Wash and the North Sea. It passes the sturdy English towns of Bedford, Huntingdon, St Ives, Ely, Gildsey and King's Lynn, whose inhabitants see the river which flows only one way – downstream – and not the river which flows in an eternal circle. Its name derives from the Sanskrit for "water". It is a hundred-and-fifty-six miles long. Its catchment is 2,067 square miles. It has several tributaries, including the Ouzel, the Ivel, the Cam, the Little Ouse and the Leem. The Leem flows into the Ouse below Gildsey. The Leem flows into the Ouse, and the Ouse flows . . . flows to . . . And by the Leem, in the year 1943, lived a lock-keeper.

16

Longitude 0°

A park bench. A bench in Greenwich Park, some fifty yards from the line of zero longitude. Onset of winter twilight; the park soon to close. Trees turning to silhouettes; flame-pink and pigeon-grey sky. A couple on the bench, striking intense attitudes (she passive yet tenacious; he, on the edge of the seat, indignant, importunate) which suggest, despite the trappings of advanced years (thick winter coats, scarves, a begrudgingly docile golden retriever lashed by its lead to one arm of the bench) a lovers' tiff. She is silent, as if having already spoken. He speaks. He wants to know, it seems, what she means, what on earth this is all— He demands an explanation. He addresses her in the manner of a schoolmaster addressing a recalcitrant child. The experienced observer of park-bench lovers' tiffs might say that the woman has had something to confess.

He remonstrates. She holds her ground. Is this that familiar drama, the "It's time we broke it off", the "It's time we never met again" drama? Or is it that equally much-repeated scene, the "You see – there's Another" routine? That outrage on his part; that hand-waving, question-firing. The patent symptoms of male jealousy? Yet, suddenly curbing his agitation, as if urged by a new consideration, he moves closer to the woman, grasps her shoulders (this schoolmaster can be human too) as though to shake her from some trance. The passer-by might catch the words "doctor – you must go to a doctor". So then, it is that other well known amorous crisis: the "Darling, I think I'm – " crisis. But these words of his are not spoken with their usual air of masculine bluster (First, I want to know for sure, first I –) but with a kind of desperation – can it be that our park-bench gallant is going to weep? – with the kind of anguish with which one begs, one prays –

She is leaving him; she is forsaking him. That's what he is thinking. But this is no ordinary separation. Not the kind where one or the other will get up and walk away.

Waning light through the trees. A park-keeper's bell. The park must close soon. Soon, everyone must be gone. Purple dusk descending on the Observatory, on the locked-up collections of antique chronometers, astrolabes, sextants, telescopes – instruments for measuring the universe. Glimmering lights on the Thames. Here, in this former royal hunting park where Henry VIII, they say, wooed Anne Boleyn, where in more august, Imperial times the nannies of the well-to-do wheeled their charges to and fro to the sound of band music and swapped their nanny-gossip, he is constrained to utter to his wife those often-used yet mystical, sometimes miracle-working words,

"I love you, I love you." He is constrained to hug his wife as though to confirm she is still there. For in the twilight it seems that, without moving, she is receding, fading, becoming ghostly.

She doesn't explain. She says, "Wait – you see." Her eyes are blue and smoky. She doesn't say, "This is only a joke." He doesn't know how to play this crazy game she is playing. In his confusion he starts to affect once more a pedagogic pose, to adopt the position of a certain practical-minded headmaster and teacher of physics. To everything a positive answer. The park-keeper's bell. He repeats: "I think you should see the doctor. I want you to go to the doctor." He believes: there is a condition called schizophrenia. He believes: it was because people were ignorant of such things that they once believed in – He believes: this is Mary; this is a bench; this is a dog. The last thing he wants to believe is that he's in fairy-land.

17

About the Lock-keeper

And by the Leem lived a lock-keeper. Who was my father. Who was a phlegmatic yet sentimental man. Who told me, when I was even younger than you, that there was no one walking the world who hadn't once sucked . . . And that the stars . . . Who was wounded at the third battle of Ypres. And had a brother killed in the same battle. Who when asked about his memories of the War, would invariably reply that he remembered nothing. Yet who when he was not asked would sometimes recount bizarre anecdotes of those immemorial trenches and mudscapes, as if speaking of things remote and fantastical in which his involvement was purely speculative. How, for example, the Flanders eels, countless numbers of which had for ever made their abode in those watery and low-lying regions, undeterred by the cataclysmic conflict that was devastating their haunts, found their way into flooded saps and even into shell craters, where there was no shortage of well-ripened food . . .

Who trapped eels himself in his native Fens. Who showed me as a boy all the various ways of cooking eels – poached in vinegar and water; in a white sauce; in a green sauce; in pies; in a stew with onion and celery; jellied, with horseradish; chopped, skewered and roasted on an open fire – and so I became just as partial as he to their subtle and versatile flesh. And so did my brother. But my mother, Fenwoman though she was and far from squeamish, could not abide them. She would scream if she saw a not quite dead eel begin to slither on the kitchen table . . .

Who when he returned from the Great War in 1918, not only wounded in the knee but profoundly dazed in the mind, was shunted for four years from this hospital to that. But was despatched in due course to Kessling Hall, until recently country mansion of the Atkinson family, but now converted as a convalescent home for war invalids. Who spent many weeks in the spring and summer of 1922, sitting on the tree-girt and secluded lawns of that curative establishment amongst several other be-scarred, be-crutched and be-patched-up victims, all of whom in that scene of apparent tranquillity (and four years after the guns had stopped) were desperately attempting to find their peace-time bearings.

Who fell in love with one of the nurses. Who came home from the war, a wounded soldier, and married the nurse who nursed him back to health. A story-book romance. Who, delivered from the holocaust, could scarcely believe that this enchanted chapter of events was happening to him. Whose love was returned – with surprising readiness. Who married, in August 1922, this woman whom for several weeks his numbed brain had registered only as "nurse, brunette" and who even after his return to lucidity – and notwithstanding their growing mutual affection – was reluctant to disclose her name. Who discovered only after a while that this white-aproned, war-volunteer, now regular nurse, who was familiar in more ways than one with Kessling Hall, was the daughter of a well known – indeed notorious – and come-down-in-the-world brewer.

Who through the mediation of this woman (her father's residual influence with the then still extant Leem Drainage and Navigation Board) acquired the post of keeper of the New

Atkinson Lock and Sluice. Who learnt, so it seemed to the boy who used to go with him to trap eels, to find both solace and mysterious, never quite suppressed vexation in this situation: fixed home, flowing river, flat land; beautiful wife. Who became the father of two sons (born 1923 and 1927), the first of whom turned out to be a semi-moron who loved his motor-cycle.

And then this former nurse, this beautiful woman who was my mother, this unlooked-for gift from a dream-world between war and familiar life, this brewer's daughter who – setting aside her practical virtues – was blessed with beauty of mind as well as body, with imagination, with hidden depths, with the art (drawn in part from her husband but perhaps derived too from her great-aunts Dora and Louisa who were avid readers of far-fetched tales in verse and prose) of telling stories, died suddenly.

My father, on the Leem tow-path, seen in profile against the Fenland sky. A series of rounded, time-worn outlines. Straight nose which goes blunt; chin which perhaps once had a point; neck tending towards the creased and convexly rippled (do you recognise your teacher? Do you see, Price, how we revert to type?) But the eyes (in full-face as he about-turns), shifting, harassed, on the look-out, belying that impression of bumpy stolidity. And that incessant pacing . . .

For many years I wondered what made my father pace up and down like a tethered dog; why even at night he could be seen, a mere half-form, mooching by the lock-pen. For many years I wondered – until the body of a boy (your age, Price) whom I had played a part in murdering, floated against the sluice.

18

In Loco Parentis

It's true, children, your commendable headmaster, Lewis Scott, is a secret tippler. In the bottom drawer of that green filing cabinet to the right of his office window, behind a stack of virgin report sheets: one – no, two – bottles of J & B.

He pours into pale blue institutional teacups. Pushes one across the desk to me.

A diligent, a persevering man. And good with kids too . . . As each one of his own brood made its entrance into the world, that questioning glance, half curious, half condescending, amidst celebratory staff-room effusions, to his senior-junior colleague (and respected sparring partner): And why not you, Tom? Why have you never?

(It's Mary. You see –)

With fatherhood, authority; with fatherhood, patronage. Even over his older-by-five-years Head of History. Ah yes, granted, Tom, twenty years in the classroom and you learn a bit about children – but when you've some of your own . . . With fatherhood, a growing tendency to be ubiquitously fatherly, even to his grown-up assistant staff.

Pushes the cup of whisky towards me like a genial pater allowing his son (who's in for a dressing-down) the adult privilege of stiff liquor. Eyes me archly, a trifle regretfully, as if indeed I am a troublesome child, one of his difficult pupils. Now this behaviour of yours – it can't go on.

And who knows? These preposterous lessons. The – regrettably early – signs of a mind in relapse. Second childhood . . .

Children, beware the paternal instinct (yes, Price, I understand your distrust) whenever it appears in your officially approved and professionally trained mentors. In what direction is it working, whose welfare is it serving? This desire to protect and provide, this desire to point the way; this desire to hold sway amongst children, where life is always beginning, where the world is still to come . . .

"So you see, Tom" (with palms held candidly open) "I have no choice."

"Of course not. I understand fully. What you are saying is that even if certain – circumstances – had not arisen, you would still now be demanding my retirement. Not your decision. Policy."

He looks at me as if I've ungraciously refused a handsome offer.

"Or put it slightly differently. These circumstances – which I won't discuss, since it's plain you don't want them discussed – provide a very convenient opportunity for carrying out, un-resisted, a long-harboured intention."

"Now that's not true. And be careful what you say. I've already said there's no question of a vendetta."

"Perhaps not, but, whatever the reasons, I'm not going to be bamboozled by – circumstances – into leaving quietly, picking up my pension and not protesting against the relegation of my subject in the curriculum."

"One might argue that you've already waived your responsi-bilities to the curriculum by turning your lessons into these – story-telling sessions."

"Perhaps history *is* just story-telling."

"I see. Whatever that means. Have some more scotch. I thought the standard line was that the past actually had some-thing to teach us. By learning from – "

"If that were so, history would be the record of inexorable progress, wouldn't it? The future would be an ever more glowing prospect."

(Price would love that: "glowing".)

He straightens in his chair. Looks at me through black-rimmed glasses. As if he'd dare to say, Well, isn't it? Isn't it?

But he doesn't say it. He's not giving one of his cheery morning assembly addresses now. He swallows whisky.

"Lew, do you know what my students dream about?"

"For God's sake, Tom. You mean it's not just stories? It's dreams too?"

133

"Seriously. Do you know what my – what our, your – students dream about?"

"I hardly think – "

"It came up, a while ago, in my 'A' level group. Nine out of sixteen said they've dreamt of a nuclear war. In several cases a recurring nightmare. They dream about the end of the world."

"Is this – ?"

"It came up – we had this count of dreams – because one of the group, Price – "

"I know Price. Wears that stuff, doesn't he? He's been told – "

"He's an intelligent kid."

"All the more reason – "

"Price suddenly announced in the middle of a class that history was a fairy-tale – you see, perhaps he's on your side. And then he said – which led us on to his and the rest of the class's nightmares: The only important thing about history is that history has reached the stage where it might be coming to an end."

"Well, isn't that an argument for – ?"

"And I began quite seriously to think, Lew: what does education do, what does it have to offer, when deprived of its necessary partner, the future, and faced instead with – no future at all?"

His eyes narrow. His face makes that expression teachers make when a student offers downright insolence, throws everything back where it came from. (I know it too, Lew. I do it too. Feel the same muscles clench. Pace up and down and fume, just like a schoolmaster. With Price, for example.)

He gets up, cup in hand. Moves to the window. Darkness falling. Looming tower-blocks. How we stick to our posts, how we cling to the curriculum.

He turns, stern, recriminative.

"Perhaps this only proves one thing, Tom. Have you ever stopped to think that it's the study of your precious subject that inspires such – gloom? Yes, you may be right, we don't learn from the past. What's more, what we pick up from dwelling on it is a defeatist, jaundiced outlook . . ."

So it's all right, children. No need to be afraid. Lewis is here. He'll look after you. To all these morbid dreams, a simple answer: the nuclear fall-out shelter.

He runs a palm across his forehead, which is grained and polished, like old wood.

"I've always said it – " He's never said it. But he's thought it. He's saying it now. And now we know:

"History breeds pessimism."

"Can't accept that. In this respect, history is as empirical as anything you teach. If history shows that the scale of human calamity increases. If the evidence of history corroborates what my students sense by intuition – "

He sits again. Pours more scotch.

"So what are you saying – that you have these dreams too?"

No, Lew, I don't dream about the end of the world. Perhaps because, unlike my students, I'm not a child (fifty-three this year). I don't expect, demand a future. And there are ways and ways, a thousand million ways, in which the world comes to an end . . .

Shall I tell you my dream? It's how it's supposed to happen: telling your dreams. They're trying it on Mary. In that place which modernity forbids we call an asylum. First you tell your dreams. First you speak all your innermost fears. Then all the rest follows – the whole story. Even back to when you were a little –

We could try it, Lewis. See if it works. The night before us. This bottle to help. You could say, So why did it happen, Tom? And I could say, These ulcers, Lew? This whisky-drinking? This ossified optimism, with its ever more palpable touch of the Victorian Papa?

My dream's different. Less spectacular. But I dream it over and over again. The setting's a suburban supermarket on a winter's evening. Dusk falling. You see, I have to tell it like a story. It's a Friday night, a busy night. Long queues at the check-outs; cash registers bleeping. All the Mums with families to feed have got their weekend supplies. All the couples with cars to load are eager to be home. They've got all the good things that supermarkets provide. They've got their canned soups and frozen meat, their breakfast cereals and scrubbed vegetables in polythene bags; they've got their cat food, dog food, washing powder, paper tissues, cling film and aluminium foil. But there's something someone hasn't got. Because amid the jostling trolleys, baskets and commotion a woman suddenly begins to wail. She screams and screams and won't stop . . .

"Lewis, tell me something. Our business is children. Do you believe in children?"

19

About my Grandfather

Could he be blamed, my grandfather, Ernest Richard Atkinson, for being a renegade, a rebel? Could he be blamed for showing but scant interest in his future prospect as head of the Atkinson Brewery and the Atkinson Water Transport Company? Could he be blamed – having been sent by his father, Arthur Atkinson M.P., to Emmanuel College, Cambridge, to receive the finest education any Atkinson had so far received – for squandering the time in undergraduate whims, for flirting with ideas (European socialism, Fabianism, the writings of Marx) directly aimed at his father's Tory principles; for spending large parts of his vacations in nefarious sojourns in London, where he was called upon by the police to explain his presence at a rally of the unemployed (he was there "out of curiosity") and whence he brought back to Kessling Hall in the year 1895 the woman, Rachel Williams, daughter of an ill-paid journalist, to whom, he brazenly declared (omitting to mention other ladies with whom he had toyed), he had already engaged himself?

Born in those memorable floods of '74, born amidst whispering and aspersion, born, moreover, at a time when the sales of (a suspiciously weak) Atkinson Ale were showing signs of decline, was it entirely his fault that he was disposed to be wayward and obstinate? And was it entirely surprising that when, in 1904, at the still youthful if mellowed age of thirty, the father by now of an eight-year-old daughter, Helen, he became director of both the Brewery and the Water Transport Company, he should accept his inescapable fate with misgiving, with reluctance and a good deal of hard thinking?

For Ernest Richard, my grandfather, was the first of the brewing Atkinsons to assume his legacy without the assurance of its inevitable expansion, without the incentive of Progress, without the knowledge that in his latter days he would be a richer and more influential man than in his youth. The profits of Atkinson beer were not the only thing to decline after that flood year of 1874. Because that last quarter of the nineteenth century, which, children, we could analyse at length if it happened to be our "A" level special subject, and which is apt to be seen as a culminatory period leading to that mythical long hot Edwardian summer so dear to the collective memory of the English, was, if the truth be known, a period of economic deterioration from which we have never recovered. A period in which the owner of a Water Transport Company, when water transport and inland navigation were falling nationally into neglect and losing, indeed, their fight against the ever-spreading railways, could scarcely view the future with confidence.

How did Arthur Atkinson, who was not a master of the present but a servant of the future, endure, in his later years, these implacable trends? By applying himself more and more to his political activities (five times re-elected for Gildsey), by being a staunch advocate of forward imperial policies (for here, after all, expansion was still possible), by reminding his Fenland constituents of the wide world and their national destiny; by becoming a caricature statesman – by alienating his son.

And how did Ernest Atkinson confront the same writing on the wall? By remembering, after an errant and experimental youth, his origins.

In 1904, while Balfour and Loubet were raising the Kaiser's hackles by signing the Anglo-French Entente, Ernest Atkinson saw as no Atkinson had clearly seen for four generations the essential desolation of the Fens. Affected perhaps by the watery circumstances of his birth, he wished that he might return to the former days of the untamed swamps, when all was yet to be done, when something was still to be made from nothing; and there was revived in him the spirit of his great-great-grandfather, William Atkinson, standing amidst the barley-corn. Since a brewer he must be, albeit a brewer of fading fortunes, what else could he do but serve faithfully his trade and brew better beer? What finer cause could there be to labour in than the supplying of this harsh world with a means of merriment?

But does merriment belong to him who gives it? Testimonies from those times – amply confirmed by his last years, and by the photographs which I still possess of my maternal grandfather (brooding brows, deep-set, glowering eyes) – suggest that even in his restless youth Ernest Atkinson was a melancholy, a moody man. That the flightiness of those early years was merely pursued – as is so often the case – to combat inner gravity; that his dabbling with socialist doctrines was not done solely to spite his father but out of an inclination (true to his name) to take the world in earnest; that he dedicated himself to the manufacture of merriment because despondency urged him, and because – but this is mere speculation, mere history teacher's conjecture – he had learnt such dark things (what death-bed confessions preceded old Arthur to the grave in 1904?) about his far-reaching progenitors that he wished for nothing more than to be an honest and unambitious purveyor of barrels of happiness.

In 1905 Ernest Atkinson proceeded to sell off most of the Water Transport Company's stock and the larger part of the Gildsey Dock (snapped up by the Gas and Coke Company as the site of a future works), whilst retaining the barges and lighters for the malt carriage from Kessling and pooling his remaining water-borne interests in the Gildsey Pleasure Boat Company: three steam-launches, the *St Gunnhilda*, the *St Guthlac* and the *Fen Queen*. Trips to Ely, Cambridge and King's Lynn. For pleasure, mind you.

At the same time he entered into lengthy consultations with his under-brewers, experimented, with a research chemist's finesse, with different hops, yeasts and sugars, with temperatures and proportions, and produced in 1906 a New Ale which the lip-smacking die-hards of The Swan and The Bargeman, or those of them whose memories stretched that far, declared to be the equal – no, the superior – of the Atkinson Ales of the middle of the old century.

But the Gildsey folk at large did not approve of Ernest's retrenching policies, which seemed to bring dishonour on their once flourishing town. They did not approve of an Atkinson who, be he a brewer in name, actually rolled up his sleeves and committed the indignity of conducting trial mashings and fermentations. For such was Ernest's style; and it was even said that in out-buildings specially converted for the purpose at Kessling Hall he concocted brews of a much more powerful character than any that issued from the Gildsey brewery. Not only this, but drank large quantities of the stuff himself. They resented his attempt – unpatriotic shirking they called it in this time of arms-racing and gunboat-sending – to shun the political sphere in which his father had so distinguished himself. But reserved the right to spread the rumour nonetheless that Ernest was a socialist sympathiser. They drank Ernest's New Ale, but they seemed to have lost the simple faith that the spirit of festivity could be poured at any time from a brown bottle and was not the prerogative, as it had been for the last time in Gildsey on Mafeking night, of occasions of national celebration.

Added to my grandfather's (conjectural) inward sorrowfulness was the knowledge that even when they are offered merriment people do not necessarily want it.

Added to my grandfather's inward sorrowfulness was the continuing fall in the Brewery profits.

Added to my grandfather's (surely no longer conjectural) inward sorrowfulness was the succumbing of his wife, Rachel, my grandmother, to a severe asthmatic complaint for which the damp atmosphere of the Fens may have been partly to blame, and her subsequent early death in April, 1908.

Ah, what stocks of merriment we need, what deep draughts of it are required to counter the griefs life has in store . . .

People who drew simple-minded comparisons and conclusions, people whose sense of history was crude, who believed that the past is always tugging at the sleeve of the present, people of the sort who claimed they had seen Sarah Atkinson when Sarah Atkinson was dead – began to speak again of a curse upon the Atkinsons . . .

And Ernest Atkinson, in mourning at Kessling Hall, mixing, for consolation, the wort of a still unperfected but potent beer and assisted by a twelve-year-old daughter, began to speak of his "Special".

In November, 1909, at a public meeting held in Gildsey Town Hall, my bereaved grandfather announced the return of his family to the political arena by declaring his intention to stand as Liberal candidate during the general election then considered imminent. Outlining his creed, he inveighed against the Conservative tradition which for so long had gripped his home town. Without disclaiming his one-time socialist propensities, he approved the recent Liberal reforms and championed Lloyd George's "enlightened and level-headed policies". He did not shrink from accusing his own father (muttered protests), from berating him as one of those who had fed the people with dreams of inflated and no longer tenable grandeur, who had intoxicated them with visions of Empire (which ought to have been clouded for ever by the disgraces of the South African War), thus diverting their minds from matters nearer home. Whilst he, the son of the father, advocated restraint, realism, the restoration of simplicity and sufficiency, and, alluding to his station in life as the proprietor of a brewery – a joke which fell on stony ground – a return from pompous solemnity to honest jollity.

He described – I have in my possession a verbatim copy of this brave and doomed speech – how it was conscience alone and no love of taking public stances (heckles from rear) that had spurred him into the political field. How fear for the future had already soured his pleasure-giving role of brewer. How he foresaw in the years ahead catastrophic consequences unless the present mood of jingoism was curbed and the military poker-playing of the nations halted. How civilisation (had Ernest inherited the prophetic gifts of Sarah? Or was he, as many suspected and attested with nudges to their neighbours, just plain drunk?) faced the greatest crisis of its history. How if no one took steps . . . an inferno . . .

Further and louder heckling, mingled with smiles from the more knowing representatives of conservatism who see that in one stroke and at the very outset Ernest has ruined his electoral chances. A speaker from the floor rises to be heard: "If your father, sir, intoxicated our minds with imperialism, what are you doing with that stuff that comes out of your brewery?" Laughter, applause. Another speaker, with apophthegmatic

140

brevity: "Mr Chairman, drunkenness ill befits a brewer!" More laughter, intenser applause. "Or abusing his own father!" (from another). "Or his country!" (another still). Howling, jeering; hammering of the Chairman's hammer ("I must ask that gentleman in the audience to withdraw his – ").

My grandfather (amidst uproar): "I warn you . . . if you will not listen . . . I foresee a . . . if . . . I foresee . . ."

But as he returns to the uncanny quiet of Cable House, knowing his reputation to have been cast away, as he clasps his daughter Helen, now thirteen years old, with an intensity – if anyone had been there to witness it – suggesting a man clutching his only comfort, he reflects perhaps on that cuttingly invoked word: drunkenness.

Drunkenness. Not merriment – drunkenness.

And, retiring to the leaden seclusion of Kessling Hall, and dictating to his daughter who diligently enters in a notebook figures, quantities and even the names of certain additional ingredients which have remained and always will remain secrets, he perfects his "Special".

Children, something of my grandfather's fulminating and faltering rhetoric infects my teacherly oratory. Something of his predicament, before that Town Hall assembly, those heckles, those jeers, revives itself in my classroom confrontations, when I face resentment and hostility over the desk-tops. And yet in whom is it that I observe today my grandfather's inward melancholy and fear for the future? In a curly-haired lad called Price.

20

The Explanation of Explanation

Whom I call to order, whom I come on strong with: "Right, Price. That's enough. You'll see me after school." (His unveiled disgust at my crude authoritarianism, this clumsy recourse to the Heavy Hand.) But that "stuff your past" . . . Pedagogic panic.

141

Teach them about revolution and they— Fears of revolt in the classroom, fed by fears of persecution from on high (Lewis wants a word), inflamed by fears of anarchy in his private life (anarchy? His wife's got religion, she's turned to the Lord). Play the despot. Take it out on— Tyranny and insecurity:

"So wipe that smirk off, Price" (actually he's not smirking) "and come and see me at four o'clock."

And now Price stands by my desk, at the end of lessons, playing his part perfectly too: the shame-faced – but unrepentant – offender.

"You can't have it both ways, Price. You opted for History. Now and then you actually produce some good work. You can't come to history lessons and have no time for history. You can't engage with me on specific points about the French Revolution – no harm in that – but at the same time want to dismiss the whole subject."

The history room at four o'clock. School dispersed; winter dark beyond the windows. Empty desks; scuff marks; chalk motes. We go through the motions, the teacher-student charade. Discipline above all. We look – or at least I do – for mutual ground, for opportunities for saying, Hang it all, let's be reasonable . . . and, For goodness' sake, must we be like this . . . But only discover that what we're forced to be, what we have to be – is on opposite sides.

"Well?"

Price shrugs. "You made things plain in the lesson. It's your show. You're the chief. You do the explaining."

"I see. So that undoubtedly intelligent mind of yours chooses dumb insolence. Very well, if the position's so clear – then let's not be vague. If I'm the chief, if I'm the one who gives the lessons, then I have the right not to have my lessons interrupted."

Price says nothing, but round his lips hovers a faint, unsettling smile.

"And if my lessons get interrupted then I have the right to know – which is why I've brought you here – why."

The smile remains.

"So how about *you* doing some explaining?"

But Price doesn't have to explain. Doesn't have to do anything more than stand there with that hint of mockery on his face. Because the situation denounces itself (my autocratic posturing): oppressor and oppressed. Because the roles are decided. (Consider this, Price, just in passing: how so much of history is a settling for roles, how so much of it happened because no one said what they really –)

Amateur dramatics. Keep him in after school: make something happen.

"Well?"

"Well – that's simple, sir. I interrupted – because I wanted to."

"Of course. And it's a free country. No good, Price. Because I ask myself why does only Price choose to interrupt, out of a class of sixteen others, who, by and large, are a pleasant bunch – "

"You mean they do what they're told."

"One interpretation. But what about your explanation?"

"I'm here to learn, sir."

"I'm touched by your trust and humility – which seem so lacking during lesson-time. But since you wish me to do your explaining for you, let me try. As I see it, your underlying complaint is not with the form or manner of my lessons or anything so narrowly particular. If that were the case we could indeed debate method and approach – all very healthy and proper – we could even come to the amicable conclusion that we hold different views. Your protest is rather purer, more radical than this. Your thesis – am I right? – is that history, as such, is a red herring; the past is irrelevant. The present alone is vital. The logical end of your view is that we should not waste time learning about the French Revolution – which, nonetheless, it strikes me, is a subject, given its flavour of subversion, you don't find so unengaging. We should instead be sitting down and sorting out Afghanistan, Iran, Northern Ireland, the ills of this worn-out Great Britain of ours."

I get up from my desk. Begin to pace the room as I speak, not looking at Price. Blathering again. Talking too much. Rhetorical hand-sweeps over empty desks. Use the stage-space. Speak into air. Any moment now Price will say: what are you pacing around for like a ham performer? Stop acting the school teacher.

"A laudable proposition, Price. And I believe there's an

opportunity for this sort of discussion in your General Studies periods with Mr Wallace."

"He's an old – "

"Careful. As far as I'm concerned in this matter, we come up against a quite practical obstacle. Namely, the syllabus. Namely that I'm paid to be a history teacher and to teach the history syllabus, that the history syllabus includes – amongst other irrelevancies – the French Revolution, and that's what we do."

(Get out of this role. Get off this stage.)

"Great! I'm glad you've got it all so worked out!"

Said with venom, said with exasperation, said with a kind of forlorn anguish, as I walk back up the desk aisle and momentarily lose my poise.

Now – now is your opportunity.

"Price, it sometimes occurs to me that there's something – on your mind. That we haven't even touched on. That we're saying the wrong things. If I can – "

A hand raised – but not in rhetorical gesture. A hand raised, almost unconsciously, to touch Price's shoulder.

Rapid chain-reaction in Price's eyes. Alarm. Hasty defensive shutter-drawing; equally hasty switch to offensive. Lip-tightening.

"If there's any way I can help – "

Stop at the window. Look out at the darkness. Silence.

"Don't know, sir. Do you think history 'helps'?"

"Price?"

"What I mean is – I don't understand this 'can I help' bit. I didn't know that was on the syllabus either."

Self-protective summary: the kid's just anti. Against everything. To hell with him.

Price's form, behind mine, reflected in the window. Standing by my desk where I stand to face my class. Ghostly schoolboy in his teacher's place in a ghostly classroom floating in the dark . . .

But how we forget what it's like, to be like that. To be sixteen, and floating, floating . . . How we forget. How we stick to the syllabus. Until –

(Price, there are things on *my* mind.)

"All right. You're quite right. Offers of help aren't on the

144

syllabus. Shall we skip my out-of-order display of concern? On the other hand, I haven't kept you behind for extra tuition. I'd still like an explanation."

Still with my back turned to him. He edges towards the rear of the classroom, as if (a momentary delusion on my part?) worried about me. People who stand at second-storey windows . . .

"So?"

Badly timed.

"You know what your trouble is, sir? You're hooked on explanation. Explain, explain. Everything's got to have an explanation."

A human instinct, Price. A definitive trait. Goes with living.

"But you said: You do the — "

"Because I can do without explanations — "

I turn round. His lip is quivering.

"Because I don't want explanations — "

Twisted features trying to reform. Trepidation trying to hide. Voice struggling to release some punch-line. Has he been saving this one up?

"Because explaining's a way of avoiding the facts while you pretend to get near to them — "

Very good, Price. Very profound. One for the Price Book of Anarchistical Aphorisms. But that frightened face — ?

"And people only explain when things are wrong, don't they, not when they're right? So the more explaining you hear, the more you think things must be pretty bad that they need so much explaining."

Silence. The pale warpaint resumes its composure. The lip controls itself. But his eyes don't meet mine.

He looks at his watch.

"Can I go now, sir? It's getting late."

So, message annunciated. So. Is that why you bothered to come to my little disciplinary rendezvous? To deliver a Challenge. Class-spokesman's Manifesto. The Price Explanation of Explanation. Something to make old Cricky think. And he will. He does . . .

"Yes, it's getting late."

"Can I go then?"

"Price, I— Yes, you can go."

He moves briskly, snubbingly to the door. Turns before exiting:

"So see you at tomorrow's lesson."

21

Aux Armes

At which the Spokesman, returned from the camp of the Despot, invested (my tactical blundering) with the aura of martyr and champion, has gained esteem and attention. Is a focus for commotion. So what did he say? And what did you say? And what's he like, by the way, when you get him on his own? Is he really – you know – a bit off his head . . . ?

At which there are murmurings and stirrings. A mood of temerity. At which the whole class has grown tired of this tedious discussion of causes, preliminaries; analytical debate. Explanation, explanation. Talk, talk. The National Assembly; its feasibility; its components; its cast-list of characters. The constitutional options; dialogue; rhetoric and reality; theory and practice; history and histrionics . . .

Hey, we thought revolution was about action. About barricades and blood. So what about it?

See how you've roused them, Price. See how you've worked them up. But for the right reasons? Against History? Against the syllabus? But it's not the syllabus that's wrong, it's just that it dawdles, it's just that it's slow getting to the exciting bits. Schoolboy relish for history – battles and beheadings. (Me too once, in my inky-black uniform.)

What you wanted, Price? Down with the past; away with the past. But see how they want the old, old story. See how they're rushing to be knocking down again that big, bad legendary Bastille. Action and atavism. Get out the costumes. When History provides our mock-up for protest . . .

The Spokesman remains silent amidst the clamourings. Eyes his teacher. Revolutionary paradoxes: when the subject's revolution, how do you rise up against it? When the past tries to demolish itself, how do you demolish the past? Faint hint of that twisted face, unsteady lip. At the next lesson (Declaration of the Rights of Man) he'll throw in, for good measure, the end of the world.

But what about the barricades and the bloodshed. And what about the guillotines? Come on.

So you want drama. You want action? You want the apocalyptic note? Then let me tell you

22

About Coronation Ale

He retreats to Kessling Hall, a brewer by trade, a politician by erroneous aspiration. A brewer: a fermenter.

In the election of January 1910 my grandfather polls only eleven hundred votes and, notwithstanding his name and his being Gildsey-born, is passed over in favour of an outsider, John Sikes, a Yorkshireman, quickly bustled in to snap up an easy seat, and duly returned as Conservative member, albeit under a Liberal government. My grandfather accepts defeat, having expected, perhaps, nothing more; having already resigned himself to the rôle of a political Cassandra and the loss of his candidate's deposit.

But though he accepts defeat he does not accept inaction. He waits for the moment to give the people what they want.

And finds it, in the summer of 1911.

In the summer of 1911, as you will surely know if you have learnt by heart your Monarchs of Great Britain and their Dates, good old gadabout King Edward was dead and diligent family-man – but still King and Emperor – George V had acceded. And when a king accedes he must be crowned, in order to give his people an occasion for rejoicing and for the expression of their loyal fervour.

And how convenient, how fitting that such an occasion should exist at such a time. When the Dreadnought programme, even under a Liberal government, had been doubled; when the Kaiser – monster of presumption – was committing indiscretions all over Europe; as Britons entered this second, momentous decade of the twentieth century.

In June 1911, during the preparations in Gildsey for celebrating the coronation of George V, amidst the hanging of flags, the building of bonfires, the arranging of floral mottoes and planning of banquets, my grandfather, the morose and unpopular brewer of the town, proposed to make his own contribution to the festivities by producing a commemorative bottled ale, to be called, appropriately enough, Coronation Ale; the first thousand bottles to be issued free, but no drop to pass any man's lips till the king was indeed crowned.

Though it had already passed, in a form known simply as "Special", my grandfather's lips. And perhaps too the budding lips of Helen Atkinson, my mother.

Warmed by patriotic zeal and softened by a mood of reconciliation (so, when it comes to it, the peevish brewer can say his God Save the King like any man), the townspeople chose to forget for a moment their differences with Ernest Atkinson. The jubilant day drew near. They cast their minds back to other times when they had been licensed to swill beer in a noble cause; to the Diamond and Golden Jubilee Ales, even to the Grand '51, and so to those halcyon days when the fortunes of the town had bloomed. Had those days gone for ever? Could this National Occasion – so Ernest Atkinson ventured, addressing the Celebrations Committee, with no hint of politics but with a curious glint in his eye – not include a local one? For was it not, he pointed out, the glint becoming curiouser, almost exactly one hundred years ago that Thomas Atkinson received, to the great grudgingness (uneasy laughter amongst the committee members) of certain Gildsey factions, the Leem Navigation, thus inaugurating the process by which this once obscure Fenland town gained its place in the Nation – if not, indeed, the World?

What was in this Coronation Ale, offered in a dark brown bottle of a shape narrower and more elongated than the beer bottle of later days, with "Atkinson – Gildsey" embossed upon it and a label bearing a large crown, centre, and a continuous border of alternating smaller crowns and union jacks? Nectar? Poison? Merriment? Madness? The bottled-up manias of His Majesty's subjects?

Rest assured, it was no ordinary ale that they drank by the Ouse while in Westminster crowds thronged, guns fired and the Abbey bells pealed. For when the men of Gildsey jostled into The Pike and Eel and The Jolly Bargeman to be amongst the privileged first one thousand to receive their bottle gratis and to raise their glasses in decent good cheer to toast the King, they discovered that this patriotic liquor hurled them with astonishing rapidity through the normally gradual and containable stages of intoxication: pleasure, satisfaction, well-being, elation, light-headedness, hot-headedness, befuddlement, distraction, delirium, irascibility, pugnaciousness, imbalance, incapacity – all in the gamut of a single bottle. And if a second bottle was broached –

Precise accounts of the events of that day are hard to track down. Partly because it was a day that Gildsey wished to forget; partly for the more pertinent reason that many of those who might have acted as reliable witnesses were, at the time, hopelessly drunk.

With alarming frequency the women of the town were called upon to restrain displays of intemperance in their menfolk, only to succumb themselves to the temptation of tasting this brew which had such remarkable effect. The landlords of the town's twenty-three public houses began to fear for the respectability and physical safety of their establishments. A parade of school-children down Water Street demonstrating their innocent, flag-waving allegiance to the new Monarch, was marred by the raucous – and possibly obscene – choruses emanating from The Swan and The Pike and Eel. Sky-rockets and Roman candles intended for a dazzling evening display were let off in broad daylight and along alarming trajectories. A horrific incidence of shipwreck and drowning almost occurred when the *St Guthlac*, whose steersman had quaffed his bottle, as had a good many of his passengers, took a zig-zagging career across the river, pennants aflutter and steam-horn braying, and was almost run down by the *Fen Queen*, under a similar state of captaincy.

Drunkenness. While the bells of St Gunnhilda's ring in the new reign. Drunkenness in many sudden and wonderful forms.

A deputation of the two senior police officers of the town addressed themselves, in the canvas structure known as the "Coronation Pavilion", to Ernest Atkinson, to express their urgent view that in the name of law and order the public houses of the town should be closed, and to ask, in the meantime, what on earth was in those bottles, and was there no antidote? To which Ernest is said to have replied, with a detectable mimicking of his election speech style, that it would be a most deplorable action, to suppress, on this of all days, a gesture intended only to do honour to King and Country; that though he was responsible for the beer, he could hardly be held responsible for those (these were his words) who did not drink it wisely. And to illustrate this latter point, he proceeded, before the eyes of the police chiefs, to drain in one draught a bottle of the ale in question (of which several crates had penetrated the Coronation Pavilion) without the slightest visible effect, thus giving the lie to the slanders made at that same election speech and proving the adage that it takes more than his own beer to get a brewer drunk. The officers were cordially invited to try for themselves. Being in their best ceremonial uniforms, they declined.

To these same senior officers it had soon regrettably to be reported that a number of their constables had yielded to the general intoxication and tasted the extraordinary potion. A young reveller had attempted to climb a flag-pole and broken a leg. The Processions and Events were falling into disarray. And numerous participating citizens who even on this day should have maintained a necessary degree of sobriety, had failed to do so, including the members of the Gildsey Free Trade Brass Band, whose much rehearsed programme suffered from wild improvisations and whose rendering of Elgar's Cockaigne Overture broke down irredeemably.

It was now a question of some difficulty, for those still able to judge the matter, whether prohibiting the supply of this by now clamoured-for beer might not lead to even greater uproar than that caused by its consumption.

During the course of this riotous afternoon several of those

150

invited to attend the Coronation Banquet (at eight, in the Great Chamber of the Town Hall) began to wonder how (given that they too had drunk –) they might conceivably excuse themselves from such a dignified gathering. But no Coronation Banquet was to occur. For the worst of this outrageous day was yet to come.

No one knows how it started. Whether the alarm was first given by individuals (and was ignored as one of innumerable hoaxes and hallucinations) or whether the whole town as a body was suddenly aware of the palpable fact. But as twilight descended on this more than festive day it became evident that the brewery, the New Atkinson Brewery, built in 1849 by George and Alfred Atkinson, was on fire. Palls of thickening smoke were rapidly followed by leaping flames, then by the loud crackings and burstings that signal an advanced conflagration.

A crowd rushed and swarmed. The Coronation Banquet, in the face of such a dire emergency, was summarily cancelled. The Gildsey Fire Brigade (founder, Alfred Atkinson) was called out in full complement. But whether this stalwart body, with its three engines and two auxiliary tenders, was of any use on this disastrous night is to be doubted. For not only had the Fire Station been improvidently undermanned throughout the day (one of the engines having been decked out with ribbons and flags as part of the celebratory procession) but almost every fireman, struggling now just as much to sober himself as to get into his cumbersome fireman's garb, had drunk his share of the Ale; with the result that when the engines at last arrived, in ragged order, with much clanging of bells, and in one case still festooned with patriotic rosettes, the brewery was already past saving. And it was claimed by several eyewitnesses that the gallant crews devoted much more of their energy to a variety of insubordinate antics (such as playing their hoses upon the watching crowd) than they ever did to the fire.

So the fire burned. Subsuming all bonfires and all other pyrotechnic displays arranged for this joyous evening. The crowd, indeed, eyes glazed as much by their intake of ale as by the glare of the flames, watched as if this were not their town

151

brewery being burnt to the ground but some elaborate spectacle expressly arranged for their delight and contemplation. And perhaps it was. The ineptitudes of the Fire Brigade were cheered and encouraged. Few accounts speak of dismay, of panic, even of apprehended danger. When the fire performed particularly impressive stunts (a row of upper windows bursting all at once like a ship's broadside) it did so amidst hearty applause; and when, at twelve midnight (for that was the last hour ever to be registered on its lofty clock face) the brewery chimney trembled, tottered and, with its Italianate friezes and paralysed iron clock-hands, sank swiftly, vertically, into the blazing shell of the brewery, it was to the accompaniment of a resounding ovation, notwithstanding the fact that if the chimney had chosen to adopt a different angle of collapse it might have crushed several score of the spectators.

An unearthly glare lit all that night the clustered rooftops of Gildsey. On the oily-black surface of the Ouse fiery necklaces scattered and rethreaded themselves. In the deserted, garlanded market-place the paving stones throbbed, and in the Town Hall where the places were laid for a banquet that was never to be, the shadows of the tall municipal window frames quivered on the walls. For miles around, across the flat unimpeded outlook of the Fens, the fire could be seen, like some meteoric visitation – a gift to Fenland superstition; and on the morning of the twenty-third of June, in place of the familiar chimney, a great cloud of smoke, lingering for many days.

Was it the case – for no sooner had the blaze gone out than the talk began to be fanned – that this Coronation Ale, which so fired internally those who drank it, had found a means to manifest its power externally and in a process of spontaneous combustion engulfed in flames its own source? Had this pheno-menal ale, intended to regale the people on a day of national festivity, only exposed the inflammatory folly of their jingoistic ardour and revealed to them that they preferred destruction to rejoicing? And was that the meaning of Ernest's cryptic and bitter remark when in the autumn of 1914 he left Gildsey for ever: "You have enjoyed one conflagration, you will see another"? Had the brewery fire been started – as was widely credited – by drunken revellers who, bursting into the buildings in search of further supplies of the ale and, accidentally or otherwise, starting a fire, had discovered a new and more consuming thirst? Or was the counter-theory true, that the fire was started by the town authorities as a desperate means both of preventing a night of wholesale lawlessness and of destroying at one go all stocks of the offending brew? For, indeed, after the razing of the brewery, no more Coronation Ale was ever seen (or drunk) again (with one exception). And the secret of its concoction – remained a secret.

Did the burning of the brewery give final and positive proof of the notion that a curse lay on the Atkinson family? Yet if it did, how did this accord with that other theory that sprang up quietly at first but with greater boldness in the ensuing years when Ernest, having made no plans to rebuild, sold his remaining business assets and retired – all too guiltily it seemed – to Kessling Hall? That Ernest himself, under cover of getting the whole town drunk, had set fire to the brewery. Because he wished to get his hands on the massive insurance sums.

And because, children (allow your history teacher his fanciful but not ill-researched surmise), far from being the victim of a curse he was glad to be its instrument. Because he saw no future for this firm of Atkinson and its one-time empire, let alone for these people who courted disaster. Because he wanted nothing better than to see this brewery utterly destroyed and finished with. To wipe the slate clean.

So, perhaps, he thought, that October day in 1914, in the ample back seat of a Daimler limousine, beside his only daughter (a beauty of eighteen), being driven from Gildsey to Kessling, where once there was no Hall, no Maltings and no barge-pool. So he pondered, passing through those flat fringes of the Leem so similar to the low country between the Lys and the Yser where so many lives were soon to be extinguished and where Henry Crick was to be wounded in the knee. What had the Atkinsons achieved, he perhaps asked himself, by bringing the wide world to a backwater?

And – I put it to you, children – were Ernest and all the beer-producing Atkinsons doing anything more, if on a grander scale, than what Freddie Parr's father did when he took to drink? Trying to assuage emptiness. Lifting sunken spirits. Kindling fire and ferment out of watery nothing . . .

The verdict of the official investigators and the insurance company inspectors: an accident.

To get his hands on the insurance money. To get his own back on the town which booed his speech and never elected him M.P. To make fools of them all (for they sobered up soon enough). Who knows if the whole thing had not been a monstrous trick and, had they been able to find him on that fateful night, they wouldn't have taken him and cast him into the midst of the flames?

For where, indeed, was Ernest Atkinson while his brewery was ablaze? Not in evidence. Though everyone assumed he must be there, amongst the gaggle of astonished and agitated dignitaries, many in their banqueting regalia, toasting themselves in an unanticipated fashion before the fire, no one, afterwards, could distinctly remember having seen him. Though he was there in the Coronation Pavilion and popped up again (quelling certain fears) in the morning to view the still red-hot ruins, no one could quite account for him in the interval. A most implicating absence.

Yet while Ernest had been making himself scarce, another and not unrelated presence had apparently stood in. For, dismiss it if you will as yet another hallucination brought on by the mixture of flames and ale, but more than one member of that crowd of fire-watchers recalled encountering a woman – a woman who put them suddenly in mind of a preposterous old story. And when, indeed, at about eleven-thirty, when, Ernest being looked for and not being found, two police constables (whether sober, is not known) were despatched to Cable House, it was to find a solitary maid, Jane Shaw (all the other servants having departed to watch the blaze), in a highly wrought condition; who swore blind, first that she had touched none of that dreadful beer and, second, that she had gone up to the top room in order to see the fire, because she feared for her safety in the streets, and she had seen – she had *seen* – Sarah Atkinson. Because she knew her from that portrait hanging in the Town

Hall, not to mention other pictures in the house. Because she'd heard all those silly old tales, and now she knew they were true. Sarah was standing before the window, where the leaping flames could be seen assailing the top of the chimney, which was soon to disappear, and she was saying with a grin on her face and a pertinence that had eluded, long ago, her husband and two devoted sons: "Fire! Smoke! Burning!"

23

Quatorze Juillet

But let us not overestimate the actual character or the actual achievements of the Fall of the Bastille. Seven prisoners released (that was all the fortress contained): two madmen, four forgers and a hapless roué. Seven heads – the governor and six of the defending garrison – paraded on pikes. Two hundred or so of the besiegers killed or wounded. The stones of the Bastille itself, a mountain of rubble, carried away by professional contractors and disposed of at a tidy profit . . .

No, the significance of this tawdry conquest lies not in its tangible gains but in its symbolic value. The king's citadel captured by the king's people. Hence that famous tricoloured flag – the red and blue of the city of Paris holding under close guard the white of the house of Bourbon – which became the portable token of revolution, just as the fallen Bastille became its historical archetype. Of revolution. Though it was to be waved in the decades to come through two Empires and to find itself flying more and more before the gusty and oppressive winds of nationalism, and even to be crossed in fellowship, in 1904, with the likewise red, white and blue flag of (the old enemy) imperialist and monarchical Britain.

Ah, the idols and icons of history, ah, the emblems and totems of yesterday. How when we knock down one, another rises in its place. How we can't get away – even if you can, Price – from our fairy-tales. How even in your teacher's childhood (if you can picture such a thing), during a great Depression which returns to haunt us in our own unprosperous times, Empire Day was regularly celebrated with no small enthusiasm (and no reference to brewery fires).

And we all know what the French do (seven heads on pikes and a mountain of rubble) every July the fourteenth.

24

Child's Play

But on the fourteenth of July, 1940, the French people had no taste for their Bastille Day and no taste for celebrating their imperishable victory over tyranny. On the fourteenth of July, 1940, France lay, as she had lain for three weeks, under a German occupation swiftly imposed against swiftly evaporating resistance. Because – so posterity points its accusing finger – either that old traitor and defeatist, Marshal Pétain (who blamed the collapse on nothing less than the poisonous spirit of La Révolution), sold his country down the line; or – not to foist everything on a single scapegoat – because previous successive onslaughts, of bitter memory, from across the Rhine had already knocked the stuffing out of the glorious, Bastille-taking French people.

In July, 1940, a German army occupies the land which in 1914 to '18 a million-and-a-half Frenchmen had given their lives to defend and for which Pétain himself had heroically struggled at Verdun. In July, 1940, Hitler contemplates – as in 1805 Napoleon had contemplated – the invasion of England. Only to put it off and go marching off to Russia. Just as Napoleon once did.

Now who says history doesn't go in circles?

And in July, 1940, as Hitler conferred with Goering, and as tearful evacuees filtered into Fenland villages to become butts for the jibes of local children, Tom Crick (future history teacher), Freddie Parr, Peter Baine, Terry Coe (friends of the first-named) and Dick Crick, all in assorted woollen swimming-trunks and, with the exception of Freddie Parr, wet-haired and muddy-limbed, together with Mary Metcalf and Shirley Alford (cotton skirts and blouses of various shades, white ankle-socks and sandals), are convened on the banks of the Hockwell Lode and engaged in matters little affected by (and little affecting) the muffled noises-off of world events.

For beneath the woollen swimming-trunks of Tom Crick, Freddie Parr, Peter Baine and Terry Coe unmistakable swellings are apparent, provoking the curiosity of Mary Metcalf and, less brazenly, of Shirley Alford, whose eyes, as much as they are persuaded to look, are also impelled to look away, for complicated reasons which simultaneously bring a glow to her cheeks.

And Mary Metcalf says, "Show us, show us." (Ritual words in a ritual confrontation, which make the woollen-covered swellings swell a little further.)

And Freddie Parr says, "First you must – "

Bicycles recumbent in long grass. Larks twittering. Aeroplane drones (a nation at war). A more than half drained bottle of whisky, cradled now, with a certain pointedness, between Freddie's thighs but previously passed among those assembled, by way of encouragement. Peter Baine has drunk, Terry Coe has drunk, your history teacher has drunk, Freddie Parr has drunk (more than anyone else), but Dick has refused most rigidly and so, in coyer vein, has Shirley Alford; while Mary Metcalf, wise already, it seems, to the delicacies of situations in which ladies are offered intoxicating drink by gentlemen, but still under the sway of her ruling curiosity, merely tilts the bottle sufficiently to sting the tip of her tongue and says, thrusting it back, "Ugh!"

And this whisky, it should be added, is the genuine Scotch article, stolen with much subterfuge by Freddie from his father. For the days of black-marketeering and illicit American imports are yet to come.

Baked mud smells, river smells, a hot-blue sky, a warm wind . . . Not to mince matters, children, and to offer you, in passing, an impromptu theory, sexuality reveals itself more readily, more precociously, in a flat land, in a land of watery prostration, than in, say, a mountainous or forested landscape, where nature's own phallic thrustings inhibit man's, or in the landscape of towns and cities where a thousand artificial erections (a brewery chimney, a tower block) detract from our animal urges.

In short, children, I wish to point out that (despite the availability and variety of contraception – despite the lowering age for the incidence of pregnancy amongst schoolgirls – and despite the apparent quicker maturition, physically, sexually and – yes, Price – even mentally, of today's juveniles) your present generation has no monopoly –

And this little game of tease and dare beside the Hockwell Lode which had been begun before several times but had never reached its culmination (however you picture that) was only prevented from doing so partly by the innate timidity behind the outward bravado of those engaged (average age, excluding Dick, thirteen and a half); and partly because on this hot and flagrant July afternoon, when things might indeed have already gone further, they were constrained by the watching presence of my brother, who, not being one for company and being at the best of times inscrutable, uncommunicative and difficult to be with, had never before participated in these proceedings. So it was impossible to tell how he viewed them.

"First," says Freddie, "you must take off your sandals and socks." With which Mary and even Shirley Alford have no difficulty in complying.

A stylised pause in which Mary's eyes remain on our swellings and Shirley's flicker heavenward.

"And then you must take off – " But under the influence perhaps of his father's whisky, or from sheer impatience, Freddie dispenses with the usual itemising by which this game is enabled never to reach its conclusion and says, with a distinct leer " – *all* your clothes."

Which produces consternation in both Mary and Shirley, though more so in Shirley. For those previously carefully separated intermediate stages – "your blouse", "your skirt" – did at least allow for compromise solutions: for audacity to falter on either side, for stipulations to be made ("so far, no further") or counter-bargains to be demanded ("only if you first – ") or for a general descent into giggles or belligerence. For this game which is impelled by mutual curiosity has also the aspect of mutual opposition.

"That's not how we played it," says Shirley.

"It's how we play it now," says Freddie, taking a swig of whisky and patting his still covered protuberance. "Change of rules."

Mary – followed, hesitantly, by Shirley – begins to remove her blouse and skirt. Though it is to be noticed that in doing this she looks, not at Freddie, Peter Baine, Terry Coe or me, nor at our tell-tale swimming-trunks but at Dick who sits, watching, like some mute adjudicator, knees drawn up, on the top of the bank.

The discarding of skirt and blouse places Shirley at a disadvantage. For whereas Mary's developing anatomy requires that she wears the skimpiest of brassieres, Shirley wears no such garment. Her flat, modest nipples present nothing different from what we are familiar with on our own rib-cages. And so, at this point, Shirley looks sheepish and all eyes turn to Mary.

Mary takes off her brassiere and immediately wraps her arms around her shoulders.

"And now your – " But Freddie can never bring himself to say without a great deal of facial distortion and the threat of giggles, the word "knickers".

Mary shakes her head, still hugging her shoulders. "No. We're equal now." (Hers and Shirley's flannel knickers for our swimming-trunks). "You've got to do something." And looks hard at Freddie's swelling which possibly contracts under the gaze.

Silence. Licking of dry lips.

Then Freddie Parr leans forward suddenly, pulls Mary's right hand from her left shoulder, presses it against his swimming-trunks and says: "There, you've had a feel. Now – "

Whereupon Shirley, with a look of fright, scrambles for her clothes, removes herself to a distance, dresses hastily and hurries off on her bicycle, amidst jeers and cat-calls.

And now, will curiosity outweigh inhibition?

Mary, with arms once more clasped over young breasts: "You first."

Peter Baine: "But there's four of us."

Mary: "Do you want me to choose? Anyway, there's five of you."

And she looks up to where Dick still sits near the top of the bank. Alone and out of it (because Dick doesn't yet have a motor-cycle).

And Freddie Parr, in particular, takes note of that look.

"Come on then." With a note of authority. As if Shirley's departure has somehow increased her confidence, or as if that glance at Dick has imposed on the four of us a mysterious compliance.

July sunshine on the banks of the Hockwell Lode. Four pairs of swimming-trunks, two dark blue, one black, one maroon, lowered, in the sunshine, with almost maidenly meekness and with an anxiety on the part of each to be neither ahead nor behind its neighbour. Four wrinkled, irresolute and slightly sticky members revealed, amidst nests of incipient pubic hair; which attempt to stand up, go limp and stir again feebly. For whether it is the equivocal work of Freddie's stolen whisky (already having unsteadying effects on our heads and the pits of our stomachs) or merely innate bashfulness, we cannot muster between us – for all our anticipatory stiffness and for all Mary's taking her arms, by way of inducement, away from her baby breasts – a decent hard-on. And your history teacher's little instrument – you see, children, I baulk at no confession – droops utterly.

Mary, after a cursory inspection, turns her head aside. (With one accord, four pairs of swimming-trunks are swiftly pulled back up again.) She is disappointed. Her curiosity has been cheated. For such a meagre display, she is not going to pull down her own navy blue convent-school knickers.

The swimming-trunked foursome stands – or does not stand – disgraced. Freddie takes a hasty pull of whisky. Terry Coe – can it be possible? – has tears in his eyes. And your history teacher does not know where to look.

"Unless," says Mary, thinking aloud and relishing the position of absolute advantage she has now acquired, "unless you – pass a test first."

"What test?"

Four raised, apprehensive heads.

Mary looks at the surface of the Lode. "A swimming test. From the wooden bridge. Whoever swims the furthest – *under*water. I'll – show him."

"But you know I can't swim," says Freddie.

"Too bad. You'll just have to learn."

By the "wooden bridge" Mary means a narrow, rickety affair of planks and slats with a single hand rail, slung across the Lode and raised in its central section by two piers, some eight feet above the water, to allow the passage of lighters. A perfect diving platform.

"So come on." And Mary, to taunt us, takes her arms once more from her scarcely developed yet fully perceptible breasts, then puts them back again.

We get up, the whisky causing us difficulty in finding our balance and producing renewed qualms in our bellies. It is doubtful whether we are prompted any longer by the prize of glimpsing what makes Mary different from us between the legs, so much as by the desire to prove ourselves to each other. Just as Mary, perhaps, is no longer motivated by curiosity but by this undeniable power she has discovered and is wielding.

But as we turn to walk along the Lode bank to the wooden bridge we stop and both our masculine pride and Mary's feminine authority receive a check. For Dick has joined us. He has come down from the top of the bank. And not only Dick but, attached to him, concealed, if scarcely contained by his straining swimming-trunks, a tubular swelling of massive and assertive proportions.

Children, given brotherly closeness, I had had occasion enough to observe my brother's member – flopping and dangling, inert. A fair specimen, sizeable but not gross, in its umprimed state. But I had never glimpsed. I had even reflected – considering Dick's other sluggish characteristics, his potato head, his lack of words, his muddy gaze – that Dick (even though I viewed matters academically from the other side of the pubertal gates through which I had yet to pass) just wasn't interested. But I had never glimpsed –

And nor perhaps had Dick. Perhaps this occasion was for him as for us one of astonishing and traumatic discovery. For he thrusts this prodigy before him, bracing his pelvis, as if holding away from himself something he is uncertain whether to acknowledge.

"Me too. M-me swim too."

Mary's eyes – we all notice this – goggle. A flush ignites her cheeks. Her brow wrinkles. And while these symptoms take place, she considers perhaps (my swift, bitter surmise) that – quite apart from this fact of sheer and astonishing dimension – Dick is four years everyone's senior. Here, after all, wrapped in infantile trappings, is a man (a little tuft of hairs in the centre of Dick's breastbone). What other wondrous faculties might this otherwise dumb creature possess . . . ?

In Mary's eyes, rekindled – refired – curiosity. And fear. Just a touch of fear. The kind of fear which because it jostles with curiosity and because it contains something else – a touch of pity too, of strange, charitable intent – forms a dangerous mixture.

To the wooden bridge. Fast. To conceal in impetuous and desperate action the effect of this cat among the pigeons, this goat among sheep. To avoid having to stand and look any more, at least, at that little giant. Even Freddie, despite his not unreasonable protestations, hurries along the Lode bank. Because he is going to have to learn.

On the central section of the wooden bridge, five figures, in the following order, from right to left: Peter Baine, Terry Coe, Tom Crick, Freddie Parr, Dick Crick, all in sundry postures of bravado and apprehension (and in one case distinct sexual arousal) and all (with one exception) in varied states of inebriation. Five figures staring at the Hockwell Lode – a manmade water-course which drains into the River Leem which in turn drains into the River Ouse – waiting for the signal to dive.

The art of underwater swimming as practised during the fine summer spells by the male children of Hockwell, Wansham and elsewhere, is neither sophisticated nor, on the other hand, undemanding. It consists of a combination of lung-power and muscle-power; against which are pitted the murky, muddy waters of the Hockwell Lode which offer little to choose between the open-eyed and closed-eyed style of swimming and which, when unintentionally if unavoidably swallowed when air supplies give out, taste foul. It has been the subject before of challenges, mild bets and boasting. But never before of such urgent provocations as this.

Your history teacher believes he is not unskilled in this art. He believes he can beat Peter Baine and Terry Coe (has beaten them before). And as for Freddie Parr— But turbulent emotions and an unexpected rival make him tremble as he stands on the wooden slats.

Five figures on the bridge. And one on the bank (in navy blue knickers) who — still with arms clasping shoulders — shouts "Ready!" Allows a merciless pause, in which fiercely inhaled draughts of air are half wasted. Then "Go!"

The younger of the two Crick brothers dives and loses sight of his opponents. Determined that his lungs shall burst rather than that Mary shall have cause to scorn him (let alone refuse him the sight of her —), he swims deep. No breaking of the surface to disqualify him. His eyes encounter a brown and silent fog. Suspended silt. Stirred-up silt. A domain where earth and water mingle. Mysterious, indefinite, enveloping. His limbs struggle, his throat makes little gulps. He must come up (what it must be like to drown), he must come up —

And does, fifteen yards from the bridge, to gasp, gasp again, and to see Peter Baine, also gasping, some three yards behind him and Terry Coe a yard behind that. But no Mary on the adjacent bankside to proclaim Tom Crick is first, Tom Crick has won. Because what is happening at the bridge? Freddie Parr is taking a swimming lesson. Freddie, indeed, not to suffer utter humiliation, has dived in, and now he thrashes, flails, splutters, yelps, rolls, sinks, comes up again, gurgles, sinks again. Mary stands in agitation on the bank. And my brother, who has not dived in, who remains on the bridge, looks down at Freddie with an air of fascination, with an air also of someone waiting till so many seconds have elapsed, and then — as those in the water swim towards the scene — kneels, lies down on the slats, hangs over the edge, secures himself with one hand, and extends the other, without hurry, to Freddie. Who grabs it and — now in a state of humiliation greater than that he sought to avoid — is hauled up onto the bridge by the manifest strength of his rescuer's long arm.

Brief and callous inquiry-session, as Peter Baine, Terry Coe and I climb out onto the bank.

"He's all right."

"What happened?"

"His own fault."

"Did Dick push him?"

"No, he dived – sort of."

"Stupid idiot."

"Didn't have to. No one made him."

But Dick says nothing. He stands on the bridge, vacant-faced, swelling stiffer than ever.

Freddie slumps on the bank, chest heaving.

"But did you see? Did you see who won?" A petulant, insistent voice. (Because even at the risk of appearing smug, your history teacher doesn't want his achievement to go unreckoned.)

"I saw – " says Mary, wandering, disconcertingly, in the direction of her clothes.

But as she speaks a hoarse cry and a loud splash make all heads swivel.

Dick has dived. Dick has expressed his opinion that the contest is not yet over.

Ripples. Bubbles. A glimmer of sallow limbs beneath the grey-brown surface. Then nothing. For a long time nothing. For fifteen, for thirty seconds, nothing. Then nothing again. Then when nothing must surely have gone on for the utmost period allowable to it, still nothing. And, after another concessionary if amazed extension of time to nothing and while Freddie, on all fours, expels onto the grass a stream of whisky-scented vomit, still nothing. And still nothing. With the result that all (excepting Freddie) rise to their feet and Mary (neglecting the complete concealment of her nipples) lifts one hand to shield her eyes. Because, basing a spatial reckoning on the lapse of time, it is now a question of looking into the sun-glinting distance.

Blue-haze sky. Hot banks. Flat, flat Fens. Rasping rushes. Mud between the toes. Weeping willows. Mary . . .

And when it seems that this astonishing nothing has merged into that wondrous and miraculous possibility For Ever, a head

– that is, a far-off dark blob – breaks surface, some seventy – can it be eighty, can it be a hundred? – yards from where we stand. Shakes water from hair; shows no sign of discomfort, as if in emerging at that point it has done so merely out of whim and not out of necessity; travels towards the bank; pulls out behind it the (long, but finless, scaleless) body of my brother; and, without rest or pause, comes towards us, perched on its six feet of lean, potato-coloured flesh, while we watch (even Freddie, restored by his vomiting, watches) in awe.

What other prodigies can be in store to add to this aquatic marvel and that great truncheon shape inside his swimming-trunks? Will Dick claim his prize? Will Mary present it? Where will they go so Mary can drop her knickers unseen by us unworthy failures and where Dick (though he is not obliged) can unharness his – ?

But as Dick draws near us something is evident – or evident by its absence. That monstrous swelling, that trapped baton – he no longer pushes it before him. It is gone – or sunk, contracted into that indeterminate sack of baggage which requires room inside every pair of male swimming-trunks and on which, after swimming, the drips gather then fall.

What can have caused this disappearance? Can it be that Dick is afraid? Can it be that now the moment is nigh he too suffers from perverse shrinkage? Can it be that the cool waters of the Lode and his extraordinary exertions have temporarily diverted his energy and in a moment all will rise up again? Can it be that Dick's purpose in diving was expressly to suppress this rebel rod of flesh? Or – more wildly speculative still and adding a new enigma to his prolonged and wondrous immersion – can it be that Dick has achieved thereby some satisfaction, some ecstasy that even Mary cannot give, and has already – ? So that, even now, twisting strands of Dick's congealed seed are floating down towards the Leem, where they will surely float to the Ouse and thence to the sea. Or at least such would be their journey if there were no hungry fish to lap them up first.

Mary steps back, steps forward, keeps her eyes fearfully, curiously, on Dick's swimming-trunks, prepares to yield herself like a captured slave-girl to this lumbering victor. But Dick, with a watery gaze (from behind flickering eyelashes) which combines two stares – one for Mary (uncertain, possibly plaintive) and one for the rest of us (indifferent, possibly reproving) – does not claim his trophy. He checks his stride momentarily before Mary. Moves on. Picks up the bottle of whisky, which still contains three fingers or so of sun-warmed liquid. Hurls it into the Lode. Gives us all a blank glance. Tramps (avoiding the splatterings of Freddie's vomit) up the bank to his former station. Sits; raises knees; clasps them, stares over them. Sulky-sullen.

"Hey – how d'you do that?"

"My whisky. My whisky – "

"How d'you hold your breath?"

"How d'you – ?"

"You haven't, have you? You haven't done it in your – ?"

No answer. Eyelashes whirring.

"Hey, Mary, aren't you going to?"

No answer. Taut silence.

"Mary, you said – "

Mary moves towards her jettisoned clothes.

"Aren't you going to play the game? Aren't you?"

Peter Baine crosses her path, deftly snatches up the larger part of her scattered garments; dodges away; stops; holds Mary's skirt by the waistband before his own hips; wiggles hula-hula style; pulls away the skirt as Mary makes a pounce at it, in the manner of a clumsy toreador; skips backward; throws part of his bundle to Terry Coe who, quick on the uptake, catches it and proceeds to do another brief dancing-girl routine, Mary's novice's brassiere held against his chest.

A game of tag, of piggy-in-the-middle, up and down the bank, in which clothes are tossed from hand to hand and in which Mary is compelled to twist, turn and reach this way and that, all the while endeavouring to keep one arm in the covering position; but in which neither Dick who sits, lashes beating, watching, nor his brother Tom (for reasons which can only be called fraternal, but for reasons also of his own) participates.

Nor does Freddie join in. Also for reasons of his own. Because Freddie sits with one eye taking in the tag game but another, more fixed eye directed testingly at Dick. Because while the tag game is only in its earliest stages and all other eyes are diverted by it, Freddie slips off along the bank to the wooden bridge and beyond, to where, as Freddie knows, there are eel-traps. Because Freddie has another game in mind. Because when the throwing and catching and chasing have exhausted themselves and Peter Baine and Terry Coe decide to scatter Mary's clothes hither and thither so that she can at least, if with little dignity, retrieve them, Freddie suddenly runs from the direction of the wooden bridge, so quickly that there is scarcely time to see what he is carrying, and while Mary stoops, unsuspecting, to pick up her skirt, clasps her from behind, pulls forward with the clasping hand the sturdy elastic of her school-regulation knickers and with the other hand thrusts the eel, a good three-quarter pounder, inside.

Whereupon Mary, who has suddenly lost all interest in her skirt and even in the so resolutely maintained shielding of her breasts, spirals, hunches her shoulders, digs her elbows into her ribs, holds out two quivering forearms on either side of her, takes in breath but making no other sound nor any other movement to relieve her situation (not having encountered it before) freezes stock-still and wide-mouthed while something squirms, twists, writhes inside her knickers and finally (because eels are adept at extricating themselves even from the most unlikely predicaments) squeezes itself out by way of a thigh-band, flops to the grass and with unimpaired instinct snakes towards the Lode.

At which Mary breaks into a fit of prolonged and disconcertingly shrill giggles.

25

Forget the Bastille

Hey, this is good. This is juicy. Forget the Bastille. Forget the March of History. Let's have more of this. So he really put an eel

in her – ? And your brother had a big – ? And. How big exactly?
Come on, tell us –

Prurient mutterings around the class. Exchanges of leers.
Judy Dobson and Gita Khan in the front row cross their legs,
feminine-defensive, experiencing, no doubt, inside their knickers,
navy blue or otherwise, uncomfortable sensations; but, up top,
are all eager and pricked ears.

So, old over-the-hill, lost-in-the-past Cricky can let it all hang
out. So old dry-bones, set-in-his-ways Head of the History
Department doesn't mind admitting that he once –

So he really means it. He's really going to teach what he
damn well likes. Really intends to chuck out the syllabus . . .

Only Price looks wary, only Price looks begrudging. Because
I've won them over, by unfair methods? Because I've licensed
subversion?

(Class-mates beware! See what he's trying to do. See the old
dodge he's trying to accomplish. That he – is one of you. The
king is but a man, the tyrant is but flesh and blood. Do not be
fooled by this sop to common humanity. And beware this other
trick he's simultaneously playing. Distracting your insurrec-
tionary impetus, diverting your revolutionary zeal by indulging
in lewd talk and appeals to your idle curiosity –)

Now who's the rebel round here?

But supposing it's not like that, Price. Supposing it's the other
way round. Supposing it's revolutions which divert and impede
the course of our inborn curiosity. Supposing it's curiosity –
which inspires our sexual explorations and feeds our desire to
hear and tell stories – which is our natural and fundamental
state of mind. Supposing it's our insatiable and feverish desire
to know about things, to know about each other, always to be
sniff-sniffing things out, which is the true and rightful subverter
and defeats even our impulse for historical progression. Have
you ever considered that why so many historical movements,
not only revolutionary ones, fail, fail at heart, is because they
fail to take account of the complex and unpredictable forms of
our curiosity. Which doesn't want to push ahead, which always
wants to say, Hey, that's interesting, let's stop awhile, let's take

a look-see, let's retrace – let's take a different turn? What's the hurry? What's the rush? Let's *explore*.

Ah, children, consider that in every era of history, no matter how world-shaking its outward agenda, there has been no lack of curious people – astronomers and botanists, fossil-hunters and Arctic voyagers, not to mention humble historians – for whose spirit of stubborn and wayward inquiry we should not be ungrateful. Consider that the study of history is the very opposite, is the very counter-action of making it. Consider your seventeen-year-old history teacher, who while the Struggle for Europe reaches its frantic culmination, while we break through in France and the Russians race for Berlin, spares little thought for these Big Events (events of a local but still devastating nature having eclipsed for him their importance) and immerses himself instead in research work of a recondite and obsessive kind: the progress of land-reclamation (and of brewing) in the eastern Fens, the proceedings of the Leem Navigation and Drainage Board, the history, culled from living memory and from records both public and intensely private, of the Crick and Atkinson families.

And what a strange and curious tale that turned out to be . . .

Yes, there's something – is there a name for it? – that doesn't care two hoots about History, or what the history books call History. Which doesn't care two hoots about shaking the world.

And even while Price tells us where History's got to, even while we pool our nuclear nightmares, you can still find time –

So you're curious. So you're curious. You'd skip the fall of kings for a little by-the-way scurrility. Then let me tell you

26

About the Eel

Of which the specimen placed by Freddie Parr in Mary's knickers in July, 1940, was a healthy representative of the only, if abundant, freshwater species of Europe – namely *Anguilla anguilla*, the European Eel.

Now there is much that the eel can tell us about curiosity – rather more indeed than curiosity can inform us of the eel. Does it surprise you to know that only as recently as the nineteen-twenties was it discovered how baby eels are born and that throughout history controversy has raged about the still obscure life cycle of this snake-like, fish-like, highly edible, not to say phallically suggestive creature?

The Egyptians knew it, the Greeks knew it, the Romans knew it and prized its flesh; but none of these ingenious peoples could discover where the eel kept its reproductive organs, if indeed it had any, and no one could find (and no one ever will) in all the waters where the European Eel dwells, from the North Cape to the Nile, an eel bearing ripe milt.

Curiosity could not neglect this enigma. Aristotle maintained that the eel was indeed a sexless creature and that its offspring were brought forth by spontaneous generation out of mud. Pliny affirmed that when constrained by the urge to procreate, the eel rubbed itself against rocks and the young were formed from the shreds of skin thus detached. And amongst other explanations of the birth of this apparently ill-equipped species were that it sprang from putrefying matter; that it emerg d from the gills of other fishes; that it was hatched from horses' hairs dropped in water; that it issued from the cool, sweet dews of May mornings; not to mention that peculiar tradition of our own Fenland, that eels are none other than the multiplied mutations of one-time sinful monks and priests, whom St Dunstan, in a holy and miraculous rage, consigned to eternal, slithery penance, thus giving to the cathedral city of the Fens its name: Ely – the eely place.

In the eighteenth century the great Linnaeus, who was no amateur, declared that the eel was viviparous, that is to say, its eggs were fertilised internally and its young were brought forth alive – a theory exploded (though never abandoned by Linnaeus) when Francesco Redi of Pisa clearly showed that what had been taken for young eelings in the adult's womb were no more than parasitic worms.

Womb? What womb? It was not until 1777 that one Carlo

Mondini claimed to have located the minuscule organs that were, indeed, the eel's ovaries. A discovery which raised doubts in the mind of his countryman Spallanzani (a supporter of Redi contra Linnaeus) who asked the simple yet awkward question: if these were the ovaries then where were the eggs? And thus – after much refutation and counter-refutation and much hurling to and fro of scientific papers – it was not until 1850 that Mondini's discovery was confirmed (long after the poor man's death) by a Pole, Martin Rathke, who published in that year a definitive account of the female genitalia of *Anguilla anguilla*.

Witness, children, the strife, the entanglements, the consuming of energy, the tireless searching that curiosity engenders. Witness that while the Ancien Régime tottered, while Europe entered its Revolutionary phase and every generation or so came up with a new blueprint for the destiny of mankind, there were those whose own destinies were inseparably yoked to the origins of the eel.

And yet in 1850, though the ovaries had been accounted for, the testes still remained a mystery – open to all claimants – and the obscure sex life of the eel still unilluminated. Obscure or otherwise, it must have been healthy, for, notwithstanding the universal ignorance as to their reproductive processes, large numbers of young eels continued every spring to mass at the mouths of their favoured rivers – the Nile, the Danube, the Po, the Elbe, the Rhine – and to ascend upstream, just as they had done in the days of perplexed old Aristotle and before. And it is worth mentioning that in that same year, 1850, though it can only be connected by the most occult reasoning with the researches of a Polish zoologist, the eel-fare, that is the running of elvers or young eels upriver, on the English Great Ouse was on a notably large scale. Two and a half tons of elvers were caught in one day, the numerical equivalent of which can be estimated when it is considered that upwards of twelve thousand elvers go to make a pound in weight.

In 1874, when you will recall there was much flooding of that same River Ouse and my great-grandfather became not only a father but Conservative Member for Gildsey, another Pole, Szymon Syrski, Professor at the University of Lemberg, made the long delayed discovery of the eel's testes – a breakthrough for which he received more recognition than Mondini. For these same tiny eel's testes are sometimes known – no doubt at the cost of a certain jocularity – as Syrski's organs. This, however, did not prevent, in the same year, Julius Münter, Director of the Zoological Museum of Greifswald, examining some three thousand eels, declaring that none of them were male and concluding that the species reproduced itself parthenogenetically – that is, by immaculate conception.

Yet, given those two vital and most complementary organs – the ovaries and the testes – when, where and by what method do they combine to do their work?

We have not yet come to the most remarkable episode in this quasi-mythological quest for the genesis of the eel. It must be understood that in its natural habitat, the freshwaters and estuaries of Europe and North Africa, the eel assumes two distinct forms. For most of its adult life it is olive green to yellowish-brown and has a snub nose. But when it has lived for some years, its snout grows sharper, its eyes larger, its sides acquire a silvery sheen, its back becomes black and all these changes signal a journey back to the sea. Since this journey occurs in autumn and young elvers come upstream in spring, it is not unreasonable to infer that the latter are the offspring of the former and that spawning occurs in winter in coastal regions. Yet (to repeat) who has ever found a ripe female, let alone an eel's egg or a newly hatched larval eel, in the inshore waters of Europe?

In 1856 – after Rathke and before Syrski – in the warm currents of the Straits of Messina, there was caught one day a tiny fish, quite unlike an eel, which was claimed as a new genus. Forty years later a similar specimen, caught from the same Straits of Messina, was reared in captivity and demonstrated to be, despite its uneel-like form, none other than the larva of the European Eel. Yet if adult eels abounded in such vast numbers, why were their larvae such elusive rarities?

It is time to introduce into the story the figure of Johannes Schmidt, Danish oceanographer and ichthyologist. Who has heard of Johannes Schmidt? It is said that modern times do not have their Sinbads and Jasons, let alone their Drakes and

Magellans, that the days of great sea-quests went out with Cook. Johannes Schmidt is an exception. There are those who fashion history and those who contemplate it; there are those who make things happen and those who ask why. And amongst the latter there are those who regard the activities of the former as a mere impediment to their aims; who, indeed, consigning history to the background, turning their backs on its ephemeral compulsions, embark on the most fairy-tale searches after the timeless unknown. Such a man – such a votary of curiosity – was Johannes Schmidt.

In 1904, when the European powers were scrambling for colonial loot, Johannes Schmidt set out to discover the breeding ground of the European Eel. He voyaged from Iceland to the Canary Islands, from North Africa to North America, in ships which, because of his inadequate funds, were ill-suited and ill-equipped. Catching his first specimen of larva west of the Faroes – the first recorded outside the Mediterranean -- he proceeded to catch younger and younger specimens at various stations in the Atlantic. At the same time he examined and statistically classified large numbers of mature eels and was able to confirm – which had never been demonstrated before – that the European Eel was indeed one single homogenous species, *Anguilla anguilla* as distinct from its close relative, the American Eel, *Anguilla rostrata*.

From 1908 to 1910, while a crisis flared in Bosnia, Italy turned covetous eyes on Tripoli and the British people, impatient with only four Dreadnoughts a year, began to chant "We want eight and we can't wait", Schmidt cruised the length and breadth of the Mediterranean, collecting eel larvae even from such contentious waters as those off Morocco and around the excitable Balkans. He found that the larvae increased in size from west to east of the Mediterranean and concluded that the eels of the countries bordering the Mediterranean did not spawn in that sea but somewhere in the Atlantic. The larvae taken from the Atlantic, in almost all cases smaller than those from the Mediterranean, confirmed the hypothesis of an eastward migration of larvae and pointed to a breeding-ground in the western part of the ocean. Schmidt realised that to locate this elusive region it was necessary to hunt for still smaller larvae, plotting their position, until at length he would have inevitably closed in on the long-sought Birthplace of Eels.

In 1911, when a German gunboat steamed into the port of Agadir and my grandfather, whose brewery had just burnt down, in extraordinary circumstances, was winding up his affairs to live in rumour-nurturing seclusion in Kessling Hall, Johannes Schmidt persuaded various ship-owners with vessels on the transatlantic route to co-operate in the collection and classifying of larvae samples. No less than twenty-three ships were thus enlisted. Not content with this, Schmidt voyaged ceaselessly himself, in his schooner, the *Margrethe*, from the Azores to the Bermudas, from the Bermudas to the Caribbean.

Alas, that curiosity must allow history its way. Alas, that Schmidt has no choice but to hold up his search, furl the sails of the *Margrethe*, and fret impatiently while the world embarks on a four-year bout of carnage. Alas, that from 1914 to 1918 it is not the origins of its own homogeneous species of eel that concerns Europe but the heterogeneous disposition of its national interests and armed forces. Alas, that it is not the presence in the Atlantic of minute eel larvae migrating dauntlessly eastwards which is uppermost in the minds of European seafarers, but rather the presence of German U-boats migrating westwards, out of Wilhelmshaven and the Kiel Canal.

And yet it must be said that this catastrophic interval, to which such dread words as apocalypse, cataclysm, Armageddon have not unjustly been applied, does not interrupt the life cycle of the eel. In the spring the elvers still congregate in their millions at the mouth of the Po, the Danube, the Rhine and the Elbe, just as they did in Alexander's day and Charlemagne's. And even at the very epicentre of the slaughter, on the infamous Western Front itself, as one Henry Crick was able to vouch, they are not to be dissuaded. If eels, indeed, were born out of mud, here they should have teemed; if eels sprang from putrefying flesh, here should have been a bumper crop.

Nor does this four-year intermission inhibit the determination, if it tries the patience, of Johannes Schmidt. For soon after its cessation, glad that history has got its business over, he once more takes to the seas. Once more he is scooping up eel larvae – this time in the Western Atlantic. And by the early twenties – so tirelessly has he worked – he is able to declare his findings; to affirm that, taking the area where the largest number of smallest larvae have been collected to correspond to the breeding territory of the eel, then this same, long unimagined, let alone undiscovered spawning ground is to be found between latitudes 20° and 30° North and longitudes 50° and 65° West – that is to say, in that mysterious region of floating weed known as the Sargasso Sea.

So it was, children, that when my father became keeper of the Atkinson Lock and began, as his forefather Cricks had done, to trap eels in the River Leem and its adjacent drains, human knowledge, after two thousand years and more of speculation, had only just assembled the facts which could have shown him where those eels came from. Not that he ever learnt, then or later, the truth of the matter. For what did he know, in his English Fens, about a Danish biologist? Yet assuredly, had he been informed on the subject, had he been told that those same eels he lifted from his traps had got there by way of a three to four thousand mile journey from a strange marine region on the other side of the Atlantic, his eyes would have widened and his lips would have formed a distinct O.

But that is not the end of the story of the eel. Curiosity begets counter-curiosity, knowledge begets scepticism. Even granted, say the doubters of Schmidt, that the larval eel makes its way three, four, or even five thousand miles to the haunts of its sires; even granted that the young elvers, undeterred by weirs, waterfalls and lock-gates, travel up rivers and even wriggle over land to reach ancestral ponds and streams, are we to believe that the adult eel, after years of life in fresh water or brackish shallows, is suddenly both compelled and enabled to undertake this journey once more in reverse, with the sole purpose of spawning before it dies? What evidence can Schmidt produce of adult eels travelling in a westerly direction in the mid-Atlantic? (Alas, Schmidt can produce virtually nothing.)

Put the case that Schmidt is wrong in his conclusion that the European Eel is a peculiarly European species distinct from its American relative. Put the case that the differences between the so-called European Eel and the so-called American Eel are not genetic but physiological and determined by different

175

environmental factors. Might it not then be possible that the European Eel, having separated itself by so many miles from its breeding ground, does indeed perish without progeny in continental waters, but its stocks are maintained by the American Eel (so-called) which is not faced with nearly such arduous distances? And that what determines that some eels will become denizens of the new world and some of the old is merely the exact point of spawning within the breeding-ground and the prevailing currents thus brought to bear?

But why should nature have permitted such a wasteful mistake? Can Europe be the graveyard of orphaned and childless eels? Are the natural environments of America and Europe so different as to create a physiological contrast sufficiently pronounced to lead to speciological error? Can it be denied – for here centuries-old observation bears witness – that adult eels, adopting their silver costume, do indeed in the autumn take to the sea? And supposing, to offer a compromise, that these adult eels fail to reach Schmidt's critical lines of longitude and latitude, might they not spawn and die somewhere, let us say, in the eastern or mid-Atlantic; and might not their eggs, given seasonal and climatic conditions, still drift, just as the seaweed drifts, towards the vortical Sargasso; so that that marine nursery, if not a breeding-ground, is still a hatching-ground?

Curiosity will never be content. Even today, when we know so much, curiosity has not unravelled the riddle of the birth and sex life of the eel. Perhaps these are things, like many others, destined never to be learnt before the world comes to its end. Or perhaps – but here I speculate, here my own curiosity leads me by the nose – the world is so arranged that when all things are learnt, when curiosity is exhausted (so, long live curiosity), that is when the world shall have come to its end.

But even if we learn how, and what and where and when, will we ever know why? Whywhy?

A question which never baulked an eel. Any more than the distance between Europe and longitude 50°. Any more than the appearance upon the scene of man with his unique possession of precisely that unremitting question Why, and with his capacity to find in the domain of the eel, in water, not only a means of transport and power and a source of food (including eels), but a looking-glass for his curious and reflective nature.

For whether or not the silver-coated *Anguilla anguilla* ever reaches the Sargasso, whether it performs its nuptial rites there or before, nonetheless it is true that, just as the young eel is driven not only by marine currents but by an instinctual mechanism more mysterious, more impenetrable perhaps than the composition of the atom, to make for some particular watery dwelling thousands of miles from its place of birth, so the adult eel, moved by a force which outweighs vast distances and the crushing pressure of the ocean, is compelled to take again to the sea and, before it dies and leaves the world to its spawn, to return whence it came.

How long have eels been doing this? They were doing it, repeating this old, epic story, long before Aristotle put it all down to mud. They were doing it when Pliny posited his rock-rubbing theory. And Linnaeus his viviparity theory. They were doing it when they stormed the Bastille and when Napoleon and Hitler contemplated the invasion of England. And they were still doing it, still accomplishing these vast atavistic circles when on a July day in 1940 Freddie Parr picked up out of a trap one of their number (which later escaped and lived perhaps to obey the call of the far Sargasso) and placed it in Mary Metcalf's navy blue knickers.

27

About Natural History

What is this – a biology lesson?

No I prefer, in order to point a contrast, to call it Natural History.

Which doesn't go anywhere. Which cleaves to itself. Which perpetually travels back to where it came from.

Children, there's something which revolutionaries and prophets of new worlds and even humble champions of Progress (think of those Atkinsons and their poor living fossil of a Sarah) can't abide. Natural history, human nature. Those weird and wonderful commodities, those unsolved mysteries of mysteries. Because just supposing – but don't let the cat out of the bag – this natural stuff is always getting the better of the artificial stuff. Just supposing – but don't whisper it too much abroad – this unfathomable stuff we're made from, this stuff that we're always coming back to – our love of life, children, our love of life – is more anarchic, more subversive than any Tennis-Court Oath ever was. That's why these revolutions always have a whiff of the death-wish about them. That's why there's always a Terror waiting round the corner.

What every world-builder, what every revolutionary wants a monopoly in: Reality. Reality made plain. Reality with no non-sense. Reality cut down to size. Reality minus a few heads.

So shall we get back to the syllabus? Shall we get back to the 1790s and Monsieur unswerving-of-purpose Robespierre?

Children, be curious. Nothing is worse (I know it) than when curiosity stops. Nothing is more repressive than the repression of curiosity. Curiosity begets love. It weds us to the world. It's part of our perverse, madcap love for this impossible planet we inhabit. People die when curiosity goes. People have to find out, people have to know. How can there by any true revolution till we know what we're made of?

28

And Artificial History

And what does he do, faced with this scene, which began with skylarking and ended with confusion: an uncontrollably giggling

Mary; an eel taking wriggling flight (away from these crazy humans) through the grass?

Your teacher notes, in true historically-observant fashion, the look that Dick directs (after first looking at the eel) at Mary. A long and searching look you wouldn't expect from a potato-head. A stern, baffled and questioning look which makes Mary stop all of a sudden her giggling, as if at some command, and look back, just as intently, at Dick. He notes how Dick looks at Mary and then how Mary looks at Dick; and he notes how Freddie Parr catches both these looks which Dick and Mary give each other.

And in all this looking at others' looks he too has a look of his own, a look which he can't describe, not having been in a position to see it, but most probably a forlorn, a rebuffed look, bearing on top of it only the thinnest veneer of bravery. Because your history teacher (though he's never told her) is in love, it's a fact, with Mary Metcalf. And that's what made him (he can't speak for the others), when he and Freddie and Peter Baine and Terry Coe cautiously lowered their swimming-trunks, droop so plaintively. A common response, referred to by the best sexologists . . .

There's something about this scene. It's tense with the present tense. It's fraught with the here and now. It's laden with this stuff – is there a name for it? It affects your history teacher in the pit of the stomach. It gives him a feeling in his guts, which, assailed by Freddie's whisky and a mouthful or two of Lode-water, crawl and twist inside him even as the eel coils and slithers towards the safety of the Lode. It's too much for your history teacher's unpractised objectivity, or for his short-lived pubescent boldness. He escapes to his story-books.

Because he can still do that. Jump from the one realm to the other, as if they shut each other out. He hasn't begun yet to put the two together. To live an amphibious life. He hasn't begun to ask yet where the stories end and reality begins. But he will, he will.

In the late summer of 1940, while Hitler sets up shop in Paris and makes invasion plans, while over southern skies history inscribes itself in white scrolls and provides ample material for the legends of the future, he rummages amongst the books his mother left behind her – many of which belonged to that book-loving pair, Dora and Louisa Atkinson, and embarks upon the two volumes of *Hereward the Wake* (a now valuable first edition still in his possession) which Louisa gave to Dora in 1866. While the inhabitants of London and other large cities are forced to take refuge within the solid fabric of air-raid shelters and underground stations, he takes refuge in the fanciful fabric of Kingsley's yarn, in which, in misty Fenland settings (which match his misty, love-sick state of mind), history merges with fiction, fact gets blurred with fable . . .

How the wild-fowl cried, "The Wake is come again" . . . how Hereward, in his magic armour, slew Sir Frederick Warrenne at Lynn . . . how, disguised as a potter, he spied on William the Conqueror . . . how he fired the Fens and roasted the Normans . . . how he loved and married the Lady Torfrida . . . how his marriage turned sour . . .

But meanwhile that scene on the Lode bank which, like other scenes yet to come, lodges in your history teacher's memory to be exhumed at later dates. Mary, in navy blue knickers which she has shared briefly with an eel; a live fish in a woman's lap; Dick; Freddie Parr; their stares, with his own, forming an invisible cats' cradle. A bottle hurled into the muddy Lode; Dick on the wooden bridge; Freddie in the water . . .

Now who says history doesn't go in circles?

29

Detective Work

So I took the bottle which I'd hidden in my room and put it where Dick would see it.

Because it's strong stuff, this curiosity. It gets the better even of fear, it gets the better of our better judgement. And even though I could have chucked that bottle in the river and been done with it, there's no keeping down that old detective spirit;

and I couldn't hold at bay for ever that question: What are you going to do?

I put the bottle in Dick's room, on his bedside-table. And then – because though curiosity can get the better of fear, it doesn't stop you being scared – I went to my own room along the landing, shut the door, locked it, put a chair against it, sat and waited.

Six p.m. Bulletin time. Down below Dad tunes in, punctually as ever, to his crackling communiqués. But he must think that my evening retreat to my bedroom is a good sign (so the lad's getting over this bad business, settling down again to his books), for he takes care not to turn up the volume unduly. And this consideration on his part, this muting of the war in favour of my scholarliness, only enables me to hear more clearly what in any case my ears are straining for: the wasp-buzz of Dick's approaching motor-bike down the Gildsey road.

And when Dick at length climbs the stairs – followed by an injunction from Dad which couldn't be more ineptly obliging to his brother: "Now don't disturb Tom – he's studying" – what does he do?

For a long time – nothing. He opens his door, enters. Clomp of his feet across the floorboards. Then he closes the door (abruptly? decisively?). Then silence. Only the "chunk-chunk" of Dad's spade in the vegetable patch, where, bulletin over, he's lifting another row of potatoes.

And what does your history teacher do? He presses his ear closer to the key-hole of his own door; attempts to repulse the assaults of his heartbeat; to interpret silence.

A tell-tale silence? An incriminating silence? A guilty silence?

If Dick can be touched by guilt. Because supposing he enters the room, sees the bottle, yet it sets off no sirens of significance? He sees a bottle, a bottle which once he threw into the river, with which he once – But he doesn't ask HowWhyWho? Supposing Dick's immune to guilt? To fear, doubt, remorse? To the whole mutinous crew of emotions.

But he's not immune to love . . .

And the silence doesn't last indefinitely. It's broken by more – less casual – footfalls and the sound of Dick's door-latch being raised. And now there's no restraining, despite that locked door

181

he's pressed against, your history teacher's heartbeat; there's no stopping his heart leaping right into his mouth. Because it hasn't failed to occur to him that Dick's strong, and this same, handy, possibly murderous bottle might do for another what it has already done for one.

But this raising of Dick's door-latch – it isn't the way a door-latch gets raised with a view to breaking down another door, in a state of homicidal rage. It's the work of a gentle, a stealthy, if still ponderous giant. It makes a sound – a click, a rasp – not meant to be heard. And a sound not meant to be heard is a much more tell-tale affair than plain silence. Furthermore, it's followed by more circumspect and would-be inaudible sounds, the noise of heavy-footed Dick tiptoeing, creeping, along our upstairs landing, yet not in the direction of the main staircase but in the direction of the little, narrow, winding flight of steps, guarded by its own door, which leads to our attic. And here Dick's stealth continues to advertise itself – for, even with the lightest of treads and even with the little door closed behind you, it is impossible to climb those old and dried-out wooden steps without a give-away medley of creaks, cracks and whines. Yet Dick climbs, and is gone perhaps a full minute (almost complete silence) before he descends, once more with painful caution, and sets off in reverse the same chorus of protests.

Poor Dick. He doesn't realise that it's stealth that incriminates, where not to attempt it wouldn't. He doesn't know that cunning can't be achieved by the motions of cunning, by a pantomime of cunning, any more than love can be –

Nor does he know that I've heard these hugger-mugger sounds, these furtive footfalls, these creakings of the attic stairs once before. But then, indeed, they were better concealed – drowned by the groans and shrieks of an east wind, blowing as it blows every winter, mercilessly across the unsheltered Fens.

But that winter, more mercilessly than ever . . .

And now he creeps back along the landing; and I tense myself once again behind my door, because I can't be sure – But he opens, still with elaborate care, his own door, enters and a few moments later emerges – this time with a manifest intention to make noises, because his footsteps thump with extra firmness on the way to the main stairs and as he descends he starts up (after the clumsy stealth, the clumsy nonchalance) a wheezing, wavering attempt at a whistle.

He descends. I wait. A brief appeal from Dad for assistance in the vegetable patch announces Dick's emergence from the cottage. I unlock my door. Remove the chair from in front of it. Step along the landing to Dick's room. A shipwreck of bed-linen. Little huddles of silt-smelling clothes. On the wall, above the bed, in a glass case, a stuffed pike, once weighing twenty-one pounds, caught on, of all days, November the eleventh, 1918, by John Badcock, former incumbent of the Atkinson Lock.

No bottle.

I return to the landing. Repeat – but without his laboured pussy-footing – Dick's foray to the attic. And there, amongst the musty smells and dusty lumber, the cast-out mattresses and sarcophagal packing-cases, is what I know to have been the object of his sortie. A chest. A black-laquered, smaller than average, battered but sturdy wooden chest. On its lid it bears in faded but just discernible gold lettering, the initials E. R. A. And it bears also – black channels in the film of grey dust that covers it – the marks of recent fingerings. Marks, which though recent, can be seen to a discriminating eye, to an eye possessed by the detective spirit, not all to have been made at the same time. For across some of the channels the lightest, the faintest refilming of dust has occurred. And just as a bruise can appear beneath a bruise, so here there are marks upon marks.

It's just seven days since Freddie floated down the river.

I crouch and attempt to raise the lid. Locked firm. I ponder. A black wooden chest with tarnished brass fittings, which once belonged to my grandfather and then to my mother. And then, one winter, my mother died. But before she died, she gave the key – to my brother. A black wooden chest which has stood, as long as I can remember, up here in the attic beneath the dormer window, but of whose contents I know nothing save that amongst them are –

I start, leap to my feet (almost crash my head on the low and sloping ceiling-beams). Dick's coming. He's coming up the stairs. Dick, whose charade of cunning has out-cunninged mine, has laid this trap. He's coming up the stairs to the attic, where there's only one, narrow exit –

But it's only a freak twinge in that old woodwork. Only a stray remnant of that wind . . .

I retrace my steps. Close the door to the attic steps. Return to my room. Lock the door. Think.

So my brother is a murderer. So what Mary said was true. And now Dick knows that I know he's a– So now it's a question of who's more afraid of who.

I go to the window and look down at the vegetable patch. Runner beans are in scarlet bloom. Dick and Dad are stooped over the potato plants, their heads nearly touching, so it seems that they are bent together in some confidence, some conspiracy from which I'm excluded. Dick looks up. Looks up at my window. Sees me looking down. Our gazes are linked by a taut rope of fear. His lashes dance.

Who is my brother? What's he made from?

I must find that key.

30

About the Saviour of the World

But after the Grand '51 Ale and the Prince Consort Ale and the Empress of India and the Golden and Diamond Jubilee Ales, not to mention the notorious Coronation Ale of 1911, no Armistice Ale flowed in the Fenlands in November, 1918. The River Leem flowed, into the Ouse, past the Atkinson Lock, past the Hockwell Lode, where later Freddie Parr would pick up an eel . . . But no Victory Ale flowed to refresh the patriotic citizens of Gildsey and its low-lying hinterland. Because, for one thing, there was no brewery to make it; and for another, a large part of the beer-drinking population was no more.

Perhaps they might have forgiven Ernest Atkinson. Perhaps they might have been prepared to excuse his warning diatribe

184

from the town hall rostrum and his even more outrageous experiment in prophetical admonition in that summer of 1911. Perhaps they might have declared themselves chastened. But they did not want, now it was, after all, all over, to sit down to a history lesson. And another thing made them not want to forgive Ernest Atkinson; and that was – his daughter.

Though – let us be clear – the people of Gildsey had no cause in that same prodigious year of 1911 when Ernest departed from them, not only under the literal smoke clouds from his own brewery, but under the darker pall of scandal, scorn, rumour and, allegation to concern themselves particularly with Helen Atkinson – then an innocent and overawed child of fifteen. But in 1914, when she is eighteen, the matter is different. For while a majority of the populace – especially now this long expected war has at last begun – is prepared to continue to revile the former brewer, a fair portion – notably the young, male, soon-to-be arms-bearing, cannon-daring portion – is in love with his daughter. And though Helen is seldom seen, living as she does with her father in that gloomy retreat at Kessling and never emerging save in his company, this in no way alters the picture. For young knights, as we know, need their damsels – especially the beleaguered, inaccessible ones in forbidden towers. And it is all still at the dreamy, chivalrous, make-believe stage, this war born in the August haze.

Shall we add to the list of indulgences – superstition, tale-telling, despondency, the bottle – to which these stick-in-the-mud Fen-dwellers are prone, another: Beauty? Especially the kind that can be invested with inspiring, exalting qualities. And need we point out how Beauty has already exerted its bewitching power both on this now tarnished Atkinson family and (by virtue of portraits with black dresses and the like) on the town which it, in turn, has for a good long century influenced?

But Helen, this last of the brewer's daughters, is surely in no danger of suffering the fate of that former beauty, the first brewer's daughter, and being turned into a local deity. Because, firstly, she is in possession of her mind, which for fifty years of her life, Sarah Atkinson was not. And, secondly, she belongs not to Gildsey and its credulous citizens, but to her father. And, though in 1914 the town would have liked to woo back this budding daughter, with her unloved father (unloved save by her) she remains.

Yet, for its own satisfaction, the town has to find some way of explaining that incongruous, twofold sequestration. It has to find a way of reconciling those two seemingly incompatible faces: the father's lugubrious, old-before-its-time countenance, with its sudden unsettling smiles and flashes of dark fire; the daughter's virgin limpidity. So it invents the easy myth that Helen, far from being swayed by filial motives, was compelled against her wishes to live with her father, indeed was forcibly imprisoned by him, away from the bright and beckoning world (bright and beckoning – in 1914), in that ogre's castle of his at Kessling.

A myth . . . Yet in every myth there is a grain of truth . . .

But what does Ernest say? We haven't heard his side of the story (we haven't heard Helen's either, but that will come out later, a little slowly and reluctantly perhaps). Does Ernest deserve this villain's part? Did he deserve those malicious barbs which followed him into his retreat? For what is the evidence? That he spoke out against the coming Chaos? That he spoke out against empire-building and flag-waving? And when words didn't work he used action, and the action seemed itself like the invoking of chaos? Yet the chaos wasn't his fault. Because *he* knew how to use that revelatory ale of his. He could drink it without its turning him into a madman. Quite the opposite: it soothed his inward melancholy and warmed and lightened his spirits. And as for that imputation that he himself had set fire to the brewery, in order to get the insurance money . . . The people had set fire to the brewery – just as the ale had inflamed their senses. And as for the insurance money, which indeed came his way – though it wasn't as much as was rumoured and a large part of it was eaten up by payments of compensation and the costly process of winding up his business – it was used in the end to endow a convalescent home for war victims, the site for which was none other than his own, once sumptuous family estate, Kessling Hall. This Kessling Hall Home (Ernest Atkinson did not wish his name to be in any way commemorated in the foundation) became in due course the East Cambridgeshire

Hospital; and today, rebuilt, expanded, with only a small portion of the original Hall still standing and used for administrative purposes, it is one of the principal psychiatric institutions of East Anglia.

But this is to jump ahead. Kessling Hall was not converted to its new purpose – and Helen Atkinson did not decide to become one of its first contingent of nurses – till 1918. And Ernest and Helen did not move into the former Lodge – a kind of miniature version of the larger house with its own small plot of enveloping trees – till the autumn of that year. So that for a good four years Ernest lived, with his daughter, the life of a determined recluse in the old hall, gradually abandoning and shutting up its rooms, letting the outbuildings fall into disrepair, gradually reducing the small retinue of servants till in 1918 there was none, save Helen herself who became housekeeper, cook – and nurse – all rolled into one.

Only once in those four years between 1914 and 1918, if we exclude those various, discreet trips to settle his affairs, did Ernest Atkinson make any public appearance in the town his grandsires had once ruled. And that, of all occasions, was in the spring of 1915 at a parade and inspection of the Royal Cambridgeshire Militia – at the Gildsey performance, that is to say, of the local travelling recruiting circus. Ernest, by some administrative bungle, quite defeating the local powers of veto, received an invitation to join the token muster of military staff and civilian bigwigs on the stand where the salute would be taken; and for some sly reason best known to himself, did not ignore it. Perhaps he saw the chance (the Gallipoli campaign had just begun) to raise again his old cry of protest, perhaps he came to scowl in silence. At any rate, in the event, he kept a low profile. Which was not difficult, with his daughter beside him.

A thronged market-square. A band going through its heart-stirring paces. Flags, bunting – But we've seen enough of this sort of thing in this town before, so if we add a lot of khaki, some old-buffer colonels with medals and shaving-brush moustaches, some bawling and shouting, some strutting recruiting sergeants, some rifles; and don't forget to deduct something too, from the background: a brewery chimney – we've got the picture.

The march-past begins. The saluting brigadier takes his position. The first ranks are composed of judiciously picked and well drilled regulars out to display just what the army, with a little spit and polish, can do with a man; the remainder – but these are the real persuaders – consist of recent, untrained and excitable recruits, apt to march in imperfect step, to flush and, in an effort not to grin when they shouldn't, to wear unduly solemn expressions.

The first ranks pass the stand and give their salute – perhaps with the barest split-second's mistiming – in the manner expected of them. But when the turn comes for the successive eyes-right from the main body of new volunteers, something is patently wrong. For before the eyes-right order comes, a good many eyes are already turned right; and not towards the saluting brigadier either, or any of the other florid-faced chiefs, but towards Helen Atkinson, who's sitting by her father on the makeshift platform amongst the civic dignitaries, to the right of the saluting point. Once they get a glimpse out of the corner of their eyes, they have to take a proper look. And once they take a proper look, they can't wrench their eyes away. Now, isn't that a prettier sight than a brass-hat with medals . . . ? And because they are constrained even to look back over their shoulders and not to want to pass this object of attention quickly, all pretence at keeping step or holding line gets abandoned, ranks behind tread on the heels of ranks in front, someone trips, a rifle falls – this march-past turns into a shambles . . .

My mother told it differently (so I never knew whom she meant or how false modesty was being dismissed): Once upon a time there was a beautiful girl at a parade of soldiers, and the silly soldiers with their rifles bumped into each other and forgot how to march because they all wanted to look at the beautiful girl. And the general turned red, and then he turned purple . . .

And the watching throng, on that spring day, had their own story: It's *his* doing – they say he's here somewhere on the platform – he's put them up to it somehow . . .

But the ones who were close enough to pick him out and might indeed have shared these accusatory sentiments, had their gazes, and their wrath, diverted: My, what a gem she's grown up to be – and what a shame, what a crying shame for her sake, that she is who she is . . .

And the town dignitaries told themselves: Something's gone wrong with our town – we can't seem to stage a Big Event any more . . .

And the army top brass said: Damn filly on the stand goes and wrecks the whole show. Mind you, quite a stunner . . .

And the *Gildsey Examiner* reported: "It would be churlish to dwell, in these urgent times, on an unfortunate disarray . . ."

And just a few, amongst the older sectors of the community (notwithstanding that we're already fifteen years into this twentieth century of hard facts and hard technology) had yet another version: It's *her*. It's her work. She stirred up those floods in '74 when she should have been lying quiet in her coffin, then she got inside those bottles of beer, drove everyone crazy and got the brewery burnt down; and now she puts the jinx on our recruiting parade . . .

But all these variants upon the same incident meant nothing to my grandfather beside the fact of his daughter's sudden power, without the need for either word or action, to make a mockery of these war-mongering proceedings – when his own words and actions had failed. And perhaps it was then, on that April day in 1915, that my grandfather fell in love (if this can be properly said about the feelings of a father) with his daughter.

After April, 1915, my grandfather never showed his face in Gildsey again. After that inauspicious parade he became not only a thoroughgoing recluse but a Worshipper of Beauty.

(This is no supposition. No wild invention. I have my grandfather's own authority: a journal, which he almost destroyed, but in the end didn't . . .)

For having done all within his power, in his own small corner of the world, to warn the world of the calamity approaching it, what more could he do now that calamity had arrived, now that, across the sea in France, the world was systematically constructing a hell-on-earth, than cling (I only paraphrase his words) to some left-over fragment of paradise?

What is happening to my grandfather? Can it be that he too

has succumbed to that old Atkinson malaise and caught Ideas? And not just any old idea, but Beauty – most Platonic of the lot. The Idea of Ideas. Can it be that my grandfather is lapsing – heaven knows – into gobbledygook?

But this is no idea. It's a living being. It's his flesh-and-blood daughter.

And there's nothing Platonic about it.

A strange thing, children, but the more the war progresses (if that's what wars do), the more it loses its fairy-tale flavour, its rally-round-the-flag, all-over-by-Christmas flavour and becomes something appalling, something indescribable, something quite unlike a fairy-tale – so the more beautiful grows this daughter. And the more despairing (of mankind) and worshipping (of his daughter) grows Ernest. Till – while George and Henry Crick join the forward march of history and end up in muddy madness – Ernest Atkinson beats a headlong retreat, backwards, inwards, to Paradise, and starts to believe that only from out of this beauty will come a Saviour of the World.

It's said that after his withdrawal into complete retirement in 1915, Ernest Atkinson's former desire to make his countrymen look to the future converted into misanthropy (though it's hardly misanthropic to endow a hospital). The terrible truths of the war, which by 1917 were beginning to come home (along with George Crick's personal effects and a letter from his C.O.) gave him no cause for self-satisfaction or for exultation over his former detractors – they only deepened his disgust for humanity. It's said, variously, that he destroyed all remaining stocks of that deadly Coronation Ale along with all records of what went into it; that he became a teetotaller; that he kept a cache of bottles but he never drank them; that he did drink them, and not only this but he and Helen continued to brew, in that private experimental brewery he'd set up at Kessling, further supplies, for purely domestic use, and that this continued imbibing, whether it calmed his Jeremiahical humour or fuelled it, certainly awoke some pretty strange urges, and drove him plain out of his wits.

In November, 1918 – when the Hall at Kessling was being prepared to receive its first batch of patients and Helen and her father were settling, just like man and wife, into the Lodge – the people of Gildsey and the Leem villages might have forgiven Ernest Atkinson. Because this founding of a hospital, to be sure, scarcely looked like the work of a madman – or a degenerate. And perhaps all those rumours –

But there's something the people of Gildsey and the Leem (and not just them but people everywhere) wanted to do more than forgive; and that was forget. They wanted to forget the nasty things that, in four years, human nature can get up to. But a Home for war victims (albeit hidden by thick woods) is a pretty big reminder (now could this just be Ernest Atkinson's gesture of revenge?). And so the simplest way not to be reminded, not to be made guilty, and at the same time not to let that man off the hook, was to say: Oh yes, he may have endowed a war hospital all right, and very fine too, but just take a peek at what's going on in that Lodge, go on, and then see what you think. Yes, we all know that there's nothing like public virtue for hiding private vice. And we don't want to hear, no, thank you very much, about a hospital that's built on shame . . .

(And of course, children, history confirms that this isn't the first time that the Atkinsons, for reasons that may or may not bear scrutiny, have established an asylum . . .)

Thus the good people, having affirmed their position and satisfied themselves on two counts, rubbed their hands and got on with sane and wholesome pursuits, such as the improvement of land drainage. The local systems had fallen into grave disrepair, not only through the deprivations of the war, but through the undeniable neglect (we must mention him again) of Ernest Atkinson, who, whilst his brewery was no more, his water transport company sold up and his agricultural interests whittled away, still held a nominal position of power on the Leem Drainage and Navigation Board.

And in a very short time they did indeed forget. They forgot about Ernest and Helen. They forgot about the Atkinsons who for a hundred years or more had ruled over their fortunes. They forgot about Coronation Ale (how easy it is to forget the awkward things). They forgot about the old world of breweries and malt barges and civic receptions – how much had been eclipsed, and so quickly, by those four dark years. Then they forgot about the war too, because that was the main point of their forgetfulness and the most awkward thing of all.

But Ernest and Helen couldn't forget – not with that Home for the shell-shocked just over their back fence. And the inmates of the Home certainly couldn't forget – because that's why they were there. Five, ten years later – ten years after the end of the war, which, of course, was to end all wars, and much talk of things of the past being things of the past – some of them are still there. And even twenty-five years later, when Henry Crick tunes in religiously to his evening bulletin and bombers set the night sky rumbling, and young Tom Crick takes a keen interest in a certain bottle, there's still a small core there – but who remembers them? – still in the throes of the old war, still trying to forget . . .

But let's not jump ahead. One way or the other at Kessling, in the years following the Great War, there are quite a few who can't forget what a mad place the world is.

Henry Crick forgets. He says: I remember nothing. But that's just a trick of the brain. That's like saying: I don't care to remember, and I don't want to talk about it. Yet it's perfectly natural that Henry Crick wants to forget, it's a perfectly good sign that he thinks he's forgotten, because that's how we get over things, by forgetting. So in June, 1921 (it wasn't a quick process), when Henry Crick starts to say in a perfectly calm and collected voice, "I remember nothing", the doctors in London and elsewhere, who for some three years now have been wondering quite what to do with Henry Crick, decide it's time he can go home. Yes, he's recovered pretty well, and it's time, now he's got rid of all those nasty memories, that he revived some nice ones. So they deliver him back to Hockwell. Here's the old village, remember? Here's the river, and the bridge, and the railway station. And here's the old home and your old Mum and Dad – they've aged a bit, but remember them? (But where's brother George?) Yes, we think you'll be all right now. Yes, it's been a long trip, but you're back now at last where you came from.

But that's just where they're wrong. Because it doesn't take much or long – just a few walks by himself along the river bank and around the fields, just a few weeks of autumn rain filling the dykes and turning the ground quaggy – and Henry Crick's crying out again for treatment. Because this flat, bare, washed-out Fenland, which ought to be the perfect home of oblivion, the perfect place for getting used to forgetting, has quite the opposite effect on our limping veteran. And maybe that's just the point: it's oblivion he'd like to forget, it's that sense of the dizzy void he can't get away from. He could do without this feeling of nothing.

Henry Crick comes home from a long walk one October afternoon, a mass of twitches, trembles, shakes and jitters, unable to speak a sensible word. They pack him off to that place at Kessling, where it looks as though he might be staying a long while. For Mr and Mrs Edward Crick it's all too much. One after the other – like two of those dazed, doomed Tommies advancing blindly into the same machine-gun skittle-alley – they topple into their graves. For poor Henry things couldn't be worse. He's back where he came from all right – in the old, old mud. But he's also at Kessling Hall, and there – But we know what happened to him there . . .

In February, 1919, shortly before her twenty-third birthday, Helen Atkinson becomes a trainee auxiliary nurse (one of fourteen at the Kessling Home). Is this her choice – or her father's wish? Or just the product of an inexorable logic? It's his hospital, after all; and she's his daughter. Every day, and sometimes at night too, lighting her way with a torch, she leaves the Lodge (which is no longer the Lodge proper, because the hospital has its own separate entrance, off the Kessling–Apton road) and, unlike the other nurses who either live-in or cycle from nearby lodgings, walks up the old Atkinson driveway to the scene of her duties. (This is something that Henry Crick won't puzzle out – when he recovers the wherewithal to puzzle things out – why she always comes and goes *that* way.) In her nurse's wimple and nurse's cloak, she bids goodbye to her wifeless father (a man of forty-four, though to look at him you'd add on at least another ten years) and disappears amongst the ranks of trees.

And Ernest Atkinson is content to watch her go. Because Ernest Atkinson (though his mind may be touched) is not – unlike a certain ancestor of his – a jealous, a possessive man.

Quite, quite the opposite. He pictures his daughter moving amongst those shattered creatures at the hospital, like some lady of the lamp. He imagines her effecting miracle cures, not by her nursely arts, but by the sheer magic of her beautiful presence. He sees, stepping out of the hospital portals, a redeemed race of men.

That's how Ernest sees it. You don't believe it? It's in that journal.

And – believe it or not – miracles happen, with Henry Crick.

Ah yes, put it down, if you like, to improved methods of therapy, the know-how of doctors, or simply the passage of time, but Henry Crick will tell you it was none other than that angel in a nurse's uniform, that white-aproned goddess. Her and her alone.

Henry Crick has discovered love. All through that spring of 1922 (it's 1922 – is that possible? Not 1917?) he is indeed in paradise. And it's no dream. Because she loves him too. She says so. And it's no airy and imaginary thing, this love. It gets more palpable, more passionate, the more Henry Crick recovers. Having missed, because of the intrusion on his time – not to say his sanity – of the affairs of the wide world, a good many of his youthful, amorous years, Henry Crick has learnt little about love (if a good deal about –), is an inexperienced lover. But Helen Atkinson teaches him. She is an able teacher (now where has she gained her knowledge?). And heals him.

Does Helen Atkinson, too, then, believe in miracles? No, but she believes in stories. She believes that they're a way of bearing what won't go away, a way of making sense of madness. Inside the nurse there lurks the mother, and in three years at the Kessling Home for Neurasthenics Helen has come to regard these poor, deranged inmates as children. Like frightened children, what they most want is to be told stories. And out of this discovery she evolves a precept: No, don't forget. Don't erase it. You can't erase it. But make it into a story. Just a story. Yes, everything's crazy. What's real? All a story. Only a story . . .

So Henry Crick, who is learning about love, learns, also, to tell those stories of old Flanders which he will tell again, more embellished, more refined, by the lockside, by the fireside and during the nocturnal lowering and raising of eel-traps, and which will lead on to other stories, till the pain, save for sporadic twinges in the knee, is almost gone. (Though other pains . . .) He retrieves that old knack of his Crick ancestors which his little trip to the trenches nearly put paid to for good and all. He even saves up, for some future time, though perhaps without knowing it, the story of this same extraordinary adventure he is now undergoing, this encounter with a nurse (for how can you explain a miracle except by saying: this is how it was?). Though he won't do that, he won't tell that story, till much, much later, till he's a dying man, and another woman is nursing him . . .

They not only become lovers, this strangely matched pair, they tell each other stories.

And what story does Henry hear issuing from the lips of Helen Atkinson?

Once upon a time there was a father who fell in love with his daughter (no let's be clear, we're not just talking about ordinary paternal affection). And the father – who'd lost his wife many years before – and the daughter lived alone in a former lodge on the edge of the grounds of a hospital. Hemmed in by tall trees and standing all by itself, this lodge was like a house in a fairy-tale – a gingerbread house, a woodcutter's cottage; but in fact the father had once been a rich and influential man – amongst other things he owned a brewery – though, one way or another, he'd fallen on bad times; and once he'd lived in the grand building which was now a hospital. Far away, across the sea, there'd been a great war and the hospital was full of soldiers, some of them wounded in their bodies but all of them wounded in the mind. And this was true even though the war had ended three years before.

Before it began, the father had spoken out against the war, which everyone felt was coming like a great adventure. He told the people that when it came it would be a terrible, a disastrous thing. But the people scoffed and scorned the father. On top of this, one night, his brewery burnt down. So he went to live, like a banished man, with his daughter in the big house in the country which would one day be a hospital.

Then the war began and became all the things the father said it would be, and the father grew sick at heart, with only his daughter to comfort him. Sometimes, in that lonely house where, to while away the heavy hours, they told each other stories and dabbled still in beer-brewing, he would tell his daughter that the world was dying; it would never be the same again. All its youth and bloom were being sucked away. But even as he said these things he could not deny (a man who was neither young nor old but ageing rapidly) that his daughter was blooming before his eyes. And even as he said these things he must have already fallen in love with his daughter. And the daughter must have known it. Because one night they stopped telling stories and fell into each other's arms, the way a father and a daughter shouldn't.

Now love, which always finds a way, has its stages. It begins with adoration. Then adoration turns to desire, and desire to cleaving, and cleaving to union. And all these stages it is possible, if it is not natural, for a father and daughter to undergo together. To all these stages the daughter assented, because indeed she adored her poor father and pitied his sorrows, and having been his close and only companion since she was a child, how should she know what was natural and what wasn't? But as for that other stage which follows union, as for the bearing of love's fruits (for this was the father's wish – he wanted a child, a very special sort of child) she baulked and trembled at this.

So in order to divert her father's designs, she sowed in his mind the plan of turning their country home, which was far too large, in any case, for just the two of them, into a hospital for victims of the war. Wasn't that a better plan? To rescue all those poor, sad cases, all of whom would be in a sense their wards, their children. They could move somewhere near, into the Lodge perhaps (no, no, she would never leave him). And she herself would become a nurse.

But this hospital, into which, indeed, the father put reawakened energies, imagining great things (even miracles), only served to remind them how evil lingers and how things of the past aren't things of the past. For though the great war ended, the broken-minded soldiers still came and remained

For them life had stopped, though they must go on living. It only deepened the father's sorrows, this home for hopelessness. And now he wanted a child more than ever. And not just a child either. Because he began to speak of this child as the Saviour of the World. For perhaps, like those poor soldier boys, his mind had become wounded too.

The daughter reasoned with the father. How would they bring up this child – he a father, and she his daughter?

Because, working each day at the hospital, she had got used to speaking reasonably about madness, as if it were the normal thing. Coming and going, through the trees, between the lodge and the hospital, she would ask herself, which is the madder place? Who is madder, the crazy soldiers, or the man in the gingerbread house? And sometimes on these journeys to and fro she would stop, while an acorn dropped, a woodpecker drilled, a breeze swung through the beech trees, and say to herself: these are the only sane interludes of my life – if this is what sanity is. She would think: the truth of it is, I'm trapped. My life's stopped too. Because when fathers love daughters and daughters love fathers it's like tying up into a knot the thread that runs into the future, it's like a stream wanting to flow backwards.

At such moments tears would often slide down her cheeks. Because, for all its being a trap, she loved her father, both in the way a daughter should and in the way a daughter shouldn't, and she didn't want to hurt him. And though she didn't want a child, yet – she wanted a child. She wanted a future. And she was used to nursing men who'd become again like helpless infants. And inside the nurse is the mother.

So she would linger amongst the trees, like a distressed damsel in the forest.

But love always finds a way. Because, by and by, there came to the hospital a wounded soldier called Henry. Life had stopped for him too; but it was about to start again. Because, by and by, he recovered, and as he recovered – though Henry would have said these two things were one and the same – he fell in love with this nurse who loved her father. And as he fell in love with her so she fell in love with him. And this second love loosened the knot of the first.

For one night the daughter said to the father: "I assent. I will have your child – if you will give me my freedom."

"Freedom?" the father said.

The daughter looked at the father.

"I love another man."

The father's face fell, but he listened to what his daughter had to say.

"I will bear your child, if first you let me marry this man and live with him, so that when the child is born it will seem like his child and will be brought up by him and me as if it were the true child of our marriage."

The father looked long and hard at the daughter.

"Is he a good man?"

"Yes, he is one of the patients at the hospital. He was very ill but now he is almost cured."

A faint light entered the father's sad eyes.

"*You* have cured him?"

The daughter said nothing.

"But he loves you?"

"Yes."

"And will you tell him, ever – this husband – whose the child really is?"

"That must be up to me."

The light in the father's eyes flickered, but did not vanish.

"And you will look after him – my son, I mean?"

"If a son it is."

"And he will be the saviour of the world?"

"He will be the saviour of the world."

So the father and the daughter were agreed. Perhaps that very night they set about begetting a child. But what the daughter really hoped (though it grieved her to deceive the father) was that first she would get a child by Henry and that the father would take it for his own. And if, failing this, she got a child by the father then she would never tell Henry whose it was and perhaps never need to. A third possibility – that she might not know herself whose child it was – she scarcely considered, being sure of her mother's instinct.

Thus the daughter tried hard by two men at the same time, both of whom she loved, to become pregnant. Though who would be the child's father would perhaps never become clear till the baby was born. All this as Henry's wounded mind became more than healed. And then one day when the moment seemed ripe – perhaps it was amidst those same woods, in secret places, where she used to stop in her distress and weep – the daughter started to tell Henry a story . . .

But when Henry heard this story (he was like a man in paradise who'd believe anything), this nurse and he were already betrothed and he'd already learnt that he was going to be a father . . .

But the story goes on, and Henry Crick's now a part of it. For not only is the day fixed for his marriage to this beautiful nurse who thereafter will cease to be a nurse but will become a mother, but both a home and future employment are provided for him, through the offices of her father, in the form of the Atkinson Lock and its adjacent cottage, whose present occupant, one John Badcock, is due to retire shortly.

All through the latter part of summer, while Europe still sorts out its peace treaties, civil war rages in Russia and a thirty-nine-year-old Mussolini is about to seize power in Italy, Henry Crick learns the arts of lock-keeping and sluice maintenance from John Badcock, a cautious and reserved man who nonetheless leaves to the arriving couple as a wedding present and memento of their predecessor a stuffed pike, weight 21lbs 4ozs, in a glass case, caught on the very day (hence its taxidermal preservation) that the Armistice was signed.

And towards the end of September, while Helen's still invisible pregnancy advances, various pieces of furniture, household articles, heirlooms and possessions begin to arrive by motor-van both from the one-time home of Henry Crick and his departed parents and the former lodge of the Kessling Hall estate. And these include – it arrives all by itself one morning in the back of a taxi and is addressed expressly to Mrs Henry Crick – a black wooden chest with brass fittings, firmly locked and bearing the initials E. R. A. Ernest knows what's in it. And Helen knows what's in it. But Henry will have to guess.

And it's here in this lockside cottage that one grey dawn in

March, under the eye of Ada Berry, the Hockwell and Apton midwife, is born the child that Ernest Atkinson wished to be the saviour of the world.

And proves to be a potato-head.

Though that he is not the saviour of the world but a potato-head Ernest Atkinson will never know . . .

But let's go back a bit – to where the light of Paradise still seems real. Henry Crick, newly married and father-to-be, sits one still and dusky Indian-summer evening outside the cottage which is his new home, gazing at the lock and the stretch of river and river bank which are his special preserve. Illumined by the presence of his beautiful and pregnant wife, this flat-vistaed domain has lost the dreadful emptiness that once it had for him, and has not yet come to show the desolation that at later times it will impart. Cocooned, furthermore, in his love for this same beautiful wife of his, he is deaf to the world's gossip. Because he knows who Ernest Atkinson is. And what is so unheard of about a child conceived out of wedlock and born within it? At this moment Henry Crick possesses the most happiness that a man perhaps can ever possess, the happiness that is set against a foil of trouble, the happiness that is driven like a wedge between past and future pains . . .

And suddenly he sees it, flickering and twisting in the fading light along the margins of the river. It comes downstream, out of the twilit distance, keeping to the far bank, moving towards the lock. It ripples, twinkles, now in, now out of the water, now mingling with the reeds; it twirls, whirls, flashes, flutters, flames, grows dim then bright again, skips, hovers, dodges, zips and seems to be saying all the time, 'Look at me – Do I have your full attention? Yes, I see I have your full attention.' For one instant it seems to take on the flickering shape of a woman. Then as it reaches the barrier of the sluice, it vanishes.

A will o' the wisp.

Henry Crick watches, amazed. So amazed that he forgets that, by tradition, will o' the wisps are bad signs. He does not doubt his eyes. But so as not to doubt his memory, he records this vision. He writes it down – one more item to add to the list of wonders he has known – in the back of his lock-keeper's log-book: "September 26th, 1922 (evening). Saw willythewisp."

It was that same day, September 26th, 1922, that the black chest with the brass fittings and the gold initials arrived at the lock cottage and that Henry Crick, on his wife's instructions (he asked no questions – happy men don't ask questions) lugged it up to the attic.

And some time before this Ernest must have explained to Helen what was inside the chest and what was its purpose. He must have explained that though, as she had affirmed, it was up to his daughter whether to tell his future son (Helen, perhaps, did not interject the words "or daughter", or even the word "grandson") the truth of his parentage, to keep a man – let alone a saviour of the world – in the dark about such things was no light deception; and he wished to make arrangements for the eventual disclosure. In his old chest – the chest that had once accompanied him as a young man on his sojourns in London – he would place a written statement addressed to this yet unborn child, explaining how it came to be. Together with this, he would place his journals, written over the years, so that – if such matters should be of value to a saviour of the world – the child might come to know more fully about the father who begot him. He would send her the chest and the key; and on his eighteenth birthday – if she chose – she was to give the key to their son.

Perhaps Helen might have said, "But by then you will still – ", but checked herself, knowing that she was looking at a sick man. Perhaps she said instead, "But why the chest?", meaning that the chest was large. To which Ernest might have replied, with even the suggestion of a wink, "On his eighteenth birthday our son will receive also a dozen bottles of our old ale. You remember – the ale we used to brew together . . ."

And perhaps it was then that he said goodbye to her – not as a father but as a lover. For they could never meet again, alone together, here in the Lodge – could they? And perhaps as Helen left to return to the lock-cottage, she wept. Because the child in her womb – so she believed then – was Henry's.

On the night of the twenty-fifth of September Ernest penned a document to his putative son, sending him a father's love and greetings, a father's confession – a father's penitence – and enjoining him to save the world, which was a place in dire need

of saving. Possibly he knew, as he wrote this, that he was mad –
because inside every madman sits a little sane man saying
"You're mad, you're mad". But perhaps this made no difference,
because by now he was already confirmed in the belief that this
world which we like to believe is sane and real is, in truth,
absurd and fantastic.

When he had finished this letter to his saviour-son, he folded
it in an envelope, unsealed (so that Helen could read it), and
placed it with the four blue cloth-bound notebooks which contained his journals in the black chest. Then he went down to the
cellar of the Lodge and brought back in stages twelve bottles of
the beer which when brewed and sold for public consumption in
1911 had been known as Coronation Ale. These, too, he placed,
carefully swathed in sacking, in the chest. Either it had already
been written or else it was at this point that he added to the
letter the words:

"P.S. The bottles are for emergencies."

Then he wrote on the envelope, "To the First-Born of Mrs
Henry Crick", wrapped the envelope and journals in more
sacking, shut the chest, locked it and the next morning had it
despatched to his daughter's home along with a sealed packet
containing the key.

How many bottles there were in the Lodge cellar is not
known. But there must have been a good deal more than twelve.
Because after my grandfather watched his chest depart in the
back of the taxi, he felt a great vacuum inside him and he started
to fill it with beer. He started to pour into this vacuum, in
quantities he had never before attempted, that extraordinary
and visionary liquor which only those who know how to drink it,
should drink – which only a Saviour of the World knows truly
how to drink.

He drank all morning: at the Atkinson Lock Mrs Henry Crick
receives a chest and – inside a small packet which also contained
a key – a simple message which read: "Call him Richard".

He drank all afternoon: at the Atkinson Lock, Henry Crick,
experiencing twinges in the knee, heaves the chest up to the
attic.

He drank, with intervals, perhaps all day. But then at some
time in the evening, leaving behind him a litter of empty beer

bottles, he began to walk from the Lodge towards the Kessling Home, following the leafy paths that once his daughter had followed on her daily journeys as a nurse. Perhaps he believed that it was there he truly belonged, with the poor soldiers, who would never get out of the past, who would never climb up into the future – while his daughter belonged with the one who'd been freed. Perhaps he was looking to take Henry Crick's place amongst the crazy soldiers, and maybe that was why he carried a gun.

At any rate, he never reached the Home. Because on the same September evening that my father saw a will o' the wisp come twinkling down the Leem, Ernest Atkinson, whose great-grandfather brought the magic barley out of Norfolk, sat down with his back against a tree, put the muzzle of a loaded shot-gun into his mouth and pulled the trigger.

31

A Teacher's Testament

Children, do you believe in education? Do you believe that the world grows up and learns? Do you believe in all this stuff about wise old men and young foolish ones? In elders and betters, in following your leader, in the lessons of experience . . . ?

Children, do you believe in children? That they come trailing clouds of glory, that they bring with them little parcels of paradise, that locked in their bosoms is a glimpse of what the world might just one day be?

What is a history teacher? He's someone who teaches mistakes. While others say, Here's how to do it, he says, And here's what goes wrong. While others tell you, This is the way, this is the path, he says, And here are a few bungles, botches, blunders and fiascos . . . It doesn't work out; it's human to err (so what do we need, a God to watch over us and forgive us our sins?). He's a self-contradiction (since everyone knows that what you learn from history is that nobody –). He's an obstructive instructor, a treacherous tutor. Maybe he's a bad influence. Maybe he's not good to have around . . .

Darkness. A school playground. Darkness in the classrooms, in the assembly hall, in the science block, the gym, the library. Only a single light still burns in the office wing.

A teacher walks, with unsteady gait, across the playground. The teacher is a little drunk. The teacher won't be teaching any more. He's in no fit state for that. The teacher's been to see the Head. He loiters in the kid's playground, under veiled suburban stars . . .

Children, some brief observations on drunkenness (made whilst in a state of drunkenness). A predominantly adult phenomenon. The very young, by and large, don't. Don't have to. Because children don't need to feel they are once again like children . . . How it makes the world seem like a toy. How it makes the bad seem not so bad. How it makes reality seem not so really real . . . Its sociological and ideological implications. A let-out for the march of history (Look – we can still be merry!). A subject for eclectic research (perhaps you'd like to pursue it some time?): the French wine and champagne industry during the French Revolution. Consumption up or down?

"Sir?"

It's Price. His pale, waxy, questioning face looms up like a haggard moon in the dark.

"Price, what are you doing still here?"

"Meeting, sir."

"What meeting?"

"Our society. The Holocaust Club – the Anti-Armageddon League. We haven't decided on a name yet."

"Just as well. Are you supposed to hold these meetings? If Lewis – "

"It's all right. We booked a room in the name of the chess club."

He falls into step beside me.

"You've seen him then, sir?"

"Seen him?"

Price nods towards that floating square of light.

"You knew?"

"Everyone knew."

"Yes, I've seen him. As a matter of fact, I've been drinking his whisky."

"So have you got the push?"

"What do you think, Price?"

"We could organise a protest, sir. Petition the education authority. Write to that shitty local paper – "

"I'm flattered. But – "

(But why this sudden solicitude? This solidarity? These extra-respectful "sirs"? From you of all –)

"I just want to say, sir, that we're all – the whole class – I mean, really sorry about everything."

"Well that's all right, Price. I'm not getting the sack. I'm being retired."

"And. And these – new lessons you've been giving. Quite something."

Stories, Price. Fairy-tales.

"And we're sorry – about Mrs Crick."

"That's okay too. But she's heard about you, did you know that? I've told her about you. You're the sort of student a teacher talks to his wife about."

"How is she, sir?"

The teacher doesn't answer.

We reach the school-gates. The teacher stands, on swaying legs.

"Look, Price, have you got to go straight home? Will they worry where you've got to? I've just had three cups of scotch. I think I need more. Come and have a drink with me."

"Okay." (A little warily.) "All right. But does he really keep a stock of booze up there?"

"It's not a crime. Your headmaster needs protecting. He'd like to be your lord protector, but it's he who – I shouldn't be saying this."

"Sure . . . The Duke's Head, sir? You know I'm under eighteen?"

"Price, are you really telling me that you've never – ?"

The Duke's Head. Garish warmth on a cold night. A background of space-invader gurgles and fruit-machine hiccupings. A corner table. A semi-drunk schoolmaster and a schoolboy with a death-mask face. Drinks: for the former a large scotch; for the latter (I might have known our Price's demonstrative tastes) a slowly sipped Bloody Mary.

More shocks from South London's School for Scandal.
Pupils encouraged in after-school drinking . . .

"So what did he say to you?"

"Lewis? Oh, never mind. Tell me about this – Holocaust Club?"

"If you like." He looks hesitant, as if I'll think it's kids' stuff. "It's just an idea. It's not a protest group. We believe – in the power of fear."

"Fear, Price?"

Fear?

"Not every kid in this school would get up and join a protest. But they might be scared. We want to pool people's fear. Tell them not to hide it. Bring it out in the open. We want to say, it's okay, show your fear, add it to ours."

"But how do you – ?"

"We thought we'd start a magazine. Get people to write down their fears. You know, how they see the end of the world. The last minutes, last thoughts, the panic, what it'll be like for those who don't go straight away . . ."

He's excited. He takes a sip of blood.

"You know where we got the idea from, sir?"

"No."

"No? Not really? That lesson. You remember. When we all told our dreams . . ."

"Ah yes." (So my classes have taught something: how to be afraid.) "That lesson."

He looks at me.

"Look, I'm sorry I messed up your classes, sir. I'm sorry I cocked things up for you."

But that's what education's about, Price. (And don't look so sheepish. What's happened to the revolutionary fire? Or doesn't it work any more when the tyrant's taken a different sort of topple? When he turns out, after all, to be a bit of a sad case.)

206

It's not about empty minds waiting to be filled, nor about flatulent teachers discharging hot air. It's about the opposition of teacher and student. It's about what gets rubbed off between the persistence of the one and the resistance of the other. It's a long hard struggle against a natural resistance (because natural history never wants to learn . . .). A slow, unending process. Needs a lot of phlegm. I don't believe in quick results, in wand-waving and wonder-working. I don't even believe, as Lewis would have it, in equipping for today's real world. But I do believe in education.

Sacked school-teacher, husband of baby-snatcher, says: "I believe in education . . ."

Do you know why I became a teacher, Price? Okay – because I had this thing about history. My pet hobby-horse. But do you know what prompted me to *teach*? It was when I was in Germany in 1946. All that rubble. Tons of it. You see, it didn't take much. Just a few flattened cities. No special lessons. No tours of the death-camps. Let's just say I made the discovery that this thing called civilisation, this thing we've been working at for three thousand years, so that now and then we get bored with it and even poke fun at it, like children in school, because sometimes it takes the form of a pompous schoolmaster – is precious. An artifice – so easily knocked down – but precious.

That was thirty-four years ago. I don't know if things are better or worse than they were then. I don't know if things were better or worse then than they were in the year 0. There are myths of progress and myths of decline. And dreams of revolution . . . I don't know if my thirty-two years as a teacher have made any difference. But I do know that things looked dark then and they do now. In 1946 I had a vision of the world in ruins. (And my wife-to-be, for all I knew, was having visions too – but let's not go into that.) And now here you are, Price, in 1980, with your skull-face and your Holocaust Club, saying the world may not have much longer – and you're not much younger than I was then.

"But you want to know what Lewis said to me? Let me tell you something I said to him, I said, 'Lewis, do you believe in children?'"

"Don't get you, sir. Want another drink?"

"Nor did Lewis. I said, 'We teach them. Do you believe in them? All the things they're supposed to be. Heirs of the future, vessels of hope. Or do you believe that they'll grow up pretty quickly to be like their parents, to make the same mistakes as their parents, that the same old things will repeat themselves?' And Lewis said, 'Which do you believe?' And I said, 'I believe the latter.' And Lewis said, 'Is that what you tell your classes?' And I said, 'It's what history tells them: One day you'll be like your parents. But if in becoming like their parents, they've struggled not to be like them, if they've tried' (you see, Price, why the student must resist the teacher, the young must suspect the old) 'if they've tried and so prevented things slipping. If they haven't let the world get any *worse* – ?' "

"And do you know what Lewis said?"

"No."

" 'That's the comment of a tired old cynic who's been teaching too long.' "

All right, so it's all a struggle to preserve an artifice. It's all a struggle to make things not seem meaningless. It's all a fight against fear. You're scared, Price. No need to start a club about it. Saw it in your face. And what do you think I am right now? What do you think all my sounding off is about, and what do you think all these stories are for which I've been telling as a finale to my teaching career and which – now you tell me – have not gone unappreciated. It helps to drive out fear. I don't care what you call it – explaining, evading the facts, making up meanings, taking a larger view, putting things into perspective, dodging the here and now, education, history, fairy-tales – it helps to eliminate fear. And why do you think I'm sitting here with you now, wanting to tell you more? Don't have to go yet, do you, Price? Mum and Dad won't worry? Yes, I'll have another. Yes, I know I'm drunk. Let me tell you another. Let me tell you –

Price gets up for more drinks. The barman, collecting glasses, stops him. Looks at him suspiciously. Then at me.

"Is he over eighteen?"

"Yes." The barman stares, unconvinced. "I should know. He's my son."

– let me tell you (even behind his corpse make-up, Price goes suddenly pink), let me tell you

32

About Beauty and the Beast

Not a saviour of the world. A potato-head. Not a hope for the future. A numbskull with the dull, vacant stare of a fish . . .

And he can't be taught. Can't read, can't write. Speaks half in baby-prattle, if he speaks at all. Never asks questions, doesn't want to know. Forgets tomorrow what he's told today. At fourteen, he still sits in a junior class of the Hockwell village school, his bottom jaw hanging, blank eyes staring, the daily butt of the other kids. "Dick Crick!" they squawk. "Dick Crick! Dick Crick!" Like some name in a nursery rhyme. (Now whatever possessed his unthinking parents to call him Richard?)

Mr Ronald Allsop, village headmaster, a persevering man, confides at length in the father: "I've done all I can." And takes the time-honoured escape route of the defeated teacher: "But he's good with his hands . . . and a strong pair of shoulders . . . no shame, to be sure, in honest manual work . . ."

And the strange thing is that the father seems pleased, is almost relieved by this sorry verdict.

And the even stranger thing is that when the younger brother, Tom – who, by contrast, is a star pupil, who wins a scholarship to Gildsey Grammar School, who will go far and make his father proud (but not his mother, because his mother's dead) – attempts to succeed where the Hockwell village school has failed; when, one summer's day he gets books, pencil and paper – because he doesn't want a dummy for a brother, because he minds what his brother doesn't, that his brother has no mind, because he wants to save him from this prospect of backwardness (ah, note, children, these early pedagogic symptoms) – and sits down with Dick on the edge of the tow-path, the father promptly breaks up this makeshift tutorial and, with wide-eyed consternation and untypical vehemence, splutters to his second-born: "Don't educate him! Don't learn 'im to read!"

So Dick grows up, deft-handed, broad-shouldered, strong in body if not in mind, by the banks of the Leem. And in time goes to work on an Ouse dredger, the *Rosa II*, and thus comes to purchase, with his saved-up wages from this same daily labour, a second-hand motor-cycle, a Velocette 350, which some might say was of all things the thing Dick understood most intimately and cherished most dearly, a motor-bike, in its brainless efficiency, in its mechanical animation, bearing a pretty close resemblance to Dick himself.

But even a potato-head must sometimes wonder and think. Even a numbskull must sometimes ponder those big and teasing questions: What's life? What's it made of? Where does it come from and what's it for?

Take, for example, that time his mother disappeared without explaining and never came back again. She used to be always there. She used to produce clean clothes and daily meals. Potato-head though he was, she used to tuck him in bed and kiss him goodnight and lavish on him, indeed – or so it seemed to the curious and envious, yes envious, eyes of little Tom – a special kind of mother's affection, somehow proportionate to its not being returned. But one day she took suddenly to her own bed and a little while later was seen no more. Now where could she have gone?

(But don't you know, Dick? Didn't you see? She's in that wooden box they lowered into the frost-hardened ground in Hockwell churchyard. We all stood round, don't you remember? That was her. She's under the little ridge in the grass where father goes and puts flowers (haven't you noticed, Dick, how he's started to grow flowers amongst all those vegetables?); and sometimes, if you watch him, after placing the flowers, he kneels down and presses his head to the ground and cries his eyes out. She's under the ground, Dick, to stay.)

But Dick won't believe she can have gone where she can't be

210

retrieved. Perhaps she's hiding somewhere else. If they took her away in one box, perhaps she'll return in another. Perhaps she's curled up inside that old chest in the attic. Didn't she give him the key – just before she vanished? And if she isn't in the chest (because she isn't) then perhaps she's inside those bottles – because that's all there is in there, and some old sacking and some meaningless writing. Or perhaps what's inside the bottles will make her reappear . . .

For one day, not long after Mother's sudden and unscheduled departure, Dick takes one of the bottles and goes down to where Stott's Drain meets the southern bank of the Leem and ceremoniously drinks the contents . . .

And why Stott's Drain?

Because it's here that every evening, after first lowering them in the morning, Dad used to pull in his wicker eel-traps which, almost without fail, came up throbbing and glistening with eels. There must be something special about this murky confluence of drain and river, something special both for eels and for Dad. Because it's here, in that spring and summer after Mother's decampment that Dad takes to coming after sunset, changing his eel-fishing routine to a nocturnal vigil lit by the moon or a hurricane lamp, and measured out by cigarettes. We go with him, his sons, and learn about eel-trapping. And sometimes we pass the whole night while Dad racks his brains to tell us more and more tales, more and more wise saws and sayings (though Dick never listened, just stared at where the traps were submerged), because he doesn't want to go back to that empty cottage, to that cold bed where Mother isn't.

And it's here too, when he's older and rides a motor-cycle, that Dick will come every alternate weekday evening on his return from the *Rosa II*, entrusted now (daytime baiting having been restored) with the privileged task of gathering by himself our crops of eels. Slung across his back as he rides home along the Hockwell road, a dripping, squirming sack. Yes, there's something special, for Dick as well, about these magical eel-traps, which, lowered empty and barren, can come up again so full of slithery quickness. Perhaps the river can tell where Mother has gone and how she might return. Perhaps the river can tell the secret of life. Perhaps one day, when the traps are hauled in . . .

Dick puts the bottle (a slim bottle, dark brown, with a narrow neck) to his lips and drinks. How do I know this? Because I'm over on the other side of the river, hidden behind the crest of the opposite bank. (Now what's turned this little brother into such an apprentice spy, into such a budding detective?) Dick drinks – the whole bottle in one go. But what he drinks doesn't make his mother rise up, wriggling and jiggling, alive-alive-o, out of the river. Though its effect is extraordinary enough . . .

And take that other time, by the banks of the Hockwell Lode, when, after certain feats of underwater swimming, after certain remarkable physiological reactions, Freddie Parr took an eel (yes, there's something about these slippery creatures) and – And Dick looked at Mary and Mary looked at Dick . . . Does that moment sink without trace in the amnesiac mire of Dick's mind? No, it lingers, it reverberates. For what does Dick begin to do, dating from that memorable July day in 1940? He starts to hang around Mary Metcalf, albeit at a tentative distance. He lurks in Hockwell village, near the station, when the 4.24 train is due from Gildsey, bringing its load of returning schoolchildren, including one who wears rust-brown and, on her left breast, a red sacred heart. He haunts the route used by a certain person between Hockwell and Polt Fen. And when allowed into the circle of the other Hockwell kids (for, ever since that day by the Lode, there has been a tendency to regard Dick less with tolerant condescension than with suspicious, ostracising respect) he bestows on Mary, should she be there, more of those long, unnerving looks.

So that during that period when little Tom's undoubtedly blossoming but still innocent passion for Mary struggles through its bashful, early, railway-carriage stages, another soul, his own brother no less (ah, cause for envy indeed), also yearns and pines. Save that whilst little Tom knows very well what constrains him, though this doesn't help him to be any the bolder, Dick's plight is of a more ignorant and incurable kind. The poor lad doesn't know what he's suffering from.

Or so it's claimed. For throughout these same, so susceptible,

212

so formative months, I see no evidence of Dick's supposed affliction. Oh yes, now and then he happens to be mooching about near Hockwell Station when I (and Mary Metcalf) return from school. But nothing so significant in that. It's Mary who tells me about Dick's plaintive condition. And clearly she doesn't tell me till our relations have achieved that pitch where such candour is possible, till they have reached, indeed, the full-blown, windmill stage. By which time Dick is a mate on the *Rosa II* and seems to be struck on his motor-cycle. So that for a good year and more, either Dick has been more stealthy and more circumspect than might be credited or else – but do I think of this as Mary unfolds her tale of my brother's secret life? – perhaps the truth is not as Mary says, but the other way round. Perhaps it's not Dick who bewilderingly yet doggedly pursues Mary, but Mary who, with much more guile at her disposal, would like to be better acquainted with Dick.

"You remember – 'course you do – that day when Freddie got that eel and . . ."

(While the big blue eye of the summer sky looks down on our love-nest; while the sun shines on coppery hairs . . .)

"It was big, wasn't it? No, no – not the eel." (Teasingly, curiously): "It must have been twice as big as this . . ."

(While insect-buzzes mingle with the sound of cropping cattle . . .)

"What's he like? No, really. Did your Dad, or Mum, never . . . But he's weird, isn't he? Don't you ever feel sorry for him . . . ?"

(While poplars rustle . . .)

"Poor Dick."

"Yes, poor Dick."

And it's true, it touches me – it touches me as it can touch only a younger son with a seniority of fortune, as it can touch only a lover secure (secure?) in his love – this image of my lonesome and benighted brother. Deprived not only of brains and education but of this extra, windmill-guarded blessing. He must know, he must learn. If not how to put words together on a page, and how to convert them into speech, then this other sort of magic.

Ah love, young love. How it can't remain simple and innocent. How it wants to stretch forth and spread its gospel. (And later it shrinks and dwindles. Later it grows wary and clings to itself as if it might disappear . . .) But young love, new love, first love – How it wants to embrace everything, how sorry it feels for all those denied its simple remedy . . .

So how was I, in our Lode-side bower, while far away the world wrote its chronicle of war, while Mary told me about her widowed father and the sisters of St Gunnhilda (how hard it was to be a little Madonna) and I told Mary of my gammy-legged and likewise widowed Dad – how was I to avoid giving voice to a pitiful account of my brother? (Ah, how envy, growing contrite, turns charitable.) And how was Mary to avoid confessing that, even before that day by the Lode, to be completely honest, to be completely frank, she'd been – curious? And, putting together this pity and this curiosity, how could we avoid forming a plan?

"Yes, poor Dick."
  "Poor Dick, with only his motor-bike."

And if you add to pity and curiosity just a touch of fear – for Mary also confessed, not without a certain shiver of delight, that, along with her curiosity, she was just a weeny bit . . . and I said (ah, so sure) Dick would never hurt a fly – then you have more than a plan, you have the tangled stuff of which stories are made.

So this is the story of how Mary, aided and abetted by Tom, took upon herself Dick's education, so harshly thwarted in the past. His sentimental education, that is, his training in matters of the heart. This is the story of how Mary tried to teach my mute brute of a brother.
  Or, alternatively, of how Mary's curiosity –
  Or, alternatively, of how a little learning . . .
  It's Mary's story. Told to me on Monday and Thursday afternoons, in instalments, throughout that summer of 1943. While on Wednesday and Saturday evenings – and sometimes on Sundays too . . .

It's Mary's story, pieced together and construed by me. So how can I be sure what really – ?

Eye-witness accounts have it that when, on alternate evenings on his return from work, Dick took a detour off the Gildsey–Hockwell road onto the track running north along Stott's Drain with the object of bringing home in the shape of a sack of live eels what, in those wartime days, formed not only our staple diet but a source of clandestine income, he did not merely haul in the traps and bag what they contained. He lingered over this slimy operation. He interrupted it indeed (the Velocette keeping sentinel close by) to sit and stare at the river at his feet in a manner that could only be described as meditative, if not forlorn. As if thinking still – though she's six years gone now – of his vanished mother; or, conceivably, of another subject, also female and tantalising.

Eye-witness? Yes, because one evening, early in May, there's someone watching him. No, it's not his little brother, not this time. And it's not his resurrected mother. It's Mary. And it's I who've tipped her off about the see-and-not-be-seen properties of that farther river-bank. She watches, unobserved. But the next evening but one she's watching again, this time unconcealed. She's sitting in plain view on the visible slope of the river-bank (knees drawn up, hands round shins, one cheek resting on knees), but so watchfully and motionlessly that it's some while before Dick, intent on tipping eels from trap to sack, sees her.

And when he does (or so I picture it) he freezes, stock-still, in the shocked and disbelieving manner of people whose thoughts have suddenly taken material form.

Mary shouts across the water: "Hello, Dick."

Dick says nothing. Then, after a volume of river water which can never be calculated has slid between them: "Hello."

"Got many?"

"Ma-many?"

"Eels."

A difficult point. Since Dick is being asked, by implication, to count. A testing process at the best of times. He can scurry to ten, stumble, with luck, to twenty. At the best of times eels

215

twined together in the bottom of a sack don't make easy counting. And under those watching eyes . . .

So he nods. Gives a shrewd answer.

"S-some."

Mary lifts her cheek from her knee.

"You see, if you've got any to spare . . . My Dad's fond of eels. So am I. We eat fish every Friday, you know. If you could spare a couple? One big one would do." She nuzzles her chin on her knees. "Haven't you got a nice eel for me?"

Now Dick understands this, or thinks he understands it – because to understand is itself confusing. That is, he understands not only the simple substance of the request, but something profoundly, amazingly deeper. He understands that he, Dick, is being asked to offer her, Mary – yes, it's either Mary or a mirage – a Gift. This is something that no person (if we exclude the rituals of family birthdays when Dick – good with his hands – produced for his Mum such wonders as a money-box made from a cocoa tin) has ever sought of him before. A gift. A gift. Something of his own that another would value. And so momentous is this concept that he is rendered quite incapable of making it actual.

He sits on the river-bank, a twitching sack between his knees. The river flows, unblinking, by.

"Well, never mind," Mary says at length, getting to her feet and brushing down her wartime curtain-fabric skirt. "Another time maybe." And then, perhaps with one of those narrow, knowing looks of hers, which even forty feet of river do not weaken: "I can come again, can't I? You'll be here – on Friday, won't you?"

And this drops into Dick's scheme of things yet another monumental notion. For not only does it suggest that this creature on the far shore takes an interest in him and watches his movements (but then hasn't Dick watched hers?), it suggests something more astounding and unprecedented still, so astounding that in order to appreciate it, Dick has simultaneously to discover for himself previously unimagined mental territory.

It has the air of what other people call (though Dick's never heard the word) an assignation. It unveils that heady realm, known already to countless initiates (including young Tom),

216

to which the password, when uttered in a certain breathy way, may be some such innocent phrase as "Meet me . . .", "See you . . .", "I'll be there if . . ."

It's something you can't get from motor-bikes.

"Ye-yes," he says. "He-here."

She leaves, with a darting smile, before he can say more.

And there's something strange about her departure. She goes, but she doesn't go, exactly. There's something left behind. A feeling. A beautiful feeling. It lingers in the soft evening air. It lingers as Dick rides home, along the Hockwell road, on his back the sack of eels which are in no situation to be experiencing beautiful feelings. And it lingers that evening in the cottage (I observe but don't tell Mary), where Dick, with lashes working furiously, picks and pecks at his eel supper and Dad is driven to ask: "What's up, Dick? What's the matter – not well?"

Now when did Dick ever lose his appetite or ever find anything exceptional in a May evening?

Once again (that very Friday) Dick visits the eel-traps at Stott's Drain. Once again the creature appears, like some conjured genie, on the far bank. Once again, the river flows mutely between them, evoking the plight of Hero and Leander. Again the creature asks, in her maidenly and water-borne voice, for the gift of an eel. And this time she has something with her. A pail. A milking pail (into which before now, before Harold Metcalf's reproving hand slapped hers for stooping to such lowly work, Mary has attempted to squirt the frothing milk of her father's Friesians).

Now clearly she means business. She means to have her gift of an eel. Because she's brought something along to take it home in . . .

"That one," says Mary, "that's a nice one." As Dick, like a gormless fishmonger, holds up, item by item, the contents of his sack.

"You wa-want?"

"Yes please – if it's all right. Please."

Though how do you convey an eel across a river? For, certainly, the last thing it will do is swim across and deliver itself.

217

Dick looks at Mary, gift in hand.

But Mary has an answer to this too. She's been counting on this. She puts down her pail. Settles into her knees-up position.

"You can swim. I've seen you swim – before."

And – if indeed it has ever sunk completely into the Lethe of Dick's brain – it returns again now, it rises, buoyantly and pungently, to the surface: that memory which disturbs and confuses, goads and exacerbates the beautiful feeling. Another eel, in a certain position of intimate proximity . . .

At least six swarms of May midges float over the river, at least a dozen swallows flitter like cupids along the surface of the Leem, taking their evening sips of water and exposing their cherub-breasts to the evening sun, while, fixed and still, Mary stares at Dick and Dick stares at Mary. While, far from still, the chosen eel (it's not so big, but it's no tiddler either) squirms and strains in Dick's grip. And while, if the truth be known, Mary too, beneath her skirt, squirms and tenses just a little (possessing a very good memory). For though it may not be clear from her present behaviour, Mary doesn't entirely like eels. Hasn't liked them ever since –

But there's nothing to say that we shouldn't be drawn by, even desire, what makes us recoil . . .

Mary moves at last. Turns her head in a gesture of impatience and disappointment as if about to make her departure. And no sooner does she do this than Dick, with his free hand, whips off his Wellington boots and plunges, torpedo-fashion, into the river. Not only plunges, but in the very same instant, it seems, reappears on the further side, without having broken surface in between, and clambers out, streaming and mud-stained, like some diluvian creature, still grasping, what's more, in his right hand, a quite dumbfounded eel (it's a remarkable grip that can not only hold an eel but keep holding it under water); so that Mary leaps up, squeals, steps back then forward again, giggles at her own squeal, laughs away her giggle, before recovering her former poise.

But now Dick must present his gift and Mary must receive it. He picks up the pail (yes, he guesses its purpose), half fills it at the water's edge, and drops in the eel. Then, eyelashes beating

218

so hard that they turn into spray the drops descending from his hair, he hands the pail to Mary.

Mary takes it; peers inside.

And a strange thing follows. For despite her qualms regarding eels, for which there are very good reasons, she has to admit that, returned to its native element, no longer wriggling and writhing but curled up passively round the bottom of the pail in a state of semi-shock, this eel is not an unhandsome creature. It's sleek and smooth-skinned. It has little glimmering amber eyes which, for all one knows, could be the windows of a tiny eel-soul. It has little panting gills and, behind them, delicate whirring pectoral fins not unreminiscent of Dick's whirring eyelashes . . .

Mary bends over the pail. Dick bends also; draws nearer.

"Thank you," says Mary. "Thank you. It's beautiful." As if she means to take it home and feed it, in a glass bowl, on the daintiest tit-bits.

"Bootiful," says Dick, looking at Mary. A word he's never used before.

And that's how Dick began to go awooing along the Hockwell Lode. Or, if you prefer, that's how Mary inaugurated a course of instruction . . .

(Let's not go into the details of how, that same evening, Dick wanted to walk with Mary back to Polt Fen Farm. But Mary said no – in his sopping wet state? And with no Wellington boots? But promised to meet him again the next day. Or of how, on Mary's parting, Dick had no option but to swim back the way he came, across this Fenland Hellespont, to his abandoned and – who knows? – jealousy-smitten motor-bike; and, having to account later for his arrival home in a sodden condition, explained that he had swerved into a ditch to avoid an ill-driven farm truck – a story which might have been more plausible and shown an untypical streak of cunning if only his bike had shown also a splash or two of mud. Or of how Mary, in parting from Dick, strode back, pail in hand, towards Polt Fen, while Dick watched, but as soon as she had slipped from Dick's gaze, stopped by one of the drains which join the Hockwell Lode and tipped the eel discreetly into it, where, doubtless, recovering

219

from this spell in the limelight of human intrigue, it continued its obscure and anonymous eel-existence . . .)

But how well does Dick learn? Does he progress? Does he make a keen and responsive pupil? And does Mary prove an able teacher?

And meanwhile, as on Wednesday and Saturday evenings he makes way so generously and tactfully for Dick and waits for the emergence of a new, improved brother, how does little Tom occupy his surplus time? You've guessed it, children. In studies of his own. As a matter of fact, in this burgeoning summer of 1943, while the scales of war tip (victory in Africa, German withdrawals in the east), he's reading for the first time old Carlyle's *French Revolution*.

Does Dick confide in his seemingly heedless, book-burrowing brother about this enlightening liaison of his? Does he offer, while we begin to win the war, excited communiqués of his own? No. But every Wednesday and Saturday evening, on his return from the dredger, he goes through a routine formerly not to be imagined of him. He takes a bath. In our old white-enamel tub, before the kitchen range, he attacks his body with soapy water and a scrubbing brush. With steamy and splish-splashing determination he attempts to expunge from his person, like some incriminating stain, all vestige of that stubborn and degrading smell of silt.

Now see what happens when you dabble in education . . .

But to no avail. Because, scrub and rub though he might, there is still – others can detect it – that residual whiff of the river-bed; and step though he does after these brisk ablutions into clean clothes, he only wraps himself once more in the old contamination. For Mrs Forbes, a Hockwell matron, who for a weekly stipend takes in the Crick laundry, can never quite, though no niggard with her suds and rinsings, expel from Dick's garments that tell-tale odour.

But thus, to his mind, cleansed and purified, his hair combed, slicked and even larded with brilliantine, a hasty supper crammed into his belly, Dick rides off, without a word, every Wednesday and Saturday evening. Dad watches. He does not mistake the signs; even regards them with a certain satisfaction (so, he's normal, in that respect, after all . . .). But Dad doesn't know, and it's just as well, who it is that Dick goes awooing on these twice-weekly sorties. Nor does he know that the reason why his younger son never sees Mary Metcalf after Dick's return from work is so that Dick's education –

So, is he learning? For if he's learning shouldn't this course of lessons be coming to some completion? How much longer is it going to go on? To what advanced and proficient stages is it going to be taken? And supposing it's not such a simple matter of teacher and pupil; supposing Mary's out to learn a thing or two as well. (Ah, how charity, turning again to jealousy . . .)

And, if he's learning, if he's making headway, why these troubled and baffled looks? For they start to appear, as instruction continues, on Dick's blank and impervious face which has scarcely registered such things before. Merest shadows, slightest furrows. An outsider might not see them. But a brother can. And who can say what internal tumult the slightest surface ruffles on the likes of Dick might portend? Is he learning that it's hard to learn? Is there something he doesn't understand? Is he learning that if he'd never set out to learn he'd never have learnt that it's all beyond him?

Why does he hang his head and gaze at the ground? Why, returning on these long summer evenings, does he loiter as of old with his motor-bike by the lean-to, tinker with it, whisper to it, as to some chromium-plated confessor?

Can it be that knowledge has indeed dawned and that Dick, for so long ignorant even of this fact, realises that he's not like other people? He's defective; he's a botched job. And this being the case, perhaps it's time the truth were faced. Perhaps it's time (he confides to his long-suffering Velocette) something better were found to replace this abortive experiment called Dick Crick . . .

Yet he must be learning, or he must be learning and yet not learning and this whole course of lessons has got more serious – and more dangerous – than we imagined. Because one day, over supper (not eels this time, but spam fritters), Dick asks, as if there's something Mary's said he wants to verify:

"Wh-where do ba-babies come from?"

Panic fills Dad's eyes. He looks at Dick. He looks at me – an interrogating, almost accusatory, yet strangely pleading look.

221

Outside, beyond the kitchen window, louring summer rain clouds are marauding the horizon.

"Where do they come from?" he echoes, looking now neither at Dick nor at me, but frantically around the kitchen as if for inspiration (they're baked in the oven . . . they appear one morning in the bread bin . . .).

At length, laying down his knife and fork, swallowing the lump of spam that has lodged temporarily in the pouch of his cheek, he says, with an air of solemn resignation (no yarns this time, no fibs about storks or gooseberry bushes):

"They come from love, Dick. They're made with – Love."

He releases the mystic word then shuts tight his lips – as if it must do its best to cross the dizzy gulf to Dick and not come fluttering back for assistance.

But Dick wants answers, not more conundrums.

"Love," he says. (He's heard this bare little syllable before but never –) "What's lu-love?"

At which Dad's clamped lips open again to form for a moment that old gaping zero.

"Love, Dick, is a feeling. A good feeling. It's like the feeling you felt for your poor Mum. Like the feeling she felt for you."

He looks at his plate. His plate seems to flash back rapid alarm signals.

"That's to say – it's a very important thing. It's a Wonderful Thing. It's the most Wonderful Thing there is – "

A sudden patter of rain. The first thick drops which herald a May downpour plop onto the vegetable patch and slide lachrymosely down the window. That evening Dad (assisted by Dick) will raise the sluice, cranking with extra violence the sluice engine.

Dick sits at the supper table. His big hands, his twenty years, belie the look on his face of a lost little boy.

"Lu-love," he says. Another difficult word.

Who Says?

"But you've got to be kidding, sir. This 'one day you'll be grown up too' stuff, this 'one day you'll be like your parents' crap. Even supposing that's how it is – who says we're going to be around long enough to be parents anyway . . . ?"

The Duke's Head. Mock red velvet. Mock Tudor oak, framing mock Georgian coach-lamps. Amidst the period anomalies, electronic growls, TV-game bleepings. How we advance . . . how we still need our babies' rattles . . .

And how our momentarily commiserative and compliant Price has regained his old confrontationary zeal. Only took a single Bloody Mary. He gulps at a second. (Whatever happened to beer and merriment?)

"And who says if we *are* around that we'll want to have children – the way things are going? Who says there's going to be any world to bring them into?"

(But if nobody has children there won't be any world anyway . . .)

"Who says we'll want to bring children into whatever world there is?"

He looks at me, this founding president of the Holocaust Club, this angry, frightened and denunciatory kid.

(Yes, yes, it's our fault, Price. The old ones. We haven't been vigilant. We've let the world slip away. Should have saved it.)

"Supposing you could have children now, sir, just supposing . . . would you?"

And forgets. And remembers again at once. And flushes; looks confused, guilty, aghast. Wipes a smear of tomato juice from his lip.

A fruit machine vomits. The space invaders close in.

"Sorry. I didn't – "

Too Big

But it's all right, Price. Because, you see, once I had a child. No, I'm talking literally. I'm not talking about now, I'm talking about the year 1943 (now would you have said that was a particularly rosy year for civilisation?). And perhaps I'd better rephrase things: Once Mary had a child. Her menstrual cycle, of which she was so proud and so unsecretive, stopped cycling; she missed a period, and then, bit by bit, things started to happen inside her, just as they're supposed to. And, at sixteen, in the year 1943, amongst all those not-so-much-older-than-me soldiers, sailors and airmen who were hastily sowing their seed and putting something by for posterity during this time of universal crisis (how nature spurs the breeding instinct when the species is threatened) I too faced the prospect of precipitate paternity.

Or would have done. Had not Dick asked, over the kitchen table, a certain question . . . Because how did I know, hearing it all from Mary, just how far those lessons were going every Wednesday and Saturday evening . . . ?

He wants to give her another eel. Another gift from him to her. He keeps on asking, his skin scrubbed and his hair glistening, when would she like another eel? So that Mary is obliged at length to say that there are other things besides eels . . . But then – since they're speaking of eels (and Dick is there to learn) – has Dick never wondered why there is never any shortage of eels, how you can keep pulling them out of rivers by the trapful but there are always more the next time? In other words, where do all the little eels come from?

At which Dick pricks up his ears. And Mary begins to explain. But quickly realises she's picked a bad example; because once she gets beyond saying there are Mummy and Daddy eels (though how do you tell which is which?), she gets into deep water. Because the truth is no one knows exactly how – She comes up against that zoological enigma which so confounded the learned men of old.

And thus I, in due course, make the acquaintance (browsings in the Gildsey Reference Library: By the way, Mary, do you know how eels really – ?) of the intrepid Johannes Schmidt . . .

So Mary decides she'd better not beat about the bush. She starts to talk about Holes and Things.

But Dick doesn't want a biology lesson. What he wants is Lu-lu-love. He wants the Wonderful Thing. Because he asked his Dad. And his Dad never said anything about Holes and Things. And Mary says, but they're all part (it's getting confusing) of the Wonderful Thing. And Dick says what's wonderful about putting something in a hole? And Mary says wouldn't he like to try and see? Now if he were to show her his . . .

And the result of all this is that, after much difficult coaxing – for Dick won't consent at first to such a bizarre operation, and even when he feels an undeniable fire kindling between his legs he's inclined, as once before, to leap into the nearest water to put it out – the result of all this is that it proves Too Big.

Or that's Mary's story. Because first of all Mary's version went like this: We never actually – I just wanted to –

So Mary says that Dick shouldn't worry – that he's too big. It's not his fault and it's not a disaster. For has it never occurred to him that perhaps it's she who's Too Small? And perhaps one day – now he knows all about it, now he's fully versed in the matter – he'll find someone else who's – just right for him.

But, far from reassuring him, far from setting him on the right track and bringing to a close at last this course of instruction, this conjures up before Dick unsuspected complexities. For can it be that this so private business can be done with more than one? This Wonderful Thing – so random and inconstant? Can it be that others – ? That Mary – ?

So she doesn't want him. He's defective, he's no good.

His eyelashes start to whir. His fingers start to clench. He protests, in garbled and stumbling language, to his apparently cooling sweetheart; a protest which couched in plain words might amount to some such uncompromising statement as: Now let's get this clear, you're the only one I love. And since you're the only one I love, then make me a baby. Because that's what love's for, isn't it? Dad says so. And that's what I want. And let's have none of this cock-and-bull nonsense about having to put things into holes.

And, just for good measure, with his big, bewildered hands, he shakes her hard by the shoulders . . .

And what can Mary say? That she can't give him love (let alone a baby)? Because love is what she's giving right now to his little brother? He's the only one she— Not only love (though she can't be sure just yet) but a baby too. So she says, Yes, all right, she'll make him a baby. She's scared by that shaking. And it's not the last one. Yes, yes, of course, she didn't mean to. They'll love each other, yes, and have a baby . . .

A tall order. She'll have to pretend there's such a thing as immaculate conception (and perhaps there is: it seems to work for eels). But then there'll be no real danger, because it really is too big, there's no way that *that* – that that *thing*. And sooner or later, Dick'll just have to realise, he'll just have to accept the fact that no baby's going to appear.

So every time now that Dick goes awooing, even if he can't put his Thing inside, he puts his loving arms round Mary and tries hard to have a baby. He puts his loving hands on Mary's tummy, which, according to Mary, is the place where babies first make their presence known. And after all those shakings (though his free hand sometimes wanders, disconcertingly, towards Mary's shoulder, towards Mary's neck), he's as gentle and as trusting as a lamb, waiting for his baby to come.

And a baby does come . . .

Or that's Mary's story. Because how did I know, how could I be a hundred per cent sure that when Mary said Dick's was too big, it really was too big? And that Mary hadn't proved to herself that it wasn't Too Big, in fact was just right, at the very beginning of our little educational experiment?

And suppose it – the baby that is, this baby you couldn't yet see or touch, which was just a funny feeling inside Mary – was mine, what was Mary going to say to Dick? Because you can't hide a thing like a baby, even from a numbskull. And what would Dick do – ? And given that all along there's this margin of doubt, given that all along it might be – it just might be – really Dick's, then – for God's sake – what should *I* do?

But Mary swears, she crosses her heart and hopes to die, that it isn't Dick's. And down by the Hockwell Lode we still cling and cleave and sigh. So we've made a little one. And it's on the way. But we love each other, don't we? Yes we love each other. And love takes its course, doesn't it? It means we'll have to tell the world, that's all, and face the music. And then get married. It happens all the time. It's an old, old story . . .

Yes, he's persuaded, he's convinced, he's emboldened; and, let's admit it, your history teacher's even a teeny bit proud of what (that's assuming –) he can do.

But sooner or later, because soon it'll start to show – and never mind about telling the world – someone's got to speak to someone.

And we know who spoke first and to whom. We know what she said. We know she steered a straight course between these two amorous brothers to a convenient third party, named Parr. And we know that she did it to protect me.

We know what Dick did. He went out and got Freddie drunk, then pushed him in the river, after first knocking him on the head with a bottle.

And we know what little Tom, whose initiative in this whole affair is so conspicuous by its absence, did. He watched; weighed evidence. Put facts together. Saw a new bruise on an old bruise. Fished a bottle – Ah yes, he's hooked by now, it's got serious, this historical method, this explanation-hunting. It's a way of getting at the truth – or, as you would have it, Price, a way of coming up with just another story, a way of dodging reality . . .

But it's no longer story-time in the land of the Leem. Reality's already imposed itself in the form of a sodden corpse. And it's going to get more pressing, more palpable still . . .

And let's not get the impression that our little keen-eyed sleuth, our junior investigator into questions of cause and effect is being cool, calm and scientific. We know he's not. He's scared. He locks his door against his brother. He's got a nasty feeling in his guts.

And we know what he does, in spite of the evidence he himself has gathered (ah, traitor to his own method) on that day when the Gildsey Coroner's Court records that happy word "Accident" and, rushing off to tell the glad tidings, he encounters a Mary whose notion of cause and effect proves less pliable than his.

Throws a tantrum (tears up grass). Gets – and wants to be – beside himself.

Now why can't everything happen by accident? No history. No guilt, no blame. Just accidents. Accidents . . .

But Mary isn't planning on any self-escapology. She's sitting, still as stone, by the old windmill, and quite inside herself. So inside herself, she might never emerge again. And inside Mary who's sitting so inside herself, another little being is sitting there too.

And then from out of these doubly internal and locked-up regions Mary says: "I know what I'm going to do."

35

Unknown Country

So one day, after teaching the French Revolution, I come home to find that my wife's committed a revolutionary – a miraculous – act . . .

I turn the key in the lock. I hear what sounds like a baby's cry. I think: our golden retriever, Paddy, has some whine-inducing dog-malady. But I hear it again. I enter the living-room. And there she is, sitting on the sofa, at half-past four on a

Friday afternoon, waiting for me to arrive, with a child in her arms.

"I told you. Look, I told you, didn't I? There! I said I was going to have one."

And she's not wearing the looks of a villainous child-thief, she's not wearing the looks of a vicious criminal. She's wearing the looks of a young mother who's never been a mother before. Her face has shed a succession of masks (menopausal wife, ex-age-care officer, history teacher's life-long, long-suffering mate); she's all innocence and maidenhood. A Madonna – and child.

"Christ almighty – !"

Now tread carefully, history teacher. Maybe this isn't your province. Maybe this is where history dissolves, chronology goes backwards. That's your wife over there; you know, Mary, the one you thought you knew. But maybe this is unknown country.

"Mary, what on earth – ?"

"I told you – "

"How – ?"

There's no denying it, she's serene, she's seraphic. Fifty-two years old. She's beautiful.

"Look. Come and look."

"Where did you get it?"

"From God. I got it from God."

"Mary, are you all right?"

"Look."

Your history teacher stands in the doorway, presenting, before this bizarre Nativity, the posture of an awe-struck shepherd (outside, in the night, his flock of pupils are dispersed, having learnt about the dawn of a new age). In his right hand – in place of a crook – his front door key; in his left hand – in place of a lantern – his worn and battered teacher's briefcase, humble emblem of his trade.

He steps forward. Approaches the sofa. But he does not stoop before the blanket-wrapped bundle (a pink, puckered face, tiny groping hands), kneel down, place palms together and let his eyes fill with wondering reverence.

His eyes fill with disbelief. The baby howls. But it's real.

"Mary, you'd better explain."

"You've made him cry."

"Where did you – ?"

"I told you."

"That– That's utter nonsense."

"There, there. Ssh now . . ."

A girl with a doll.

"You've got to tell me. You've taken that baby from some-where – "

"Don't frighten him."

She looks at her husband with wide-open, dreaming eyes.

Then an astonishing scene ensues, confounding all affinities with a mock Adoration. Worthy, rather, the attention of the N.S.P.C.C. The husband makes a grab at the baby. The wife clutches it – now bawling frenziedly – to her breast. Thwarted, the husband starts to shake his wife. The rocking motion has the inadvertent effect of quietening the baby; but now the wife starts to scream.

"You've got to explain."

But this is no way of getting explanations – shaking them out by force.

The husband's hands move again to the baby. He pulls. The wife stops screaming, pulls back.

"Give it to me!"

"No."

"It's someone else's. You must have stolen it."

"No. He's mine. Ours."

Observe, children, your history teacher in action. Yes – for all his droning on, for all his talk-and-chalk – in spontaneous action. Observe him locked in elemental violence. Witness, for contrast, the fastidious surroundings which offset this central whirlwind: a room still preserving its late Regency features, tastefully furnished over a period of thirty years with items to match: old porcelain, leather bindings, Cruickshank prints. A veritable museum. Witness the Chelsea vase on the Sheraton table which, jostled by the sofa which in turn is jostled by the motions of this desperate tug-of-war, topples from its perch and disintegrates on the floor. Observe too the golden retriever, roused from its favourite napping place in a corner of the

230

kitchen, which enters and adds the din of its barking to the racket of screams, baby-hollers and tinkling antiques.

"And the bruises, Mr Crick – to the baby's arms and upper body?"

"They were made in my attempts to take the baby from my wife. My intention being to return it at once to whoever it was taken from."

"From which we may conclude that your wife resisted these attempts – and thus too, such an intention . . . ?"

The wife pulls. The husband pulls. Baby blankets unravel. The dog barks, wanting to join the game. The wife's face contorts – like the baby's. As the husband pulls he cannot suppress the sensation that he is pulling away part of his wife. He is tearing the life out of her.

And perhaps he is. For, yielding the baby at last to his stronger grip, the wife collapses, slumps onto the sofa, buries her face in the seat cushion, sobs, turns her head, reaches out with one arm, wails: "He's my baby! He's my baby . . ."

At which the husband, cast now not in the role of an amazed shepherd but of a ruthless Herod, is driven to think: And supposing, and just supposing . . .

He holds the baby. He places on its forehead an unthinking, an instinctive soothing hand. Sssh-ssh. He holds the baby but he wants to hold his wife. He can't hold the baby and hold his wife too. But if he relinquishes the baby in order to hold his wife, his wife may seize the baby.

He steps forward. He deposits the baby on the lowered flap of a rosewood bureau, out of reach of both wife and snapping dog. He sits on the sofa, raises his wife, clasps her, starts to say extraordinary things:

"You're *my* baby. You're *my* baby . . ."

Can you imagine, children? Your learned and sagacious Cricky – mouthing such stuff? But look closer, children – your Cricky's crying.

He rocks her, this baby of his, this former protectress of his perpetuated schooldays.

"Mary, explain – "

The golden retriever, left out of things, nuzzles its head on the sofa; yaps, growls. Your history teacher gives it a sharp, a sudden, a ferocious kick.

"How? Why? Why?"

"God told me. God . . ."

But God doesn't talk any more. Didn't you know that, Mary? He stopped talking long ago. He doesn't even watch any more, up there in the sky. We've grown up now, and we don't need him any more, our Father in Heaven. We can fend for ourselves. He's left us alone to make what we will of the world. In Greenwich, in the midst of a vast city, where once they built an observatory precisely to stare back at God, you can't even see at night, above the aurora of the street-lamps, God's suspended stars.

God's for simple, backward people in godforsaken places.

"Mary, whose baby is it?"

"I've told you."

"Where did it come from?"

(Still rocking, while broken china litters the floor, while on the mantelpiece a carriage clock strikes half-past four, while a dog whimpers with a cracked jaw and a baby wails and wriggles precariously on an escritoire.)

"He told me . . ."

"*Mary.*"

"All right, all right. I got him from Safeways. I got him from Safeways in Lewisham."

36

About Nothing

Don't apologise, Price. Though perhaps we'd better drink up and go. It doesn't help, after all, does it, this drunkenness? I know what you feel. Yes, the end of the world's on the cards again – maybe this time it's for real. But the feeling's not new.

Saxon hermits felt it. They felt it when they built the pyramids to try to prove it wasn't true. My father felt it in the mud at Ypres. My grandfather felt it and drowned it with suicidal beer. Mary felt it . . . It's the old, old feeling, that everything might amount to nothing.

37

Le Jour de Gras

The guillotines are hissing in the Place de la Révolution. They have been hissing now for months and will go on hissing for some months yet. Who can stop them hissing? Who can curb their unappeasable appetite? And who can stop the hunger in the faces of the crowd who watch, wet their lips, jeer and cheer. Yes, children, this is the fact that every schoolboy knows about the French Revolution. That it was all to do with guillotines. This is what makes even the most bored and insouciant pupil find History just a little bit engrossing. That hiss-hiss of the descending blades. And yes, old gap-toothed crones really did sit and do their knitting beneath the scaffold; and, yes, there were several recorded instances of corpses that wriggled, kicked – rolled their eyes, moved their lips, screamed – after the head was severed from the body.

Shall we watch, children? Not just once to see what it's like, but over and over again, for months on end? Shall we watch the crop of heads mounting in the baskets? Or are you beginning to feel sick already? Are you beginning to feel that History is all made nonsense by that sensation in the pit of your stomach, that tingling in your finger-tips and that swimming feeling in your head and knees? It's called terror, children. The feeling that all is nothing. There is your subject, your lesson for today.

Or would you prefer to turn your back and walk away? Shall we leave the guillotines to go on working by themselves, shall we leave History to its own devices, and would you prefer, after all, a fairy-tale instead?

Then let me tell you (I hope it won't remind you of that dreadful hissing in the distance)

38

About the East Wind

It has its birth in the Arctic Ocean, north of Siberia. It steals round the northerly tip of the Urals, unleashes itself across the North European and Finnish Plains, gathers itself up again in the Baltic, attempts to sever the neck of Denmark and (if it has lost by now any of its scything keenness, it has it honed back again by the waves of the North Sea) assails the east coast of England. And some people say that the Wash, that gaping wound in the backbone of Britain, is not formed by the effects of tides and rivers and geology, but is simply the first bite the East Wind takes out of the defenceless shoreline with its ice-whetted incisors.

The East Wind blew particularly bitingly in January, 1937. And it blew in with it not only the breath of the Arctic and of half a frozen Europe, but also the influenza, called by some, who claimed to know, the Asian or Russian influenza, or, perversely, for such a wintry malady, the Spanish influenza, but called by most, including those, who weren't so few, who succumbed to it and died, plainly and briefly, the Flu.

It laid low several pupils of the Hockwell Village School, one of whom, poor little Roger Pearce, never recovered. It afflicted Walter Dangerfield, the General Store-keeper and Mrs Finch, landlady of the Volunteer Inn. Jack Parr caught a dose but his stalwart wife and plentiful hot whisky pulled him through. Two old people in Apton got it and were dead within a week. And another in Wansham; and another in Sudchurch. In Gildsey the General Hospital improvised a special ward; likewise the Kessling Hall Hospital, albeit designated for mental patients. Doctors Fry of Apton and Bright of Newhithe, to name but two of their hard-pressed profession, had a busy time of it, not to mention the labours of the district nurses. And just to show that physicianship does not confer immunity, Doctor Fry, poor overworked soul who should have retired long ago to Bournemouth or Torquay, went down with a severe bout and was left with a permanent chest complaint.

Henry Crick escaped. And Dick Crick never got it (or if he did, never knew it). But your history teacher was put to bed one Friday and didn't get up till the following Wednesday, during which interval the stories which his mother told him, in her inimitable fashion, to soothe and console him, failed to perform their normal office. For, far from issuing from his mother to confer on him their balm, they seemed instead to be rising up to envelop and overwhelm her, casting round her their menacing miasmas, so that through his hours of fever he strove to cleave a passage through to a mother who was becoming less and less real, more and more besieged by fiction. But he couldn't, because these same stories had taken hold of parts of his own body and of the infinitely treacherous bedclothes; they were running coded messages along his bloodstream and performing non-stop variations of themselves inside his skull, so that he himself was in danger of becoming – a figment . . . Until, on the Monday morning, he awoke to find his mother perfectly real and palpable, not to say smiling and relieved, sitting on the bed and about to suggest a little light sustenance; while outside the window, beyond the frost-rimmed glass (for with his fever that malign east wind seems to have dropped too), across a room whose outer coldness presents a happy contrast to now cosy and trustworthy blankets, the morning sun is shining on a flat and stable world that is also lucidly real and clear. There is the distant tower of Ely; and there is the distant chug – throaty in the frosty air – of the 8.25 to Lynn. And he finds it hard to believe that such plainly immaterial things as stories should ever have proved so predatory and besetting . . .

But. But. Now it's his mother's turn to take to her bed. The flu has flown from him to her. And that wind, after a week or so's glassy lull, has revived again with redoubled force. It's booming in the chimneys; it's rattling the window panes; it sharpens the icicles on the eaves; it shears off the surface of the Leem and deposits it on the concrete tow-path where it turns to a hard and perilous film; it sends bone-chilling darts through every crack and cranny of the cottage. Yet amidst all this, amidst this onslaught of cold, his mother sweats and tosses, just as he once did. And now, in all fairness, it should be his turn to sit beside her, comfort and soothe. But it won't do any good. Because there was prophecy in little Tom's fever-dreams. Because, though no one knows it yet, his mother won't get up out of that bed again. Because, in a word, she's dying.

Though no one knows it yet. The fever runs its course. But when it departs it doesn't leave a restored, a recognisable mother, washed up on the safe shores of recovery and not minding if she does have some milky porridge with a large dollop of treacle. It leaves a changed, sunken woman, not at all like the woman of before. Moreover, the wind which announced your history teacher's recovery by ceasing and letting the sun shine on spangled winter tranquillity, doesn't cease for her. It continues to scream and howl. It's a terrible wind.

And it was because that wind didn't stop, though it did for him, because that wind didn't stop though the fever did, that your history teacher, without being told and mere child of nine though he was, knew.

Perhaps the wind wouldn't stop till she –

And it was plain that Dad knew too. Because of that brightness in his face. For in those days of Mother's gradual decline an imperturbable good cheer wrapped his features, a benign smile moulded his lips, a gleam lodged in his eye. As if, by his adopting consistently and resolutely enough this posture of optimism, reality might be persuaded to follow suit; as if by never showing that he recognised the truth, the truth might turn out not to be the truth after all.

But who knows what he did with this rigid mask all those hours that he sat, unseen by us, watching and waiting, behind the closed bedroom door? For whether or not it would have done any good for little Tom to sit too by his mother – telling her or not telling her curative stories – it is Dad who monopolises this vigilant function. All through the day he watches, while down below, Dick, aged nearly fourteen but like his brother excused on compassionate grounds from school, chips ice from the lock-gates with fingers that do not seem to feel the cold;

superintends, with stolid efficiency, the passage upstream of rime-coated lighters, but only shrugs uncommunicatively before the inquiries of the chilled-to-the-marrow lightermen who have heard that Mrs Crick is proper poorly, leaving it to his otherwise unassisting brother (swathed in two coats, scarf, mittens and his father's outsize balaclava helmet, and trying not to snivel) to offer the gallant lies: "She's not so bad, Mr Bailey, thank you. We think she's getting better . . ."

All through the night he watches; while in our room Dick snores and I lie awake listening for sounds across the passage-way and praying (yes, praying: Please G.·d, please, let this not be happening . . . Please God, if you don't let Mummy die, I'll . . . I'll . . .), and the wind comes and goes, howls and whimpers, but doesn't stop, and the cottage, creaking and groaning, seems more and more like a ship far out at sea that has lost its rudder.

It's only occasionally and guardedly, as if smitten with some peculiar form of jealousy, that he lets us enter the sick-room. He ushers us in, sometimes with a finger to his lips, as if into the presence of something rare and priceless, as if to behold the crown jewels. He smiles fixedly. He smiles exactly the sort of oafish smile a father smiles when a new little baby's just been born. And that's just what Mother looks like – like a little helpless baby tucked up under the sheets. A little baby with an old woman's voice.

What's become of my beautiful, grown-up Mummy? We sit, one on either side of the bed, Dick on the left, I on the right; Dad, in his chair, drawn up at the foot, one of his hands clutching Mother's blanket-wrapped ankle. She croaks, after a long pause in which it seems she will never quite find enough breath to speak, "Well this . . . is a fine . . . state of things . . . isn't it?" With an air of almost-levity. But her eyes say something different. They say: Look children, your mother's dying. In a little while she won't be here any more. It's a unique, a momentous event. Unique and momentous, not to say unexpected, for your mother too. It only happens once, it won't be repeated for you. Note it, observe it.

(And I did, children, very carefully. And though, indeed, it only happened once, it's gone on happening, the way unique and momentous things do, for ever and ever, as long as there's a memory for them to happen in . . .)

Dick sits, unmoving, by the bed; his lashes flicker. But I turn round to look at Dad. Whose face beams back; whose eyes twinkle: Isn't she lovely? Isn't she wonderful? Isn't she a beautiful baby?

(When is the mask going to drop? Not yet. Not yet.)

We troop out. We troop in again. Between our rationed visits Dad remains at his station, nursing this woman who once, years ago, nursed him; emerging only to descend to the kitchen, to concoct soups and hot drinks and refill hot water bottles; or to carry downstairs other kinds of vessels – Mother's poor last feeble passings – whose contents he empties down the lavatory.

I think: Can this go on for ever? This being-on-the-edgeness. This trance of Dad's. This wind. This hearing Mother say, A fine state of things, when it isn't.

I pray to God: Please God, don't let it go on like this for ever. Please God, if it's got to happen, make Mummy be no more. Let it be over, let it be done with . . .

Now how could I be praying this when only a while ago I was praying . . . ?

But it doesn't go on for ever. The fact that it's not going to go on for ever is announced, in the first place, by Doctor Bright who on one of his medicinal visits doesn't, as is his wont, thrust his stethoscope back into his bag, utter a few grave if calm instructions and depart at once with the air of a man in justified haste (Don't you know I've got other patients to see? Don't you know there's a flu epidemic?). He is slow to leave. He accepts Dad's offer of a cup of tea in the kitchen. I officiate with the kettle. He engages Dad, or attempts to do so, in conversation. Not doctor's talk, mind you (unless something's already been said up in the bedroom), but a groping effort at casual chit-chat.

For example, after first stirring his tea much more than is necessary, then cocking an eye, out of the kitchen window, towards the hen-coop:

"Do they keep laying then, even in this weather?"

Dad: "Yes, they lays. Not much. But they lays. Bless 'em."

(One of my jobs during Dad's nursing duties: to fling daily handfuls of feed into the coop, and to remove with cold fingers from under the bellies of resigned and apparently frost-proof hens, the odd warm egg. Warm. Incredibly warm . . .)

But there's something about the very by-the-wayness of this talk; there's something about the slope of Doctor Bright's shoulders and the fact that his stethoscope, apparently forgotten, is still dangling round his neck, as if he might use it at any moment, instead of that overworked spoon, for his tea; there's something about the way Dad starts without knowing it to rub his knee, so that Doctor Bright gratefully latches on once more to a professional topic; there's something about the way they concern themselves with such curious intentness with this knee (an old wound, always worse in cold weather) while, up above, Mother . . . There's something about all this which doesn't deceive even nine-year-old Tom (". . . and we're fighting fit again, are we, young soldier?" – as Doctor Bright at last packs away his stethoscope); which fills him with far from by-the-way feelings.

Dad walks with Doctor Bright to his car, via the back path round the edge of the vegetable patch to avoid those treacherous glaciers on the tow-path. I watch him return, from the kitchen window. His mask has gone. His face doesn't have any expression at all. He pauses on the path, unaware that he's being observed, apparently heedless of the bitter cold. His shoulders start to shake. His head is turned. He's not shivering. It's not the effect of the icy wind. Little abrupt spasms are seizing him by the neck.

I start back from the window. I run up the stairs and open the door where Mother is. Her eyes move. Open. Her eyes look at me. But the strange thing is that she says, "Dick?"

And it's announced, in the second place, by Dad's entering our room late that night and shaking Dick into wakefulness. It takes a long time to haul Dick from his oblivious slumbers, and while the rousing goes on I pretend I'm asleep too. But I half open one eye and in the beam of light from the open door I read the time on our bedroom wall-clock – an elaborate affair with a wooden face shaped like a plump, perching owl (perpetually chased by a ravenous yet lifeless pike three feet further along the wall). The

239

hour hand is straight between the owl's eyes. It's ten minutes past midnight, on the morning of the twenty-fifth of January, 1937.

"Dick, your mother wants to see you. Dick – "

He won't let Dick slip back into his cocoon of sleep. He shakes him; pulls off the covers. Makes him stumble out, in his pyjamas, into the freezing draughts of the room. Fetches his dressing-gown from the hook behind the door.

"Your mother wants to see you. Quiet. Be quiet."

He leaves Dick to step for a moment towards my bed. I sense him stooping over me. I feign the deep breathing of undisturbed sleep. Outside the wind utters its own restless gasps. Then he returns to Dick and propels him without another word out of our room, shutting the door behind him.

So this is the hour of my mother's death. Then why only Dick? Then why should Dick and not I – ?

But it can't be the hour of my mother's death. Because a few seconds later I hear the door across the passage open again, then close, and footsteps make their way downstairs. They're Dad's footsteps. So Dick is alone with Mother.

The wind moans and judders at the window, masking other sounds. Your history teacher tumbles from his bed, tiptoes across the floor, crouches by the door, not minding the icy fingers which play about his toes, and listens. He hears the faint, laboured tones of his mother, but distinguishes scarcely a word. However, these are not the tones of valediction but of earnest injunction. He makes out (or does he? Did he supply them six years later?) the words "Open" and "Eighteen". He hears Dick – for it cannot be Mother, she cannot have got so miraculously to her feet again – cross the room and (or so he fits actions to sounds) pull out a drawer in the chest of drawers which stands in the far corner of the parental bedroom, fumble amongst its contents, then return to the bedside. His mother's voice drops, even from its previous husky level (all this while Dick, it seems, says nothing); then rises again to a sudden desperate intensity:

"Dick . . . Dick . . . darling Dick . . ."

And from Dick a single, blockish, vaguely inquisitive "Mummy?".

240

Now why Dick? Why his name – even when his brother Tom opened the door?

But no time to think further on the matter. No time – as this baffled eavesdropper has almost a mind to do – to burst open doors, to dash across the passage, to fling himself upon his mother's brittle form and to demand, why not him? Why this exclusion? Some last word for him too?

Because he hears the latch on that farther door being lifted: Dick is coming out. And at the same time he catches Dad's tread at the foot of the stairs. So all along he's been loitering there? Straining perhaps, too, to hear?

He darts back to his bed; and almost simultaneously with Dick's opening the door and entering, dives beneath the covers and resumes the attitude (though with a heartbeat no sleeper ever had) of unbroken repose.

And almost simultaneously with Dick's reappearance, Dad's tread hastily mounts the stairs and Dad enters again through the door that Dick has not yet shut. He ushers Dick back to bed, just as surely as he roused him before. And Dick, who throughout this strange episode must have remained in a state verging on somnambulism, so that, come daylight perhaps, it will all seem like a dream, is in no condition to resist Dad's bidding or to ask him (Dick, who never asked questions – till he asked one big and fatal one) what all this is about.

Yet Dad, while he busily tucks the blankets round Dick, has the unmistakable air of a man who'd like to ask questions, who'd like to make sure of something. Yet restrains himself; thinks twice about it . . . Better to rely on this sleepy stupor, better to rely on this inveterate ignorance. "Go to sleep now, Dick. Go to sleep . . ."

As if he might be saying, "And forget everything, forget everything . . ."

There's something Dick knows that perhaps he shouldn't. There's something Dick's come by Dad would rather he hadn't.

And so there is. Because after Dad leaves – after first checking once more that little Tom is sound asleep – Dick puts something, something that rattles metallically, something that must have been clenched all along in one of his over-large hands, on his bedside cabinet.

A brass key.

I wait for the rhythm of Dick's snores to return. I creep out of bed and in the shivery darkness feel that mysterious object on the bedside cabinet. A key. Yes, a key. I return to my bed. I lie awake. No more sleep for me that night. I listen to the wind. I hear carried on its blasts and thus rendered somehow crazy and random like the sound of a bell flying through the air, the chimes of Hockwell church. The thinnest of gauzy lights penetrates the room from under the door. So the light is on, across the passage, where Dad sits with Mother. I imagine I hear – but surely it is some trick of this deranging wind – the sound of subdued human sobs.

Ah, wild, pitiless wind, blowing through the small hours of the twenty-fifth of January, 1937. In such a wind Saint Gunnhilda would have crouched in her wattle cell, hearing the roaring of the Devil. In such a wind old Jacob Crick would have cowered in one of his windmills (its sails removed, tail-pole lashed to the ground), expecting at any moment the whole creaking edifice to be blown to kingdom come . . .

Dawn breaks on the morning of January the twenty-fifth. Dick – who just as unfailingly as he sleeps soundly at night is unfailingly aroused by the first glimmering of day – wakes. His clenched eyes part. They stare at a brass key. So it wasn't a dream; it really happened. Then they stare at me, awake in the other bed, staring also at the key and at Dick staring at the key. And no sooner does Dick's stare catch mine than a hand shoots out from beneath the bedclothes, grabs the key and plucks it out of sight – as if the very swiftness of this action will make it seem that it never occurred and no key had ever been there in the first place.

Now if Dick had never caught me staring so intently at the key perhaps he would never have come to the conclusion – or given away so plainly that he had done so – that this key must be a special key.

But I don't mean to leave things here. I get out of bed. As if to defend his territory, Dick gets out of bed too. The key is either wrapped inside his fist or lodged in some fold of pillow or sheet.

His eyes flutter. I am about to say – in a voice neither too importunate nor too mildly disinterested – "Dick, what's that key?"

But I don't. Because it's at this precise moment that Dad opens the door and, since he finds us both out of bed and close enough to each other to come within the span of his arms, gathers us in that crushing, never-to-be-forgotten embrace which can only be described as maternal; and with a face already anointed and now turning rapidly again to liquid, says, "Children" (yes, he called us that), "your mother's gone. She's gone. Gone."

Gone.

And so too – because despite this rending announcement everything around us is strangely steady and still: the Leem is calm, the sky beyond the window is smooth, clear oyster-pink – has the wind.

So we buried Mother in Hockwell churchyard. And Dad began to grow flowers in a corner of the vegetable patch to place upon her grave. Though, flowers or no flowers, scarcely a day passed by during those following months when he did not visit that patch of bumpy grass behind the church and loiter there, abandoning his lock-keeper's duty for a duty that he clearly regarded as more consuming and imperative. Sometimes I went with him, watched him at a distance, this strange man who was also my father. And during these sorrowful excursions of Dad's, Dick – excused now more or less permanently from school on account of both his classroom ineptitude and the recent loss sustained by his family – learnt, as he'd begun to do when Mother first took to her bed, to take command of the lock. To acquire (no one told him, it came by instinct) the knacks and know-how of the waterside; to deal with lighters and barges; to maintain that precarious yet vital relationship between river and sluice. And thus it was during this period – this period not only of graveside meditations but of moonlit eel-fishing and sleepless moochings on the tow-path – that the already thin spectre of Dick's education faded and vanished altogether; that headmaster Allsop concluded and Henry Crick agreed, that if there was little brain there was no lack of serviceable brawn. And that there arose between Dad and Dick, now that they shared the same labours, a kind of special bond; but a bond, which if you observed closely, was built not so much on trust and co-operation as on the desire of the former to keep a close and careful watch on the latter.

Thus, urged by both natural inclination and his father's attentions, Dick grew up to be a true descendant (so one might have said) of his dogged, water-taming, land-preserving Crick ancestors.

Save that Dick –

But all this is to leap ahead – and to pass over the immediate effects of that terrible January dawn.

Now Dad, it is to be noted, while he clasped us so fervently in his arms, did not utter the word "dead". The word he used was "gone". And throughout the succeeding days, despite Doctor Bright's arrival to complete the death certificate, despite Mother's transference from bed to coffin and, with due accompanying ritual, to her grave, he never let pass his lips either the word "dead" or the word "death".

And while there is much to be commended in the use of that euphemism "Gone" before two sons, one too young perhaps and the other too doltish to understand, there is also much to be questioned. For "Gone", in such circumstances, is a far more elusive word. To little Tom, whose whole life might have been different if his father had told him what his infant heart was already braced to accept – that his own Mum was dead, no more, finished, extinct – this word "Gone" carried the suggestion of some conscious, if perverse decision on his mother's part, as if she had not ceased absolutely to exist but was somewhere very far away, inaccessible, invisible, yet still there.

"Gone", in other words, echoed with mystery. Whilst "dead" is a blunt word for a blunt and natural phenomenon. "Gone" – awesome and open-ended – required Explanation. It made your infant history teacher's mind – which was getting on quite well with "What" and "How" first throb to the gong-beat of Whywhywhy. (And we know what that led to.) It made him set out, in ways of which he was scarcely conscious and over which he had scarcely any control, to find again, at least to revive in some new form (ah, bashful, yearning railway journeys . . .) the image of his departed Mummy.

And thus little Tom's reaction to his Mother's death, for all its protracted after-effects, was perhaps no different in essence from the crude response of his brother, which had it ever been voiced – amidst all his blinking bafflement – might have amounted to: "Well, if she's gone, when is she coming back?"

And as for Dad: had he used that word "Gone" merely out of consideration for his children? For if he really believed himself that Mother was no more and not somewhere where communication, if ever so distant, were still possible, what was he doing making these repeated trips to the graveyard and standing there, with his lips moving *as if he were talking to someone*; and telling us, furthermore, about a far-off place called Heaven?

And so all three surviving occupants of the Atkinson Lock cottage were perhaps united in a common belief: that Mother who was dead wasn't really dead at all, that from some hidden vantage point she still watched over them and held the cottage under her protection.

Ah, Fenland superstition. The dead are dead, aren't they? The past is done with, isn't it?

But sometimes there are ways of unlocking that sealed-up domain, of exposing to the corrosive air its secret contents. And Dick had a key.

Which he hid. For when, after making that fateful if ill-judged announcement, Dad led us both across the upstairs passage – because he wouldn't deny or spare us this final privilege – to take our last look at Mother, little Tom fell into such a fit of wailing and blubbering – which did nothing to help Dad's own steadily welling tears – that he quite forgot about that hastily snatched-from-view key. And before grief allowed him to re-member it, Dick plainly took steps to conceal it. For – while Dad is in mournful conference with Doctor Bright and Dick carries out more ice-chipping on the lock gates – Tom conducts a distraught yet rigorous search of Dick's bed and its surround-ings. He feels for lumps in the pillow and amongst the blankets;

245

lifts the mattress; scans every inch of floor beneath the bed; explores the frugal contents (several cocoa tins, the skull of a water rat) of Dick's rickety bedside cabinet; checks cupboards and drawers.

No key.

Yet one day – to be precise, five days after Mother's death and only two after her interment in Hockwell churchyard, by which time that word "Gone", which on the occasion of that final view of Mother perhaps held for Dick no tearful implications (Gone? But she's right there. She's only decided to lie still for a while) had begun to exert its power – I hear Dick mount the attic stairs. I hear Dick and I hear the wind. For it's come back. But it's not the wind that's making those creaks. From the foot of the main staircase I hear those tell-tale sounds which I am destined to hear years later from behind a locked and barricaded door. Dick descends. I mount the main stairs, feigning a casual need to go to our bedroom. Dick's hands are empty. But his eyelids are twitching, less, it seems, at coming face to face with me (even eyelids have their nuances) than on account of some inward puzzlement or disappointment.

And one day, after school, ascending again to our bedroom, who should I discover within it but Dad, who starts guiltily at my entrance, as if caught in some stealthy act, as if he were *looking for something*, and to cover his confusion yet no doubt with another purpose too, says: "I was thinking. Perhaps it's time you had a bedroom of your own. Perhaps it's time we moved you into the back room."

And then (by now Mother's been Gone nearly three weeks and still hasn't come back) Dick makes another ascent to the attic. He should be dutifully exercising his newly acquired office of deputy lock-keeper. For Dad has left once more to walk through Hockwell village (where curtains will be plucked and people will observe: There he goes, there goes poor Henry Crick again) to his rendezvous in the churchyard. But scarcely is he out of sight than Dick leaves his post of trust and, with an air of resolution rare for Dick, enters the cottage and climbs the stairs.

I skulk meanwhile in the kitchen, my hands daubed with flour. For if Dick can step into Dad's lock-keeper shoes, I put about me Mother's apron. On this chill Saturday afternoon I am endeavouring to make scones as Mother once made them. I am engaged in culinary necromancy. With the aid of that swaddling apron, with the aid of the mixing bowl which she once held in the crook of her elbow, with the aid of the wooden spoon which she once – , I am trying to conjure, to absorb into myself, the spirit of my dead Mummy. So that when Dad returns, pinched with cold from all that standing around in the graveyard, he will bite into his warm scone and –

But I have tried this remedy before. My kitchen travesties have only brought pain to my father's heart. And stomach. While he smiles at me thinly for the tenderness of the gesture, my leaden and hapless scones have stuck in his already lump-laden throat . . .

And there'll be no scones today, in any case, like Mother made or not. Because Dick comes down the stairs and catching me, all ears, in the kitchen doorway, grips me by the shoulders and jostles me along the hallway to the front door. The cold air of the tow-path strikes my oven-toasted face.

"You do," says Dick, flinging out a hand to indicate the lock. "You do. I go."

By which I gather that Dick is delegating in turn the power delegated to him. He wants me to mind the lock – me with my flour-covered hands – while he apparently has business of his own.

"Yes, Dick," I say, "all right." More with the intention of not appearing to question this curious command than of obeying it. For there's something undoubtedly fraught about Dick's voice, and, moreover, there's something – something bulging and hard – hidden under his navy blue sweater, held there by a cradling hand. I see what it is when, while I pretend to be busy in the kitchen, removing Mother's apron, he quickly transfers it, first to the little hall table and then, after donning his coat, to his coat pocket.

A bottle. A bottle of all things. Brown glass . . .

Buttoning his coat with his left hand, thrusting his right into the already loaded pocket so that its cargo can no longer be spotted, he steps out onto the tow-path and turns, without a further word, in a downstream direction.

I emerge too onto the tow-path and watch him stride away along the southern bank of the river, with the slightly hunched and encumbered gait of someone walking with something much on his mind – which is not Dick's way of walking at all.

A backward glance. I adopt an air of vaguely vexed responsibility.

But my concern is not with my dubiously conferred – and, for a ten-year-old with a fetish for his mother's apron, unlikely – assignment.

That afternoon (raw, misty: an unmelted frost) the Atkinson Lock cottage lay deserted. Neither lock-keeper nor lock-keeper's sons were in occupation – though each, in his own way, was intently occupied. If the lightermen of the Gildsey Coal Company had chosen that time to require admittance through the lock, they would have had to assist themselves. And if Mrs Henry Crick did indeed still linger in some unseen way about her former home – though how could she have been in three places at once: in the cottage, in the churchyard, and in that bottle Dick was carrying? – she would have smelt, with spiritual nostrils to match those of a certain fire-sniffing forbear, the smell (for I forgot one little thing) of over-baking, nearly burning scones.

What hope for stealth in a flat land? What hope for detective work in the featureless Fens? What hope even for a four-foot high, ten-year-old detective in this level country where all is conspicuous and nothing is hidden from God? . . . Were it not for the fact that drained land sinks and the rivers get raised; and this means high banks.

For while Dick walks, with that walk that is not his usual walk, along the crest of the southern bank of the Leem, who walks simultaneously on the northern side? Though not along its crest but, concealed, on its landward side – having first crossed the river by the lock and sluice and, by means of a little hasty sprinting, drawn level with his brother. Who scrambles every so often up the hoary northern slope of this northern bank, pokes a furtive head above the ridge to check on the other's progress, then scrambles, slips, slides back down again? Who, when his brother on the southern side halts at a certain watery junction, namely the mouth of Stott's Drain, halts also on his side; not only halts, but in perhaps the very spot where six years later Mary Metcalf will make her own observations of this same brother, clambers to just beneath the summit of that northern-facing slope and lies chest down, sniper fashion, on the frost-sugared grass – a position scarcely wise for a boy only recently recovered from a bout of flu? But so warmed is he from running and scrambling and by the heat of curiosity, and so scornful, anyway, of any discomfort the world can muster after the loss of a mother, that he feels neither cold nor damp.

Dick stares at the water. Stares around him at the wintry landscape as if to confirm that he's quite alone. Then he takes the bottle out of his coat pocket and stares at that too.

Across the river, while ice melts beneath him, his brother thinks: So Mother's secret legacy to Dick is nothing more than a few old bottles . . . So that chest up in the attic is no more than a fancy beer-crate.

No more? Dick unscrews the stopper from the bottle; lifts the bottle to his lips. Never in his life, so far as I know, has Dick drunk a bottle of beer. Even an ordinary bottle of beer . . .

He swallows; wipes his mouth. Squats down on the bank. Stares hard at the river. Swallows again; drains with a sudden voracity the whole bottle. Stares. Tries suddenly to get up, but squats down again. Tries again; falls; staggers at last to his feet. Breaks suddenly into a wild laugh, then into wailing, wordless, unmelodious song. Does a sort of dance, a slow and clumsy waltz with himself; laughs again; hoots, cackles. And then, simultaneously cutting short his dance, stops hooting and cackling, sinks to his knees, puts a hand to his belly; feels his arms, his legs, his head to see if they are still there. His eyelids have never whirred so fast. A look of disbelief – of guilt, terror – crosses his face. A look not unlike the look he will give on a certain day by the Hockwell Lode, when something inside his woollen bathing trunks starts to stir unsuspectedly. He sits, but can't stay still, as if he'd never guessed quite what dangerous stuff he was made of, and he has to get away from it. But the only way to get away from it is to leap out of his own skin. He bobs and bounces, wriggles and rolls his eyes (across the river, his younger brother can hardly keep still either, and his eyes pop too in amazement). Then he realises he's still clutching the bottle. It's not him at all; it's the stuff inside the bottle. But how could his mother − ? As a last, parting gift − ? And with a confused and anguished cry − as if, for all his terror, he is throwing away some potential parcel of bliss, some part of his own unconsummated flesh − he hurls the bottle in a lofty, arcing trajectory into the river. Where, floating, tilting, slowly replacing its former potent contents with plain river-water, it sinks . . .

And that's why Dick never touched again a drop of anything out of a bottle, including Freddie Parr's proffered tots of purloined whisky. And why, perhaps, though he still possessed the key, he never opened again that extraordinary chest, till he realised how its contents might help him.

Minus the bottle, Dick still reels and staggers, still can't decide whether to sit or stand, to move this way or that. Against a background of toneless beet fields, against the mistily receding perspective of Stott's Drain, against the grey neutrality of the winter sky, he makes a bizarre, an engrossing picture . . . But careful, little detective. Perhaps you've seen enough. Time to make your secret get-away. Time to slip back to the cottage, before either Dad or Dick returns so that neither will suspect −

And so he does − slips literally, aided by those frost sprinklings which quicken his descent down the bank and almost result in a sprained ankle − and, with clothes wet from lying on winter grass and thoughts in a whirl from what he has witnessed, returns along the foot of the northern bank.

But something else happens after that strange performance of Dick's with the bottle. Something else starts to make itself felt, faintly and scarcely noticed at first, after the plunging of that same brown-glass vessel, like a mock-Excalibur, into the river. A breeze gets up. It gets stronger by the minute. It disperses the mists. It ruffles the Leem. No doubt it rustles the holly bushes in Hockwell churchyard and shakes the ivy on Hockwell church tower. It's blowing hard, fanning raw embers from the ashes of the western sky, by the time I get back − to rescue from the oven, before they too catch fire, a dozen blackened scones.

The East Wind.

39

Stupid

And that same East Wind – or rather not the same, but its summer sibling, its winsome, hot-breathed sister (for, as any Fenman will tell you, the East Wind isn't just one wind, it's twins, and one twin kills and the other ripens) – was blowing one Thursday afternoon in August, 1943, blowing, in visible waves, across the poppy-splashed wheat fields of Polt Fen Farm, blowing through the poplars by the Hockwell Lode, making their dry leaves shimmer and jingle, as I followed the familiar route yet again to our decapitated windmill.

Because though we had made no more arrangements to meet, because though the last time we had met, Mary walked away as if our windmill assignations were over for ever, and a whole week had passed since then – a whole week since Freddie Parr was accorded an official cause of death – I still hoped to find Mary. And I had to talk. Because for three days now I'd been playing this game of fear with Dick, this bottle game, and I didn't know if Dick was more afraid of me or I of him. And it couldn't go on like this. So should we tell? Own up? Go to the police? Because, sooner or later, all our little secrets are going to come out, aren't they? Should we tell, Mary? Mary, what – ?

(You see, children, even then, the historian's besetting sin: how he ponders contingencies, how he's no good at action.)

And another thing, since we're speaking of secrets, that bottle came out of a chest, an old chest up in the attic which belonged to my grandfather, and Dick's the only one with a –

But I stop at the edge of the poplar spinney. For though it's gone five o'clock, though it's late in that magic interval – three to five-thirty – in which, in those never-to-come-again times, we would regularly meet, Mary is indeed at the windmill. And she's doing something very strange.

She's standing at the very edge of the brick emplacement, where it drops, five feet or so, beside the old scoop-wheel housing to the end of the grassed-over drain. She stands, hair tousled by the breeze, and then, throwing her arms forwards and upwards, she jumps. Her skirt billows; brown knees glisten. And she lands in what seems a perversely awkward posture, body stiff, legs apart, not seeming to cushion her fall but rather to resist it. Then, letting her body sink, she squats on the grass, clasps her arms round her stomach. Then gets up and repeats the whole process. And again. And again.

I loiter in the trembling poplar spinney, trying to interpret this bizarre ritual. Is this some kind of solitary game? Some kind of exercise routine? And hadn't she better be careful? After all – with that baby inside her?

I cross the wedge of pasture between the spinney and windmill. Warm wafts of meadowsweet sail through the air. The wind carries away my first shout, so that by the time Mary's aware of my arrival, she's poised again for another jump.

"Mary, what are you – ?"

She hasn't expected me to appear. I see that straight away. A little wince of vexation tightens her face. She's come all alone to the windmill. On private business.

"You'd better go away, Tom Crick. You'd better just get you gone."

"What's all this this jumping? You'll hurt yourself."

"Stupid. Go away!"

"I've come to talk – "

And she jumps again, ignoring me, as if in serious practice for something, swinging her arms, screwing her eyes resolutely; as if she's not going to be deterred, as if this jumping's more important than anything else. And lands, in that abrupt, staggering fashion, then sinks onto her haunches.

I run to help her up. There's a little bruised depression in the grass from her successive landings, as if she's been jumping like this for a good while already.

"Why – ? Isn't it dangerous? With – "

"Stupid. Get away."

And then, as Mary turns her head, I see that her face, for all the weeks of summer tanning it's had, is pale, and it's glistening with sweat. Not the trickly sweat of exercise and heat, but a cold-looking dew of sweat. What's more, in the corner of each of Mary's eyes are bright, exasperated drops which aren't sweat at all.

"Stupid! Stupid!"

Like a scolding, pestered mother. Like a –

I realise.

(Ah, children, your history teacher in the making. So clever at analysing events. So good at discerning the truth . . .)

"So you're – ?"

"Yes. Stupid. Out of my way."

"You really mean – ?"

(So little aware, till now, that Mary can be a real Mummy, that that thing in Mary's tummy is really there. But she can. It is. He'll see.)

She clambers once more, panting, past the weed-choked culvert, onto the brick emplacement.

And I don't stop her. I don't put out restraining hands or shout outraged words. For while, for the second time in two weeks, reality comes up, just as the ground comes up to meet Mary, and gives me a dizzying jolt, and while as the ground meets Mary it seems simultaneously to leave me, to make my vision reel and my stomach turn – what hard and sharp little thought am I nonetheless thinking?

It must be Dick's. If she wants to kill – if she wants to get rid of. It must be Dick's. Because she doesn't want the baby of a– Because she wouldn't kill our –

And as she turns again that waxy, glistening face, I catch her by the arm and suddenly scream, "It's Dick's, isn't it? All along. Dick's. Dick's!"

"Why don't you just get out of here?"

She heads once more to her jumping-off point.

"Mary, don't. Don't do it."

The way one talks to a suicide.

"Don't jump."

She jumps. Crouches. Grunts. Walks back to jump again.

I grab her arm.

"Stop it. Stop doing it."

She shakes off my grip. Her face is fierce, teeth set. The wind whips her hair about her eyes.

"It's Dick's, isn't it? Dick's, Dick's!"

She gets back onto the emplacement.

"All right. It's Dick's."

(So, little father-to-be: satisfied?)

She moves to the edge to jump again.

"Mary, I think he knows I know. Mary, talk to me. Oh Christ— I came to tell you. I think we— There's this chest—"

(Mary, if you'd just stop this—)

But Mary isn't listening. Because, before she can jump again, before another jolt can do its work, her knees suddenly give beneath her, she gropes to steady herself against the tarred boards of the windmill. Squats, drops her head.

I scramble onto the emplacement. Crouch beside her. Put an arm around her. There's this cold intensity about her skin. I can almost feel, transmitting itself to me, the tingling of her nerve-ends.

"Something's happened," she says, looking up with the ghost of a laugh. "Works, after all."

Then she says, tears suddenly starting in her eyes: "Not Dick's. Ours. Ours. You understand?"

The wind blows, fluttering poplar leaves and scarlet poppies and Mary's nut-brown hair. It blows, ripening East Anglian corn, turning Fenland wheat fields with its oven-gusts to the colour of the loaves they will one day become. But though it's a warm wind, though it's slackening now in any case, because it's getting on for evening, it might as well be that cold, relentless wind of winter . . .

We crawl into the shell of the old windmill. Where once we sowed love (Mary—such hard justice?), we wait for its precipitate fruit-fall. I lean against the desiccated boards. Mary leans in my arms. She pulls up her skirt.

"Not much blood. Something's just happened inside. Just. Have to wait . . . See."

She can't get up. Makes her sick.

We wait (whispers and whimpers; flapping of the wind; squealing of swallows) while an hour or more passes. And nothing happens.

I venture: "Mary, maybe it's – all right. Maybe it's not going to happen."

(But that's what we're waiting for, isn't it? For Nothing to happen. For something to unhappen.)

She shakes her head. Knickers, blood-stained, round her knees. Done now. No undoing.

"Do you – understand?"

Yes, I understand. Because if this baby had never . . . Then Dick would never . . . And Freddie . . . Because cause, effect . . . Because Mary said, I know what I'm going to . . .

I understand, but I don't understand this mellowing August sunshine, this harvest wind, this scent of meadowsweet, and, up above – where once, in Thomas Atkinson's day, the wooden sails turned, draining, draining – this cruel circle of cornflower sky.

Evening draws on. The wind fades.

Cradling Mary in my arms, invoking the bedtime voice of my mother (but I'm the infant, and she –) I start to say, in the frail tones of grown-ups who in the midst of crisis try to maintain before their children that all is well: "Do you remember, Mary, when we first came here, when we, when – ?"

(Do you remember, Mary, long ago, long ago? When there were no TV sets or tower blocks, no rockets to the moon, no contraceptive pills, no tranquillisers or pocket calculators, no supermarkets or comprehensive schools, no nuclear missiles . . . when there were steam-trains and fairy-tales . . . when the lighters passing on the Leem still bore on their prows, from olden times, two crossed yellow ears of barley? Do you remember, that windmill? That journey we made to Wash Fen Mere . . . ?)

But Mary's not interested. Her face is white and clammy. Her eyes clench. She's not interested in stories. Not curious.

Windmill-refuge, windmill-shelter. How could its already ruined walls protect us now? How could its wooden embrace comfort us now?

But we lay there, waiting, that golden August evening, as if it was the last place on earth. Because that's what I thought, despite wheat fields and poppies and cornflower heavens: everything's coming to an end.

40

About Contemporary Nightmares

"And people are all getting into their cars, sir, and taking to the streets. They think they're going to get away somewhere safe. They think that, even though they've been told it's pointless. My parents push me and my sister into our car. They don't think about food or clothes or nothing. Then as soon as we get to the main road it's blocked with cars. People are honking their horns and screaming and wailing. And I think, this is how it's going to end – we're all going to die in a great big traffic jam . . ."

". . . and I have this dream that when the warning goes I'm miles from anyone I know. I've got to get to them. I just want to see them before – But . . ."

". . . they announce it on the telly. You know: you've got four minutes . . . But no one seems to notice. No one moves. My Dad's snoring in his chair. I'm screaming. My mum just sits there wanting to know what's happened to Crossroads . . ."

". . . all the buildings go red-hot and then they go white and all the people go red too and white . . ."

("You couldn't see that – you'd be dead. Stupid.")

". . . an' my baby brother's writhing about all burnt an' that an' I know I've gotta kill him . . ."

"Suicide pills, sir. We sit round and all take them together . . ."

". . . and no one wants to be first to leave the shelter . . ."

"Funny thing is, in my dream I'm the only one left. I'm not hurt. But everywhere there's just this dust. And I'm walking round thinking it won't ever be, it can't ever be . . ."

A Feeling in the Guts

But all the stories were once real. And all the events of history, the battles and costume-pieces, once really happened. All the stories were once a feeling in the guts. I've got a feeling in the guts right now, Price – no I don't want another drink. Hadn't we better be on our way? And you've got a feeling. About Nothing. And Mary certainly had a feeling, that August evening . . .

One day, Price, one day in the future, you'll say: There was once this history teacher, who gave these crazy lessons, and whose wife – Other realities will come along.

But when the world is about to end there'll be no more reality, only stories. All there'll be left to us will be stories. Stories will be our only reality. We'll sit down, in our shelter, and tell stories to some imaginary Prince Shahriyar, hoping it will never . . .

Huddled in our windmill. Whispers. Whimpers. The wind dies; the shadows of the poplars lengthen. Little cramps – not so little cramps – in Mary's guts. And Mary says at last, because it's not working, it's not happening: "We've got to go to Martha Clay's."

So, children, since these fairy-tales aren't all sweet and cosy (just dip into your Brothers Grimm), since no fairy-tale is complete without one, let me tell you

About the Witch

Who was called Martha Clay. Who was Bill Clay's wife (or so it was said). Who lived in Bill Clay's cottage on the far side of Wash Fen Mere. Who made potions and predictions (or so it was claimed). And who also got rid of love-children . . .

But first, before I tell you about Martha, let me tell you about our Fen geese . . .

By which I don't mean the feathered, beaked and web-footed kind. Not the black-necked Canadas. Not the Grey-lags, Pink-foots or White-fronts winging their way from the Arctic, driven by migratory urges no less mysterious than those of their watery fellow-wanderer, *Anguilla anguilla*. Not those honking, cackling, V-forming squadrons which from time immemorial have sought the sanctuary of the Fens and given the Fen-people their ancient sign of welcome – a split goose-feather. No. On an August evening in 1943 no such geese were to be seen, for the time for geese is winter. And in any case in 1943 we had our new kind of geese. Noisy too and formation-flying, following their own migratory paths across the North Sea; made of aluminium and steel, wooden struts and perspex; and with the trick of laying explosive and inflammatory eggs while still in mid-air.

They were taking to the wing, these twentieth-century skeins, leaving their scattered daytime roosts (for they were night-fliers) and forming, as geese should do, black soulful silhouettes against the fires of the sunset, as Mary and I (Mary white-faced, numb-lipped, catching every third breath) made our way from the Hockwell Lode to Wash Fen Mere. But we scarcely noticed them, having other things on our minds, and having grown used in any case to these throbbing evening flights, as if they were a natural phenomenon, as if they were real geese. As Mary and I journeyed to Martha Clay's they were setting off, in the direction of Hamburg, Nuremberg or Berlin. And all the brave pilots and navigators and gunners and bomb-aimers had hearts and had once sucked mothers' milk, and all the citizens of Hamburg and Nuremberg had hearts also and once sucked mothers' milk too.

Ah children, this artificial stuff, this man-made stuff. In 1793 the Apocalypse came to Paris (just a few thousand heads); in 1917 it came to the swamps of Flanders. But In August, 1943, (yes, history soberly records that, despite that earlier bloodbath, the deathtoll in the First War was smaller than in the Second, and included few civilians) it came in the form of detonating goose eggs to Hamburg, Nuremberg and Berlin . . .

But of all this no thought (our own end of the world to face) on that August evening.

Love. Lu-love. Lu-lu-love. Does it ward off evil? Will its magic word suspend indefinitely the link between cause and effect? Will it help those citizens of Hamburg and Berlin, clutching in anticipation their loved ones and whispering loving words in their feeble cellars and backyard bunkers? Will it disperse these brainstorm-firestorms of realisation: This is your doing, it wouldn't have happened if – This ain't no accident, you've cooked your goose . . .

Along the Fenland tracks, across the Fenland dykes, by willow holts and sallow clumps, by paths and short-cuts and plank-bridges known only to us, being children of the Fens. Like Hereward and Torfrida (ah, cosy-thrilling late-night readings), fleeing through the marshes after the sack of Ely. Their love too, so the story goes, had sustained them in that hour of calamity. But this is no story . . .

It's a long way to Martha's cottage. Round the southern fringe of the Mere, northwards to the neck of meadow between the Mere and the long easterly loop the Ouse makes below Newhithe. Sunset-pyres on our left. On our right, speared armies of reeds. Out in the midst of the Mere, smoke from Bill Clay's marsh-hut. So Bill Clay's there, after his summer fashion. So Martha's alone. Down Mary's leg two sudden unfurling ribbons of blood, one outpacing the other, smeared by the swish of the long grass. We stop, for a pause of wincing, hard breathing and transfixed looks. Anticipatory visions: spilt onto the marsh grass, a bloody tadpole, a gooey sheep's heart. Is it going to – ? Now? Christ, Mary, if we're stuck out here in the dark. Twilight thickening. The time of owls and will o' the wisps. Right time to arrive at a witch's. Hold my hand, Mary. Hold on, Mary. Love you, Mary, love you, Mary. Keep going, Mary. Are we going to get there? (Do we want to get there?)

But we do get there. And we meet Martha Clay . . .

No pointed hat, no broomstick, no grinning black cat on shoulder (only a yapping, slavering, grizzled brute of a dog, straining at a rope tether, which signals our arrival and brings Martha out of doors, oil lamp in hand). I see a small woman with a large round head. I see a woman wearing mud-caked gumboots. Wearing a heavy grey skirt that might have been made from a horse blanket. Wearing a series of underskirts, their tattered edges just visible, once white perhaps, now the colour of old teeth. Wearing a greasy blouse, stiff and sticky as weather-worn sail-cloth, sleeves rolled up to the elbows. And over both the blouse and the grey skirt – as if, in between turns as a witch, she doubles as a charwoman – a faded, floral-pattern, full-length apron.

And as we meet Martha, we meet Martha's smell . . .

But enough of Martha's costume. (And enough of that smell!) That face! Small, moist, needly eyes. Leather purse of a mouth. Nose: bony (but in no way hooked). Forehead: bumpy-shiny, tobacco-hued. Hair: waxy-grey, pulled tight down to her scalp by a knot at the neck stuck through with two lengths of quill. And those cheeks! Those cheeks! They're not just round and ruddy. They're not just red. They don't merely suggest alternate and continual exposure over several decades, without any intermediate stages, to winter gales and scorching sun. They're bladders of fire. They're fleshy pimentos. They're over-ripe tomatoes.

And, speaking of over-ripeness, this smell . . .

"Well now, well now." She holds up the oil lamp. "What brings you to owd Martha? Martha don' git many callers this time o' day. Martha don' git many callers at all. What brings you to owd Martha?"

Taking in all the while Mary's blood-stained skirt, her stricken posture . . .

I've resolved to be a bold spokesman:

"We want you to – "

"Henry Crick's bor, ent we? Tom Crick. Dick's brother. Pal o' Freddie Parr's, ent we?"

"We – "

"An' it's Harold Metcalf's gal, ent it? As goes to conven' school. All prim an' proper. Well now, what brings you to Martha?"

"Mary's – "

"Cos Martha don' git many vis'tors."

"We've heard that you – "

"O, save it up, bor! I got eyes in me head, hevn't I? You're a-goin' to say that little missy here's got somethin' she wants to git rid o'. An' by the look on it, it's already bin tryin' to git rid on itself. Is that what you're a-goin' to say?"

I nod.

"Well now. Well now. An' are we sure on't? Proper sure? Cos, you see, 'ow does Martha know missy ent jist hevin' a bad month on it? Ent jist got the owd bleedy-peedies. Cos thass what a lot on 'em thinks. Young gals. Convent gals. Little drop o' blood an' they thinks they's done something wicked. Thinks they mussa got a bubby. Don' know 'ow you gits a bubby, but they comes grizzlin' to Martha anyways."

She looks with twinkling eyes from Mary to me, then back to Mary again.

"So what I'm askin' you two young folks, what I'm askin' is what makes you sure, what makes you – ?"

"Because – we did it!" Mary blurts out in a wavering voice. "Because we did it together. What you have to do."

"Well now. That be different." She lets out a long, satisfied chuckle. "So Tom Crick an' Mary Metcalf. Now that be different. Shut yer noise, Cuff!" (to the yapping, rope-jerking dog). "So we did it together, did we, the two on us?"

Mary gives an involuntary gasp. Clutches herself.

"You know, my owd Bill says young Freddie don' come no more. To c'llect the birds. Wi' the bottles. My Bill's missin' his bottles."

261

Mary groans.

"We haven't got anything," I say. "To give. But we could get you something – anything. Please. Please, Martha."

"'Plee-eese, Martha, Plee-eese.' Mrs Clay to you, bor. Where's yer manners? Mrs Clay."

Mary sinks to her knees.

"Thass right, gal, you drop. You faint right away if you can. 'Tent goin' to be so much fun gittin' it out as it were puttin' it in. Well, bor, best git her inside, ent we?"

Children, have you ever stepped into another world? Have you ever turned a corner to where Now and Long Ago are the same and time seems to be going on in some other place? If you ever go to the Fenland Museum in Gildsey (opened in 1964 on a site in Market Street once occupied by the old Gildsey Corn Exchange) you will see a full-scale mock-up of an old Fen cottage. But it won't begin to tell you, it won't begin to convey in the slightest . . .

Once-white plaster over wattle and daub. Earth floor, hardtrodden. A turf-fire burning in a brick fireplace. Smell of turf-smoke, smothering even Martha's Martha-smell (which consists, to be sure, of a good part of turf-smoke). A grid-iron, spits, griddles, pots, trivets; a vast kettle. Set into the fireplace, a rudimentary oven. Two solid-back wooden chairs and a trestle table. Half drawn across one portion of the room, a filthy curtain, part concealing a sheepskin covered bed. A rough wooden dresser. Lamps. Guttered candles in saucers. And that's all. Because the rest – it's not like a home at all. It's full of things people wouldn't keep inside a home – or that people wouldn't keep at all. Two monster-barrelled flintlock fowling guns slung on hooks on the fireplace wall. Nets, spades, poles, scythes, sickles, pails. Hanging from a ceiling beam, like amputated, mummified legs, a pair of long leather waders. But take a look at that ceiling! Look what else it's hung with. It's hung with dead birds. Mallard – a duck and drake – teal, plover, snipe. It's hung with strips of fur and eel-skin, a bloody-mouthed water-rat dangling by its hairy tail. It's hung with nameable and unnameable bunches of leaves, grasses, roots, seed-pods, in every stage of freshness and desiccation. With misshapen things blackened with smoke that you don't like to ask what they are. With all manner of bags and pouches that you don't like to ask what's inside.

On the dresser, incongruous items: aluminium saucepans, a tin of Cerebos salt; pinned to the edge of a shelf, a yellowed photograph cut from a newspaper: Churchill, with a belligerent cigar. Impossible intruders, stray objects from some exhibition of the far-away future . . .

But then we've already stepped into a different world. The one where things come to a stop; the one where the past will go on happening . . .

"You best git you on the bed, gal. An' take down them drawers . . ."

Not there! Not on that pile of stinking sheepskin!

"An' you best make yisself useful, bor. Hot water. There, the kettle. Stoke the fire. More water from the pump."

Martha's hands: the fingernails, like old pewter.

Mary stumbles feebly towards the bed. Martha follows. She doesn't draw the curtain. I look away.

"Thass right, bor. You turn yer head. Don' s'pose we was so bashful when we did it together, was we? Now gal, you better tell Martha what you bin a-doin' to yisself to make sich a mess. Was it the pokin' about? Or was it the jumpin' and jouncin'?"

I go out with a pail and a jug to find the pump. The dog barks. It's almost dark. We'll be here all night. We'll be here for ever. When I re-enter, Martha's holding Mary's soaked, twisted knickers like a piece of limp meat.

"Whass matter, bor?"

She steps past me to the doorway.

"Here, Cuff. You go chew on this."

She throws the bloody bundle into the twilight.

"Now, bor, you boil water."

She goes to the dresser and from one of the cupboards removes a bottle, a rag, a basin and a piece of rolled up oilskin. Then she takes a pot from beside the fire and tips into it from jars on the dresser a sprinkle of this and a sprinkle of that, and then from

263

the bunches hanging from the ceiling-beams a handful of this and a handful of that.

No spells, no incantations.

She puts the pot by the hearth. She crosses to the bed and folds out the oilcloth over the sheepskins.

"Now, gal, you jist shift yer little arse onto this. Then swaller some o' this. Martha's med'cin. Don' matter if you don' like it."

She holds out the bottle. Mary drinks, chokes, drinks. Two bulging eyes look suddenly at me over the neck of the bottle.

"Right down. There. Look at Martha, look straight at Martha. Well, you're a pretty 'un. Right down. Martha's med'cin. Do you good. Look at Martha."

Mary goes limp, delivers the bottle back into Martha's hands. Her eyes remain open. For a moment I think: Martha's poisoned her, she's killed her. Now she's coming over to me – to deal with little Hansel, who happens to be stationed conveniently near the oven.

"Now – how's that kettle, bor? She's all right. You help me git this table beside the bed."

We carry the table. Mary doesn't move. Blood on the oilcloth. Then Martha lights a lamp with a splint from the fire and puts the lamp and then a candle in a dish on the table. She returns to the fireplace, pours water from the now faintly hissing kettle into the pot of mysterious ingredients and puts both kettle and pot back on the grid-iron. She takes a pail and places it by the foot of the bed. Then she reaches up for one of the leather bags that hang from the ceiling. There are things wrapped in a cloth. Things that look like long spoons, tongs, bottle-brushes, shoe-horns.

"Martha's little tool kit. You'd be s'prised, bor. You'd be s'prised how many."

She lays the things out, surgeon-fashion, on the table. By this time the kettle is steaming. She tells me to pour the contents of the pot into the basin, to add water from the kettle and bring the basin to the table. I carry over a steaming, flotsammed, tea-coloured broth and set it down. She puts each item from the bag into the basin. Then she pushes the lit candle in its dish to the end of the table, by Mary's head. She lifts Mary's arm and places it so that it's resting on the table by the candle. Mary's arm doesn't resist. Then she leans forward and speaks into Mary's ear. Mary doesn't move, or change the direction of her stare, but her eyes blink at Martha's words.

"Now gal, Martha don' wanna hurt you. Martha's goin' to help you. But if she hurts you anyways, you jist put your hand over the candle. Right over the flame."

Mary blinks.

Martha lifts her head, sniffs the steam rising from the basin, dips her hands into it, then looks at me.

"An' you best make yisself scarce, bor. You best sit you outside quiet an' not git in owd Martha's way. An' stop that blubberin'."

(Because I'm blubbering.)

"Here."

She holds out to me the bottle from which Mary's drunk. I shake my head. The next moment the bottle's thrust between my lips and I swallow involuntarily.

"Now. Make yisself useful. Know how to pluck?" She cocks her head towards the gallery of fowl suspended from the ceiling. I nod mesmerically (by the kitchen door, after Mother's patient instructions – after Dad had wrung its neck – plucking the russet feathers from the old hen that had ceased to lay).

"Take one on 'em birds an' pluck it for Martha. Ent nothin' like a bit o' pluckin', eh? Is there now?"

I go to the beam and reach up for the emerald-headed drake mallard.

"No, bor. You take the duck." She chuckles, draws the curtain. "You take the duck!"

And so, while inside Martha Clay ministers, as only she can minister, to Mary, your future history teacher sits outside and begins dutifully to pluck a duck. It's a moonless August night. Shoals of stars, silver geese, swim through the sky. His head starts to spin. The duck he's holding in his hand isn't a duck, it's a hen. He's sitting in the sunny space between the chicken coop and the kitchen door, where Mother stands, in her apron. But the hen's not dead, it's still alive. Its wings start to flap and it starts to lay eggs (so it hadn't stopped laying after all). A

265

copious, unending stream of eggs, so many that he has to collect
them with the help of his mother and her apron. But Mother
says they're not really eggs, they're fallen stars. And so they are,
twinkling and winking on the ground. They carry the fallen
stars into the chicken coop. Which isn't a chicken coop at all.
It's the shell of the old wooden windmill by the Hockwell Lode.
And Mary's inside lying naked with her knees up. Mother discreetly retires. And Mary starts to explain about her menstrual
cycle and about the wonders inside her hole and how babies
get to be born. She says, "I've got eggs, you know." And he,
ignorant but eager to learn, says, "What, like hens?" And Mary
laughs. And then she screams and then she says she's the
mother of God –

I drop the duck I'm holding (it's a duck after all). It's not a
dream. What you wake up into can't be a dream. It's dark. I'm
here; it's now. I'm sitting (my head slumped drowsily forward)
on a bench outside a cottage where Martha Clay, a reputed
witch . . .

And Mary. Mary's woken too out of whatever home-brewed
anaesthesia, whatever witch-induced hypnosis she's been under,
into a dream that isn't a dream, and – is saying her prayers.
She's saying them with a terrible involuntary persistence.

I rush to the door. Hesitate. Move instead to a little window
that must look over the curtained-off bed. Children, there
are things which happen outside dreams which should only
happen in them. A pipe – no, a piece of sedge, a length of hollow
reed – is stuck into Mary's hole. The other end is in Martha's
mouth. Crouching low, her head between Mary's gory knees,
her eyes closed in concentration, Martha is sucking with all her
might. Those cheeks – those blood-bag cheeks working like
bellows.

I go into the cottage. I pull back the filthy curtain. Martha
appears to have just spat something into the pail. I yell, "Mary!"
But Mary doesn't hear me. Her name bounces back to me. She
doesn't know me. She's a little convent girl, staunchly saying
her prayers:

"HolyMaryMotherofGodHolyMaryMotherofGodHoly-
MaryMotherof – "

The candle is snuffed under Mary's hand. I nearly trip over the pail. In the pail is what the future's made of. I rush out again to be sick.

43

Not So Final

He half puts out a hand to help me onto the street. He's embarrassed, he's solicitous. His teacher's drunk . . . (And how is it our disruptive Price evinces such temperance and rectitude? When I succumb to just another one, he asks for straight tomato juice). Teachers shouldn't be drunk. They should be upright, exemplary, magisterial and sober. Ridiculous for that. Not for playing the clown. The pupil shouldn't have to guide the master. The would-be revolutionary shouldn't have to prop his surrogate tyrant . . .

How it makes the bad seem not so . . . How it makes reality . . . My maternal ancestors, Price, built an empire on strong liquor . . .

"By the way, Price, you'll be pleased to know, he wants to get rid of History. Not just me, the subject. Get rid of the whole caboodle – "

A broad, sweeping and unbalancing gesture towards the unmoved twentieth-century streets of south-east London.

"Don't think I should drive, do you, Price? No? Sorry – no lift. I'll get the bus. Leave the car at the school."

"They'll have locked the gates anyway. I'll come with you to the bus stop."

We tread the pavement.

"Steady."

At the bus stop I perorate – ". . . the whole caboodle, the whole . . ." – he's smitten with more awkwardness and gravity. As my number 53 approaches to scoop me up, a taut "Goodbye then, sir. Take care, sir."

"Goodbye – hey, Price, not so final. Not so solemn. I've got till the end of term. And we've got our French Revolution to finish

267

still. Have you forgotten? Hey, Price," (from the platform as my bus carts me away) "don't let him do it!"

And History scarcely finds time to mention that on the eve of the French Revolution Louis XVI mourned his first-born.

44

Begin Again

We take the baby to the car. By some freak, it's asleep. Hasn't even wet itself. I think for a moment: it's dead with shock. Mary sits in the back seat and clutches it and I drive. What follows is like a parody of those panic drives to hospitals made by young husbands with wives in the throes of precipitate labour. Save that in our case we already have the baby and we are rushing to return it.

From the back seat Mary offers a running confession:

"It was easy. Easy. I saw her come in. She left the pram near the turnstiles. That was risking it, wasn't it? I was by the fruit counter, heading for the check-out. Crowded. One of those big prams, not a pushchair. Maybe she'd just got a few things to get, and she thought – with that big pram and all those people. I watched her go up one of the aisles. Didn't think I would ever. But then I put down my basket. Didn't get any shopping, after all. Got a. Instead. I looked up the aisle. Went over to the pram. Looked. I got hold of the handle. Pushed, pressed, the way they do. I said, 'Here I am. Off we go then.' Nobody would've known. Nobody would've known that I wasn't the real – "

Mary, you're fifty-two.

"And I knew it was all right. Because it smiled. When I pushed, it smiled. Didn't you? Didn't cry. Did you? Then I wheeled the pram round the corner and into the lift to the multi-storey. I put my bags in the boot and the baby in the back seat with some of the blankets. Know that's wrong. Supposed to strap them in, aren't you? But it didn't cry. Didn't cry at all . . ."

268

But she says all this as if only pretending, under some sort of hypnosis, to be a woman confessing to a crime. The truth is so different, no one would believe it. The truth is a miracle. God came down to Safeways and left her a gift, a free product. A babe in the bulrushes. He said, Go on, I command you. Take. It's yours . . .

(It's what she'll tell a presiding magistrate and a practising psychiatrist. To her husband alone – a sort of practising historian – she gives the unreal, historical facts.)

"Psychological disturbance there may have been. Yet the account given to the husband seems perfectly lucid."

Ah, but if you had been there, your worship . . .

"Would you recognise her, Mary – I mean the mother – again?"

"Yes. Yes, of course . . ."

I see her in the driving mirror. Her eyes are brilliant and clear. Yes, she'll continue this trumped-up narrative (. . . and just drove off. No hue and cry. No chasing police cars . . .), she'll play this part of the cranky child-thief. But in reality . . .

As if we're not in the same space. As if there's a glass plate between us. She in the back seat, I her cabby. Where to, lady?

(Where to? Where to now?)

Or she the picked-up suspect in the back of the squad car, I the already interrogating officer:

"So you left the pram? So then you drove home . . ?"

(But we'll know, soon enough, about squad cars and rides to the station.)

The lights of Shooter's Hill, of Blackheath, Lewisham. A Friday evening in the suburbs. Heavy traffic in Lewisham High Street. Should I sound my horn, flash my lights? Make way, this is an emergency!

But why this haste? Why this wild car-dash? When a simple phone call. Why this need to return to the scene of the.

A quarter past five. We reach the multi-storey. Park on level three.

"So this is where you – ?"

It's called reconstructing the crime. From last to first. It's an analogue of the historical method. It's an analogue of how you discover how you've become what you are. If you're lucky you might find out why. If you're lucky – but it's impossible – you might get back to where you can begin again. Revolution.

I park the car. Turn off the engine.

"Now give me the baby, Mary. We're here now, Mary. I'll take the baby now."

As if I'm talking to another baby.

"Mary, I'll take – "

She hands it over, in a trance. But it's still there really, still in her arms. Always will be.

I hold it. Incredibly, it goes on sleeping. It won't know. All this will be its dream.

"Now we're going to go back to Safeways. To where you – "

We're going to retrace our steps. We're going to go back . . .

She walks with dazed confidence. You'll see, you'll see. God's waiting. He'll explain. That other yarn I told you in the car – all nonsense.

"So you pushed the pram along here, from the lift?"

No prowling policemen. No distant hubbub.

So perhaps it never.

Or perhaps the scene has already shifted: A tearful woman sits in a police station. A constable offers unconsolatory tea. A phone-summoned husband arrives, wild-eyed. A pram awaits forensic inspection . . . Meanwhile the shoppers return to their shopping. Drama over. The wire trolleys fill . . .

We'll arrive with our cock-and-bull story. Woman? What Woman? What baby? We never –

I'm wrong. As we come out of the lift and turn the corner by Mothercare and the kiddies' play centre: a knot of people visible outside Safeways. Police helmets. Security staff. Gaggles of onlookers watching from the entrances of W. H. Smith and Marks and Spencer.

So the drama's not over. The Mother, perhaps, refusing to budge. From where she last – Though it's an hour since. Still doesn't believe. It can't have really. Hoping for a miracle.

Which she's going to get. Come on, Mary. Be brave, be brave. We're going to restore – we're going to return. Keep walking Mary. Only a few paces. Back. To go forward.

Or –

Yes, I've thought of this too. She'll tear Mary's eyes out. The crowd will set upon us. I know about mobs (how, for example, in revolutionary Paris . . .). Spitting and scratching. A Lewisham lynching.

But it doesn't happen like that. It happens as if it's all on a stage. The crowd parts. "Please, please – we've got the baby. The missing baby." The crowd hushes. The mother occupies the centre of the scene. I see her. She's standing beside a policeman and a policewoman, both in attitudes of patient persuasion. She's young. Still in her teens. She can't be any age. A kid. Only a kid. A kid.

She turns. Red-rimmed, emptied eyes. She sees me. Or rather, she sees the baby. And hears it (before such an audience, it wakes up, suddenly bawls its part). She sees only the baby. She doesn't see me, or Mary behind. She doesn't see the crowd – mute, blurred faces on a backcloth. She steps forward. She knows, without thinking, her role. She takes her child, not caring who I am, or how or what or where or why. Her face spills over. She starts to sob ecstatically words which only moments before were sobbed in agony: "My baby, my baby, my baby . . ."

And it's then that Mary groans, snaps, topples out of her trance, falls into my arms. I totter, rock, an unaccustomed pillar of support.

(Mary, my darling, my angel, my strength –)

"My name is Crick. My wife took the baby. Yes. My wife's – not very well. We've brought it back now. So it's all right now. Please, is that all?"

But it's not all. As you know. Though it's over, that's not the end of it. "This way, sir, please – and Mrs Crick." They want to know how and where and why. They want to find out, to know what really. (Officers, I'm familiar with all this, it's the stuff of my trade. You see, I'm a –) "Very well, sir, shall we make a start?" But officers, there are different versions. (There are

271

always different versions: for example, 1789: bread riots, or the millennium.) There's her first explanation and then what she told me in the car. "Look, sir, shall we go back to the beginning?" The beginning. But where's that? How far – ? Very well, I confess that my wife, with intention so to do, took a baby from an unminded pram. Very well (this far back?): I confess my responsibility, jointly with my wife, for the death of three people (that is, if, in the second instance, we are truly speaking of a person – we're still uncertain, aren't we, of the status of the embryo? – and if, in the third, what we're speaking of was indeed a death . . .).

But what does it matter. She's got her baby back. That's the only thing that – And my wife, as you see, officers, is in no fit –

But not so fast, Mr History Teacher. You can't change your tune. You can't set yourself up to be a classroom sleuth and then want to skip the process when it's your turn for investigation. *Historia*, or Inquiry (as in Natural History). You're not saying all this was an accident, are you, sir? And none of this talk of miracles. We want an explanation . . .

And we want our story. Yes, we can't do without stories. Even when the police have finished and legal proceedings have taken their course, the press-men want their stories . . . Read this. Stole a baby. Right outside Safeways. What kind of a woman – ? Said God told her. Well, would you credit it? A psychiatrist testifies – yes, yes, but never mind the clever-talk. And her husband a schoolteacher. (Not for long he won't be.) To think of our children – ! He'll lose his job (she's lost her mind) . . . Hey, is there more? A quarter-page photo of the relieved Mother and the innocent Babe. How I felt when . . . Hey, this is good stuff, this is real-life drama. Let's have more.

45

About the Pike

And Dick, while I watch, clambers onto his bed and, reaching up to the precariously perched glass and mahogany case, containing the stuffed and mounted carcase of a twenty-one-pound pike, caught on Armistice Day by John Badcock, puts his hand through one of the side panels, which, since the signing of the Armistice, has lost its glass, and thus (even Dick's large, bony hand passes with ease) into the gaping and befanged jaws of this same memorable specimen . . .

Alive and not alive. Dead yet unperished. A ghost . . . Those restless nights, when Dick and I slept in the same room, and even my mother's stories . . .

Moonlight on the staring eyes, on the icicle teeth. "Nov. 1918": that's before I was – Yet it is as it was, was as it is. I swas. It's the past! What stops but remains. Mummy, Mummy, tell me a –

Twice she and Dad removed it. But it was Dick's prize possession. (And a wedding gift.) "Only a fish. A dead fish."

Pike. Jack, luce, *Esox lucius*: Pike. They're killers. Mere-monsters, Freshwater-wolves. The teeth rake backwards towards the gullet, so what goes in, can't – They'll tackle coots, water-voles, other pike. Killers. It's in their nature.

And into the jaws of a killer, the hand of a –

But Dick's no longer a creature to be feared. It's some days now since I've locked my door against him. Since we've played our see-saw game of nerves: who's more afraid of whom? Fear's been dissolved by something else. Fear's been washed away by local scandal, the after-ripples of which eddy and rebound around the communal gossip pool of Hockwell, and cannot fail to ruffle even Dick's duck's-back senses; since there's a deep end to this gossip-pool, and Dick's brother's in it.

So the poor thing got taken to hospital. Very nearly – Sepsi-what-dyamecallit of the womb. Martha Clay! Martha Clay! That old– And her a convent girl. Bless us, what's happening to the world. (A world war's happening to it.) First Freddie Parr. And now her Dad's shut her away for her pains. Or maybe it's her as doesn't want to show her face. And it was young Tom Crick, they say, would you believe . . . ?

Yes, it's common knowledge. But only I know about that night in Martha's cottage. What I saw through the window. And that dawn. That dawn. I carried the pail, down to the Ouse. Because Martha said: "You gotta do it, bor. Only you. No one else. In the river, mind. An' when you throws it, don't you look. Nothin' but bad luck if you looks." So I carried the pail across the mist-wrapped, dew-soaked meadows. Larks were trilling somewhere above the mist, but I was stumbling through a mist of tears. I climbed the river wall, descended to the water's edge. I turned my head away. But then I looked. I howled. A farewell glance. A red spittle, floating, frothing, slowly sinking. Borne on the slow Ouse currents. Borne downstream. Borne all the way (but for the Ouse eels . . .) to the Wash. Where it all comes out.

He grips me by the arm. His grip wants to tell me something. His lashes fan his eyes. He says, "C-come with Dick. D-Dick show." He leads me up the stairs to his room.

And where's Dad, on this dull and sullen yet revelatory Sunday morning? On his way, at this very moment, to Polt Fen Farm. To make due representations, to make reparations by word of mouth to Harold Metcalf. Though God knows what he'll say to him, since he hasn't found a way yet of having matters out with his son. His good-scholar son (not the other one). His pride-and-hope and so-full-of-promise younger son. Something stops his paternal wrath. He opens his mouth to speak but something sticks – a kind of deadening phlegm – in his throat and turns his lips into a sad, mute circle. We all go wrong. It all goes wrong. All scooped into the net of trouble. So is it time then, time at last, to tell that whole story? For his son's weeping confession, one of his own? He broods by the lock-gate. Rehearses a dialogue that never gets performed: So it was serious, after all. Dead serious. But if you, I mean, if she was – Why didn't you just – ? Not such a bad match – even starting it the hard way – you and Metcalf's girl. Though old Metcalf would have had his piece to say. So why? . . . Trouble upon trouble. First Freddie. And now. But it's a punishment, that's what it is. A punishment for non-vigilance. For neglect of duty.

And so, with eyes alert (yet guilty) and adopting the posture of one not shirking his bounden duty, he sets off on a rickety bicycle to see Harold Metcalf. Who, being a farmer of lofty if unrealised ambitions, will not waste the opportunity to play the high and mighty squire, not to mention the outraged father, before Dad's humbled and suppliant serf. He'll return red-faced and dry-voiced, like a schoolboy from a summary caning:

"But is *she* all right, Dad?"

"Don't know, Tom. Can't say. He damned my – my appur-tenance – for asking. Leastways, Tom, I see you care."

"Dad, Dad I – I'm afraid there's more."

"More, Tom? More?"

Because Dad doesn't know yet . . .

He thrusts his hand into the mouth of the pike – which being dead and stuffed, does not snap shut its jaws, as once it must have done, with fatal results, on John Badcock's bait, but leaves them obligingly open – and pulls out a key. A brass key. A stubby, important-looking key. He gets down off the bed and holds it out to me in his palm. He says nothing, but I know this is Dick's confession. Yes – since you know anyway. I. Freddie.

But it's not just this. Something has a hold of him. Something as inescapable and inexplicable as the sudden grip of love. His face is a-quiver with un-Dick-like importunacy. He wants releasing. He's got a key in his hand. For the first time in his life, the forgetful flux of Dick's experience has congealed around him into imprisoning solidity. He's as fixed as that pike on the wall. He's made things happen. Things have hap-pened because of him. He can't understand. He's stuck in the past.

"Y-you loved?"

"Yes, Dick. Me too."

But this is only the first, the easier question.

"Wh-wh-wh-? Wh-whose?"

What shall I tell him? Which will crush him least? What does one stunned and guilt-laden brother tell another?

"It was your baby, Dick."

A sudden, brief spasm, as if pride and remorse contest with each other only to cancel each other out, crosses his face.

He looks at the key, still held in his palm. He doesn't look at me. He looks hard at the key as if it's the key to all the riddles of life.

"Take."

I take.

"We go up now and open it. D-Dick want know."

46

About my Grandfather's Chest

How strange it becomes. How larger than life it becomes. These eighteenth-century dandies with their perukes and brocade. These whiskered Victorians with their whaleboned womenfolk. (These wild creatures – look, in the streets – with Phrygian caps and human heads on pike-staffs . . .) How strange, how extraordinary, how impossible, becomes the flat, mundane stuff of our lives. It needs looking into. How it gets . . . How it becomes . . . Children, the world is madder, madder than you'd ever think. Discover it for yourselves . . .

Once I toyed, once I dabbled in history. Schoolboy stuff. Harmless stuff, textbook stuff. But it never got serious – my studies never began in earnest – until one August afternoon, a prisoner myself of irreversibly historical events, I unlocked the past inside a black wooden chest . . .

It contains eleven bottles wrapped and padded with old sacking, ten of which are stoppered and full, one of which is empty

276

and which in the process of losing its stopper has journeyed surreptitiously to the Hockwell footbridge, been used first to intoxicate then to bludgeon, travelled back again by river, been plucked out, examined; secreted in one bedroom, then conspicuously placed in another; and been carried back, with ponderous stealth, to its attic resting-place by the self-same hand which first took it thence; thus illustrating that all sins come home to roost, and thus qualifying itself to be regarded in any inquiry into the death of Freddie Parr (but Freddie Parr – don't we know? – died by accident) as Exhibit Number One.

It contains four thick, well dog-eared notebooks, bound in blue-marbled paste-board, evidently bundled together at one time by a canvas strap which has since been untied. It contains an envelope (from which, to judge by its crumpled state, the contents have, on some previous occasion or occasions, been removed and replaced) on which is written, in the same thick, sloping hand which seems to fill the notebooks: "To the First-Born of Mrs Henry Crick" . . .

Dick breathes his hee-haw breath over my shoulder. I ignore discreetly the empty bottle (Yes, we've seen that before, we know all about that; it's only a murder weapon; it's only the reason why we come to be stooped over this derelict chest). I take up one of the dusty, stoppered bottles. Dick's breathing quickens. For one moment I think he thinks I'm about to raise it and, in an act of poetic, if brutal justice, crash it down on Dick's skull. (So it's true – he *is* more afraid . . .)

But his agitation has a different meaning.

"D-don't open. D-don't drink – "

(Yet we know that too: a certain wintry scene, an ice-fringed river – six years ago. Yes, Dick – so you remember? There's potent, there's fiery stuff inside.)

I put back the bottle. I pick up the envelope. The notebooks will come later (midnight porings . . . the start of a quest . . . a bedtime story to cap them all . . .)

A questioning, almost deferential glance: "It's for you, Dick. It's addressed to you. Shall I – ?"

Lash-fluttering consent: It's all right, go ahead. You see, I can't— Never could –

I take out the letter. There are three well crammed pages. I read. Dick breathes. I don't read aloud. There are words, whole sentences Dick wouldn't– I read while Dick watches. The attic timbers murmur. Even on a still and windless August morning something stirs their old, creaking bones. It takes perhaps ten minutes to read (much, much longer to digest) the letter. You can hear the slightest sounds – you can almost hear, from the direction of Polt Fen Farm, the distant tirades of Farmer Metcalf before the hapless supplications of Henry Crick – while I read the letter. And when I've read it the first thing I say is: "It's from your grandfather, Dick."

Though it's not as simple as that.

"It's from your mother's father."

And the second thing I say – it spills out almost before I have decided to say it – is: "Dick, I'm sorry. I lied to you. It wasn't your baby. It was my baby."

He stares at me. Because it's Dick's stare, it's impossible to tell what he's thinking. But a sticky dew starts to collect in the corners of his eyes. Though it's not like tears. It's like some strange, unknown secretion that has nothing to do with Dick. When it overflows onto his cheek he almost flinches in surprise.

"Listen, Dick, listen very carefully. It was my baby. Mine and Mary's." More of the strange liquid spills from his eyes. "But it's nobody's baby now, is it? Nobody's."

Attic-murmurs. Creaking assents.

"Listen – it was a good thing it wasn't your baby. Yes, a good thing. Because it says here – your, I mean, our grandfather says – he says that you shouldn't have any babies. Because – you won't need to. Dick, you know how babies get born?"

"Lu-lu-lu-"

The tears have reached the corners of his mouth.

"You know every baby has to have a Mummy and Daddy. Nobody gets born without a Mummy and Daddy. We both have – both had – a Mummy and Daddy. And they had Mummies and Daddies too. But – sometimes it's not as simple as that. Sometimes when a person wants to be a Mummy or

Daddy and they want someone to be a Mummy or Daddy with, they choose someone who's already their own Mummy or Daddy. Or their own Mummy or Daddy chooses them. It's not supposed to happen, Dick. It's not – usual. Do you see?"

He doesn't see. I'm talking gibberish.

"It's as though you, Dick, wanted to make a baby – with your own Mummy."

His lashes start their humming-bird act.

"Lu-"

"It's not supposed to happen. Not – natural. But if it does and if a baby gets born, then that baby might be – unusual. And any babies that baby has when it grows up to be a Mummy or Daddy might be – unusual too. Dick, you're a baby – I mean, you were a baby – like that. Your grandfather – my grandfather – was also your father."

He stares.

"My father isn't your father."

His chest starts to heave, to wheeze.

"Though your mother was my mother."

The wheeze grows hoarser.

"You and your mother had the same father."

And hoarser still.

"Before your mother and my father . . ."

But I've run out of variations. And Dick seems to be running out of air. In the dim light of the attic he is gasping for breath, as if suddenly finding himself in some element not his own.

So he understands? Or understands, at least, what he's already half-guessed. That he's a bungle. Something that shouldn't be. There's been a mix-up somewhere and he's the result.

Suddenly he blurts out, as if it's all his fault, as if he, being the effect, is to blame for the cause:

"S-s-sorry, Tom. S-s-sorry."

"Listen. Calm down, Dick. Wait. This is what your gran – your father – wanted to say to you. You're not to have babies. Because – because of what I just said. But it's all right that you won't have babies. You're an – unusual person, Dick. You're a special sort of person. It doesn't matter that you can't have babies. Because you're going to be – "

279

How can I put this into any other words? How can I preface, interpret, explain (your father was not only your grandfather, he must have been quite mad –):

"Because, Dick, you're going to be – you're going to be – the Saviour of the World."

He doesn't speak. He doesn't utter a word all through that Sunday lunch-time (no one's thought of food, no one's got an appetite). When his Dad – when the man he used to call his Dad – returns, he avoids his eye, keeps a wary distance; beats a sudden retreat to the lean-to and a companionable motorcycle.

But his Dad (that is, the man who –) scarcely notices. Preoccupied: face still stinging from the verbal slaps of the Master of Polt Fen.

And in any case, he's not given to talking, is he, this son who isn't a – ? A dumb-dumb, isn't he? A sieve-brain, isn't he? And he's had enough of pretending otherwise. Enough of having lessons.

Better not to learn. Better never to know. But once you've . . .

(A saviour, Dick? A saviour is someone who . . . The world? The world is – everything. An emergency? An emergency is – when things get –)

But don't shun *him*, Dick. Don't shun your own – I mean – He's the one who never wanted you to be educated. Your protector, your guardian. I'm the one who had to ask questions, who had to dig up the truth (my recipe for emergencies: explain your way out). He would have kept you, happily, in the dark. Must have hunted for that key too . . . Never thought that a dead fish . . .

"Dad, there's more . . ."

Much more. How to begin?

"Freddie Parr . . ."

And supposing I'd followed his own example? Guarded his ignorance just as he'd guarded Dick's. This trusting and forbearing man who though not the real father of his older son, is sometimes not unlike him (bovine in deed, slow in speech); who

280

stares, open-mouthed, at this, his true and younger son – his brainy, his gifted son – as if in non-recognition.

"He knows, Dad. Dick knows . . ."

A turn on the tow-path suggested. A turn on the tow-path urgently enjoined. (A turn! Twenty, thirty turns. But who's counting?) On that old fretful yet therapeutic tow-path, on that old agitatory-placatory tow-path. Up, down. Up, down.

So this is the day that he always knew would come. That he always hoped might never. (He's prepared it perhaps a hundred times, taken the imaginary initiative: Tom, take a turn with me on the tow-path . . . But that was without unforeseen complications.) So this is how it turns out to be. Well. Well then: let it rain, let it pour trouble . . .

Smoothly sliding Leem. Late-summer level (sluice well-lowered). Colour: glaucous-green. Motionless willows. Cracks of milky light break the warm lead-roofing of the sky.

Up and down. Father and son – father and only son – in close confabulation. What are they saying? When the son completes his ravelled resumé – in which he omits to mention four blue-bound notebooks safely stowed amongst his school-work in his bedroom, but freely offers to hand over a certain letter (response: "I don't wanna see no letter, Tom. I never wanted to see inside that chest . . .") – does the father fill the gaps (gaps! – chasms!) in the narrative with a tale of his own? How he and Helen Atkinson – ? How he and the brewer's daughter – ? No. He seems to have lost his story-telling knack. He seems to remember nothing.

Up and down. Now away from the cottage, now towards it, as if perpetually torn between setting out on a journey and return-ing home. Up and down, as if stalking some runaway decision. At each about-face the father flexes his knee. At each outward sortie the son cannot help looking across the glaucous-green Leem in the direction of Polt Fen. Even now, she's there. And *her* recipe for emergencies . . . ?

Up and down. And as they walk, the other son – the son who's not a son – skulks, listening, in the lean-to.

Listening? Not wanting to listen? Spying? Not wanting to

look? Thinking (thinking?)?: It's all up. I'm denounced; they'll turn me over.

And they know he's in there. Because just as this son-who's-not-a-son takes advantage of the lean-to in order to hide from his non-father, so the non-father, escorted by his true-son, in dictating the turning-points of these tow-path promenades, studiously keeps his distance from the lean-to . . .

Yet observe more closely. For with each successive ambulation, that critical turning-point at the cottage end of this two-way beat, though at first occurring some several yards from the lean-to, draws, slowly, warily, agonisingly nearer to it. The process of turning itself becomes more laboured, more vexed, as if the subject of some dreadful test. Until the father, almost overbalancing under the sway of contrary efforts, allowing his face at the same time to become a mass of watery convulsions, leaves his true-son standing and rushes, hobbles, towards his non-son's temporary refuge, crying all the while: "Dick – my poor Dick" (yes, *my* Dick) " – Dick!"

But Dick isn't there.

He's in the kitchen. Or – so we deduce later – that's where he must have been.

For even as Dad, in his distraught state, scuttles into the cottage by the front door, true-son at his heels, Dick, who at some stage, while the backs of the tow-path walkers were turned, must have stolen into it (ah, the cunning, *in extremis*, of a potato-head), steals out again, by the back door, and returns to the lean-to. While father and son search each room for him, he ties across his back a familiar sack, redolent of its usual contents but now heavily, awkwardly but deliberately laden with something else. He wheels out his Velocette; mounts and starts it.

All this, undetected. For it is not until father and son have ascended, with inevitable logic, to the attic and discovered the chest open and void save for a single, empty beer bottle, that they are informed by the noise of the starting motor-bike of their deception. They descend the attic stairs. Hearing the bike already rounding the cottage, they scurry into the true-son's bedroom at the rear of the cottage, in time to see, from the window, Dick turn out of the cottage-track onto the Gildsey road, on his back a grotesque hump formed by ten bottles of beer inside a sack.

It's too late for shouting. Which doesn't stop Dad, head thrust through the window (a window beneath which, amongst folders of school-work, lurk four blue notebooks), screaming a desperate and strident "Di-i-i-ck!". His face, even when this cry dies on the air, remains a twisted mask. He plainly believes that his son – that Dick is riding away for good. But I believe otherwise. I can temper his despair. I am about to say that Dick – for reasons too complex to explain with brevity – must be heading for Stott's Drain.

But from our vantage at the bedroom window we can see where the Stott's Drain track joins the Gildsey road; and Dick rides straight by it. His fleeing, hump-backed form gets smaller and smaller.

I see him now, I see him still, on the arrow-straight road, under an opaque sky, between the sombre beet fields. My – Riding, riding, his birthright on his back, the legacy of the Atkinsons on his back . . . For a moment it seems that he's riding into – that he's already in – some oblivious never-never composed for always and only of straight road, flat fields, of monotony, unchangingness and the annihilating throb of a motor-bike engine. Then I say to Dad – whose head has sunk onto the windowsill: "I think he's going to the dredger."

47

Goodnight

She doesn't look up as I leave. She allows herself to be kissed and gently embraced, with neither reciprocation nor resistance, so that the touch of my lips on her temple, on the submissive crown of her head, is like a goodnight kiss to a child. She sits by a strange bed. She doesn't lift an eye or a hand as I give a last look through the wire-strengthened glass of the ward doors. She doesn't stare forlornly from behind protective bars as I walk across wet, institutional asphalt towards the gates.

The feeling of permanent departure is all within. The sense that it is not I who am leaving but really she who is receding, into the obscure and irrecoverable distance, while I stand, arms outstretched, is belied by my movement, her passivity. By the outwardly functional nature of my visit (to deposit my wife, along with certain personal articles, pending psychiatric treatment). It's belied by the cheery prognosis offered by the ward sister (oh yes, visiting's informal – any time between two and seven, within reason . . . and don't worry, Mr Crick, your wife will be out soon . . .). By the reflections of pale sunlight (blue holes in a scudding March sky) – gleaming off wet, slightly steaming asphalt.

First it was a story – what our parents told us, at bedtime. Then it becomes real, then it becomes here and now. Then it becomes a story again. Second childhood. Goodnight kisses . . .

She doesn't grieve at my departure. She grieves for her baby. The baby they took away from her and won't give back. That baby who, as everyone knows, was sent by God. Who will save us all.

First there is nothing; then there is happening; a state of emergency. And after the happening, only the telling of it. But sometimes the happening won't stop and let itself be turned into memory. So she's still in the midst of events (a supermarket adventure, something in her arms, a courtroom in which she proclaims in a loud and clear voice: "God told – ") which have not ceased. Which is why it's impossible to get through. Which is why she cannot cross into the safe, sane realm of hindsight and answer the questions of the white-coated doctors: "Now tell us, Mrs Crick, you can tell us everything, you can tell . . ."

He walks across wet asphalt, bearing a suitcase, as if leaving on a journey. But the suitcase is empty. A selection of his wife's clothing along with various belongings (the rules are strict: no article which might be used to cause injury either to other patients and staff or to the patient's own person) now in the keeping of the hospital authorities. He made the choice. She

284

wasn't interested. A survival-kit of mementoes. A tortoise-shell hair-brush (could that be used to inflict personal injury?), bought – do you remember? – in a Gildsey jumble shop during the icy winter in which we were – A leather writing-case. A small mother-of-pearl box – but this *she* chose, this she produced suddenly as if from nowhere (he calculated: when did she last hide it away? It must have been in that same cruel winter) – containing a silver crucifix on a chain. Attached still to the lining of the lid, an inscription in the scrupulous hand of Harold Metcalf: "Upon your Confirmation, With All My Love to My Darling Mary, May 10th, 1941 . . ."

He walks towards the exit-gates. His historian's eye takes in, on a grass island amidst the asphalt, the stone statue of some founder or benefactor (leonine-featured, hand on breast of frock-coat); notes, on the pink granite plinth, beneath dates and honorifics, the word which modern preference for plain "Hospital" or, begrudgingly, "Mental Hospital", cannot, in justice to this worthy's memory, erase: ". . . Asylum."

What they called in days gone by . . .

He passes through the gates which (since it is informally permitted) he will repeatedly re-enter, in order to visit his wife, who's yet not his wife, who's only a story; with whom, in the cloistered precincts of this asylum, that is hospital, he will play his plaintive do-you-remember game. Do you remember, the train: Hockwell to Gildsey, Gildsey to Hockwell? Rust-red and inky-black? Do you remember beet fields? Poplar trees? A walk by the frozen Ouse . . . ? Avoiding in these memory-jogging journeys so many no-go areas, emergency zones and long, long vistas in which nothing happens – save schoolmastering and age-concern.

So you, after all – a history teacher – afraid to tread, when it comes to it, the mine-fields of the past –

(No, no, not afraid – no, I've told it all, told it all, unabridged – to my class. No explosions yet – unless Price . . .)

While he offers this whispered and desperate nostalgia she stares out of the ward window. Enclosed within the circle of a crucifix.

And perhaps amnesia's best, perhaps amnesia's the cure for all . . .

Acquitted on grounds of extenuating circumstances (the voluntary return of the child to its parent) and of diminished responsibility (but we all know about these witness-box stunts, these get-you-off lightly psychiatrists) on the charge of kid-napping, and thus spared a possible prison sentence, she sits – in this other prison – protesting still, to her white-coated interrogators, that God –

In another age, in olden times, they might have called her holy (or else have burnt her as a witch). One who hears the voice of – One to whom – They might have allowed her the full scope of her mania: her anchorite's cell, her ascetic's liberties, her visions and ravings . . . Now she gets benefit of psychiatry.

She stares before her, out of the tall ward window. She's made a certain corner of the ward her own. Her post, her station. The ward smells of crazy old women. Beyond the window, on fine days, other patients, in coats, exercise on the asphalt.

She stares imperiously and knowingly (the common ruse of the inmate: it's *they* who are mad, not me) at these frail, doomed playground children.

Her eyes are bright. They blink (yes, I remember – that other life). Her arms hold nothing . . .

He can't sleep. His bed's empty and marooned in a black sea. He's afraid of the dark. And when he does sleep – what dreams! He's alone in this sepulchral house with its spilling shelves of books and its period bric-à-brac (you and your Regency retreat – you and your historical props). Alone, save for a dog, which shrinks away from him, draws cautiously near again, shrinks away again – a vet's wire brace only recently removed from its lower jaw. An injured retriever, with which amicable relations have to be re-established slowly, tenta-tively, never quite completely. ("So how come your dog's got a broken jaw?" "I'm afraid I kicked it. You see – if you haven't read your local paper . . .")

He sits up all night. Reads. Smokes. Works his way down a whisky bottle. Marks essays and piles of notes (the last har-vestings of thirty-two years). Drunken red-ink scrawls: More care. Try harder. Good. Fair. Poor. To comfort himself he tells himself stories. He repeats the stories he's told his class. Ah, the contrast of these hollow nights and his well thronged days: classroom chatter, playground bedlam . . . But not long now before even they –

On weekend mornings – before afternoon visits – in the gusty Lenten weather, he walks in Greenwich Park. With a still wary dog. Wolfe keeps his vigil. Fresh sunshine falls on old splendour. The old palace, the Naval College. Green grass and white stone. So pristine and clean. So lovingly preserved (and by act of law, and out of public expense) in a world which –

Ah Mary (ah Price), we all wander from the real world, we all come to our asylums.

The March wind tears holes in racing cloud-sails. Blue sky blooms over longitude 0°.

Ah Mary. Love. Lu-love.

48

And Adieu

"And finally it's my sad duty to have to bid farewell to Mr Crick who – "

Duty! Duty! Ah, that so well pitched, that so strategic word. Suggestive of the righteous judge, suggestive of the stern policeman. Not my desire, oh no, my duty. Suggestive too of the corollary (for we all know, don't we?): *he* failed in his duty, his schoolmaster's duty.

" – who after fourteen years as a pillar of the school – "

Pillar! Pillar!

" – is leaving us this Easter – for personal reasons – "

Poised on the edge of the dais, gripping the lonely bowsprit of the lectern, he seems to his entourage of assistant staff to be rising and falling, breasting a swell of words, a (vaguely mutinous) sea of children.

"Fourteen years I do not have to tell you is a long time. And that does not include the eight years before that during which

287

Mr Crick taught at the school which was the predecessor of this one. Mr Crick has seen a good many of you come and go. The children he first taught now have children of their own. Some of your parents, it's quite possible, may well remember being his pupils. So let us not dwell on this unhappy departure – "

Unhappy! Again, so diplomatic.

" – but – as Mr Crick, as our head of history, would no doubt have us do – look to the past and give due credit to his long and valued service. And let us reflect – "

He's going to make a speech, a sermon of it. Murmurings from the back of the hall. He's going to baste his victim (who sits at the back of the dais like a trussed-up chicken) with rhetoric.

" – as Mr Crick would doubtless also have us do, on how time passes – "

The elegiac note. Ah, how we age. Ah, *sic transit*. (Invisible to that sea of children, invisible to Lewis himself, yet an abiding image, to his watching staff, of their stalwart chief: a pink patch of spreading baldness – amidst wiry greyness – bobbing before a lectern.)

" – these school years of yours, which may seem long enough to you, are soon over, believe me. They're precious. They're vital. So don't waste them, don't spurn them. Build on them. Lay found – "

But apparently the sea – or a turbid, restless part of it – doesn't wish to convert itself to metaphorical brickwork. For from the midst of its furthest reaches – only now does Lewis, with a momentary pause, acknowledge the clamour that has all the time been gathering – rises a decided squall. A noise as of whipped-up waves starts to strike the resonant air of the assembly hall and turns itself into a regular, repeated, if ill-orchestrated beating:

"Fear is here! Fear is here!"

It's the watchword – it's the official rallying cry – of the Holocaust Club (banned by Lewis two weeks hitherto as an "uneducational activity"). It gathers rhythm. Modulates into the staccato chant of a football crowd:

"Fear is here! Fear is here!"

Lewis perseveres.

"Build on them. Make the most of them. Don't let the time come when, not so long from now perhaps, you'll say, If only I'd – "

"Feeear! Feeear!"

"Because, believe me, what you build now will be your security later – "

"Fear is here!"

But he won't be beaten. Won't be drowned out. A few trouble-makers at the back of the hall shan't stop Lewis. He positively rises, lifting one moral-stressing arm from the lectern, to the moment.

"As you can see – hear – there are certain elements amongst you – I know perfectly well who they are and they'll be dealt with – certain prophets of doom – who wish to disrupt this vital and constructive process I speak of. Who wish to spread among us a spirit of hopelessness and alarm. I do not propose to be intimidated – nor should you be – by their childish, yes, childish activities – "

"Fear is here! Fear is – "

It continues, checks, trips over itself, continues again. Behind the headmaster's back his rearguard of staff look uncomfortably at each other.

"And I'm not going to tolerate such outrageous behaviour at the very moment when we are paying tribute to one of our senior – "

Ah sanctimony! Ah tenacity!

"Don't listen to their nonsense, the rest of you. Don't be fooled. Don't be afraid. There's no need to be afraid!"

He seems to dip and sway, clinging to the lectern, an undaunted Canute.

A vision of Lewis, here on this same precarious dais. At a special – an emergency assembly. While sirens wail outside, his hands are raised to enjoin trust and calm. It's all right. Don't be afraid. Lewis will save you. Follow me – into our special bunker. (Yes, didn't you know? It's specially provided, specially constructed. School and shelter. School as sanctuary. Places for children only – and one for me.) Follow me, my little ones, through the portals of pure future . . .

"Don't be . . . Don't be . . ."

But the clamour is subsiding. Insurrection is averted. So are they more afraid of him?

"And so I call on Mr Crick – can we have silence and respect (oh piety) for Mr Crick? I know who you are and you'll be punished. I call on Mr Crick to give you his own farewell. Mr Crick. Mr Crick!"

Mr Crick rises to his feet, creeps towards the front of the dais. He hasn't expected this. He's expected the quickly bustled exit, the swift public execution. Lewis turns to him. His face is bathed in sweat. It looks scared (This is your doing, isn't it, Tom? You –). Yet it's flushed with a glow of undeniable triumph, of proven lordliness. See, they heed me. See, they're guided by me.

Yes, the rebel voices are stilled. Silence for Mr Crick. But what is this? From the centre point of the recent eruption, in the midst of the silence, comes a sudden solitary cry, strangely urgent and imperative, devoid of schoolboy insolence: "No cuts! Keep Crick!"

Price.

Crick doesn't know what to say. He clears his throat.

"Children – "

49

About Empire-building

– who will inherit the world . . .

When the children of the French Revolution threw off their tyrannical father Louis XVI and their wicked step-mother Marie Antoinette (who, as it turned out, were only like figures in a puppet show, you could pull off their heads, just like that), they thought they were free. But after a while they discovered that they were orphans, and the world which they thought was theirs was really bare and comfortless. So they went running to their foster-father Napoleon Bonaparte, who was waiting by the old puppet theatre; who'd dreamed up for them a new drama based on old themes and who promised them an empire, a purpose, a destiny – a future.

Children, there's this thing called civilisation. It's built of hopes and dreams. It's only an idea. It's not real. It's artificial. No one ever said it was real. It's not natural, no one ever said it was natural. It's built by the learning process; by trial and error. It breaks easily. No one ever said it couldn't fall to bits. And no one ever said it would last for ever.

Once upon a time people believed in the end of the world. Look in the old books: see how many times and on how many pretexts the end of the world has been prophesied and foreseen, calculated and imagined. But that, of course, was superstition. The world grew up. It didn't end. People threw off superstition as they threw off their parents. They said, Don't believe that old mumbo-jumbo. You can change the world, you can make it better. The heavens won't fall. It was true. For a little while – it didn't start so long ago, only a few generations ago – the world went through its revolutionary, progressive phase; and the world believed it would never end, it would go on getting better. But then the end of the world came back again, not as an idea or a belief but as something the world had manufactured for itself all the time it was growing up.

Which only goes to show that if the end of the world didn't exist it would be necessary to invent it.

There's this thing called progress. But it doesn't progress. It doesn't go anywhere. Because as progress progresses the world can slip away. It's progress if you can stop the world slipping away. My humble model for progress is the reclamation of land. Which is repeatedly, never-endingly retrieving what is lost. A dogged and vigilant business. A dull yet valuable business. A hard, inglorious business. But you shouldn't go mistaking the reclamation of land for the building of empires.

50

The Whole Story

He opens his eyes, and his eyes tell him that he's not in the familiar room (yellowed wallpaper, mahogany wardrobe) in the Atkinson Lock cottage, where every morning (every morning with a few exceptions) he would be up with the dawn – that is, if he had not already quitted the bed for the dark lock-side and the chain of cigarettes – and where even before he was on his feet a conspiracy of signs, the rustle of wind about the eaves, the patter or lack of it of rain, even the weather-wise cluckings of his hens, would tell him whether today was a day when a good sluice-keeper should have a mind to his sluice.

He opens his eyes, and his eyes, or rather his limbs and the feel of a strange mattress beneath him tell him that he's not in the brass-framed double bed (purchased in 1922, from Thorpe Bros, Gildsey), which years ago – ten to be precise – became a bed for one only, so empty, so cold, so hard to sleep in, so impossible to abandon. He's not in that large, comforting and comfortless bed because (now his memory returns) that same bed stands at this very moment – or attempts vainly to float – in a good half-fathom of treacherous water. And since the bedroom is on the first floor it follows that the larger part of the cottage is occupied by this liquid and uninvited guest and that the goods and chattels pertaining to it are either submerged and awash or, by a process astonishing to contemplate – witness the absent lean-to; witness the hen-coop, gone with all its weather-wise but not weatherproof hens; witness the vanished vegetable patch (and flower garden) of Henry Crick – carried clean away or erased by mud. That, in short, the Atkinson Lock cottage is a waterlogged ruin. That the Atkinson Lock, with its companion sluice, built by Thomas Atkinson in 1815, rebuilt by Arthur Atkinson after the deluge of 1874, is no more. And will never be rebuilt again. For what has become, in this war-shadowed, petrol-driven twentieth century, of the once bustling river-traffic between Gildsey and Kessling? (Ask Henry Crick.) The River Leem, in future years, though at present indistinguishable from an inland ocean, will become a weed-strangled, sludge-choked stream, navigable only to Hockwell railway bridge, a mere catchwater, thence beyond, for its tributary drains.

He opens his eyes. It's not his bed. It's not the marriage bed of Henry and Helen Crick (and death-bed of the latter), but the marriage bed of his newly wedded son and daughter-in-law, who have vacated it for his sake and are sleeping as best they can, and in turns, on the floor in the next room. And it's not the old bedroom at the cottage, but the bedroom of the narrow, two-up, two-down terraced house in Church Lane, Gildsey (look out of the window and you can see, above the rooftops, the tower of St Gunnhilda's), bought for the young couple with begrudging magnanimity by the bride's widower father. And it's just as well, at present, that this house happens to stand on the higher ancient ground neighbouring the church (still known unofficially, but with historical accuracy as "The Island"), because large parts of Gildsey, no less than the Atkinson Lock cottage, are inundated, and Water Street, once again, is a street of water.

He remembers where he is. He sees the unfamiliar curtain, half drawn over an unfamiliar view; he sees the bedside cabinet transformed into a medicine trolley (cough mixtures, bowls, towels and a kettle – but it's past all that, it's reached the somnolent, delirious stage). He sees it all. But perhaps in his mind, which has grown so extraordinarily vivid and mutinous, he's neither in his son's marriage bed nor his own but still on the wind-lashed slate roof of the old cottage, having clambered there from the attic window, watching water surge and slap beneath the guttering, watching debris – a five-bar gate, a whole willow tree – casually cruise by, watching the cataract where once a lock and sluice – , watching a world that has sunk without trace, as if some giant plug has been knocked from its hidden bilges.

He's still straddling the ridge, where he's been now for a whole night and most of a day, in the midst of a roaring gale, feeling the uncurbable sensation (surely this bed too is tilting, moving?) that the roof, the cottage beneath him, must at any moment shudder, heave, unmoor itself from solid ground and bear him away like an impromptu Noah. He's still huddling against the chimney-stack for protection from the wind, clad in an old army great-coat (though it's soaked through and his teeth chatter like a monkey's) first worn, as befits a great coat, in the so-called Great War – so that he presents to his rescuers, who at last come, in a labouring motor-launch (and some of them are soldiers too), the image of a beleaguered sentry sticking like a khaki limpet to his slithery station, or a sailor – though it's the wrong uniform and (or so it ought to be) the wrong geography – determined to go down with his ship.

The launch draws near. It carries a sergeant of engineers and two sappers. It carries lifebuoys, ropes, tackle, sand-bags, first-aid packs, an urn of hot soup, a keg of rum. It carries a whole shivering family of four, huddled under blankets, picked up from a farm east of Newhithe, with – of all things – a half-drowned cocker spaniel rescued with them. And it bears volunteer rescue-worker Tom Crick. Who, while the launch bucks and rolls and spray breaks over its bows, can scarcely believe his inability to act as extemporary pilot, there being an absence of familiar landmarks, and can scarcely credit when at last they draw near, that this is the old cottage and that that grotesque gargoyle on the roof, who – now help is at hand – adamantly refuses to budge, is his own father.

"Lots of them the same," says the sergeant, who in only forty-eight hours, in two wild March days and two wild, sleepless March nights, seems to have acquired a knowledge of flood-victims worthy of a lifetime's study, " – they do and they don't want to be rescued. You'd best talk him down, sir."

So the son – an ex-serviceman who finds it strange to be addressed as "sir" by a sergeant – shouts through cupped hands to the huddle on the roof: "Dad, it's me! Dad, come down. It's me!" And when the huddle doesn't answer: "There's nothing you can do, Dad. There's nothing . . ."

And the huddle on the roof (and in the fever-rocked bed) sees a launch perform a tricky docking operation where once swallows made their nests and sees a landing-party of two balloon-chested, slithering soldiers start to clamber towards him as if to seize his last remaining unsurrendered toehold of territory.

It's March 18th, 1947. The war's over. But the hardship's not over. The ration book still stands on the mantelpiece. And show us, please, the fruits of our victory. Uncle Sam will give us time to pay. Gandhi wants his India back. Ah dreams, ah schemes. View it all through the memory of a forty-eight-year-old man, born in Victoria's reign, wounded at Ypres and to die in 1947 of broncho-pneumonia. What happened to that yarn our grandfathers spun us?

And now, to cap it all, comes one of the hardest winters and, to follow it, one of the most calamitous floods on record.

She was right: it would be a bad thaw. The Boards and Committees bungled: 60,000 acres under water, 15,000 homeless, 20,000 tons of potatoes . . . But we've seen all this before. For example, in 1874 . . .

And the lock gone, and the cottage. And a black trunk, inscribed E. R. A., carried off to sea.

It's his fault. ("His fault for not getting out when he should've," scowls the sergeant.) If he'd taken more care, if he'd been more vigilant. He might have saved the sluice. He might have saved the world. Or if Dick had been there to help. Strong, stupid Dick . . .

He opens his eyes. A woman's face bends over him. Smoky eyes; a stray lock of chestnut hair. A woman's hand touches his brow. He sees the face of a nurse. Nurse. Brunette. So he's not on that floundering rooftop. He's not where the world – He's rescued, he's safe. Amongst the wounded soldiers. She stoops, she's saying something. She's so lovely; it's a miracle. She's trying to get him to tell . . .

But instead of words he delivers a ragged fusillade of coughs. His breath rasps; his lips are livid. He brings up into the bowl held out for him a rust-stained gobbet.

"Don't speak . . . don't try to speak."

She holds the bowl and with her free arm supports his juddering shoulders. When the coughs subside she returns the bowl to the bedside-table and eases him back onto the pillows. She wipes a trail of sputum from his mouth. Presses his hand. She's tended him like this for six days. She's found in this stricken father-in-law a kind of calling, a purpose (and perhaps her true atonement); so that her husband, who sits at the foot of the bed, hands held uselessly between his knees, feels excluded and unworthy, a clumsy gooseberry to this scene of painful intimacy.

She has no illusions. It's real, this coming of things to their limits, this invasion by Nothing of the fragile islands of life. She's been this way before. And prayers won't help you. And miracles don't happen. She'll become a practical person, a realistic person. She won't ever tell about the time when— She'll find work one day in age-care. She'll minister to those near the end of their days. She'll move with her husband to the big city, but in her heart she'll always remain in the flat fens. They'll take with them this marriage bed which is also a death bed; and of the two of them she'll always be the stronger, the more enduring . . .

"Don't speak . . . don't try to speak."

But he wants to speak . . . Yes, yes, it's true, he didn't want to speak, not then, didn't want to talk. Didn't want to know any more. After that business with Tom and Mary. And Dick. After Dick—

It flowed back into him once more. Reclaimed him. Phlegm. The old Crick phlegm. True, it had been seeping back, trickling back, ever since she— But now it repossessed him quite, extinguishing even that old story-telling flame inside him. He didn't want to tell stories any more. Didn't want to believe any more in stories. And Tom—yes, he knew—had those notebooks. Tom was poring over them, itching to know more, making trips to Gildsey and the Kessling Hospital. But he didn't even want to open those blue-bound pages.

Phlegm flowed back. The drift of the river. The tedium of the tow-path. You can stand on level ground and let the mind go numb. Father and son lived together, scarcely sharing lives. He talked to chickens, Tom pursued history. Till Tom got his call-up papers. (History chased him.) Just as his father did thirty years before. How it goes in— But this war was over (no six weeks' rifle training then off to merry hell), and Henry Crick no longer listened anyway, so as to hear the wide world, to his six o'clock bulletins. And then he was all alone, with the mute river; and—

till Harold Metcalf called one day with a story that needed an ending – phlegm enveloped him . . .

And now it's choking him, filling the cavities of his lungs, welling in his throat. He's escaped the flood, but he's drowning . . .

He gasps. His face is a purple flush. His nostrils flare.

"Don't speak . . ."

Beyond the window the bells of St Gunnhilda's strike the half hour. (But only Tom, apprentice historian, notes the exact time: four-thirty, March 25th, 1947.) Those bells, those damn bells, gonging and echoing through the vaults of his delirium. But don't damn church bells, Henry Crick. Not on your death-bed. (Because this is your death-bed.) Remember God on your death-bed. Pray to God on your death-bed. And think yourself lucky these aren't medieval times, when the bells tolled incessantly during the days of flood. Pray. Pray. The waters are rising. Pray to St Gunnhilda for deliverance . . .

The bells chime. So he's not still on that slippery roof. And he's not – He's in the house in Church Lane, Gildsey that Tom and – But just for a moment he thought he was drowning. And just for a moment he thought that face, bending over him . . .

But it was only a vision, Henry Crick, it was only an image of that magic tale that must be told at last, that struggles for utterance in your breathless throat. Because, yes, it's true, when you drown you see it all pass before you. And now's the time, now's the only time, to tell the whole –

He beckons with a weak arm to his son so far away at the end of the bed. But the son, prompted by some look in his father's eyes, has already drawn near; and the lovely girl who bends over him (yes it's Mary, and this must be their marriage-bed, how things go in –) is already grasping with such a strong, sure grip not just his own dying man's hand but little Tom's too.

The lips tremble, form a quivering circle.

Once upon a time –

51

About Phlegm

Or mucus. Or slime. An ambiguous substance. Neither liquid nor solid: a viscous semi-fluid. Benign (lubricant, cleansing, mollifying, protective), yet disagreeable (a universal mark of disgust: to spit). It resists inflammation; retains and disperses moisture. When fire breaks out in the body (or in the soul) phlegm rushes to the scene. It tackles emergencies. When all is quiet it does maintenance work on drains and hydrants.

Its soggy and suppressive virtues make it inimical to inspiration or cheer. It deters the sanguine and the choleric and inclines towards melancholy. A preponderance of phlegm may produce the following marks of temperament: stolidity; sobriety; patience; level-headedness; calm. But also their counterparts: indolence; dullness; fatalism; indifference; stupor.

An ambiguous humour, said to be characteristic of the insular and bronchitic English. It affects the elderly; is gathered with experience. To the sick and fevered it brings equivocal comfort. Eases yet obstructs; assists yet overwhelms. According to ancient tradition the phlegmatic or watery disposition is to be remedied by infusions of strengthening liquors. A specific in all cases (though never a permanent or predictable one): the administration of alcohol.

52

About the *Rosa II*

So we mount our bicycles and ride to Hockwell Station. Dad first, me following. We're in time for the 6.30 King's Lynn. The air is heavy and muggy but we wait in the stuffy waiting-room (so as not to be spied – though neither of us says as much – from the nearby watch-tower of the Hockwell signal-box). The 6.30 is punctual. We load our bikes into the guard's wagon. The guard, one of a former ring of railway employees engaged in an illicit freight service (bagged water-fowl one way, Bourbon whisky the other) strikes up: "You're Henry Crick, ent you? The one as found poor Jack Parr's – " But Henry Crick doesn't want to talk. Henry Crick looks as if he's seen a ghost. We travel three stops to Downham Market where we detrain and cycle upwards of a mile, to Staithe Ferry, on the east bank of the Ouse, in the vicinity of which we have reason to believe is anchored – and so it is, a quarter of a mile or so upstream in the middle of the tidal channel – the *Rosa II*.

A dredger, children. A mud-sucker. A sludge-extractor. A battered, rusting, sixty-foot hulk with – where on most vessels the superstructure steps down in more or less graceful, more or less shapely style towards the deck – a monstrous deformity: the befouled and beclogged bucket-ladder with its befouled and beclogged winding apparatus.

Why so evocative a name for so unsightly a craft? Why so fragrant an emblem for so noisome a task? Rosa. Rosa? Who could have chosen such a name? Rosa. Rosa II. The humblest ship has its whiff of romance. Steamers chug to exotic havens, corvettes ride out on their perilous duties (for we're back in that summer of '43). But a dredger, a dredger.

And who would choose dredging for their calling? Who would opt for this endless and stationary war against mud? This dredgery-drudgery, sludgery-sloggery. It would sap even the stoutest spirit. It would dull even the brightest soul.

And yet it has to be done. Because it won't go away. It gathers, congeals, no matter what's going on in the busy world above. Because silt, as we know, is the builder and destroyer of land, the subverter of rivers, the foe of drainage. There's no simple solution. We have to keep scooping, scooping up from the depths this remorseless stuff that time leaves behind.

Consider the plight of Stanley Booth, dredger skipper, master of the *Rosa II*, who in the autumn of 1941 needs a good dredger's mate. Someone to share his skipper's burdens, someone to take away the weight of twenty-five years' Ouse dredging (for Stanley

Booth has no love left for his trade), to ease the toils of this rusting, lifetime's liability of the *Rosa II*. Dredger's mates come, to be sure – Stan Booth has employed over twenty. But they also go – off, now, to fight this other war where the enemy, at least, is human. They can't stick this life of mud.

He advertises – yet again – in the *Gildsey Examiner*. And receives an inquiry from a Mr H. Crick on behalf of his son – a young but seemingly unpromising applicant, since the army do not want him and he cannot write a letter for himself. The youth, indeed, turns out to be a semi-imbecile. His powers of conversation are limited (but then Stan Booth is no great chin-wagger), his mental arithmetic wanting. And yet, to Stan Booth's surprise, he is strong and dextrous, docile and dependable; and, what is more to the point, seems to have a natural instinct for the principles of dredging.

Stan Booth is only too glad to pay his new hireling's wages. And not only his wages but, since this lucky find looks set to stay, to offer certain sums in advance so that his young helper can buy the second-hand Velocette motor-cycle which will bear him to his labours much more promptly than the means at first employed (milk lorry to Newhithe, early bus to Staithe Ferry). And many times indeed the early-arriving mate dutifully starts up the bucket-ladder alone on those days (which become more frequent) when the skipper is disinclined to be punctual.

Stan Booth is happy. His young apprentice is happy. Yes, happy. For how else explain (can it be that this new assistant, so assiduous and reliable, actually *enjoys* his labours?) that strange singing, that out-of-tune yet contented wheezing which he sometimes emits amidst the clattering of the ladder and the slurp-slurp-slurp of discharging silt? (Now who ever heard of a *merry* dredgerman?)

So it's not surprising that Stan Booth should quite regularly, at about the middle of the morning, feel free to leave the Rosa and its cacophonous machinery under such rapt and zealous supervision, and, taking the dredger's dinghy (thus marooning his trusty companion) make his way to the nearest waterside pub.

For Stan Booth, too, was a drinking man . . .

*

A further ride along the bumpy, summer-hardened Ouse embankment. Past ditching works, pumping equipment, an idle bulldozer, not to mention a concrete pill-box or two, hastily erected in 1940 and now, so general opinion feels confident in asserting, unlikely to be used. Then a halt and a rapid dismounting. For not only have we drawn opposite the *Rosa II*, but there, standing riderless but erect on the brow of the embankment, identifiable, in fact, long before we reach it, is a Velocette motor-cycle.

So my hunch was accurate. But goes uncongratulated. Dad still wears, despite his cyclist's flush, his witness-of-a-ghost look. We gaze down the bank and exchange significant glances. The motor-cycle keeps guard over what is clearly a makeshift mooring: two angle-iron stakes driven into the slope of the bank, ropes trailing from each. A contrivance, no doubt, of the two-man crew of the *Rosa* to save the trouble, during favourable states of tide, of rowing all the way from the Staithe Ferry landing-stage. And the tide is plainly favourable at present. Because the river is high, and the green-fronded ends of the ropes snake languidly into water which is uncertain which way to flow. A simple matter, therefore, to conclude that the dinghy now tied up to the *Rosa*'s hull, just upstream of its attendant sludge barge, is the same that but a while ago must have been tethered to the bank.

Nothing stirs on the dredger. Over an hour has passed since Dick departed, sack on back, down the Gildsey road. A trio of seagulls perches on the idle bucket-ladder. Wasting no time, Dad fills his lungs, puts hands to mouth and repeats the cry uttered from my bedroom window. "Di-i-i-ick!" A good, professional bellow this time – the cry of a man used to hailing lighters on the mist-bound Leem, and surely audible across the water on this still and torpid summer evening. But Dick doesn't appear. The cry reverberates as if in some empty room.

He shouts again, allowing a pause, as if planning, if necessary, on regular shouts at ten-second intervals. The three seagulls, unmoved, nonchalantly arch their wings; then suddenly take squawking to the air. And then we see him. We see, that is, a figure – and there's no mistaking Dick's figure – emerge from the bowels of the dredger and lumber, like some half awake animal disturbed in hibernation, towards the nearside rail.

We can't see his face, we can't read his expression (Dick – expression?). But we don't have to guess at the cause of that lurching gait or that strange lolling of his head as he stares at us across the water. He raises to his lips what can only be a bottle and ostentatiously quaffs.

"Di-ick! Di-ick – for God's sake, boy, come back!"

But Dick is obeying other, authentically paternal instructions.

In case of emergency –

He throws the bottle, emptied, over the side and ducks out of sight, as if to fetch another from his hidden hoard. The gulls swoop, wheel and return to their perch. The floating eyesore of the dredger, bucket-ladder raised in the non-operative position, presents to us its lop-sided, rotten-toothed grin.

Dad turns to me. "You have a go."

He stands, recovering his breath, watching my own loud-hailing efforts like an instructor appraising a novice.

My cries (did you hear them, Dick?) die on the air.

"No good. We'll go back to the ferry. We'll get a boat and go out and get him."

We pick up our bikes. We mount and ride off along the bank, the Ouse this time on our left.

A ferry no longer operates at Staithe Ferry. A new three-pier road bridge, built in the mid-thirties north of the village, has made the former, centuries-old mode of crossing redundant. There remain some cottages, a boatyard, a landing-stage and, next to the old ferry point, the half-timbered Ferry Inn.

The cindered forecourt of the Inn is almost deserted, but it is well past the Sunday opening time and a grey Ford saloon parked at a careless angle and displaying on its rear seat a pair of U.S. Air Force forage caps, suggests a roistering party of our American allies. We lean our bikes against the white-washed Inn wall – where a rust-pocked enamel sign still announces ghostly ferry charges – and make for the bar door. But even as we do so a sudden eruption of noise, breaking the languor of the evening, stops us in our tracks.

A series of rattles and grindings, a medley of explosive, mechanical retchings and hiccups issues from upriver. Followed, to the accompaniment of various raucous sub-noises, by a persistent rhythmic hubbub: Chung-gha-chung-gha-chung-gha! The dredger has started. Dick has started the dredger.

We stand for several seconds on the forecourt beneath the motionless inn sign in frozen appreciation of this fact. Then turn again, with renewed urgency, to the door. But we do not need to open it. For who should emerge at this same moment, closely followed, in trim crew-cuts and shirt-sleeve order, by two U.S.A.A.F. aircraftmen, but Stan Booth, skipper of the *Rosa II*, bafflement on his bleary face and whisky on his breath.

He stares through us – at the source of this sound which has clearly activated even his drink-sedated senses – and only after his eyes have corroborated his ears (the bucket-ladder is dipped and turning; wisps of oily smoke are dispersing above the dredger) do they register our own gaping presence.

"What the – ?"

But – wait a moment – hasn't he seen this man before? This is Henry Crick, isn't it? He who on his son's behalf – A glimmer of realisation combined with a vague ripple of relief crosses the dredger-skipper's face.

"Mr Crick, I know your lad's a bit – " (he taps a plump finger to his temple in place of a word) " – but can't 'ee tell a Sunday from the rest of the week?"

He stops, looks suddenly, with uncertainty, at the assembled company.

" 'Tis Sunday, ent it?"

We concur. It's Sunday, without a doubt.

"An' 'tis him on board, ent it?"

Something in our faces is draining the relief from his.

We concur again.

"So what the – ?"

Upon the threshold of the Ferry Inn (licensee, so the inscribed lintel proclaims, J. M. Todd) Dad attempts the mammoth task of explanation. Attempts. Gives up. Grimacing and stuttering, he pushes me forward (tacitly acknowledging my schoolboy adroitness, my powers of intelligible exposition).

"You tell him, Tom, you tell him for God's sake."

I open my mouth. I review in my mind a dozen possible starting-points; I foresee confusion and incredulity; I realise the

303

utter impossibility of encapsulating, in the space of a moment, the causes of my brother's (my whose?) presence, this listless evening, on the *Rosa II*. I settle for succinct fabrication.

"He's gone barmy."

(Forgive me, Dick. To malign your final gesture, your last recourse, with the taint of madness, to rob it of reality. I, if anyone, knew there was reason in your plight. I, your brother. Your brother. Your brother?)

"He's gone barmy. He got himself drunk and rode off on his bike. We d-don't know," (ah, truthfulness at last!) "what he might do."

Stan Booth's face darkens with a frown. Behind him the two clean-cut U.S.A.A.F boys seem to puzzle over this strange English word, "barmy".

(From the Old English "beorm", children, meaning the froth on fermenting beer.)

Meanwhile, beside me, Dad undergoes a series of scarcely detectable yet agonising spasms. Faced with this statement of mine, in one sense a master-stroke of quick-thinking, in another a patent evasion, a reminder of his own inability when the moment comes (that unconfiding walk on the tow-path) to speak, he can stand no more. The stretched tissue of silence and concealment gives way. He breaks down. (And so too breaks down – it won't be patched, won't truly be mended till Tom Crick marries Mary Metcalf – the harmonious relationship of father and son.)

All but dropping to his knees on the penitential cinders, beneath the gallows-like inn sign, he splutters:

"And he killed Freddie Parr. You know, Freddie Parr who drowned. Killed him. Murdered him. And he's not my son. I mean, he is my son. I mean. O God! O Jesus Christ God help me!"

His eyes moisten. A stray ghost of a breeze makes the sign-board creak and lifts a strand of his thin hair.

Stan Booth draws a slow breath. The two aircraftmen (later we learn their names are Nat and Joe) adopt dumb-struck expressions, inwardly revising perhaps those guide-books issued to U.S. servicemen in which they are officially advised that the inhabitants of rural England are reserved and unexcitable.

No one rushes to fetch the police. No one believes him. The truth is so much stranger than –

"You mean this guy on the boat killed a guy?"

A small roundel is stuck on the windscreen of the nearby Ford. The silhouette of a giant cactus, in blood-red, against an orange background. The legend, in turquoise: "Arizona: Queen of the Desert".

Sniffing the unmistakable scent of crisis, other occupants of the Ferry Inn have emerged onto the forecourt. The pipe-sucking landlord – J. M. Todd himself. Two wizened-featured locals with the air of regular bar-haunters.

And all the time as this group-tableau forms, the noise of the dredger continues, like a tocsin. The sound which every weekday must be so familiar to the inhabitants of Staithe Ferry that they scarcely heed it – reminding them as it does that all is normal, the Ouse is undergoing its ever-needed, never-ending decongestion – now rattles out on a Sunday, when it should be absent. From which it can be inferred that all is not normal.

Stan Booth speaks.

"Beats me. Beats me, blust it! All right, we'll take a boat an' go out there."

A general movement to the landing-stage. A two-bench rowing-boat bobs on the high water as if expressly waiting for us. Stan Booth, directing operations, takes by way of a first precaution a packet of cigarettes from his shirt pocket and lights up. Camel brand: compliments of aircraftmen Nat and Joe. He puffs, eyeing the run of the tide, weighing up, perhaps, two eventualities – that a latent maniac is about to sabotage his dredger, that he's about to lose, because of some weird family rumpus, the best dredger's mate he ever had – then gives orders for embarkation. Dad offers to row. Stan Booth gives him a strange, pitying look and directs him to the after-bench. My intimacy with events begs a place beside him. The two Americans clamour for inclusion – something, given the circumstances and the boat's dimensions, no wise coxswain would permit. Stan Booth forbids, then yields. Only the combination of his own state of whisky-bemusement, the favourable tide, which is still just on the flood, their persistent

305

pleas ("Maybe you're gonna need some help, if this guy's, like violent"), and – possibly most important – the implicit bribery of further packs of Camels and tots of whisky, allows a boat intended to carry with ease and safety no more than three, to leave its moorings with five.

Before boarding, one of the aircraftmen races back to the parked Ford. He returns with a pair of field glasses. Black bakelite. U.S. Air Force issue. "Hey, fellers, we could use these." He slings the binoculars by their leather strap around his neck, like a camera-primed tourist about to take a trip round the bay. Clambering into the boat, he gives a flashing grin and a jerk of a salute to Dad and me. "Hi, I'm Nat Tucker, this is Joe Shulberg. We're from Tucson. Tucson, Arizona." He gets out his own pack of Camels. Stan Booth spits on his palms. Dad slips the painter. We shove off.

It's not like our little old Leem. It's like a sea. It's the Great Ouse, which flows into the Wash. Which once merged with the Rhine. It has a salty, unparochial tang. Viewed from a small boat veering into midstream, its banks seem far off, like miniature coasts.

We nose towards the dredger, impelled as much by the push of the tide as the labouring oar-beats of Stan Booth. The light, veiled all day by the clammy summer cloud, is starting to dim. Not that we need yet strain our eyes. For, as any boatman will tell you, light lingers longest where there's water. It's over land that the shadows thicken fastest. It's the watery places of the world that last yield up to night. And not that we have much to look upon: the approaching bulk of the dredger (from our little boat it seems so much bigger, more monstrous than it did from dry land); the receding Ferry Inn and the road bridge behind us; to either side the blank and cryptic ramparts of the banks, cutting out the distance as if they conceal the fact that there is nothing behind them.

A low and liquid world, a scarcely substantial world. So different (ah, even then, errant curiosity) from the fierce sierras, the cowboy bluffs and canyons of Arizona . . .

The aircraftman with the field glasses (Nat? Joe?) directs them on the *Rosa*.

"Can't see nothin' at all." His face is fresh and pleased with itself.

He catches my glance.

"Here, kid, you wanna take a look?"

Over Stan Booth's heaving shoulders, he holds out the field glasses as if offering the eternal gum and chocolate. Grins. "Go ahead." As if I'm some goggling aborigine who's never seen before such a marvel of the new world.

Two years from now I'll be in uniform like him.

Stan Booth says, "Siddown!" He strains at the oars.

Above the noise of the dredger – literally above it, for it issues out of the cloudy sky – comes another sound, throbbing, reson-ant, oppressive, but too familiar – or too little to do with present concerns – to make Dad or me or Stan Booth, sweating over the oars, raise our eyes. Only the two aircraftmen, drawn by their own choosing but with no going back (the dredger is getting close now) into this aquatic adventure, feel obliged to show their attachment to larger matters and to register their alleg-iance, already announced by their uniforms, to the skies.

"Thar they go!" (Joe? Nat?)

"Yih-hoo! Give 'em hell, boys!" (The other one.)

Conditions favourable, despite low cloud over the North Sea coast. An anti-cyclone, perhaps, pushing from the continent, already clearing the skies of Germany. Before the night is out, stars.

And, besides, this war doesn't stop for Sundays. Doesn't take a break for church-going or weekend recreation (or even for one little case of murder). There's no let-up for the citizens of Hamburg and Berlin, who in honour of the Lord's day are going to get hell.

They thunder past, screened by decorous cloud. Then the din of the dredger reasserts itself. Chung-gha-chung-gha! Louder now, because we're getting near – less than a hundred yards.

And with the sound, a smell also. The smell of something hauled from primitive depths. The smell that haunts Dick's bedroom.

*

He's here. He knows his place. He knows his station. He keeps the ladder turning, the buckets scooping. The noise of the churning machinery drowns the fleeting aerial clamour of global strife. He hears no bombers, sees no bombers. And the smell of silt is the smell of sanctuary, is the smell of amnesia. He's here, he's now. Not there or then. No past, no future. He's the mate of the *Rosa II*.

And he's the saviour of the world . . .

Fifty, forty yards. The water is rumbling, juddering. Beneath the *Rosa* the giant snout of the bucket-ladder is biting, gnawing with its rotating teeth into the soft, defenceless belly of the river-bed. Thirty yards. Dad can't restrain himself from another bout of hailing. Cupping his hands once more, he yells against the competition of the ladder. "Dick, we're coming! We're coming – to take you home, Dick! Home!" Twenty yards. "Dick, we'll – "

And then –

Then.

But memory can't keep fixed and clear those final moments. Memory can't even be sure whether what I saw, I saw first in anticipation before I actually saw it, as if I had witnessed it somewhere already – a memory before it occurred. Dick's head and shoulders (for we're close enough now to have to crane our necks to view the *Rosa*'s deck) appear above the dredger's rail about three yards forward of the steadily spewing sludge-chute. For a second he stares at the approaching boat. For the same second I see what he must see: an overladen dinghy, three familiar faces and two inexplicable (inexplicable?) attendants in uniform. In uniform. He scurries forward of our intended point of contact with the dredger's hull just downstream of the sludge-barge, so that we pass wide and abeam of him. Above the uproar comes the distinct chink of glass against metal.

Was it Nat, or Joe who spoke first? "Hey feller, take it easy!" Or Stan Booth (wrenching head over shoulder): "Dick, Dick bor, blust it! Turn off the blusted ladder!" Or was it Dad who shouted before either of these (to the further astonishment of our American visitors, not to say Stan Booth): "Dick, it's all right! Dick, I'll be your father . . ."

Was it really the case (but how could I have been sure, in that fading light, at that bobbing distance?) that his eyelids were quite motionless and that his gaze, luminous and intent, ceased at a certain point to be aimed at us, but turned to contemplate the rippling, furling, vibrant surface of the Ouse? Did he move first or did I shout first? And did I really shout aloud, or did the words only ring in my brain (and echo ever after)?

"Dick – don't do it!"

But we all saw, we all agreed – whisky-fuddled or sober – what happened next.

He turns. He lurches to the fo'c'sle, to the very prow of the *Rosa* (which is not, like many a prow, sharp and nobly arched, designed to cleave and affright the waves, but stubby, rounded and dented, and crowned by a derrick for hoisting the sling-lines of the bucket-ladder). He clambers onto the rail; stands, shoeless, upon it, disdaining the hand-hold of the adjacent derrick stanchions. Stretches to full height. For a moment he perches, poises, teeters on the rail, the dull glow of the western sky behind him. And then he plunges. In a long, reaching, powerful arc. Sufficiently long and reaching to quite discount the later theory that he must have become entangled in the anchor-chain or the sling-lines; sufficiently reaching and powerful for us to observe his body, in its flight through the air, form a single, taut and seemingly limbless continuum, so that an expert on diving might have judged that here indeed was a natural, here indeed was a fish of a man.

And punctures the water, with scarcely a splash. And is gone.

Gone. Stan Booth digs in an oar to bring the dinghy around. We watch, wait for the up-bobbing head. Watch and start to distrust our eyes. Watch and drift down on the current (yes, the tide has turned, the ebb has begun); cross and recross an imaginary line projecting downstream from the *Rosa*'s bows. Shout into the watery gloom (even the aircraftmen from far-off Arizona give vent to repeated and strangely impassioned "Dick!"'s, as if beseeching some old buddy). Shout; shout again. All, that is, except a sixteen-year-old boy who, sitting crammed beside his father in the stern of the dinghy, goes implacably silent. Because he knows (though he doesn't say; he'll never say: a secret he and Mary will share for ever): there'll be no bobbing top-knot. There'll come no answering gurgling, rescue-me cry. He's on his way. Obeying instinct. Returning. The Ouse flows to the sea . . .

Dad takes the oars from a fatigued Stan Booth. The dredger, unmanned, still determinedly dredges. We scan and scour the water (later, in the light of dawn, the laid-bare banks, the slimy piers of the road bridge). We row back against the current, tie up to the *Rosa* and climb aboard. No wet and shivering Dick (our last, thin hope) who has tricked us all and, swimming in a circle, clambered back on deck. Stan Booth shuts off at last the bucket-ladder engine. The sudden, dripping quiet strikes like a knell. "Someone best explain." We trip over empty bottles. Peer from the rails. Ribbons of mist. Obscurity. On the bank in the thickening dusk, in the will o' the wisp dusk, abandoned but vigilant, a motor-cycle.